CRIMES OF THE FATHER

CRIMES OF THE FATHER

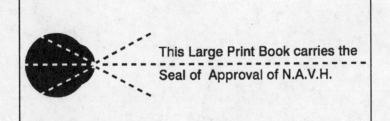

CRIMES OF THE FATHER

THOMAS KENEALLY

THORNDIKE PRESS
A part of Gale, a Cengage Company

Farmington Hills, Mich • San Francisco • New York • Waterville, Maine
Meriden, Conn • Mason, Ohio • Chicago

LIBRARY OF CONGRESS CIP DATA ON FILE.
CATALOGUING IN PUBLICATION FOR THIS BOOK
IS AVAILABLE FROM THE LIBRARY OF CONGRESS.

ISBN-13: 978-1-4328-4424-0 (hardcover)
ISBN-10: 1-4328-4424-5 (hardcover)

Published in 2017 by arrangement with Atria Books, an imprint of Simon & Schuster, Inc.

Printed in Mexico
1 2 3 4 5 6 7 21 20 19 18 17

AUTHOR'S NOTE

I suppose you could call me a child of the Church. It defined me and gave my young life any higher meaning it possessed. I was certainly one of several generations of children to be introduced early to the deranging Catholic addiction to guilt and the possible neuroses that lurked in the confessional — Pope Pius X's edict of 1910 that seven years was the age at which a child was fit to confess made sure of that. In the confessional I encountered irritable priests, priests bored by the task, priests of admirable and tireless compassion, priests who actually tried to temper my religious over-enthusiasm, and priests who seemed at best eccentric messes themselves. But I never encountered any greater perils, of the kind for which plentiful evidence exists, those dangers that encouraged the English author and former seminarian John Cornwell to call the confessional a venue for pedophiliac priests to groom children for abuse.

At an immature age, I chose to study for the priesthood, and I would like to put on record my thanks for the more generous and openhanded aspects of that training. It was not, however, an education designed to encourage a callow young man to achieve full maturity as a sentient and generous male adult. I was too innocent to understand that the education to make me a celibate strayed easily into stereotyping half of my species — women — as a perilous massed threat to priestly purity; or that the attendant emotional dwarfing could create, encourage, or license the young men whose abusive tendencies are mourned in this novel.

Those who trained me nonetheless proceeded in good faith. I might well have been a doctrinaire catastrophe if I had lasted, or else a whiskey priest, but a nervous collapse after I was ordained a deacon, accompanied by a long spate of disabling mental exhaustion and inertia, saved me from finding out. I left a few months before my ordination as a priest. By then I had been partly humanized by some of my wiser fellow seminarians and priests.

I felt compelled to leave, but I did so with the conviction I was letting down not only the universal Church but also the traditions of my Irish-Australian clan. Like some characters in this novel, I too had heard about the Mass stones of western Ireland, and I knew the worth of the despised Irish because I saw it amongst my own people, now transplanted to Australia. I knew that persecution had made us associate our identity with the Church. I knew that it was true, in fact, to say that some of my forebears in North Cork had starved instead of taking the chance of Famine soup and becoming Protestants — all for the sake of "the auld faith." I knew that the struggles of the Irish had continued in the New World, that there were places I could not get a job in the 1950s because of my name and religion, and that my father and other kin of his had volunteered to fight in the Second World War in part to show that Catholics were reputable citizens like anyone else.

In the seminary not only did I have problems with belief in such theological fables as the Virgin Birth, but I was also shocked out of my own arrogant piety, in particular by seeing the callous way the institution treated young men who left. Some of these men were unwell — mentally or physically — yet even when that ill health stemmed from conditions at the seminary, they were cast back on their families with minimal financial or pastoral support. The rest of us were told to avoid them. Much later, as the abuse cases emerged, setting off an era of scandals, I saw a connection between the way the Church treated these young "failed" priests — with nominal care and no responsibility — and the way the victims of abuse were being "helped" and maneuvered.

As a writer and former seminarian, I was asked in 2002 to write an article for the *New Yorker* on child abuse in the Catholic Church. In researching it I spoke to priests in both the United States and Australia who were friends of mine, and one of them, an Australian stationed in the US, predicted two outcomes for the Church in its failing to address the matters of both pedophilia and underage abuse. One was Frank Docherty's message as narrated in this book: if the Church did not face up to the problem, and act according to its highest principles, the civil arm of society would ultimately force it to do so. The second was that a time would come when all priests would bear the opprobrium of the crimes committed and covered up. Both these prophecies of my venerated and now deceased friend turned out to be, as they say, on the money.

My friend was certainly not the only honest, striving priest to foresee these perils, to be scandalized by what had happened, and to appreciate what was coming. He, like a number of my friends in the priesthood, possessed a genuine spirituality and a social conscience — a taste for what St. Paul said was the first commandment: fraternal love. I wanted, therefore, to write about the spirituality of such priests, even though a fellow former seminarian jokingly warned me that spirituality was a rare animal amongst Catholic clergy. I was, however, lucky enough to know many priests with whom it was more than a pretense, and so, for good or ill, I based my main character, Docherty, on priests I have admired, none of them sadly the kind who are likely to be made bishops.

I have come to realize that if you leave the Church, the Church may not leave you. Even so, I am afraid that despite my arm's-length admiration of spirituality, I am what you would call a cultural Catholic, one of a subspecies despised by the more doctrinaire and totalitarian Church officials. I got the idea from those agnostic Jewish folk who celebrate Passover to commemorate their fellow humans whose lives were ended by barbarous decrees in the 1940s. In the same spirit I attend all the rites of passage of my esteemed late father and mother's numerous Irish-Australian clans, both of which had American wings as well. I am grateful to celebrate the Last Supper and, in the name of people now gone, and much nobler than I, take the host, the sacrament. A deity could not be more appalled at my unworthy welcome to the Eucharist than by the celebration of the Mass by abusive priests. Many of the Church's ayatollahs will queue to call me a delicatessen Catholic. Perhaps the Church is lucky still to have a delicatessen. But to say so is just the beginning of a tiresome debate in which the legalistic certainties of some priests and many bishops fall like axes; falling, as they always do, on divorcées, homosexuals, users of contraception, and all the other outcasts who might hanker to take Communion.

I have taken the liberty of setting this novel in the 1990s, when the pattern that would mark the Church's circumstances in the new twenty-first century was beginning to emerge, yet when the voices of the victims did not have the force they have now gathered. I chose that time setting in the interests of making Docherty something of a prophet, as my dear friend in the United States was in 2002.

Though I am far from saintly or free from

shame myself, I have — like many Catholics at birth — been profoundly shocked by what has happened, by the hubris of notable Church leaders, and by the fact that the Church, faced with this crisis, reached not for the compassion of Christ but for the best lawyers available. I am not the only one. On a recent visit to Listowel Writers' Week in Kerry, I noticed how thoroughly — more thoroughly than in the United States and Australia — the Irish Church has lost the west of Ireland, the land of our observant forebears. The most devout are the most profoundly scathed by these scandals. Much was required of them and of the rest of us as Catholics. Observance and innocence were required of us. But at the higher level of the priesthood such rigor lapsed, and the lapses were hidden to the limit of criminality. That, I suppose, is the story of this book.

A PLEA FROM
FATHER FRANK DOCHERTY

1996

Monastery of the Congregation of the
  Divine Charity, 2214
Kitchener Boulevard, Waterloo, Ontario
  N2J AO1, CANADA

16 June 1996

His Eminence Cardinal John Charles
  Condon
Cardinal Archbishop of Sydney
Polding Centre
133 Liverpool St
NSW 2000
AUSTRALIA

Your Eminence,

Re: Dr. Francis Dominic Docherty
CCD, formerly of the archdiocese of
Sydney

Please accept my most reverent respects. I am the above-mentioned Frank Docherty, Australian-born, Canadian resident, and incardinated at the moment in the diocese of Hamilton, Ontario, Canada, where I live in my Order's house, performing many parish duties at the Church of All Souls in Framborough Street, but also working as an associate professor in the Psychology Department of the University of Waterloo. There I specialize in developmental psychology and am accredited to conduct a clinical practice as well as being involved in the clinical training of doctoral students.

The Very Reverend Eugene Egan, Bishop of Hamilton, will attest to my record as a priest of this diocese. On his authority and with his backing, I have embarked on a study of the problem of clerical child abusers, whether that abuse be pedophilia or assaults upon minors. As required by their bishops, I give consultations to a number of priests from eastern Canada who face psychosexual problems. I hope I shall have concluded my present research, and made a helpful contribution in that research area, within the next three years.

Your records will show that the reason the cardinal archbishop of the archdiocese of Sydney, Norbert Scanlon, canceled my faculties to administer the sacraments in 1972 involved no reprehensible behavior on my part. Like many a young person at that time, I was vociferously involved in human rights issues, which, in the spirit of the Second Vatican Council, I have never seen as separate from matters of dogma. I also took an unambiguous position on apartheid and the Vietnam War, opponents of which were wrongly seen by some Catholics of the early 1970s as communists. I was denounced by members of the laity, who believed sincerely but wrongly that I was undermining the papal magisterium and exalting individual conscience over its authority.

Given that I was advocating no more than Christ himself had advocated, I felt they were wrong in their condemnations of me to the archdiocese. I still claim, with respect, that this was so. Therefore, I would be grateful if you would review my situation when my academic career in Ontario comes to an end, and allow me to return to Sydney, my home city — indeed, the city in which my mother is ageing, to resume priestly functions there under the aegis of my congregation, to which I have belonged since adolescence, the *Congregatio Caritatis Divini* — the Congregation of the Divine Charity.

I am coming to Sydney at the beginning of July to speak at a Council of the Clergy, and to see my relatives, and I would be happy to discuss the matter with you then, at a time of your convenience.

Your sincere servant,
Frank Docherty CCD

1
DOCHERTY COMES
TO AUSTRALIA

July 1, 1996

Sarah Fagan was driving a cab. Some might think her cab-driving a pathetic attempt to meet men. In fact, it was a genuine attempt to allow a recovery of her brain, which was depleted, and a revival of her spirit, which had been rendered numb from all that had happened to her.

Driving was an art, but it also allowed intellectual vacuity, plain rituals of conversation. And if Sarah did not want to converse on the issue of why a woman like her was driving a cab, she would say, "We're all filling in for my husband, who has cancer." The "we're all" implied a tough family hanging together in a crisis; that she was not, therefore, in favor of being messed around by passengers. She suspected that a decision about whether she would stay in neutral gear for the rest of her life, or might pull herself out of it, would most probably arise not from conscious thought or frantic self-analysis, but with her brain muted by routine. Listening to and exchanging banalities with her passengers, she hoped she would hear some healing neutral words. She might then learn to live in the same room as the tiger, the flesh-tearing fury.

A Friday morning at Sydney Airport provided taxi drivers with lots of fares. The line of cabs was prodigious by seven o'clock, with a dozen ahead of her. But the stream of morning arrivals kept it moving, and as Sarah was a cabdriver more for the therapy of it than for sustenance she was unfazed by the wait.

When eventually the last cab in front of her had cleared off, Sarah's fare proved to be a tall, lean man, studious-looking, in his late fifties or early sixties — you couldn't tell in an age when even the old went to gymnasia and sweated themselves thin. This fellow hauled a modern suitcase on wheels and in his other hand carried a briefcase. The suitcase was not massively packed, nor the briefcase of the latest design. A sensible traveler, but neither a conventional businessman nor tourist. A chiropractor, she thought, or a health-shop owner.

"Good morning," he said as she got out

18

and came around the cab to watch him putting his bags briskly into the boot, whose lid she had released. When he was finished, he set out walking around the car to take the other front seat, as was the custom with Australian men of his age, a residual gesture of egalitarianism. It was only then he noticed she was a woman and was struck by doubt.

"What should I do?" he asked her in a level, earnest voice. "Would you like me to sit in the back?"

She told him it was his choice, he was the passenger. So, after weighing the matter, he took the front seat. She asked him where to, and he said Gladesville — he believed he knew the way, he said, since he used to live in the area. He mentioned a street. "We'll work it out as we go," he said.

She pulled out and asked him if it had been a good flight, and he said it had been passable — given the time change, he preferred to fly by day than by night. But he hadn't had a choice this time.

Where had he come from?

"Vancouver," he told her.

"Oh," she said vaguely, because all points of departure were equal to her. She liked these conversations, but did not want to take on any of their weight. "They say it's a little like Sydney," she remembered to contribute.

"Yes," he said, "it is like Sydney, and yet they're both their own places. They're like siblings, very much the same and very much different."

It was what she wanted to hear. Something unchallenging, which still transcended plainness.

"So you're pleased to be home."

"Proud Australian boy," he said. "Though I live in Canada."

She asked when he was going back and he said in three weeks' time. His mother had a few mobility problems, he said. She was old enough to warrant his coming to see her.

Did he live in Vancouver? No, he said. Ontario, over in the east. Flat country but very pleasant. She asked him what the winters were like and he laughed. "Unspeakable. Sometimes I think it's amazing that any Canadian survived before 1900." He shook his head. "And yet, when you live there you just take it as it comes. Pretty much the way Australians accept their summers."

Apart from such superficial issues as geography and weather, she generally left her passengers free of inquiry. It was astonishing, however, how many would offer

20

particulars without her asking. Humans were natural confessors, and she was sure it was this, rather than the sophistication of police forces, that landed many people in the criminal dock.

He said, "Things have certainly changed in Australia."

"In what way?" she asked. She wondered if it was wise to ask.

"Well, it was all freckle-faced Celts and Anglo-Saxons when I was a kid. Now the faces are Asian, Middle Eastern. And women driving cabs. The old crustaceans around me when I was a kid wouldn't have considered them safe enough drivers!"

"You haven't seen it in Canada?"

"Not particularly. Well, yes. There's an Ojibwe woman in Waterloo who drives for her husband because he's got diabetes. You see, I live in a sort of big country town. But also . . . well, I always thought the Canadians a bit more progressive." And then he laughed. "In a backwards sort of way."

She said nothing.

"Are you driving for your husband?" he asked.

She did laugh at that, and was aware it wasn't an entirely kindly laugh. She said, "Why would I need a taxi owner for a husband to make it all right for me to drive a cab?"

He held up a hand. "You're quite right; forgive me. I'm a sexist brute. Women in Canada tell me I am all the time."

"You can get cured of that, you know!" she said, a little tersely.

In the silence that followed she wondered idly if he was married. She was not going to ask. He asked her about the present Australian government, but he was treading water and she gave a simple answer, discontented with politicians in the Australian way that expects no prophets ever to emerge from the desert.

She went left beside Hyde Park, reached Chinatown, and crossed the Glebe Island Bridge. It was only when she turned into Rozelle that he recognized familiar landmarks on Victoria Road. "My father and uncle owned that pub," he told her. "If I called it an old stamping ground, you'd asked me what I stamped on it. But at least I'm familiar with it."

He had a weird sense of humor, she thought. She said, "We're close now." For some reason she said it for her own comfort. This one was just a notch too subtle for conversation. Whereas she could live with "my old stamping ground," she found "I don't know what I stamped on it" harder. She wanted clichés, not a smart-aleck expatriate who turned them on their head. "Not far," she said, but again to reassure herself.

She had an opening to ask him what he did for a living, for she still couldn't guess and she was certain he didn't own pubs. She had a feeling the answer would be at least mildly interesting, but she resisted saying anything because it would allow him the right of a question in return.

The morning beamed down on her windscreen and she put on her sunglasses.

"Ah," he said, "Sydney light."

"Isn't it just like Canadian light?" she asked.

"The light there on a bright cold day, twenty below freezing — it's big honest light, too. The rays doubled up by reflections off the snow. So it's like Sydney light but without the inconvenience of snow."

She said, "The Canadians must appreciate you telling them that. I don't think."

He laughed. A low, short laugh. He was looking out of the window and drinking in what he could see of the suburbs and their shops and pubs, just like a returned, easily satisfied patriot. She took an exit and he was on familiar ground and could guide her.

"I don't know what number it is," he told her. "It's a big sandstone place."

They rolled along suburban streets and he watched schoolboys in cricket-style hats, brown shirts and shorts, and the little girls in their checked uniforms. At last he pointed to a nineteenth-century mansion that stood behind a reclusive, high-shrubbed, high-treed garden. She could see the Celtic cross at the apex of the facade and a smaller metal version above the front door. Convents sported such icons. So did monasteries. She felt a pulse of revulsion. The poisoned cross still boasting of its triumph over the suburb. Atop a smug garden and a smug antipodean sandstone mansion.

She punched the meter off and jabbed the button that released the boot.

"That's fine. Father, Brother, whichever you are. The trip's on me. Don't forget your bag." It would have been good to end it there and maintain functional, cold politeness. But she couldn't. "Just get out, will you?" she told him.

He was mystified. "No," he said earnestly, "the freeloading days for priests are gone. And they gave me taxi money especially for the airport."

He pushed a fifty-dollar note towards her but she would not take it. She sat stiffly and clung to the wheel. He tucked the note into a recess between the two seats.

"I insist," he murmured.

Eyes fixed ahead, she said, with a deliberately chosen profanity, "Just fuck off, will you? Just get your bag and go."

She could see out of the corner of her eye that he was examining her face, as she fixed her gaze blankly on a couple of young mothers and their children across the street. She knew he was skimming through a number of options in his head — the job of a supposed general practitioner of the soul. Meanwhile, she both wanted him to react to her so she could unleash truer insults and passionately wanted him to vanish to save her the grief.

He said simply as he opened the door, "Just let me get my bag. And . . . I'm sorry I made you angry."

It happened that Docherty knew well how ambiguous the Celtic cross, once the symbol of one of the most oppressed peoples in Europe, could be for the damaged. One of the purposes of his journey was to warn Australian clergy of this enlarging rage now loose in the world. If nobody listened, he believed such rage would grow to fill the sky. This woman was clearly one of those damaged in the shadow of that sign. And no Southern Baptist, no Marxist, hated the sight of the Celtic cross with the intimate hostility that he could tell was in her. For he had encountered this before. Symptoms of unutterable harm. She had achieved equilibrium, he understood, driving her cab, but perhaps to her own surprise her effort of calm had been disrupted by getting too close to the gate of a suburban monastery.

Quickly, he took one of his professional cards from his pocket, wrote his Sydney contacts on it, and dropped it through the window onto the passenger seat. Then he fetched his bags from the angrily sprung trunk and made for the gate without looking back.

2
THE CASE OF
SARAH FAGAN, VICTIM

Early 1970s

Sarah did a remarkably sedate U-turn and set off for the city. She was not fit to drive, and she ignored the hopeful commuters in Drummoyne and Rozelle who held out their arms to her. If she could make it to the Regent Hotel, she could wait in the long queue there and compose herself.

Her family was back with her. The sight of the Celtic cross so close had done that. Her mother had been a fervent Catholic, her father and brothers merely tribally so. Their belief was like belief in the stars: it did not endow their lives with any further light for all that. Her brothers were loud, her father watchful for wrongs done him, which the world seemed to deliver in daily doses and for which he frequently blamed her mother or her. That part of Sarah's life was ordinary and predictable. It was everything else that wasn't.

Her father and brothers had that awful man-ness. The boys had sympathy for their mother. They mocked their sister's pretensions routinely. Something in them, or the nature of the household, made them take a sort of glee in the world's imperfectness, and when it came to imperfectness they had a model in their father.

He was a former seaman who had gone into the navy when he was barely more than a child and had learned there too much about drinking. Offloaded by various captains, he'd sought a discharge and worked as a bricklayer; and the Fagans would have been comfortable had he done the job properly. But he was let go from sites for failing to lay his daily quota, or to excise the cement from between the bricks with the usual stylishness of brickies. It was a craft he could have mastered had it not been for the boozing.

Not that any of this made Sarah exceptional. She knew — she could in some cases read the signs — a number of girls in her class who lived in the same uneasy state of emotional excess and occasional dread that marked drinkers' households. And so, despite having seen wholesome films about families who blithely resolved all crises in a couple of movie reels, she knew, too, that the exchanges between her mother and father were bitter but predictable, offering neither the comforts of homeliness nor any hint of exaltation.

It seemed to Sarah there were thousands of men and women caught in this joyless net, though at least for nonbelievers there was a chance of escape. She got used to spotting at Mass the families who had emerged from an apogee of alcoholic disorder and were now temporarily gusted along on new hope, on the promises of a repentant father, cowed himself by the dimmest memory of his own paroxysms of mayhem; soon an edged, heated insult, a readjustment, one thrown punch would teach that entire family once more how business was really conducted.

She hated the squalor of her home. Her parents rented; if he had not been consumed by "that beastly stuff" (her mother's phrase) they would have owned their house like other people.

Then there was a supremely humiliating night. The house was quiet and he came home and could be heard shuffling in the hallway as a prelude to . . . what? His dropping into oblivion, his pissing in a sink, or some new invention of booze-maddened disruption. But he remained silent. He came to her bedroom nearly soundlessly. It was his thunderous breathing, not his shoes, that woke her. She understood so much by that time — she knew the Latin vocative of a swag of nouns, and the neatness of Pythagoras; she could recite the Chinese dynasties and debate the causes of the First World War. She was barely conscious when she found his hand on her breast, and when she drew in breath to cry out, he covered her mouth with his other hand. She could smell brick dust on it, beer, a trace of his own excreta, as if he lacked the consciousness to clean himself properly. She could feel the calluses indenting her face. That was how her mother, suddenly standing at the door, caught him, caught her. Her mother roared like thunder and he lifted his hand off his daughter's breast, though the act could not be reversed and took all the divine music out of Pythagoras.

Her mother advanced and dragged him upwards by the back of his shirt.

"Leave a man alone," he nearly managed to say.

He was the lucky one. He would barely remember in the morning. Her mother told Sarah that he didn't know what he was doing. She quizzed her daughter about whether it had happened before, and when Sarah let out a little negative bleat, her mother hugged her and said it was not her fault and she must protect herself as women did, and the best protection was to tell another woman. Me, said her mother. This exchange excruciated and steeled the young Sarah.

She began to get to school early and stay as long as she could. She was always ready to run errands for the nuns; she lingered at netball. The joy of knowing things revived in her. Her father had lost her — she did not want his company and he was chastened, and the chastening remained even in his worst bouts: it was profounder than the base needs alcohol stirred in men.

Much later she realized how nineteenth century her family was: the men the brutes, the women the madonnas, the fathers drinking what they could not afford and taking from that armory of liquor every implement of imaginative malice, unpredictably cutting and maiming edges. Still, getting the kids to tyke, RC, rock-chopper schools, the schools of the ancestors — for some reason that was essential to her father, automatic to him, and to her mother.

There was by then a modern phenomenon of middle-class, wine-ingesting women, who'd had the time in suburban nullity to digest the promises and defiance of Betty Friedan's "Woman: the Fourth Dimension," which appeared in magazines in the mid-1960s, and to be drawn up into the anger of Greer and assurances that the old model of marriage was done with. They told their husbands to iron their own bloody under-wear and shirts, and, while they were at it, to feed the kids. But Sarah's mother re-mained the pietà, the suffering monument. She represented for Sarah what marriage was; her father symbolized sex — and both were piteous and despicable.

Her name was Sarah Fagan. But she intended to change even that. And not through the expedient of marriage.

Sarah was fourteen when she ran an errand to the presbytery, with a message from one of the older nuns to the polished young priest who was curate to the parish priest, himself a monsignor. The housekeeper left her waiting at the door and went to get the younger priest. He bounced downstairs but-toning his cassock. His neat brown hair was brushed flat, his cassock impeccably black, no scurf, no tobacco flakes or ashes.

"You caught me watching television," he told her with a smile. Some priests looked almost as disheveled as her father, but there was another kind who smelled of soap and some hair preparation or aftershave. Fragrant priests. This man was that kind. And in the presbytery front hall there was none of the dusty, musky smell of the house she lived in, humid with her mother's unhappiness and her brothers' imaginings; home, too, of the tropic of shame that she could never again mention to her mother.

The priest read the note she gave him. He looked up. "Mother Alphonsus says you are very competent," he told her. "And that you've helped them a great deal with their office work. I've been asking for someone to help us — running messages, organizing files. I promise it's not because I'm lazy or watching TV all the time."

At that second she loved the Church, the sane face of Mother Alphonsus, the ordered face of this priest. Father Leo Shannon.

He led her upstairs to a room with a desk, filing cabinets, a picture on the wall of a saint she could not identify, and a settee under the window. The floorboards were varnished but there was a mat spread as neatly as a little lawn. He showed her how the parish filing was done — letters from the archdiocese, the replies, files on parishioners, references for job-seekers, notices of bereavements and of parish social events, as well as bills paid and donations received. I will not look in the Fagan dossier, Sarah decided. In fact, there was an embarrassing question to which she did not want the answer. What did Father Shannon know about her family?

"I know I can depend on you not to snoop inside the files," he told her as if he had perceived her thoughts. "They are confidential, and I keep your mother's file as secret as I wish to keep the others. That's why I asked Mother Alphonsus for an entirely reliable girl."

He further confided to her, "To tell you the truth, the monsignor is so busy on God's matters, and with golf on Mondays, that he has let the church records slip a little. You are going to help me get them under management."

He said that, about the monsignor not having time, with a kindly irony, but again he had taken her into a secret, as he had when he'd confessed to watching television. She was flattered to be confided in.

As she was alienated from her own household, the presbytery became Sarah's vision of home. Everything shone; the carpets were vacuumed; the walls were white and sparsely decorated with portraits of recent popes, reproductions of Raphael's Madonna and child, bright statuary, and photographs of various clergy. She would in time come to see this ecclesiastic decor as sterile, but it seemed to her then to be a space made for devotion and in which good works might flourish. She wanted it because she did not want what was at home: a marriage sacred only in its origins, a venue of unpredictable tears and gestures and of such low exuberance as her brothers' farting contests.

Father Shannon and Sarah worked cooperatively. He would give her a letter and tell her which folder to put it in and under what alphabetic listing. Financials — electricity, gas bills, rates — she filed in their own drawer, to be used for the parish's financial statements by the honorary treasurer. The priest told her she was a fast learner. Passing papers, dressed in his collarless white shirt and black trousers and impeccable shoes, he said like a confession, "I just can't stand things not being in order."

And it was obvious to her, his hunger for orderliness.

Over time, the monsignor himself asked her to run errands when he was in, to take notes to various parishioners, generally members of his parish council, occupiers of neat brick bungalows, owners of good cars.

Men of substance. Or else to the ladies of the sodality who did the altar. But the monsignor was out a lot, and what she did above all was work for Father Shannon.

In between these tasks, said Father Shannon, she was welcome to attend to her homework. So, within the presbytery, sitting in its dusted chairs, on its polished wood, she did her trigonometry and her French.

3
DOCHERTY IN SYDNEY

July 1996

After Frank first left Australia in 1972, sent to the Order's "house," or monastery, in Ontario, it was seven years before he returned.

International airfares were high in that decade, and the truth was that eventually he found his mix of priestly work and academia in Canada satisfying. Docherty's graduate studies at Sydney University had been based around psychology and sociology, so when he found himself close to a good provincial university in a regional town in Ontario, at the desire of both the superior of his Order and of the local bishop he proceeded to his doctorate.

The other monks in the Order's house were either indifferent or amused by the expulsion Docherty himself found hard to live with. Occasionally one might say, after too much evening beer, "Come on, Frank. Come clean with us. Did you fall for some Aussie woman?"

Some Aussie woman. Maureen Breslin. He did not know whether to grieve for her. To rejoice in being separated from her, he thought, would be sinister indeed, because it treated a living, splendid woman as if she were temptation incarnate. In private, he applied meditation and his Gandhi-ist principles to prove to himself that he had not been hard done by. The world was one of forced migrations. Look at the bloody relocations of 1947 across India and Pakistan. And in no sense could this part of Ontario where the house was located be depicted as a bitter land of exile. He came to miss Australia and his mother and the sight of Maureen only with occasional spasms of grief and not, as he had expected, continuously.

In the 1980s, as the price of travel fell, he came home twice for visits during the North American summer. On the first of these, he found that his friends the Breslins were of the same mind as him. Willing without embarrassment to make room for the intense attraction he and Maureen Breslin shared, but not wanting to make a meal of analyzing it. North Americans had a tendency to want to analyze mysteries, but Australians pragmatically thought not only that mysteries were beyond analysis, but that analysis would break their ineffable clockwork. He was grateful for this new level of friendship. Critics would say it made a eunuch of him. Well, that came with the job.

His last visit had been three years before, for which his brother, Declan, paid his plane fare so that Docherty could visit their mother, who was by then living in a retirement village run by the Little Sisters of the Poor and had some weeks earlier broken her hip. The resultant shock had provoked a transient ischemic episode, which mimicked the symptoms of a stroke but whose effects then eased. The paralysis of the left side of her face and body ameliorated after two days, and she was already well recovered by the time Docherty arrived. Her nurses said it had been a sad thing to see her when she was demoralized, and that his visit had elated her.

Declan Docherty was a lawyer in Melbourne who had become an industrial relations specialist. During Frank's 1993 visit Declan took his brother to the Melbourne Christmas and Sydney New Year Ashes Tests, and some of the Adelaide Test as well. Cricket did not seem a luxury to Frank, raucous though it might sometimes be and as malicious as the aim of pace bowlers might sometimes seem.

Everywhere they walked during lunch and adjournments and rain breaks at the Test at the Melbourne Cricket Ground, and in the members' stand of the Sydney Cricket Ground, Declan was stopped by other lawyers, men from the corporates, and union officials, and he took this frequency of greeting with a calm social grace. Declan was known for having friends on both sides of the fence, and bringing about satisfactory results with his well-paid interventions. A former New South Wales Labor minister confided with vinous breath to Docherty that his brother had a large hand in designing industrial relations systems for sundry businesses, which gave industrial peace for years at a time. It was not a matter of surprise to Docherty — he knew his little brother was clever, flexible of thought, amiable, earnest, learned.

By an implicit arrangement the two of them never spoke of the Church — Declan and his wife had let their weekly attendance at Mass slide. The fact seemed to make Declan more edgy in his brother's company than Docherty wanted him to be. Docherty even had a sneaking sympathy for the omission — Declan was far too bright to be browbeaten or soft-soaped by your average deadening, authoritarian sermon, and Docherty knew as well as anyone in the archdiocese of Sydney that there was not a lot of encouragement for original material, for breaking new ground. It was by no means impossible to find somewhere a priest whose sermon was exhilarating, but there was the investment of time for uncertain results. Indeed, Docherty's semiblasphemous idea was that since the threat of Hell for missing Mass had failed to compel Declan's generation, it was the duty of the Church to offer something so enriched with meaning and communal solace that people would dislike missing it.

Frank and Declan's mother, born Helen Quinlan, was a handsome woman, a Queensland country girl and Depression-era survivor. She had been, by accounts of Docherty's aunts, a lively girl, star of the convent netball team. At a dance at the Catholic Club in the bitterest year of the Depression, she had met a handsome, exuberant young man, James Docherty, who described himself as a pub broker and horse dealer, and was from the same town and parish, Rockhampton on the Barrier Reef.

Jim Docherty was fanciful, eloquent,

frolicsome — and a fundamentally unreliable father. Before his death, at every turn of his fortunes Helen had seemed skeptical of him. Certainly she had reason: he was capable now and again of taking the family to the financial edge, due to his dreams of impossible riches based on chancy propositions, which included — in line with his Irish heritage — cheap but chancy country pubs in hamlets beyond Adaminaby or Cobar, and expensive and unreliable racehorses. To pay him credit, however, after he had moved his wife and young sons to Sydney, he had given them stability, for he'd become an adequately affluent man: he and his brother Tim were partners in three pubs in Rozelle, Alexandria, and Leichhardt.

His premature death at barely more than fifty, which would have been an economic catastrophe for half the families of the boys Frank went to school with at the Christian Brothers, left his mother financially secure. She remained a dynamic woman who didn't resign from vivacity, social life, a certain acerbic flirtatiousness, and all the rest, but she never remarried, something that was a subtle relief to her sons when they were in high school and imbued not only with the first stirrings of sex but with the baleful influence of Irish sexual puritanism.

Helen had been careful with her encouragement of her husband, and — seeing that a repute for cleverness had not helped him much — she applied the same reticence to her boys. Declan told his brother during the Melbourne Test in 1993 that when he was named dux of their school in North Sydney, his mother had kissed him on the forehead and said, "That's it, then. You've done very well!" Unlike more gushy mothers, that was the extent of her adoration. Declan and Frank had enough wit to know that had they possessed the sort of mother who kept referring to their academic supremacy, it would have become tiresome, an embarrassment. And yet they could have tolerated at least one or two more references to it. It was the case in most families — indeed Frank had not encountered one in which it was not the case — that the woman dominated all imagination and concern, and provided a high emotional spur.

On that bright July afternoon of the day of Docherty's arrival, at the reception of the complex in which Helen now lived, he asked to be connected to her room. She answered and told him to wait there — she proposed that they walk in the garden. As he waited, he was overcome once more by a pleasant, torpid reflection that it was part of his good fortune he had a mother who did not take him too seriously, who did not exalt his earnestness of soul into a sign of coming magnificence on either the ecclesiastical or the mystical scale. It did not mean that her love or admiration for him was in any way qualified. He knew from his previous visit that she had, amongst the reduced set of icons on her dresser, photographs of Declan's family, and of Frank in his doctoral gown. What she doubted was not her children's talent, but the capacity of the world to adapt itself to them, and Docherty knew that had been a wise doubt in his case.

When she appeared, she had a pink bloom in her face. She walked with a cane held casually, even stylishly. He knew from the liveliness of her face that her acerbity was at its best and her spirits robust. She still looked young to be in a retirement home.

"Well, you're back," she said, with a trace of imputation that he was forcing himself on her attention.

He laughed. "Yes, Mater." He had taken in his adolescence to calling her Mater in the manner of the English public schoolboys he'd read about in the British comics that had made their way to the colonies after the Second World War. Docherty kissed her and

44

she hugged him with one arm. Her nature accounted for that.

"I believe you're in good shape?" he said.

"I'm not repeating stories three times anymore, if that's what you mean. Did you have a good flight from the Arctic?"

"We were attacked at takeoff by polar bears, but Biggles and Ginger shot them and we got clear just in time."

"Ha-ha! The smart aleck is back! I know there aren't polar bears in Ontario. But there's everything that goes with them. Ice on the roof. Probably ice in the soul, as well. And God knows what it must do to people's joints."

"You've got to get Declan to bring you over there. I know you're game enough for the trip. You'll be surprised how pleasant the summers are."

"I'm saving up to fly first class," she told him and gave a wink. "It may take a while." Like many Australians of her generation, she was a climatic nationalist, no matter how many sun melanomas the patriots had to show for it. "But, I have to say, it's good that you're here," she continued. "You're my first son, you know. Given birth to in uncertain times, let me tell you."

"I kind of remembered all that, Mater. Now, I have to speak at this conference

45

tomorrow, and hope to see you in the days after. Perhaps I can take you for a spin in the car."

"What car?" she asked.

"The monastery clunker. As your first son I owe you everything. Including the best clunkers I can summon up."

"Yes," she said, "you do owe me everything." She gave a dry grin. Such was his mother in a sentimental mood, and her voice evoked multitudes of forgotten banalities and crises and tenderness. It did not evoke, however, meanness or a chastising subtext, as some parental voices did. Helen was a woman of reliable parts, of surfaces that would not shift. But if you wanted someone to gild the lily of affection, she wasn't the one.

They walked in the garden. He told her he had written a letter to the cardinal archbishop pleading to be allowed to return. And he reminded her that he was speaking at the Sydney Council of the Clergy.

"About kiddy-fiddlers?" she asked. "I'm not certain that'll win His Eminence over."

"What do you think will?"

"Tell him your mother's going to get very angry if he doesn't have you back. Can you imagine: me as the plaintive old mummy of her priest-son, weeping on the *7.30 Report*

46

for a sight of her boy? Rachel weeping for her children. I'll make him seem a monster."

"I'll warn him," Docherty assured her.

She looked at him sideways with her warm irony — that is, with love — and took him to the dining room for tea. Along the way she introduced him to lively old biddies and blokes, old-fashioned Australians arguing politics, chortling bitterly at satirical cartoons in the *Herald*. And she continued with her grievance. "When you think of all the drongos and dolts the old cardinal could have thrown out! Well, thank God for the jet plane yet. Remember the letter your old grandfather in Ireland sent your father. 'I think there may be an eternal decree,' " she recited, " 'that I shall never again in this world look upon the faces of my exiled children.' Breaks your heart, eh? On the other hand, a Cork farmer, able to write like that! Imagine. We've got baccalaureates who can't write their way out of a paper bag these days."

"The cleverer we become," said Docherty with a smile, "the less literate."

She was obviously a hub of organization amongst the people in the home. She arranged the tickets for the Sydney Theatre Company and the occasional opera. It was her love of cricket that had imbued him, and she was the resident authority — she could recall the major statistics of every Test since 1928.

"Do you think Sydney will be congenial to you?" she asked. "In the future, I mean."

"Well, the fellows at the monastery seem inoffensive, and of course I'll have an easier time of it when I finish this research project. Going to the cricket — without being caught in a riot, for example, as in Calcutta. And seeing my old mum now and then."

She warned him — at least it sounded like a warning, "I'm not going to be one of those priest's mothers who thinks their son should live for them."

"No," Docherty conceded. "I don't want you to be, either. But I do daydream of taking you for rides to the Blue Mountains."

"And I want you to take me out to dinner so I can complain at length about how economic rationalism is destroying the so-called commonwealth of Australia." She had always called it that, the commonwealth. "And how the mongrel Murdoch press is cheapening debate by mistaking insults for arguments and editorial for news. And how an auxiliary bishop here refused Communion to a nun who talked about the ordination of women. That sort of thing! Meaty subjects."

Her extended left arm trembled as she recited her log, a portent of any number of bad possibilities.

"Do you have any shakes?"

"Side effect of my injections of zoledronic acid."

"Is it really?"

"My prognosis is that I'll live forever with the old Quinlan heart, tough as a bookmaker's satchel and about the same size."

He remembered an argument between his father and mother in which Jim Docherty had accused his wife of being cold. Even back then Frank had thought, in a kind of angry protest, No! Cold was a description he would not countenance. It was that she treasured her emotions too keenly to easily express them. His father was the sentimental man who could reinforce one feeling with another — a success with a racehorse with the general well-being of tipsiness, for example, not that he was in any way a habitual drunkard. But with that emotional glibness of his, every grand sentiment had to be emphasized, placed in bold type, and this was only exacerbated by an accretion of booze.

In the later afternoon Docherty drove his mother up to the great headland of Manly and she talked about the night the Japanese miniature submarines had penetrated the Sydney boom gate to attack the USS *Chicago*. Looking down the harbor from North Head, they discussed the Australian cricket team and praised Adam Gilchrist and his phenomenal talents. And they were content.

The following morning, Docherty served Mass at a side altar of the chapel for an old German priest he had met at dinner the night before. Gunter Eismann had worked for many years in New Guinea. He was, on the authority of his advancing years, ironic about the whole missionary project: he had found in large part, as Docherty himself had years earlier in India, that the target population had marked him more permanently than he had them.

Eismann had great simplicity of soul, and was one of those lucky people who seemed to have become increasingly childlike and untroubled, a type sometimes encountered in monasteries. Yet Docherty thought he appeared fragile, too, as if a pit of serpents threatening this elderly man's spiritual peace lay beneath a wafer-thin film of composure. He had told Docherty the previous night that during the war he had served as a member of a U-boat crew for two years before he was captured, and that in his POW camp he had been drawn into the orbit of and influenced by a Benedictine monk who had visited.

For a man in Eismann's situation, to be a member of a religious order was a good arrangement, as abnormal as the outside world might consider it. He was looked after, had brother priests who understood him, and was not overburdened with work. He went out to short-staffed parishes on the weekend, as most of the Order did, and no doubt gave calm, unremarkable, Teutonic-inflected sermons about a God of love.

That morning, while Docherty said his Mass, the first he'd had a chance to celebrate in some days, he fell into contemplation. By now, in the last few weeks of his fifties, Docherty sometimes felt that despite his dependence on conversation and contact with other humans, he wished to take comfort only from the liturgy, from the rite of the Mass, and from sitting by the hour in chapel, or taking a walk in the presence of . . . of what? . . . Of the Crucial, of the essential element, the sexless, person-less Utter, or — as Catholics used to describe it — the Divine Presence.

Nearly everything Docherty had believed when he became a seminarian seemed now to push up against the limits of the absurd. Was the Virgin Mary a virgin? Was Christ God or a prophet of God? And the great circus of the canonization of saints — what was to be made of that? The po-faced searching for three miracles, as if so many suspensions of the natural law were either credible or in fact desirable. He simply knew that all these were at best kindly myths, hinting at transcendence. It was the transcendence he still felt at the rim of the Ultimate, which in his case meant sitting in an empty church in the Divine Presence, waiting, as he saw it, for it to come out and meet him.

He accepted that via the vagaries of empires and emigrations, an Irish inheritance had been reborn in a string of antipodean colonies, and through an accident of fate his life lay with a particular religious tradition — the Catholic one — though it so easily could have lain with another. Born a cricket-mad Bengali, for example, he would have seen the world through the lens of Durga, Krishna, Shiva, while still knowing the difference between a seamer, a yorker, an outswinger, a googly, and a leg-break. Born a cricket-mad Sydneysider of parents who were products of the massive Irish immigration to Queensland, and you saw the world through the imagery of incarnation and resurrection, and knew every delivery in the menu of balls a bowler might serve up to a right- or left-handed batsman, including Shane Warne's flipper.

Through performing the sacraments — baptisms, weddings, visits to the dying — Docherty was aware that he was reaching towards both an indefinable but, to him, essential realm, as well as celebrating human solidarity: the whole species embroiled in life and death, but further in a celebration of the Beyond, the Unutterable, the I Am Who I Am. Though it was not an *I*, Docherty thought, because it was not a person. Not a he, she, or it; not a first, second, or third person. It was the Am, and the Am resided in people's minds. Because of religion's institutional pomposities, it was in the mind in some cases as the great Not There, the great Absence. But even then, Docherty thought, a Not There-ness in the world was so huge a fact, it was almost itself a There-ness. He didn't often run these principles of his past people, because they could sound smug if wrongly delivered. But they were not smug as he perceived them.

He was relaxed with the question, therefore, of why he should feel the promise of transcendence when he was an entirely accidental creature, an inhabitant of a random star; the only star on which Christ had died, as far as was known, or rather been killed off — as the scapegoats and the outsiders and the tellers of truth always are, generation by generation. Christ lashed the Pharisees and the Sadducees, the rival political parties, theological camps, liturgical opponents, the Pharisees being corporate hypocrites and the Sadducees toffs. But Docherty knew the spiritual children of both factions were found in the curia in Rome and, in some cases, amongst bishops. For the sake of their power, their comfort, and the avoidance of scandals that should have been spoken about and damned by them, they created new scapegoats, new Christs, new sacrifices.

Apart from this, he let the question lie as to whether the Utter noticed the human rites, the services of ritual connections between humans, between them and It. "It" could, he chose to believe, be approached, be crudely experienced through ritual and meditation. He could not live without these, let alone see any greater reason for being a priest. He simply knew that this was his version of a religion, a religion that was once coextensive with the worldview but no longer was. Yet it was *his*, Docherty's, balm to practice it, a balm in this life whatever befell him in the next — oblivion, or transport, or vision in whatever gradations.

The truth was he had to be modest. He knew the suspicion he attracted from his brethren in the wider priesthood. He was a priest who ponced around academia all week, dealing with unhealthy and distasteful subjects, and helped out at a local parish on the weekend — how graceful of him! But his order was very grateful for the professorial salary he contributed to the finances of the monastery.

4
MAUREEN BRESLIN
REMEMBERS THE 1960s

I was born into an Irish-Catholic family from Sydney. I belonged to that generation of Irish-Catholic women of the New World (the United States, Canada, Australia, New Zealand, and elsewhere) who were the first to go to university and acquire a degree almost as a matter of course rather than miraculous exception.

One summer day in 1959 I took a ship with a friend and fellow newly minted graduate, Momo Griffen, and we embarked for the barely foreseen, never previously experienced cold of a London winter, which we were sure would give glamorous relief to us children of torrid Australian summers. Momo and I had booked a passage on the brave understanding that we wanted to escape the constraints of suburban Sydney, and the narrow Australian definition of what a woman was meant to be in the — looking back on it — suburban idyll of the reign of

Prime Minister Robert Gordon Menzies.

Escape was so frightening, however, that we were delighted to meet Damian Breslin and a few of the other boys from the university students union on our first day at sea. Damian, then and since, represented safe ground to me, and he and the others shared our objectives: not only to see the Tower of London, but to get to our grandparents' villages in Kildare, Killarney, Tipperary, and Cork. It was as if at that stage of the development of the Australian personality we almost believed that half our soul had been left behind in the Northern Hemisphere, and we must find it.

I was unprepared for the scale of the great British damp and frigidity. I thought we had those things in the Australian winter and that it would be at worst a variation in scale. It was meteorological murder. But I liked the fraternity of it all over there — the shared squalor, the competitions to find another shilling for the gas heater, the warming of our conversation over flagons of South African wine, which I, who would later become so politically exacting about that place, drank as though it were an unambiguous form of sunlight, barely understanding the term "apartheid." I worked in a school in Peckham; Momo, who stayed in England in the end, as a physiotherapist at Great Ormond Street Hospital.

Momo, Damian, and I went, with a sense of belonging and equally of not — a sense we were already used to from our London experience — by the Fishguard Ferry to Ireland and were surprised by the enhanced squalor and gloom of Dublin, and its little River Liffey we'd read about in *Ulysses*. It was a river that ran as hugely in our mythology as the Nile. My grandfather's rendition of "The Foggy Dew" had done it — he had been, as Protestants accused us of being, a Cork republican. "But the Angelus bell o'er the Liffey's swell rang out in the foggy dew . . ." Yet the river through Dublin made Melbourne's much-mocked Yarra River look like the Mississippi. Child beggars who put out their hands and called jovially, said in your wake, if you ignored them, "Fook you, mister! Fook you, miss!" Nuns at Bethlehem College had told our class that the Irish never took the name of the Lord in vain. We had been told that they combined that abstention from cursing and blasphemy with their saintliness and their scholarship. We couldn't see much of that in autumn Dublin, though.

The cold and the gray followed us as we clung to the idea that we would find the true Irish, the ones further west. And in a sense we did when we stayed in farm bed-and-breakfasts. These people seemed far more familiar to us than the British, and there was in each case a warm welcome for Australians, if you endured the hours of rain and mist between destinations. We encountered the Irish kindness that all travelers wish to bring home from that squalid, dim, wonderful place. A farmer who offered us a whiskey toddy, made according to his own recipe, said one night, "Sure, if you don't have it you won't know what you've missed out on!" The following night he outdid himself. "I been takin' this stuff three months for me cold, and praise be to Jesus, it hasn't done me the slightest good."

We went north by bus, and in Galway City found people still singing the songs of our grandparents. We attended a solemn high Mass, and Damian and I argued whether the fondlings and all the rest we had been up to in the deep nights, creeping to each other from separate rooms, were serious enough to keep us from taking Communion.

Generally we decided they were, but the most important point, which confirmed and gave me a sense of my unarguable destiny as a Catholic, was something I saw on a roadside in Donegal. On the Donegal coast, which, though gloomy, was magical and bespoke something ancient and somehow familiar to us, something our ancestors saw and thus shared with us, we saw a Mass stone. I could understand who I was then. That poor wet stone, with a fading Mass sign "IHS" scratched in it, represented the map and history of my faith. Mass said by a priest on the run in Ireland's penal times, when the faith of our fathers was forbidden by law, and celebrated on that stone in front of the barefooted, shawled, and huddled poor, with gales threatening from the Atlantic and a lookout on either hill to scour for dragoons coming to punish this outlawed ritual. This stone is my inheritance, I thought. An inheritance of the oppressed, too. How could I let the people who stood here, hungry and ill-clothed and yearning for peat fires, go from my life? How could I sunder the connection with them and their strife?

In no way did this stop Damian and me fornicating, or near-fornicating, that night in Glencolumbkille amongst the holy stones. "Fornication" is an overcolorful term for our sometimes inconclusive and partially achieved ecstasies. I, who had escaped the Sydney suburbs, had fallen for a boy from those same suburbs.

A year later, we returned to Sydney and were married, and quite quickly had two children, Niall and Rosie.

Certainly Damian and I were not so 1960s as to be unfaithful to each other, though we both had ample chance at this hectic time, when marriage was considered not only a stale entity but a doomed one. But the sexual rule I was sure would be changed, and that I longed to see changed, was the long-held proscription of contraception. The benign John XXIII had put in place a commission into birth control before dying in 1963. Paul VI would make the ruling on the matter, and women looked forward to it with confidence.

There was method to my sexual conservatism in the free-range orchard of love that was the 1960s. The doctrine of original sin, the most reliable doctrine of all the Church's catalogue, the doctrine of my own fallibility, told me that I could not tolerate an open marriage — that it was a condition available only to a kind of saint in a perfectly equal partnership, in which the partners lacked any sense of grievance against each other, any ammunition to use in hours of rancor. Perhaps it only worked in those not given to rancor in the first place. The much talked about "open marriage" was in fact a condition that required extraordinarily trusting and calm natures on both sides, the sorts of natures people believed we were achieving at the time, and that many people believed could be achieved by walking through the gates of clarity — by dropping acid; that is, by tripping.

In any case, much of the free-love ethos turned out to be unreliable news, part of the great fancifulness of that decade. A man whispered to me at a party in North Sydney — he smelled of a rather sweet hemp instead of that quasi-industrial odor of tobacco — "I've never rooted the sister of a priest before." The fact that my brother was a priest apparently added to my allure, even though at the time I'd had too much wine. We used to drink Asti Spumante, which seemed to connect us to the glamour of northern Italy, and a Moselle named Ben Ean, which we hoped would endow us with sophistication. Though the madness of that whisper attracted me in a way it shouldn't have, especially given its bullish, boorish impudence, I did not succumb. I did not, as that American term has it, come across. To come across was to ford the Rubicon, and I didn't want, and was grateful I fundamentally did not need, to come across. If I started it, anyhow, I might get a taste for it, and we had two children. I was not a free-floating woman.

If I'd said any of that to my propositioner, I would have been laughed out of the court of the era as too suburban and square. I was a Catholic, but I enjoyed appearing a liberal Catholic — worldly, even anticlerical — looking to the Church to affirm us after the centuries we, with bowed heads, had spent affirming it. Now we were the kind who stood comfortably in secular, multistranded society and said that Catholicism was changing, that there were extraordinary manifestations of liberation theology amongst priests and Catholics in Latin America. In the months and years after his death we spoke fluently of the ways in which Pope John XXIII (God help and remember him) had changed things, had proposed we learn from the world instead of fearing it, and how things would change further still, allowing us fearless travel.

Damian and I were still embarrassed and unforthcoming with friends about our own sexual travails, our attempts to use the so-called rhythm method, a fussy process of birth control not involving prophylactics, the use of which had been depicted, earlier in the 1960s, as a mortal sin capable of plunging us into Hell's pit. Don't ask me to justify such fear, or the role of conscience in all this, or that of reason. Such a rigmarole of taking temperatures and checking the consistency of cervical mucus, unmagical and unerotic procedures. You had to be born when we were, to have grown up with a totalitarian Church as we did, to know why we were such uncool subjects of its sexual admonitions in the age of rock 'n' roll and flowers in the hair. But the two of us need only look to our family histories to see that fertility came easily to our sort of people, the immigrated children of the Irish peasantry and small farmers. I feel sorry for the apparently unfertile young men and women now who must attend fertility clinics, but by contrast we made efforts between babies to concentrate our sex into the twelve or so days when I was supposedly infertile and thus entitled to have joy without incurring nearly assured motherhood.

Love, as it is extolled in its classic sense, does not normally await the taking of temperatures. Heloise and Abelard did not let a thermometer and charted basal temperatures stand between them. There was no messing about with thermometers between the Irish patriot of my grandfather's generation Charles Stewart Parnell ("A great man, Protestant as he was!") and his favorite squeeze, Kitty O'Shea. But Damian and I, banking the tide of desire, took clinical account of the time of day and month.

So then what could one do in mercy to each other if the temperature variation did go wrong? One must surely give the poor man some relief. For there is something plainly engrossing and peculiarly innocent in the sight of the man at the mercy of his arousal. But this, too, was against the rules of the Church, which deemed there was only one *vas,* receptacle, into which seed was meant to flow.

It became apparent to us that since we'd broken the edicts of God's Church by taking temperatures, we might as well forget the thermometer, and for a time we did use prophylactics and stopped going to Communion. I know the young now would not think twice about taking Communion while using contraception, or indeed exploring their mutual possibilities in any way they choose. Love has conquered all, including the Vatican. And I myself, knowing what I know now about the men who consecrated the Host and gave Communion, their unfitness for it all . . .

My older brother rescued me from a lot of mental stress. His name was Father Leo Shannon, and it was confidently predicted that he would end up a bishop. He had the wit to sense from peripheral remarks made by Damian and me, and from various theological arguments Damian had picked with him, that in that period after 1963 we were having doubts about the Church's dicta on marriage. He surprised us by recommending a confessor to me, a priest who would go easy on me.

Leo was considered a sensible man by the big end of the Catholic community, the Christian Brothers boys who had become judges and surgeons and received papal knighthoods. He had a gift for seeming to harbor liberal opinions while remaining every inch the cleric, a man of the Vatican way. He was a type — the smooth priest whom the laity felt privileged to speak to; the sort of cleric who was a great administrator of a parish and whose sermons were eloquently unremarkable and concentrated strictly on dogma. He belonged to that school of thought which proposed that the basic doctrines — the Resurrection, the Trinity, transubstantiation, the heavenly status of the Virgin Mary, the sacraments, and the love of Christ and his Mother — were best imbued by plain reiteration, with only an occasional gesture towards modernity, but never Modernism. He was little concerned with the reinterpretation of dogma in the light of Darwin, Freud, the Big Bang, and had none of the sort of theological pizzazz some of us liked in other priests. Leo had a strong liturgical sense, too — he liked the ceremony of it all and honored that, laid stress on it, since in his childhood it had helped raise the faithful above the level of their normal dour and economically straitened lives. "One of the purposes of the Church," he told me later, "is to bring majesty into people's lives. The majesty's been beaten out of every other part of existence."

The priest whom he recommended was Father Frank Docherty. Leo had heard enthusiastic reports about Frank Docherty from laymen my brother respected. I called the presbytery where Father Docherty was curate and found out that he was a member of an Order named the Congregation of the Divine Charity. He lived at their monastery, but heard confessions on Saturday after-noons and evenings at the parish church. The following Saturday, I drove there to become his penitent.

We still did all that nonsense then. We knelt like children in the confessional, dimly perceiving the priest through the fine-wire grille when he opened the flap to hear our crimes, and we said the old formula, "Bless me, Father, for I have sinned." To some of them we should have said, "Bless you, Father, for you have sinned." But the idea was unthinkable then.

I told Father Docherty in as non-explicit terms as I could manage that I was back to using the rhythm method but sometimes things went awry and I did not use the proper *vas*. The pattern of our discourse, as it developed that day, was exceptional by the standards of other confessions I had made in my life. He must have known women; his knowledge surely came from more than a sister and a mother. Because he knew how to talk with women, how to validate their decisions, and unlike so many of his brothers in the clergy, he seemed to like them, in the sense that he understood and countenanced their ardors and honor, their conscientiousness.

Father Docherty told me, for example, when it was time for him to speak, "You are conscientious to a degree and not likely to make facile judgments. So I think that in all this you must follow your own conscience."

I said, "Father, if I may, that sounds very Protestant."

He laughed. It was a laugh without an edge to it. "Yes, the old argument about

68

total authority over conscience has traditionally been located in the Church, not in the individual's soul. But there was always individual conscience, as there should be. Our pope only a few years dead wrote this — I have it on a piece of paper I always carry with me, especially for confessions: 'Also among man's rights is that of being able to worship God in accordance with the right dictates of his own conscience, and to profess his religion both in private and in public.' That's John XXIII, of course. Note that he doesn't say 'the right to obey all orders that come down from above.' He doesn't say 'we'll tell you what to do.' He says 'in accordance with the right dictates of his own conscience.' "

"When did he say that?" I wanted to know. "I wasn't aware . . ."

"An encyclical letter, actually, *'Pacem in terris.'* A few years back. Insofar as the Church is a human institution, too human according to some of us, it struggles towards the light like any other organization. And I believe John XXIII took us as close as he could. Until peritonitis killed him."

I had heard discussions like this occasionally, earnest Catholics of democratic temper sipping Moselle and arguing for individual conscience and wondering if that made

69

them Protestants. But I never thought I'd have this kind of exchange in the confessional.

Father Docherty murmured, "If you didn't have the right to your own conscience, you would be less than human. You would actually sin against nature."

I coughed. Confession, the sacrament of penance, had always been for me the shame-faced muttering of failures, the allotment of a penance by the priest, then fleeing the confessional box and muttering prayers at the back of the church. I was both pathetically afraid and exhilarated by the concept of a discourse in the confessional. I could not help but tell Father Docherty that what he was saying was new for me. "I've never heard that quotation before."

"Do you think I made it up?"

"No."

"You probably wouldn't have heard it. We celibate patriarchs tend not to tell people things that might make them more independent of us."

Would my brother ever have made a statement like this? Had he even considered the idea? It was unimaginable. But I had not finished arguing, this first time I had ever argued in the confessional box, and now I protested against the right Father Frank

Docherty was trying to press on me. "We were always told the conscience was a fool," I insisted. "Hitler's conscience told him to kill Jews."

"I don't think it was exactly conscience that told him. It was doctrine. All the signs are that the Church is now ready to acknowledge the individual conscience. Indeed, if more had had the chance to exercise individual conscience, instead of obeying the state, there might not have been a Hitler. The difference between Hitler and you is that your conscience doesn't tell you to do the unreliable and the savage. It is telling you to do a quiet, kindly thing. It won't always do that. But that's why you're here. You are conscientious about humanity — yours, your husband's. We must rely on who we are and what we perceive. Anything else, depositing your entire conscience in an ancient institution in Rome, is less than human."

So he went on arguing that my conscience should have sovereignty not only over that of a parish priest and a bishop, but also, more fantastical still, over the Vatican.

Through the confessional grille I could see Father Docherty's profile. The wire of course made him near invisible to me; this grille that, as I had learned at university, was prescribed by St. Charles Borromeo to prevent Renaissance priests from being tempted into dalliances with sexually confused young women. Young women like me.

"In the end," said Father Docherty, "you can only filter these outside authorities — the state, the Church — through your own conscience. We're always saying that the greatest commandment is love. And what you tell me you did, you did from love, and I wonder how offensive that can really be to a merciful God."

I suddenly and for the first time felt that I was the confessor and he the penitent.

"But how can one tell one's conscience from what is convenient and comfortable?" I asked, like a true Catholic of my generation.

"You can tell it's your conscience if it keeps speaking to you despite all," he said. "If other choices seem morally absurd. Look, our consciences can deceive us, but they're all we have."

This was wonderful to me. I had heard it in the confessional, the international forum of absolute moral authority, and it suddenly made eminent sense. Within that strict and sometimes tyrannous space, Frank Docherty had set me free. It *is* true, as orthodox feminism has it, that the history of the confessional is a history of male authority over women's bodies. And it seemed to me that he somehow knew this and didn't want to play that trick; perhaps he'd played it once in callow times but had now got beyond it. Frank Docherty seemed a heretic to me, but he'd made me rebellious enough to believe that if I was judged with him and condemned, I was judged in good company.

5
DOCHERTY GIVES
HIS LECTURE

July 1996

Docherty had been invited to speak at the
Sydney Council of the Clergy by Dr. Gil
Heffernan, a former priest. Heffernan, a
man of considerable moral repute, was now
laicized and married, and ran the office of
the Australian Catholic Social Justice Council. Docherty had never met him, but Heffernan had been a young progressive in
Melbourne when Docherty himself was a
young progressive in Sydney. Docherty had
been sent away; Heffernan had taken his
expertise as a social scientist into the Social
Justice Council, a tolerated arm of the
Church generally considered a haven for
Catholic lefties, liberation theologists, and
ineffectual liberals. To what extent the
return to authoritarianism in 1963 by the
Vatican after the death of John XXIII had
explained the departures of some of the best

and cleverest was a question hard to measure, but the losses had been considerable.

Earlier in the year, Heffernan had read in the Toronto *Catholic Register* one of Docherty's articles debating celibacy, and asking whether it contributed to the spate of child abuse cases emerging in North America. He had also read Docherty's article in *Psychology Today,* entitled "Emotional Dwarfism and the Abusive Priest," which was based on Docherty's research and clinical work at the University of Waterloo, Ontario; and then a speech Docherty had given at Waterloo in which he outlined his findings on how the Church dealt with abuse cases, findings based on his interviews with victims, men and women, who had been sent to him for counseling.

Docherty's diocese in Canada happened to have a more progressive leadership than Sydney. He knew this for a fact because its bishop had authorized and supported his research even though his repute was still considered risqué by those who did not understand his true case — which was that as well as giving solace to victims, Docherty also advocated methods more likely to protect the name of his profession in the long run.

On the bus to town that morning of

Docherty's second day in Sydney, uncertain of his reception by an audience of his fellows, he went over his notes. He was to lecture on abuse phenomena amongst the clergy. He got out near Museum Station and walked across the park towards the sandstone mass of St. Mary's Cathedral. "Oh, the place where I worship is St. Mary's Cathedral," they used to sing in the seminary, "built on the blood of the poor." Docherty had been ordained here in the year of President Kennedy's election, a high-water mark for Irish Catholics the world over.

He saw a fairly expectant scatter of priests on the pavement around the doorway of the cathedral chapter house, a neo-Gothic hall down the hill from the neo-Gothic exuberance of the cathedral. Surely the entire conference was not taking place here?

Heffernan met him. After they'd exchanged pleasantries, he took Docherty aside by the elbow. "Look, when we authorized you to come, we thought you'd be given the main venue, which is up the road at the Sheraton. But we got orders from above." Heffernan put his thumb in the direction of the cathedral. It was a weary gesture. "And we had planned that you would have a plenary session everyone would attend, but, again . . ." He made an apologetic noise with his lips. "You've heard about the resumption of the Supreme Court hearing?"

Docherty had indeed read in his newspaper a short item about a man who intended to issue a writ of damages against the Church for abuse he had suffered as a boy.

"It's a young scientist pleading to get the Limitation Act lifted so he can sue."

"Yes," said Docherty. "So the old sub judice considerations operate."

"Yes, I'm sorry — you shouldn't refer to it."

"Of course. Don't worry yourself, Gil. Please."

"But we all need to hear this — the good, the indifferent, and the expedient of us."

"Yes," Docherty agreed. "But I can imagine the cardinal archbishop would have been against a plenary session. I'm not necessarily judging the man up the hill. And I'm certainly not comparing him to my bishop in Ontario."

"Anyhow," Heffernan said, "you will have a good and interested audience in a Gothic ambience. You'll be preaching in large part to the converted, I'm afraid."

Docherty reassured him. They had paid

his economy fare and he would do his best by them, he said. If he could, he would give it back. . . . Heffernan insisted he wasn't implying that at all. "I'll take you round to our green room," he said ironically, as if they were on a television set.

Heffernan told him on the way that a number of bishops — those who would not be attending his talk — had sent their secretaries or, in a few cases, their vicar-generals. Docherty was part-relieved that by and large he would be speaking to priests and not the hierarchy. Though the priests would, no doubt, be reporting to their superiors, it meant he'd be able to speak more directly.

There was, in fact, a hulking Western Australian bishop sitting in the green room in shirtsleeves but wearing his collar and purple stock. He rose with fraternal promptness as they entered. He was the chairman of the council, a man with a good reputation, well known for his work with the bored youth of the hinterland towns and for inventive programs for Aboriginals, in which he followed the advice of a council of Noongar tribal elders, without, it was claimed, second-guessing them. This man greeted him, said that the Council was honored to have him here, and asked if Heffernan had been discussing with him "the problem with our betters," as this bishop called it. Then he said he should get a seat, and without fuss left them. Docherty could hear a lot of talk from the hall. Engaged voices.

He went in and saw the old cedar rafters above, the sconces flowering at their bases, and the pilasters that continued the line of the rafters down to the floor. The room was filling. A few priests nodded at him, but as to a stranger. Many of them were caught up in personal exchanges with an edge of intensity to them. The subjects he was to address put everyone on edge. Him, too.

The Western Australian bishop led the congregation in a prayer that asked for wisdom and reverence for each other to infuse the session. Heffernan gave a polite tap on the microphone and the audience composed itself. There were laypeople in the hall, Docherty saw, and a number of women, members of the council or its secretariat.

Heffernan's introduction was brief: Dr. Docherty, formerly of this archdiocese, was an associate professor in developmental psychology at the University of Waterloo in Ontario. His work gave him clinical access to Catholics who complained of priestly abuse, but also to priests themselves, whether they suffered from depression or psychosexual disorders. The bishops of eastern Canada had taken an interest in his work because of its potential application to the psychological screening of men who wanted to become priests. Dr. Docherty would, he continued, also address the question of the relationship between celibacy and some of the scandalous instances of child abuse being reported from America and Ireland, and now Australia as well. "I am very pleased to see that these matters are sufficiently important to you that you have attended today. And you will give, I'm sure, a strong welcome back to his home city to Dr. Frank Docherty."

Docherty rose to an earnest barrage of applause. After the introductory formalities and a joke about jet lag, he began.

"I was asked, in part, to speak on the future of celibacy. That is, I was asked to be a prophet. But Five Dock, where I was born, statistically lacks in prophets, and I do not intend to mar its record.

"In my research, I do my best to investigate whether the training of a celibate clergy has anything to do with this alarming phenomenon of claims of abuse, many of them already proven. Is it good enough for us to tell ourselves, as some do, that acts of pedophilia and abuse occur in all manner of institutions — from the Boy Scouts of the United States and Britain to boarding schools throughout the world — and are not peculiar to the Catholic Church? The Boy Scouts, however, do not claim the authority over faith and morals that the Church does. The scale of the Church's claims, and the boast that we are urged forth by the love of Christ, compels us at least to consider whether there is anything systemic in the Church to encourage the perpetrator of reprehensible and, by the way, *criminal* acts against the young. For we should be concerned that these laws offend not only morality, but are subject to the intervention of the state, and we should not content ourselves that the repute of the Church is such in our communities that police forces and justice systems will never intervene. In many cases they already have. Increasingly, we shall not be permitted to continue to deal with these matters exclusively in-house. Indeed, the days when we could confidently depend on applying our own solutions, enlightened or not, self-serving or not, are vanishing.

"There will be more civil cases. Writs have been issued, for example, against the archdi-

81

ocese of Dallas, Texas, involving a single complainant. And a number of class actions are likely to emerge in the United States. It seems essential that the Church does not look upon these merely as an assault on its treasure, but as a claim for compassion, a test of its moral standing, and, most significantly for the individual priest, of your and my repute and effectiveness.

"As for criminal prosecutions, in Canada charges are in the process of being laid against Christian Brothers who have been accused of pedophilia by a number of former inmates of the Mount Cashel Orphanage in St. John's, Newfoundland, during the 1950s. Police were slow to react to these accusations, but the media and groups such as the National Abuse Coalition have since given the victims a forum and a level of support, and solace, they did not previously have. Legislatures have reacted to such initiatives as Congress's 1986 Child Abuse Victims' Rights Act, reducing the trauma for victims in testifying in these cases."

The mood of the audience was engaged and there were no wry mouths or shaking heads.

"I am far from being the first to issue such warnings. The American Father Gerald

Fitzgerald, a pioneer in treating abusing priests, wrote a series of letters to bishops in the United States in the early 1950s warning them of a coming crisis and urging them to take account of the fact that moving offending clergy to a new parish, or diocese, or country would not reliably prevent them from reoffending.

"The collapse of the Fianna Fáil government in Ireland due to its lack of co-operation in the extradition of abuser Father Brendan Smyth to Northern Ireland, and the resignation two years ago of Monsignor Ledwith, the president of the great Maynooth Seminary, following a sexual abuse allegation, are signs that more than stopgap policies are needed and that in issues involving pedophilia and abuse, we must make the victims the chief issue — for reasons of both humanity and governance.

"We cannot blame the media's appetite for these cases on sectarianism, on doctrinaire feminism, on the theory of the child as it arose during and after the Industrial Revolution. None of this will give solace to the victim or redemption to the Church. The condition of the world is what it is, and our response is sometimes what it should not be. Self-preservation and the protection of assets have figured, in practice, in many

North American dioceses, as if they were of more significance than the pain of the wronged victim.

"Simply to raise the issue is in some eyes an outrage. It is not my intention to outrage anyone or unsettle men in their vocations. The future of celibacy may well turn out to be more celibacy. There is a sense now, however, that the terms of trade under which a priest plies his tasks have altered. The onus and solitary nature of the priesthood are of a different order than they once were. In towns of old, in Ireland or Poland, or in Catholic cities in the booming New World, there used to be presbyteries full of priests, and a constant traffic of the community. We as children were attracted to the priesthood perhaps by the camaraderie between priests, and between these men and their community, in big parishes and big presbyteries. Those presbyteries are now a memory. The community is at work, men and women fitting themselves to the strict regimen of the new economics. So nowadays presbyteries can seem sterile houses without visitors — I know myself from relieving in them in North America — and often with one priest and none of the former vivifying human traffic. I must say I am pleased to belong and live in the fraternity of my order's house.

"Many earnest scholars interested in the future of the Church feel the need for new, transparent studies that are open to peer scrutiny. The University of Chicago has conducted one — needless to say, a confidential one — into clerical celibacy. Catholic bishops in a number of dioceses encouraged their priests to participate, for they felt it was time to be realistic about the issue. Let me say, I hold no brief for abolishing celibacy — that is not my business. An old priest once told me, 'Celibacy is the card you're dealt, and if you want to play the game, you have to take that card as well.' Based on the Chicago study, however, more than sixty percent of priests admitted to sexual experience of one kind or another."

Now the first mockery, with unease at its base, broke out. "You show me yours and I'll show you mine," someone called. There was a prurient seminarian guffaw.

"But as the Chicago study also makes clear, that is true only for those who have volunteered to comment on the end of a relationship, however temporary. There are other men who may have pursued a relationship, whether within the priesthood or not, but have chosen not to give evidence. In any case, the study concluded that the great majority of the men who did give evidence possessed a relatively high level of emotional and, if you can bear the far more pretentious term, 'psychosexual' maturity."

The interest of the audience was restored. There did not seem to be many cynics here.

"It has been my task," continued Docherty, "as a clinical psychologist, to treat men who, to use shorthand, lack that maturity; who had it blocked by a number of factors. One could argue that a by-product of celibacy is the admission into the seminaries of a number of psychosexually immature men, who are encouraged by an outdated system to maintain such immaturity as a defense against homosexuality. And within the traditional system, the sad truth is that adult women were too easily dismissed as a mere temptation, an occasion of sin. Fifty-one percent of the population, that is, written off as an inconvenience to celibacy. Not only does this offend the instincts of democracy, but it immediately turns the entire gender into a series of volatile objects. Further, the acute, often conscientious, sensibility of Catholic confessors to the sin of masturbation created a milieu in which 'the objectification of women,' as modern gender studies calls it, prevailed, giving false encouragement to those who were incapable of mature relationships or sexuality.

"This is the seminary environment in which we were all educated. I look out at you and see honest faces full of commitment and humanity, and it shows me that the innate virtues — call them sanctifying grace, if you like — can survive what many experts are now calling a bad education."

Docherty could see many of the priests taking notes. One cried heartily, "Hear, hear!" He hoped the others were not taking notes in the same way as his right-wing parishioners in Sydney used to record his "political" sermons in order to undermine him to the cardinal archbishop.

"Herein, incidentally, we have a case for a new kind of education. It is easy to be celibate because of a fear of women. We remember from our earliest instructions St. Kevin, that good Irish mystic at Glendalough in Wicklow, who, when approached by a maiden, cast her over the waterfall into the waters below. If St. Kevin could maintain his virtue only by homicide, better he had given himself to her. The minority of abusers, some of whom were themselves abused as children, suffer from the St. Kevin syndrome: they are attracted to children or the young; they find it licit to use their power to compel them, and at the end they throw them over the waterfall."

The best message I can give is near delivered, Docherty thought with relief.

There had been scandals everywhere, he continued. His audience knew that, and did not need an enumeration of the horror stories. Researchers — and Docherty named several psychologists and social scientists from Europe and the US — predicted that the majority of cases were still to emerge, and that the numbers would astound and humiliate the Church — priests and laypeople. The damage done to the repute of priests by the 4 percent of them who were guilty of these crimes, and the further unknown percentage who sheltered them, could be catastrophic if bishops and their superiors continued to pursue a policy of denial, secrecy, and legalism.

There were two options, he said. One was to try to silence victims while compensating them in a limited way. This involved the victim signing a confidentiality agreement and guaranteeing not to seek further legal redress. That is, the corporate church could defend itself against the victim the way mining companies frequently tried to do, most notoriously in the United States. The second was for the Church to make peace, as far as it could, with the victims, and to make no attempt to limit their rights. In dioceses in North America, confidentiality agreements were being broken in any case, and when they were revealed by the victims, they made the Church look niggardly, legalistic, and shifty.

"I believe that confidentiality agreements, and documents seeking to bind victims to no further action, should be cast aside because they limit the rights of those wronged. And all priests should be entitled to make their feelings known about the Church's processes, since it is their priesthood that will bear the odium if appropriate healing is not undertaken. Classically, it has been the mystique of the priesthood that has made it possible for predators to operate under its cover.

"In my studies I have been the beneficiary of the conviction of my order's superiors that the discipline of psychology can provide tools that are of use to the Church. One is to screen applicants for the seminary. It is not desirable anymore that young men should flee to the seminary because they're suffering emotional instability, developmental problems, or traumas from abuse in their own childhood. I note without prejudice that even my bishop in Ontario required such screening. The process involves an interview and a questionnaire, and I have attached to copies of this lecture the journal in which these can be accessed.

"Lastly, may I quote fellow priest and psychologist Friar Austin Carter, an American Franciscan. He writes: 'Should the Church pursue legal arrangements instead of compassion and generosity, within two decades it will face legal sanctions from civic authority. I can foresee that in Ireland, for many of us the source of our faith, the government will soon be willing to react to a church that has operated by authoritarianism towards the victims and protection for the culprits.'

"By the time we have been called to account in courts and secular inquiries, we will have scandalized those who believe, and created scorn in the hearts of those who look for an excuse to belabor us. Our priests will be under suspicion for crimes they've had no part in, and will be making restitutions into which they've been allowed no input from their bishops. The shame we already feel, even if some of us have tried to hide it, will be hammered to the door of every church by secular authorities, whereas we could have prevented and healed the harm by our own efforts and by listening not to lawyers but to the generous instincts of the spirit."

Applause in the hall stuttered at first, but quickly a number of people were on their feet, nodding in Docherty's direction. The laypeople at the back of the hall were loudest in their agreement.

A young priest, a potential careerist, thought Docherty, stood up with his hand raised. Here comes my chastisement, he thought. But the man was conciliatory and asked about false allegations. Didn't Docherty think that the Church's method of settling these matters helped to limit false accusations? And was it not appropriate that the complainant be denied the presence of a lawyer, who was not as concerned with reconciliation as he was with maximizing a settlement?

Docherty argued that by now protocols had been developed to show accurately which allegations were real, the signs and symptoms of an authentic case. The questionable psychotherapeutic practice of retrieving lost memories should not be admitted, he argued. Most clinical psychologists had great concern about these techniques and felt they had in the past led to unjust accusations, often of the subject's parents. But experts in this area were familiar with the symptoms that typified the victims of sex abuse. Those present could see notes on these manifestations in Docherty's addendum to the lecture.

It was true, too, that legal processes were very blunt instruments in delivering justice and in appeasing the feelings of misused humans. But the victim should surely be permitted to bring a representative to his or her meeting with the Church, whether it be a lawyer or not. For the Church had recourse to lawyers, and sometimes they were on the panel that negotiated terms with the victim.

To this point of history the discrediting of those with true cases against clergy, rather than the reverse, said Docherty, had characterized the whole relationship between Church and victims. Nonetheless, he conceded, the possibility of false accusation was justifiably every priest's nightmare.

Some priests stayed in knots, chatting, but the hall soon emptied except for one group. A young priest amongst them, with a lustrous black beard of a kind that would not have been allowed in Docherty's day (in case the Blood of Christ got caught in the facial hairs), approached him. He introduced himself as a member of the Missionaries of the Sacred Heart.

"Are you free for morning coffee on Friday, Dr. Docherty?" he asked pleasantly. "A few of us would very much like to talk to you further."

Docherty was used to a reception of repressed hostility to his message. He had experienced it in Canada and the US when he had been invited to speak; those who could sense the impending storm of scandal, retribution, compensation bills, and resented it all, as an Australian farmer might resent a drought. Or else they thought it an overblown issue. But there were always a troubled few who wanted to talk further. He could guess by now what they would tell him: that they had seen what could be called suspicious signs, and they had reported them, and they had been ignored.

That, Docherty knew, as he said goodbye and agreed to the future meeting, was a common story, too.

6

MONSIGNOR SHANNON FIGHTS THE GOOD FIGHT

March 1996

At the end of the summer, a few months before Docherty's visit to Sydney, Monsignor Leo Shannon enjoyed his morning swim at the Boy Charlton Pool near the Art Gallery of New South Wales before strolling across the greensward of the domain to the Cathedral House gates. The statue of Michael Kelly, a former archbishop who had once argued with guards to let him into the Quarantine Station so he could give last rites to those dying of the Spanish flu, pointed towards a sky of the most superb blue.

Monsignor Shannon went to his rooms in the Cathedral House and, after a shower, changed into a light, fawn suit, such as would not have been considered appropriate in the old days, put his purple stock over his chest, and adjusted his clerical collar.

His hair was thinning but still an evident feature, and on his lapel was the membership badge for the Order of Australia, for which he had been successfully nominated by his contacts in the business community.

He went downstairs to his office — he was the financial vicar and business manager for the archdiocese — collected from his secretary the file he needed, and was in the meeting room in the chancery ten minutes before the appointed time. There he found Peter Callaghan — a retired silk, ruddy-faced and wise, a sun-kippered Celt — studying a folder full of the same documents as those in Monsignor Shannon's dossier. The former deputy commissioner of the New South Wales Police Force, Nick Erasmo, a thin-faced, defined sort of fellow, reliable, son of the Church, was also at the table. He was a young man compared to Callaghan, extremely athletic, even ascetic, with an appropriately hawk-like, inquisitorial face. Yet he had been a wonderful cop, certainly not one to refuse enhanced police powers, but scrupulous in their administration. The normal Australian balance, this committee: a balance between law and order and savoir faire, as Monsignor Shannon thought of it.

"Do you have the check, Monsignor?" asked Callaghan, sounding a little stressed.

"All drawn up," said Shannon. "How are you, Peter?"

"This one worries me," said Callaghan, who did look worried, though he was blessedly better at looking it than actually being it. "This one is a highly educated man. He has a doctorate in laser physics."

"But I don't think that changes our approach, does it?" asked Shannon.

"No. But it might influence his expectations."

"Well, as you know, we have authorization from the company to go to seventy-five thousand dollars in this case."

"Given that Father Guest died in prison serving a sentence for pedophilia, it is hard to deny the likelihood of this claim. The man's evidence is internally coherent."

"Yes," Shannon admitted. "We know Father Guest was a delinquent."

"The account of what happened is true to the way Guest operated."

Monsignor Shannon said nothing. He was given to counsels of reticence. He did not pour fuel on fires. The note-taker came in. Pleasantries were exchanged and then, "Gentlemen," said Shannon, ordering his papers, "tell me when you're ready for him."

"I'm ready," said Callaghan. "What about you, Nick?"

"I agree he's not a typical case," said Erasmo. "But I'm ready."

Shannon saw Callaghan adopt a noncommittal, professionally skeptical face, the one he brought to all his encounters with those who claimed to be victims of clergy or of members of religious orders. Erasmo was studying the file. Shannon called the receptionist and asked her to escort Dr. Devitt into the meeting room.

The door opened and Devitt entered, in a good if disheveled suit, carrying an attaché case. He was a square-jawed man with the tan and condition of someone who surfed or cycled. His eyes were, however, fraught. The monsignor was half-amused at the way the ecclesiastical atmosphere, the austere grandeur of the cathedral chancery, got to people. That is, a conditioned awe from childhood came into play. That dread we thought we had left when we grew up could rise again in us.

"Please sit down, Mr. Devitt," growled Callaghan. "Or I should say, *Dr.* Devitt."

The chair for Devitt was at the end, beyond a swath of polished wood. He would face Shannon, Callaghan, and Erasmo.

Devitt said, somewhat skeptically, "Thank you."

"Dr. Devitt," said Callaghan absently and

not looking up from his papers, as if Devitt were merely one of a string of claimants and they were all being dealt with today, "did you know that I am the commissioner of the Church's process named In Compassion's Name?"

"Yes, Mr. Callaghan," said Devitt briskly, but the unsettled look was still in his eyes. He cannot be calm about the Church, felt Monsignor Shannon, with fraternal tolerance.

"I'll leave it to my fellow board members to introduce themselves," said Callaghan.

"I am Monsignor Shannon, Dr. Devitt. I am financial vicar to the cardinal archbishop."

Dr. Devitt shook his head marginally, anticlerically — so Shannon decided. Something within Shannon had been wearied by the old white-hot slurs; claimants yelling, "Who was *Christ*'s financial adviser?" — after which, if there was opportunity, Shannon would spread his hands and say, "Times change. Indeed, our Divine Lord and his apostles were all volunteer workers. But the Church was small then."

Devitt, however, went for none of the normal abuse.

Erasmo introduced himself. "You were referred to us by your lawyers?" he asked.

Dr. Devitt nodded. "And I have to say, Mr. Callaghan, it seems inequitable to me that my legal representation was not permitted to accompany me. Yet I believe I should hear you out. And discover what, in your terms, 'reconciliation' means."

"Well," said Callaghan, "we fear that lawyers, bred to confront, might inhibit the spirit of our process."

"Yet the Church engages you, Mr. Callaghan. A justifiably eminent lawyer."

"Yes, but I work pro bono, as a volunteer and son of the Church, on these matters. That alters my participation. I am not involved in a confrontation. I trust I am involved in a form of peacemaking."

Monsignor Shannon thought that he now perceived what Callaghan had been uneasy about: frequently, in a process of reconciliation, which this was above all meant to be — a process of consolation — victims (and people who were merely victims in their own mind) were healed by allowing themselves to go through the process without legal intervention, that is, without the ceaseless interruption of lawyers on picayune issues.

"This is a matter," said Peter Callaghan to the young man, "of the Church genuinely trying to make peace with its own and to

99

address their valid concerns. We hope it is a mediation in which all parties feel they are well served. Please feel free to make any notes you choose to."

Devitt unpacked his attaché case and took out a notepad. "Now, what precisely do you mean by *reconciliation,* Mr. Callaghan?" Devitt asked.

Callaghan said, in a practiced manner, "Well, first, of course, before reconciliation, we mean to protect the Church from false accusations, a consideration that does not apply in your case. Following your assessment by our psychologist, we wish to utter our regret and to offer you a warm and fraternal reentry into a community of mutual trust.

"We are here, too, to offer spiritual counseling, if you believe you need it. We wish to mark our concern for you, and our regret for the crimes of the deceased offender by making an *ex-gratia* payment — a mere gesture, I know, but something adequate to prove goodwill and compassion. A payment made on the basis of mutual respect, that is. Not wrung out of us by any arduous or antagonistic process."

Devitt said nothing for a time, then chose the moment Monsignor Shannon was drawing his breath to speak. "I'll pass on the spiritual counseling, thank you, gentlemen."

Again, he spoke levelly. There was barely a sign of pent-up fury, or, if there was, it was a new kind of fury, a matured, subtle one with a steely density. It was far easier to deal with those who raged until it ended up chastening them. This brought them to a quick resolution, either through embarrassment at what they had said, or their relief at saying it. They took the $50,000, signed their binding confidentiality statement, and often could not leave soon enough, having got out their anger. They had been believed, and thus were convinced they might now face a renewed life.

"The trouble with counseling," Devitt continued in that even tone, "is the brand of it I got from Father Guest."

"Yes," said Monsignor Shannon, and wraithlike images of Guest, whom he had known, flickered about his memory. "Your interview with our psychologist makes that clear."

But Devitt would not be prevented from telling his story. "He began quizzing me in the confessional, asking me if I'd committed sins I had not yet even thought of. I've heard from others — I don't like the word *victim,* but I'd better say victims for clarity, anyhow — that the confessional has played

101

a big part in child abuse. That's where these predators start working on a kid. You might remember that in Father Guest's cases . . . the five he went to jail for, two of them being suicides . . . they all said that. It started with that bloody confessional box. Maybe you fellows should have a look at that. It was a dating agency for Guest. It is for other monsters, too. And one with a high success rate. If you consider raping a child a success."

"The Church did not want any of that to happen to those five," said Callaghan, the capable, dry-humored but kindly man. "It does wring the heart of the Church. I have to say it wrings my heart."

"The feeling does you credit, Mr. Callaghan. By the way, I played cricket with your son and remember him as a nice boy. But back to business. Don't forget that Guest was prosecuted only because one of the victims was a nephew of a public prosecutor.

"Now, do your notes recount that when at last I told my father about this, he took the matter to the auxiliary bishop, Charlie Modena, in Penrith? Modena told him it would stop. And it did, with me. I was nearly fourteen by then, anyway — I was getting too old for Guest. You know that phrase from the Bible? 'We are legion.' Well, Guest's abused children were legion, but they weren't the demons. He was the demon. Anyhow, I'm sure you don't mind my speaking at a little length."

"No," said Callaghan, neither sympathetic nor prohibitive. "Within reason. You are a reasonable man, I know, Dr. Devitt."

Shannon said, "We spoke to Bishop Modena, who is retired now. He remembers your father coming to him with a complaint. We do not dispute your case."

"Obviously he did not report my father's claims to the police."

"You have to remember that he was a man of his time. There was no legal requirement to report . . ."

"That's right," said Devitt. "One of those merry men and women some call enablers."

"Well," said Callaghan, "that might be a little harsh in Bishop Modena's case. But we are willing to acknowledge the special circumstances of the damage done to you with an *ex gratia* payment in this case of seventy-five thousand dollars."

Devitt whistled, but there was irony in the sound.

Callaghan said calmly, looking at his papers to show he did not intend to argue, "The sum is not negotiable."

"And I have to sign that agreement, don't I?"

Callaghan passed a copy of the agreement to the monsignor, who reached and groaned a little to get it all the way down the table to Devitt.

"Excuse me if I take a little time. I was not presented with the terms previously."

He read the document, making notes on his pad.

"I see," he said, raising his eyes at last. "I take your . . . payment, then I must keep silent on all aspects of Guest's abuse of me, and on the arrangements we make here."

"As you know," Callaghan said, "the media is ready to pounce on any vulnerability of the Church and make a carnival out of it. A carnival out of you, too! The victim is useful to them only as a trigger for their story. I don't have to remind you of that, Doctor."

Devitt conceded that with a wave of the hand. "But may I be clear? Does signing the agreement mean that my lawyer and I are prohibited from disclosing the amount of the settlement to any person? And, second, if I speak of Guest's other victims, I do it under pain of prosecution and am required to repay the amount of the settlement, with interest?"

"You understand," said Monsignor Shannon, "that this is a substantial arrangement we're making. It must be protected by substantial sanctions."

Devitt sat forward. "Oh, and I forgot the big one, of course. That if I accept the sum, I am unable hereafter to take any legal action."

"We would hope that you'd feel your troubles had been allayed and your sense of having been wronged soothed by such an openhanded gesture," said the monsignor, falling back on lines that had worked in the past. He knew that Callaghan did not like him saying things like this, and using words like "soothed" and "allayed." Callaghan was, for an experienced lawyer, something of a soft touch, son of a union organizer, raised with a fairly acute sense of social justice. He had always used his air of calm austerity to cow people, but did not like insulting them.

"We would, above all, hope," said Callaghan, "that the Church's generosity signals its desire to make amends to you, one of its children, in a pact in which privacy suits all parties."

"Under pain of excommunication?" asked Devitt.

"Not by any means," Callaghan explained.

"But under legal sanction."

"I don't want to risk excommunication," declared Devitt, annoying Shannon by directing his conversation to Callaghan, as if Shannon and Erasmo were of a lesser caliber. "Despite everything, I still attend Mass and the sacraments, in the parish of a good, liberal-minded priest whose belief is like mine — that the Church is ours, too. Yet sometimes, I admit, the host is like poison in my mouth. Your confrere, Guest, gave it that taste. Even so, it would be the last blow to face threats from the Church for recounting in the future the details of what Guest did to me."

Erasmo frowned. "You're overstating it, Dr. Devitt. There'll be no such melodrama."

Callaghan said, "Yes, you're speaking speculatively, Dr. Devitt."

"Are you sure that such a secrecy clause would survive a court challenge?" Devitt asked.

"Well, it has to this hour," Callaghan murmured.

"You see," Shannon said, "in the end you can't have it both ways."

Devitt moved his gaze to Shannon and said, "I'm afraid, then, I would find it very hard to sign such a restriction on my freedom of speech. Or on my right to take further action, if I see fit. Now, you gentlemen seemed impressed by the offer of seventy-five thousand dollars. Let me tell you that it is a fragment of the damage Guest, under your protection, has done me, and the inroads he has made upon my career. For the rest of my career I'll need to contend with the stories that came out of my crack-up. There will be no post I apply for in the future in which my behavior to the team in the laser lab will not figure. But, putting that aside, it's a matter of principle, you see, not necessarily of intent to take action. I do not see why I should have to give up these options — freedom of speech and a legal recourse."

Callaghan pursed his lips, again with a sort of unconscious professionalism, and declared, "You do enunciate splendid principles. But are you sure that in continuing to pursue the Guest matter, you will help your career? Are you sure you're not going to false extremes? Now, I know from our psychologist's report that you're under stress in your marriage. I know you and your wife recently separated."

"Leave my wife out of this, please," said Devitt, but like a request, not a command. He still seemed tightly determined not to waste his anger here.

"I do apologize," Callaghan told him. "But we know there is a high divorce rate in cases such as these. The question is — and I'm sure you are dispassionate enough to consider this — can the total sum of a victim's misery be sheeted home to the Church? I simply ask this, Dr. Devitt, because the mistakes and follies of my life have been of my own making and I was never abused by a priest."

Devitt cast his eyes up in authentic contemplation. "It is true," he was willing to concede, "that I was inhibited from extending trust to my wife. My psychologist's report, which you have in your bundles there, confirms that, and lays it at the door of Father Guest. But if I thought myself entirely to blame, I would not have considered legal options or any form of mediated settlement."

Callaghan said, "Well, we're at a point where I must tell you that this is the only form of mediated settlement in which In Compassion's Name engages."

At once Shannon was uneasy at this unexpected application of the spur by his colleague. And Devitt took up the challenge.

"So you are saying, Mr. Callaghan, that it's either this forum or the court system?"

Shannon decided now, too, however, that

it was indeed time to tap down the problem. "Yes," he said. "Once again, you can't have it both ways."

"And I must emphasize, it would be very difficult for you to undertake court action," said Callaghan. "The great benefit of this system is that strict tests of evidence do not apply. Whereas in a court case you would be challenged; your very pain would be challenged and, regrettably, mocked. In any case, a jury might decide, Father Guest is dead and has already been punished for his sins. And if you think the Church would settle out of court . . . Well, the Church's policy is not to settle before the verdict. You speak of expense — this would get very expensive for you. I don't believe that court proceedings would be a good experience for you. In the meantime, the Church offers In Compassion's Name. That is its settlement."

They watched Devitt absorb and weigh all this. He rose. "Thank you, Mr. Callaghan and gentlemen. I'm sure there's a great deal of truth to what you say, and it will be a severe test. But, you see, I can't take your offer on terms of stygian confidentiality."

Erasmo and Monsignor Shannon exchanged glances at this pretentious adjective. *"Stygian?"*

"I can only seek a form of justice that's

visible," Devitt announced, "and brings the Church to account."

"It's moot," Callaghan warned him. "Father Guest is an individual. He is not the Church."

"I intend to make a point that he was abetted and assisted by the Church."

"But as you must realize, Dr. Devitt," Callaghan said, frowning but avuncular, "the Church's assets are held by a trust, and it's from the resources of that trust you are now to be paid. It's axiomatic, however, that since a trust is not a legal person it cannot sue or be sued."

"Look," said Devitt, "I know you're a decent fellow, Mr. Callaghan, and no doubt you're convinced you're helping your Church out of a corner. I know you believe this confidentiality agreement should best suit all parties. But it doesn't suit me. Thank you."

Devitt rose and walked to the door, then turned to them and said impeccably, "Goodbye to you, too, Monsignor, and Mr. Erasmo. Thank you."

He went out and they sat inhaling and reviewing what had happened. The monsignor laughed drily. "A studied irony in his use of *monsignor,*" he said.

"Well, you don't have a son he could have

110

played cricket with," said Erasmo. "He never addressed a sentence my way."

They gathered their papers. "I hope he might be back," sighed Callaghan. "Once he's had a further talk to his lawyers."

7
DOCHERTY BECOMES A PRIEST

1960

Frank Docherty was a sensitive boy, attracted at sixteen to the poetry of Gerard Manley Hopkins, who had imbued the world with spirituality by such sentiments as "Glory be to God for dappled things."

Docherty had begun his studies for the priesthood at a time when, despite pretensions to torpor and stability, Australia was transforming itself from a white dominion into something more complex. Until then there had been largely one kind of Catholic — Irish — with a few Italians and Lebanese to leaven the mix. In the five years Docherty had spent in the Sydney seminary of the *Congregatio Caritatis Divini,* Czechs, Poles, people from the Baltic states, many Calabrians and Sicilians, and — so letters from home assured him — half the population of the Greek Islands, had arrived in White

Australia, that Anglo-Celtic fortress whose citizens consoled themselves that at least the line was being held against Asians.

During his last three years at the seminary, Docherty finished an external degree with the University of New England, where the Order kept a monastic house in which he and other seminarians could stay during the brief periods they were required to attend courses. So when his years of study were over, he had a baccalaureate, a diploma of education, and a certificate that awarded him a distinction pass in psychology.

He left the monastery to live with his mother two weeks before his ordination back in Sydney in St. Mary's Cathedral. At home, he devoured the newspapers — everything from cricket to the glamorous young Irish-Catholic politician about to make his run for the US presidency. Traveling by train and bus, Docherty saw faces that had not been in his country eight years before, and they excited him. He was a democrat by nature. His progressive, Labor-voting family combined membership in an authoritarian Church with a passionate belief in equity within society. And not merely as a political hope but as a moral duty. His father and uncle had retained the democratic impulse implanted in the Irish in the nineteenth century by the Liberator, Daniel O'Connell, who had politicized the Mass-going peasantry by allowing them to contribute pennies to his Irish Party in the parliament of Westminster, the ultimate dream being his country's self-government.

Docherty was a virgin innocent when he was ordinated. A young man who had been encouraged to believe he knew more than he did, he went to the altar and lay prostrate with the others, like the fallen who had died and were to be raised up as new beings. When his turn came, his palms were anointed with oil and bound together with a linen cloth the sacramental powers, the powers of counsel and judgment not yet unleashed from them. His hands unbound, he knelt before the cardinal archbishop and felt the man's hands firm on his skull as he pronounced the words of ordination. Then Docherty concelebrated Mass with the cardinal and the other seminarians, who were mainly from the archdiocese. He felt, that day, enlarged in a way that was, he later saw, to do in part with vanity, in part with noble but naïve hopes; and he had never quite lost this sense of exultation, a suspicion of possible transcendence, whenever he approached the altar in vestments.

Later in the century it would prove hard

to explain to young people the sense of potency that the priesthood carried then. Young Docherty was astonished and humbled by what lay ready to his hand. On ordination day, all the weird and cranky members of the priesthood one had ever known were forgotten, and the ideal of the priest — champion of his people, teller of the truth, dispenser of mercy — glimmered above the cathedral's high altar. Docherty was aware of holding great treasures, of being entrusted. His demeanor was pleasing, humble, because his mother had raised him in those terms and was watching him with her characteristic irony, ready to intrude if he developed too much priestly hubris.

There was a celebratory ordination breakfast at which his uncle Tim gave as eloquent and whimsical a speech as everyone expected. Docherty was reminded by him of the devilish, precocious, earthy deeds and utterances he had been guilty of as an infant.

As people left, he sat with his uncle, who had been drinking whiskey since before noon as if he believed that the new potency Docherty brought to the clan would moderate his blood pressure.

"Feeling pleased, are you, Tiger?"

"Happy enough," said Docherty.

"And I didn't disgrace you, did I?"

"Yes. But that's what I needed, Uncle Tim."

His uncle laughed gutturally. "Of course, all that guff was for the edification of the faithful — how I beheld a divine light in your little blackguard eyes when you were thirteen. I can't remember if I did or not. I wouldn't be surprised. How good you were at cricket — that was true. 'Australia lost a fine leg spinner and middle-order batsman when you entered the seminary,' et cetera, et cetera. Well, it did, of course."

"So, no divine light that you can remember?" asked Docherty.

"You sure you don't want a drop?" his uncle asked him. "In my experience, it's mother's milk to the clergy."

Uncle Tim was the sort of man to whom a whiskey-drinking priest was an honestly fallible and humane person. Docherty said no, without making a fuss of it.

"What I wanted to say to you, as a fellow man, is that celibacy . . . Well, it's a bugger of a sacrifice. But then marriage . . . marriage can turn out pretty much like celibacy anyhow. That's the lot of many people. And, contradictorily, given the realities of these things, we have more sex drive than we need. If God is an intelligent designer, why did he hand out enough to send us insane?

116

He could have kept the species plodding along on somewhat less of the old electricity. Meanwhile, don't idealize marriage, will you? Take my marriage."

His wife, Glenda, was talking enthusiastically at the other end of the room and laughing with Docherty's mother.

"You fall for a wholesome girl like Glenda, and you're attracted by the wholesomeness, but by something else, too. By something demonic — and you don't have to be told what it is. So you take this amiable creature as your partner, and you make things so hard for her, without even trying — just by being a bloke — that you bring misery she's never before known into her life. And all along she has a subtle hunger for something a man can't give her, something bigger and broader than we're designed for, and that brings misery as well. This happens in every marriage. In *every* marriage, believe me. So it's a strange business, and I don't have much to say to elucidate it, and I'm damn sure no priest has. But the secret is . . . the priest should know that. He should know not to pontificate."

Docherty said, "But surely the usual politeness and kindness between people — that's even more important in marriage."

"With the rightful diddly-aidle-day," said

117

Uncle Tim, as if singing the last line of "Whiskey in the Jar." "That's something about marriage they don't tell us. It's easier to be polite towards a stranger on the tram than it is to be polite to someone you've vowed to love for life. Glenda is a wonderful woman, and I am opined to be a charming bullshit artist and a fair businessman. Is that sufficient for a civilized marriage? Only if we're lucky, or saintly, or both. I say all this, of course, in the full admission that your aunt Glenda might well have been better off marrying Prawn Carey, the accountant."

This genial lecture on matrimony meant a considerable amount to Docherty. His uncle was still his uncle and had not been overcome by reverence, and could not be expected to be. Nonetheless, the newly ordained Docherty thought the older man was overstating for effect.

At the time of Docherty's seminary training, there were no public debates and no private ones, nor any debate in the soul of the individual seminarian, about the validity of celibacy. It was a given.

Docherty was little troubled by his sexuality until near his ordination: he would later believe he had been a late developer, whether for psychological or physical reasons, or both. He had been attracted occasionally, in a confused, chivalrous way, to certain girls he'd known at the convent schools near his Brothers school. He had no sisters. Were any of these, or only some of them, factors in what he thought of as his late maturation, despite his unrealistic youthful infatuations?

In the year before his ordination, however, he became strongly moved by the claims of desire. To call what overcame him fantasies was to understate the severity. They were hungers in as definite terms as hunger itself. He had a potent sense that out there, somewhere in the ether, was the other half of his body and soul, and it was undeniably female.

This perception of himself as an incomplete hemisphere seemed a far more severe challenge than ordinary sensuality. Celibacy was one of the terms of trade of the priesthood. Until now it had seemed achievable without too much fuss. But not if north sang out for south, and vice versa.

He had a confessor, Father Holland, a priest who taught the seminarians history — a good historian, too; one who would embrace with relish questions to do with scandalous and worldly popes such as John

XXII and the Borgia Pope Alexander VI, by whose fiat the globe was divided into land to the west, open to Spanish occupation, and land to the east, available to the Portuguese.

There was wistfulness in Father Holland, and it was clear it sometimes edged into depression. He was fascinated by Luther, had read his earthy *Table Talk,* with all its Germanic fart jokes. He mentioned to Docherty one day that before Luther's declaration of war on Rome, the man had been tormented by the words that consecrated the host, and had repeated them over and over to ensure that the transubstantiation of the bread and wine into the body and blood of Christ had indeed taken place.

Serving Holland's Mass on clear seminary mornings, Docherty found that the priest was cursed with the same consecration neurosis as Luther. *"Hoc . . ."* Holland would say, for the Mass was still in Latin, *"Hoc . . . hoc est . . . hoc est enim . . . hoc est enim Corpus meum . . ."*

When Docherty was struck by the great hunger, which was more than eroticism, and less arguable, he felt he must take his conscience to this priest's confessional. He tried arduously to define his exact feelings — they were so serious, so likely to end his career, he had no choice but to be honest with Holland.

"That sensation," the priest told him, "is going to occur to every priest, and if it doesn't, it should. You see, this celibacy is a complex matter. It is one thing to lay down the law to the laity. How does a man lay down the law to himself?"

Holland breathed audibly awhile, letting the question settle. "Part of the answer, they tell us, is to see celibacy not as a restriction but as a privilege. But that's only a small part of the solution. If the feeling of incompleteness doesn't pass, indeed you may have to leave. Consider this: you cannot live by the letter of the law, because the letter kills; but the spirit of the law sets free. What I mean is, you must be lenient on yourself in these matters. What sort of God expects you to suffer a nervous breakdown if you sin? The Church wants to prohibit all sexual release in adolescents for fear they'll do it all the time. Let me tell you, God understands if a good man — doing his best, obeying the rule — lapses. And you're a decent fellow. If we were not fallen people, what would be the sense of this sacrifice and these temptations? Don't feel you've got to come running to the confessional every time you're stricken with feelings of this nature."

By now the man sounded almost embarrassed.

"Another thing," said Holland, laying it down with the weight of an edict. "Some priests temper this feeling by choosing to prey on young girls and boys. This is a sin that evokes the word *'unforgivable.'* You are not troubled in that way, I hope?"

The idea was news to Docherty.

"No, I'm not troubled by any of that."

"Good," said the priest, and Docherty's experience of confessing to the seminary's historian and being absolved was all the more potent because Holland had as good as confessed his own anguish at traveling the same *via dolorosa* as Docherty.

8
DOCHERTY MEETS THE "PRIESTS AGAINST ABUSE"

July 1996

Three priests met Docherty at the coffee shop that Friday morning: the bearded young man belonging to the Missionaries of the Sacred Heart, who ran one of the Sydney parishes, and two priests of the diocese. As their stories spilled out, the specific details varied little from ones Docherty had heard during other confidential coffees he had drunk with men shocked by the behavior of others, who also had seen their reports disappear into the clerical apparatus, with at best a transfer for the offender. Docherty knew the pattern was consistent from Canada to Tasmania, because the ecclesiastical habits of mind were consistent.

One of the diocesan priests described his coming upon a priest behaving obscenely with an altar boy in a sacristy in a parish

123

where he was working. He had been so shocked he'd upbraided the more senior man, who had come to him later with lowered head and said, "I know it is disgraceful. I don't know how to make it up to that boy, but I need a chance to do so. A man is only human . . ."

The young priest admitted that — believe it or not (and Docherty believed him, because the unworldliness of some clergy could not be overstated) — back then he had barely heard of such crimes, and had accepted this man's assurance that he would seek confession, and that the altar boy would be dismissed for his own good.

"Then I found him receiving boys for private confessions in his room," the young priest went on. "And he got careless. When I wanted to run a video of *Lawrence of Arabia,* I found a tape of child pornography in the player."

This time, he went to see the archbishop. But nothing happened. The priest was moved to another parish, where, upon his semiretirement, he was given a part-time job as chaplain of a boys' school.

The priest from the Missionaries of the Sacred Heart reported that he had been so appalled by evidence that two priests had abused boys in a high school run by his order that he had written not only to his superior but, risking everything, to the Congregation of the Clergy in Rome. The priests were moved on. One was sent to England. Other than that they suffered no penalty. In an administrative sense, that was the end of the affair. The administrative sense was, this man said, all the superiors of the Order and the archdiocese seemed worried about.

"I agree with you, Dr. Docherty," said the third priest. "The contagion will explode. And I feel that we'll be all suspected, as you say, and condemned."

Docherty shared with them a certain sense of helplessness, but he knew it must not be yielded to. He wanted to say, "Endure, brothers, and they'll listen to you in the end," but he wondered whether it was too hopeful an assertion. "Look," he said in the end, "I always remind myself that Stalinism fell."

The priests laughed and Docherty joined in.

"No, I'm not comparing the Vatican to the Kremlin. But systems change quickly when the change begins. There's a cliff of indifference in front of us. One day it won't be there."

He could not let himself think otherwise.

"Surely they'll have to listen to the results of this study of yours," one of them told him, and Docherty could only say that he fervently hoped the time would come sooner or later when they would have no choice. "But it's going to take vigilance and determination from you fellows as well," he added.

"I'm willing to be vigilant," said the young priest with the beard. "I'm willing to endure. I just don't know what for. If I report a problem, nothing happens."

"Sometimes I think," said the second diocesan priest, "that we ought to form an organization — Priests Against Abuse — almost for our own protection."

"The cardinal would love that," said his colleague. "I'm not his favorite bloke to begin with." He turned to Docherty to explain. "Theological differences," he said. "The boss can't actually sack us for belonging to such a body without attracting some outrage. It's not that he's a bad fellow. He just doesn't believe it's the problem you and I know it is."

"You know what one of the problems is?" said the bearded priest. "Religious leaders see the soul as their exclusive preserve. The soul is *their* territory, they think, so to hell with psychiatry and psychology. Because they . . . we . . . . control the remission of sins. So the abuser goes to a retreat and gets absolution and really believes it won't happen to him again. But it does. The bishops don't want to face it — that the sacraments aren't everything, can't do everything. Sanctifying grace isn't enough! And isn't it interesting — we never trust the victims? We trust outsiders only if they're lawyers or insurance men."

"Nor," said the second diocesan priest, "was any of this mentioned in our training. No one warned against it as the ultimate crime. It was all about impure thoughts towards women, and sometimes towards other males. But a bit of honest heterosexuality is nothing compared to . . . Well, you can finish the sentence yourself."

"So," the priest with the beard said, "we're trying to get the word out. That we can help priests who see these things and want to report them. We keep our spirits up by writing letters to the Congregation of the Clergy. We're like Amnesty International in that way. But until someone actually answers us, that's the measure of what we can do."

Docherty nodded and drained his coffee grounds. "On your side," he assured them, "you have the fact that, sadly, the thing is not going to go away. As I said in my paper, if the Church does not face this, it will ultimately be blazingly exposed to their gaze. Then, I fear, the scandal will make the attrition of Catholics after *Humanae Vitae* look small-scale."

"When will you publish?" asked the piratical monk with the beard.

"Not for another eighteen months at least, I'm afraid. Two years, to be realistic."

"Do you think the Congregation of the Clergy will read it?"

"Naturally I hope so. But sometimes I fear it's only the social justice elements of the Church who read these things. Not the men with the power."

Docherty felt he must pay for the coffees to restore a little of the men's faith and optimism, and as they said goodbye he assured them he would keep in touch and let them know when his paper was nearing its publication.

One of them gave him a lift back to the monastery. Their conversation was somber and intermittent.

That afternoon Docherty fell into a jet-lagged sleep, full of dreams of guilt and the disapproval of prelates, from which he was awakened by the telephone. When he answered it he heard a voice he recognized instantly. The cabdriver. Its impact jolted him alert.

"Father Docherty," said the accusing voice, as if it were some sort of sleight of hand on his part that he'd picked up. "You gave me your card."

"I remember. Thanks for getting me there in one piece."

"I was tempted to take us both headfirst into a bus. Except that wouldn't have been nice for the bus driver or the ambulance men."

"I'm glad you were considerate enough not to do it."

"The rest of the world wouldn't have missed us much."

"My mother would have been cranky with you. And I've got at least two doctoral students in Canada who would have been inconvenienced."

"I was a nun," she said. "Nobody misses me. I don't miss me."

So Docherty knew that he was in serious territory and there should be no further whimsy.

"That explains everything," he told her.

"What explains everything?"

"The way priests have lorded it over nuns, anger is a natural result."

"It's not only that," she assured him. "It's

the way they dwarf you, reduce you to a spiritual bonsai. And it's the way they hide things. I'm sorry to be hostile. You might be a pleasant man, and I'm afraid I gave you the whole treatment. On the other hand, fuck you! For the complacency. That's the sanction for all the crimes."

There was silence for quite a time and he could hear her breathe. He knew he must be unintrusive and let her give full play to her anger. It would be the generous way, and the professional one. She remained silent. It was as if she could not think of the next outraged thing to say.

"Well," she said eventually. "You're sending me up, aren't you?"

"The anger you have — it's in all of us to an extent. Everyone who gets used up by the Church of the apparatchiks. The enforcers. And the legalists."

"Don't patronize me," she said, and she sizzled with contempt.

He didn't defend himself.

She said, "That's the other thing about your crowd. The smallest gesture of respect makes you smug."

"Look," he said, "would you care to meet for a coffee somewhere? I don't dare say I think I know what your problem is . . ."

"I *have* a problem and I know it. *They* . . .

they have a problem and don't. I'm carrying the shame for the lot. For them and you *and* me. Do you think that's a fair arrangement?"

Feelings of such intensity were ones he believed came from one source, though in feeling this he hoped he was not like a psychiatrist he'd met at a lecture at New York University. People whose specialty was a particular disorder had a habit of suspecting everyone they met of symptoms that only some exhibited. The psychiatrist's specialty had been cross-dressers, and Docherty had had considerable trouble persuading her that he was not a cross-dresser, since she believed that the tendency to dress up in liturgical vestments was akin to the desire to wear the accustomed and stylish clothes of women. Now he hoped he did not see an abused child in every angry adult Catholic.

Enough anger could indeed be generated by the confessional box itself, without any added wrong thrown in. Pope Pius X, by decreeing in 1910 that seven should be the age of a child's first confession, ensured that many young people felt so abused by the fear of childhood damnation and the weight of implied guilt associated with the sacrament of penance that they were angry at the practice. This well-intentioned pope had condemned infant Catholics of the twentieth century to unprecedented neuroses to do with Hell; and to questions arising from the ecclesiastical obsession with "self-abuse." Nor were priests exempt from neurosis, some thinking that even a glancing sexual thought by an adolescent had the power to cast the boy or girl who harbored it into the pit of Hell. Docherty also encountered anger about the denial of ordination, and of any real power, to women.

Still, anger on this scale could, he believed, have just the one source.

"I think we ought to meet for a coffee," he reiterated. "I think I might have at least a glimmering . . ."

She repeated the phrase ironically. "A *glimmering . . . ?* My friend, there's no *glimmering* about it!"

"Look," he told her, "I can't defend the Church to you, and I know it's futile to try. I have a hard enough time defending it to myself."

"You sound like one of those priests who'd like to leave but is too old and comfortable."

"Right on the target," he said, smiling into the phone. "I'm scared shitless of leaving. But sadly I'm also a sort of believer. I have a sense that I can't get to joy any other way.

132

Observing and dispensing the sacraments. That's my shtick!"

"Oh Jesus, now we've got Yiddish! You're a sad case."

"I think we're all sad cases," he told her.

She mimicked him in a fluting ironic voice. *"We're all sad cases.* You bastards either condemn us to the pit of Hell or patronize us."

"So, did you want to meet for that coffee?"

"Oh yes, I earn so much as a cabdriver that I can come to a posh suburb and drink latte with you."

"Is there a place near your depot?"

"Okay," she said after a long silence. "Meet me at Charlie's in Harris Street. Past the Powerhouse Museum."

"When?" he asked.

"Tomorrow," she said. "Eleven o'clock. There'll be parking."

"I'll come by bus," he said.

"Oh, the humility!" she mocked. "Don't bloody dare be late!"

And she hung up.

9
MAUREEN BRESLIN HAS
A PAINFUL ENCOUNTER

June 1996

A task of commiseration had brought Maureen Breslin to her friend Liz Cosgrove's neat little Federation house in a wooded street in Longueville. She had heard the day before that Liz's son Stephen had overdosed, apparently deliberately, and blessedly not at his family house but in his own small room in Newtown.

Maureen's friendship with Liz had waned in the thirty or so years since they had first met through Father Docherty, and the cause of that in part had been Liz's husband's unnervingly erratic behavior. So Maureen approached the house with a wistfully harbored conviction about the cause of the boy's self-destruction, and the springs that had brought it about. It was the father's fault. He had created domestic mayhem throughout Stephen and his elder brother's childhoods.

Maureen remembered Stephen had been what old-fashioned Catholics called "a child of grace" or, as they sometimes also liked to say, a child in whose face one could see the sanctifying grace. But he had fallen apart in high school, experimented with heroin, begun university, had therapy, dropped out, and taken to heroin again. Liz's love had not sufficed in the days when Matt, the boys' father, had inflicted on the household either regular sullen absences or a destructive presence. Stephen's brother had at least survived; he had become a lawyer in an NGO and, Maureen had been told, was a temperate fellow who generally avoided liquor out of terror of its malign power.

In the face of a tragic death we all write our own scenario, and this was Maureen's version. The father and his disease were to blame.

The door was answered by Paul. He blinked uncharacteristically when he saw Maureen, as if at an exceptional apparition. There was a hesitation in him. "Ah . . . Mrs. Breslin . . ." he said haltingly. "Did you want to come in?"

Liz Cosgrove appeared, haggard, behind her son.

"Oh Liz," cried Maureen, with genuine

feeling. "Oh Liz, I'm so sorry. I felt I must come in person. How we all feel for you! Your beautiful boy . . ." She remembered, of course, the fresh-faced child, not the hungry ingester of smack.

"Did you want to come in?" asked Liz, but, it seemed, as a sort of grievous challenge.

"That might not be convenient for you," said Maureen, sensing the unwelcome in her friend, and Paul's discomfort.

"Perhaps you *should* come in," said Liz — again as a dare or a taunt. Yet she didn't move from the doorway. Her neck was stringy and tense, a striver's neck; her face seemed to have absorbed too much chaos on her own hearth and, at this last blow, to be threatening to collapse.

"If you come in," Liz continued, "you'll have to live with what we're going through. And I'll tell you what I won't let you do. You can't deny anything, and you can't apologize."

"I don't know what you mean," said Maureen.

"Maybe you should go home, Mrs. Breslin," Paul Cosgrove suggested to her as Liz disappeared down the hallway. His eyes telegraphed apology.

Maureen, in the midst of her exercise in

compassion, was utterly bewildered by these pronouncements.

"Forgive me," she murmured to Paul, "but your mother's talking as if I'm somehow to blame . . ."

"You're not," said Paul. He whispered, "Don't apologize though. It will make Mum hysterical."

Liz called, "Come in, come in, for God's sake."

On impulse, and even as an egotistical urge to demonstrate her innocence, Maureen did so. Paul followed her down the hallway, saying, "I'll make some coffee."

"I'm awfully sorry, Paul," Maureen said. "It must be the hardest way to lose a brother."

"He was taken from us by the drugs before he killed himself," said Paul levelly. But he looked almost middle-aged; he did not seem to have the gait of a young man. "Sit down with Mother here." He indicated a seat in the lounge room. "I'll get the coffee. I'll put a nip in it, Mum. Would you like a nip of Jameson's in yours, Mrs. B?"

Maureen said she would have it just straight, thanks. Maureen would always remember this — he now left her to his merciless, demented mother.

"I really can't imagine how it must be for

137

you," she said to Liz.

"No. Your husband didn't beat up your kids. And your brother left them alone. At least I hope so."

"My brother? I don't understand."

"Your three are flourishing, aren't they?"

"They are. Only one of them still goes to Mass, but I've come to consider that a minor loss."

"Strange," said Liz Cosgrove, with tragic and manic emphasis. "Our families once lived or died by that. Keeping the faith. What crap! Because no one was measuring the bloody measurers, were they?"

She picked up a letter from a table nearby. "This is what Stephen left us. It's a photo-copy — the police have the original. Not that there'll be action, of course. The Knights of the Southern Cross in the police force! They'll keep it close. But they had to give it to the coroner, and they gave me a copy so I could digest it. A document like this takes years to digest. You . . . you above all . . . you should see it."

"Only if . . ." Maureen had no time to protest. Liz had slapped it into her lap. Maureen sat stupefied. Her fear was some-thing she could not define. She did not want to read it, as if the page held the infection of self-destruction and she might carry it to her middle-class children and grand-children.

Paul came in just then with the coffee and a plate of biscuits, as if there were any appetite left in this room. The distraction was welcome to Maureen, though, for he questioned her about her preferences for milk and sugar. She almost said she wanted both to buy herself a few seconds. Paul passed her a cup of black coffee while looking to his mother. "Has Mrs. B read it yet?" he asked.

"Just about to," said Liz.

Maureen took a sip of the coffee and, with no options left to her, put down the cup and lifted the suicide letter.

To all of you. If I didn't love you, I wouldn't write anything, but I know I owe you an explanation, and this is it.

I'm sorry that in wrecking my life I wrecked yours. I'm sorry for my rage. I was angry all the time, like the old man in his heyday. But the one person I go to Hell cursing is not who you expect. Monsignor Shannon. My rage was for him. And for myself as well. I take my hate for him to Hell, matched by my own self-hate. He began when I was in Year 6 — I didn't even know what he was talking about at the time, but I soon found out. Before I hit fourteen he went on to another boy. I thought of going to the Church, but it's useless — he's such a heavy figure with them. I know one thing — he'll never kill himself. Too pleased with himself. And I'm too weary to take action. I don't have the energy to keep going. The other kid, my successor, was Brian Wood. If you ever meet him, tell him to go after Shannon if he wants. He's done okay for himself, I think. He can probably afford a lawyer. Good on him.

Again, sorry, sorry. I can't face many more breaths though. Now I'm gone, you can both get on with life. The only two people I give a shit about! Don't worry, I didn't suffer. I've got a big raw dose ready.

It was signed simply "S."

Maureen looked up, stricken. She understood now. She was, by blood connection, on the side of culpability.

"Don't say a bloody thing," shouted Liz. "You may not be to blame, but if you say something I'll rip your throat out. Now go! And tell your fucking brother. Tell him. There've got to be other boys. There always are with his sort. Get out!"

Liz lowered her face, done with Maureen.

Maureen knew she had no choice but to rise. As she left the house, Paul escorting her up the hall and opening the door for her, nausea overwhelmed her. "I'm sorry, Mrs. Breslin," he whispered. "By the way, the coroner will pass on the letter to the director of public prosecutions. He has to if a third party is mentioned in that way. But the police said prosecution's unlikely . . ."

And he shut the door.

On the pavement close to their gates, Maureen vomited. She should clean it up, she knew, but she didn't have the physical or spiritual means. As she moved her hand to her mouth, she realized it still held the letter.

It was as if Liz had intended that.

10

MAUREEN BRESLIN
REFLECTS ON HER BROTHER

July 1996

I was aware that my brother, Leo, whom everyone liked, though he was considered a man's man, was entirely at home within the Church. He had worked in a string of parishes, having a gift for accommodating himself to whatever the Church decided. He adapted to the new post-Latin liturgy, though he enjoyed nothing as much as the *Missa Solemnis,* with a choir singing plain-chant and the priest singing the offertory, which Leo could do in a pleasing baritone that had been exploited, when he was just a schoolboy, for St. Patrick's Day ceremonies such as the Rose of Tralee and songs like "I'll Take You Home Again, Kathleen."

The Church in which he flourished was no longer such an Irish thing. Surplus priests from Irish seminaries, and nuns and brothers from monasteries and convents, who'd once been sent to North America and the Antipodes, were very old by the time Leo began his studies. Nowadays the Australian-born nuns and priests of all backgrounds who replaced them are growing past middle age, as is Leo himself, and there are sermons about how there's no one in the present, supposedly selfish generations to, in turn, take their place.

At various stages of our childhoods, I would guess that perhaps 40 percent of a class of girls would contemplate entering the convent, especially if they felt encouraged by nuns they admired or had a crush on. The same was the case for boys in the Catholic system who thought about becoming a priest, though the numbers reduced when these boys began to develop heroic pimples and sexual aspirations.

Leo first decided to enter the priesthood when he was nearly sixteen. The option of becoming a priest, he said, had been floating around for some time but had only just come into focus. (In the 1950s he was praised for that nifty photographic usage "into focus.")

While he was studying in the neo-Gothic seminary on the hill above the beach at Manly, he was seen as one of the young men from the archdiocese of Sydney who would be sent to the *Collegio di Propaganda Fide* in Rome. There, he would finish his studies with students from other prodigiously remote countries such as Uruguay and Nigeria. He would learn the Italian he'd need were he ever to become a cardinal. Each diocese in Australia sent two candidates, so if you were half-clever and came from one of the geographically huge but population-sparse dioceses in the bush — the vast Wilcannia-Forbes, for example — the competition for places in Rome was not so daunting. To be a city boy and be sent was a much steeper competition.

I think Leo's academic achievements were solid and were — and I say this with the greatest love and forgiveness I can marshal — unmarked by individuality or an attempt at initiative. The Church was not built for new directions. It believed its directions had been laid down, and Leo happily believed that, too, and was good at conveying the message.

Despite my mother's prayers, he was not chosen for the *Collegio,* which meant that he might have a harder time becoming a bishop. He did honest work in the parishes to which he was posted; he had a gift for administration, and was soon a financial consultant to the archdiocese's education office.

Ultimately he became an important adviser to the cardinal himself, and lived at St. Mary's Cathedral, from where he conducted the sort of active social life at which he had always been so competent. He developed an expertise with insurance through his work on the archdiocesan finances, and was a founding director of the Catholic Church's own insurance company, for which Damian called him God's broker. Thus he made many contacts in law firms and insurance companies, and would be invited to industry dinners. I had studied law before my marriage and by then had taken up an editorial post on the small staff of the *Australian Law Review*. So I sometimes met my own brother at the shindigs laid on by the larger law firms and insurance groups. But my table was, as it should have been, and as I was comfortable for it to be, one of lower status than Leo's. He would sit in a tailor-made clerical suit, study the wine labels, and set out to prove what he liked proving to the ungodly — that he was an ordinary bloke underneath it all, and as much of a success in his business as they were in theirs. Many people liked him for his mix of administrative sleekness and easy charm.

The charm would have been considered oily if it had not been based on a sincere liking for other beings, a gift of giving his full attention to the person who was consulting him.

When a sister writes such a qualified opinion — "Many people liked him" — she is giving the suggestion that she herself might not have liked him. Well, I can certainly say, as do many sisters and brothers, "We were temperamentally different." But I love him. And I was strangely proud of his capacity to be a smooth operator — that was something I seemed to have missed altogether from the family's genetic assortment. But by the mid-1970s I frequently wondered: wouldn't he have been better suited to the world of law and finance than to the business of God's truth? Was he ever attracted by the handsome women of the brokerages?

His demeanor, as far as I could read it, seemed to say that he managed such questions with the same clerical smoothness as he managed his life.

11
DOCHERTY MEETS SARAH FAGAN

July 1996

The next morning Docherty chose his clothes carefully: he didn't want to dress in full clerical garb or look exactly like a civilian when he was meeting an attractive woman. So he put on a collared shirt and wore a stock with a clerical collar beneath it. Thus he was declaring what he was without making a meal of it.

Docherty took a bus to Chinatown then walked up to the Powerhouse Museum. Past its forecourt he began scanning for Charlie's Café, and on the other side of Harris Street he saw it. As he crossed the road, he felt the old Sydney appetite for coffee dragging at the roots of his tongue. In the snows of Canada and on balmy Ontario summer evenings, he would praise his city's coffee to fellow monks, academics, or graduate students. Starbucks, having spread from Seattle

147

into Canada, would, he knew, never catch on in Sydney, since the coffee nearly everywhere in the city was already so good. A massive Italian postwar immigration had brought with it the Gaggia, and since the 1950s Sydney had gone from a tea-drinking city to an espresso-drinking one at an exponential rate.

He was not worried about being denied a coffee that morning, either. He felt that the cabdriver wanted this meeting and would be unlikely to negate it by the screams or exorbitant gestures to which she was entitled. He believed this as a professional, though behind his professional ethics and compassion for her there was in him an old-fashioned reticence about scenes.

He could see her through the front window as he approached the café. She was already seated, in jeans and the blue shirt of her taxi company, her hair severely tied behind her. She had a coffee in front of her. When he came in and nodded at her, she got up, frowning. He knew that part of her, the part stuck in its familiar misery, must have hoped he would not turn up.

She nodded him to a chair. "In normal circumstances," she said in quite a moderate voice, after the waitress had taken Docherty's order, "I'd thank you for turning up. All I've done is harangue you. So, why did you?"

"I thought I had a clue as to what might be causing you so much distress."

"So much distress," she scoffed, making a fist and hitting his forearm with it. "Not distress. *Rage,* mate! Call it what it bloody well is. *Rage!*"

"Yes. I think I could make some guesses about the rage. Without being too patronizing."

She took a sip of cappuccino and for a moment it left froth on her lips.

"Do you think I'm a good-looking woman?" she challenged him.

"I do, of course. But that isn't the issue. So why do you ask?"

"I shouldn't have any difficulty in finding a husband or lover, then, should I?"

Docherty could see no sense in buying further into this argument. The question seemed a tease, or at least a test he did not need to take. "I think we should talk about your true problems, which aren't about how you look. Shall I begin by saying what I think about your anger?"

She was surprised, perhaps by how quickly he had reached that point. She shrugged and nodded curtly but said nothing. He knew that if he did this badly, it would be painful for both of them. And there would be a scene.

"Okay," he began in a lowered voice. "I could be absolutely wrong and too swayed by my clinical experience, but I would guess that your rage comes from a violation you suffered at the hands of the clergy when you were young. Of a priest, I mean. It happens that a lot of my research and practice is in this area. You might not have felt much for years, but then the fury arrived and overcame you."

"Well, go on then," she invited him. Her large brown eyes, weighing him, were less mocking.

"I think that if you were abused as a child you would find it hard to have what are called 'normal' relationships — although I suspect that most people in 'normal' relationships only produce certain approximations. Like myself. I'm only approximately a priest. I'm a celibate monk, sure, because that's the job I took on. But I know how we all hang by a thread. However, whatever that term 'relationship' means, you don't find that possible. What happened to you *then* makes it impossible *now*. The anger, the panic — if I'm right, you know it all better than me. So you pick up a priest who's flown in from Canada and you off-load on

150

him. And fair enough, too. It's time you told someone in the business.

"So . . . am I anywhere close?"

"Well," she said, looking out of the window then returning her eyes to him. "So far you're right. You don't have all of it. But you're right in a generic sort of way."

"Of course I'd have to be wide of the exact mark. As much as these crimes are similar, they're also different from each other. I don't know you. I can't go beyond the generic."

"Guess what age I was?" she challenged him after drinking more coffee.

"I don't think we ought to turn it into a game."

"We'll turn it into a game if I say so. If it's a game, I bloody well own it."

"Very well." He shook his head. He felt the solemnity and grief. "You mean when it happened?"

"Yes. What else? When it happened."

"Somewhere between thirteen and sixteen years. But, God knows, I'm no prophet."

"No, but you're close. More than two years — fourteen onwards. Then he got a girl to replace me. And God knows where she is. Poor bitch. I think of her and I don't want her to be totally happy. Explain that."

"I think it's easy to explain. It's human.

151

Me saying that will probably only make you madder, but it's the truth. I might be a priest, I might be a psychologist, I might be a male brute, but I'm a human, too. I'm appalled as a human that all that happened to you."

She scanned him and decided to believe him for now.

"So now what? I was a ruined child. And grew up to be a ruined nun."

"Oh Jesus," said Docherty. "That is a rarer combination. But not unknown. And, I hope, not irreparable."

She was partially appeased.

"Okay, smart-arse," she challenged him. "What happened then?"

"Would you enjoy me getting it wrong?" he asked.

She made a small acquiescent squeak of the lips.

"Of course I'll get it wrong," he said. "I can only use abstract nouns like shame, rage, anxiety. You were too young and he . . . whoever he was . . . drove your psychosexual development into morbid grooves. It was as if he dammed up your development. What lies behind the wall grows stagnant. It isn't your fault at all, but sometimes you think it is, and that does nothing to lessen the rage."

He must have been accurate in part, for

she grew solemn. "Were you got at when you were young?" she asked.

"No. My being here is entirely my own work. I'm here because I wasn't got at."

"Then there's at least a chance," she conceded, "according to what I've heard, that you won't become an abuser."

"Most aren't, you know. Most of us are just confused heterosexuals. But homosexuals make good priests, too. There's an irony in that, as you know. It's the Church's secret no one dares utter."

"You don't have to be Einstein to know that," she told him.

"You don't even have to be Christ," he assured her.

"Do you understand how fake a sentiment like that sounds to the modern ear? On the streets? It might be good for the retreat house. It's utter shit to real people."

"Yes," he said. "Well, I'm old-fashioned. I actually talk like that."

"Why don't you stand up for yourself? Just because some other priest wrecked me, doesn't mean you can't push back at me."

"If you were my patient, I would. As it is, we're just talking. Human to human."

"I suppose you think I'm sexually inactive," she challenged him. This was the part, he thought, where the patient tries to shock you.

"Okay," he said. "I won't presume anything."

"I fuck men randomly. And I like it. I give signals, if I want, to someone in the cab. Other cabdrivers, too. Younger than me. Pakistani graduate students. I'm the one who makes the move, and it's quick and off he goes, never to be seen again. Never to have his face redefined for me, never to have it impose itself. I'm in charge. In your much-praised permanent relationship, is the woman ever in charge? My mother wasn't in charge for a day."

"There are some men who aren't like that, though. Power sharing is what works in most marriages. I mean, just from my observation. What would I know? But it seems people often get to that workable arrangement by argument. That's the messy human process."

"It's a risk I'm not equipped to take," she said, "and you bloody know it! Thanks to my glamorous seducer, I'm done for, and I don't want to go through the rigmarole of it. You know, *he* was younger than I am now when it happened. But that's where we come to the second reason for my rage, Father Docherty. What happens when the

154

abuser is now the one who decides the fate of the abused?"

"Decides *your* fate?"

"Not mine, but all those who come to the Church in the hope of mercy. *Mercy!* They've got a committee."

"Yes, that's become standard practice."

"And they've got a fancy name for it, but all the fancy name means is Cover Our Arses. Even so, do the poor sods who come to inform the Church and to seek its reparation deserve to have him there? Right at the heart of the process? The man who messed me up?"

"How do you mean?"

"How do I mean? This is where you'll begin washing your hands. This is when you'll scurry to your monastery and take the plane back to Canada. The monster, the man whose name turns my stomach . . . He's giving evidence right now in a court case some poor fellow's taken against the Church as a matter of principle. Reckless boy! Because I know the Church will fight to its last lawyer."

"That's true," agreed Docherty ruefully, and it did not infuriate her that he did so.

"Monsignor Leo Shannon. Know him? The Devitt case — you must have heard about it? This man, Devitt, refused the

155

terms of Cover Our Arses. The matter's in court."

Docherty flinched. What he'd known with a clinical distance had in one terrible moment become personal. He did know this man! Above all, this man was Maureen's brother. His mind surged. Maureen couldn't know about any of this, surely. No, she could not possibly know about it.

He whispered, "Surely you're not saying that Monsignor Shannon took sexual advantage of you when you were fourteen?"

"I certainly am. So, this is where you get up and leave."

"Why would I do that?"

"The closing of the ranks," she declared, so loudly that another coffee drinker noticed. She lowered her voice. "You're a bit shaken by this, aren't you?"

He thought of Maureen. A woman of probity. His professional instincts told him the cabdriver was telling a version of the truth, yet he hoped it was premature to be alarmed.

"I have to admit I am. And I can't close ranks. I'm not in the ranks. I'm a sort of outrider. I've learned not to discount any such tale as yours. You certainly don't *seem* to have a condition of pathological fantasizing, so it looks as if you're very likely telling the truth. I'm appalled for you."

"Go to hell!" But she conceded a half smile.

He thought of bland Leo Shannon, his presence in the Devitt case, no doubt dealing smoothly with barristers in the courtroom.

"I think you should see a counselor who specializes in this area," he told her after a silence. "I can give you a few names."

"For a hundred and fifty dollars an hour? On a cabdriver's pay?"

"I've known one of them to take on cases for the medical rebate. I'll speak to him. He's a friend I studied with."

"I'll think about it," she said.

"I can see why you don't wish to approach the committee here. 'In Compassion's Name,' as they call it, rightly or wrongly."

She murmured, "You're the first one I've mentioned his name to, and it's so easy. I thought beforehand saying it might kill me. Do you know him?"

Docherty's face must have given her the answer.

"My God, you do know him!"

"He's not a friend," Docherty told her, abandoning professional distance. He saw his hand on the table was trembling a little. "What would you like to do? Approach the

Church? Sue it — as this other man has?"

"I want to strip him naked. Before the eyes of the world. I want to humiliate him and have him publicly ask my pardon. Then he can suicide."

"That won't heal you. But other things can. I hope he's capable of asking anyone's pardon. I don't ask that to prejudge him, but I have a little experience of abusers. They don't like to be caught, and at a profound level they can't see that what they have done is wrong and imposes hell on their victims. Some of them even think it's educative."

She was shaking her head. He realized this analysis was not of much use to her. She had adequately vented her feelings, at least as they related to Docherty, to his membership of the clergy. He said, "Do you want to take your case to the archdiocese? Sadly, they won't let you be represented by a lawyer before the board of In Compassion's Name. They, of course, have lawyers. You should name Monsignor Shannon. Then he will not be present at the meeting. They'll protect him, of course — at least at first. It's part of the culture. But there will also be a shock for them in finding that someone they work with and respect might be guilty of such things. Your situation is far too important for me to bullshit you. You'll find that they're quite polite — at least in my experience — and they're sensible enough to know that to dismiss you out of hand isn't wise."

"That's the problem. I would lose it if they doubted me."

"It's a risk, so I wouldn't suggest approaching them until you've had professional help. You'd have to see a clinical psychologist or psychiatrist as preparation. To make it possible for you to live with limited results, because I'm afraid the results are sometimes limited. But when you're feeling up to it, the reason you must go to them is that you are not the only victim — you talked about another girl?"

He thought of the Breslins; that there was a risk they might be angry with *him* if Maureen's brother were accused. But that had to be a secondary consideration, even that — the impact of shame on Maureen if her brother's crimes were proven.

"I wish you could get exactly the result you need. It's immensely important this man be stopped. You're absolutely certain in your identification? Monsignor Leo Shannon?"

That made her angry. "Do you think I could make a mistake about it? Once or

159

twice a week for two years or more, and you think I could make a mistake; misplace a name and face? Fuck you!"

"I'm sorry," Docherty said. "And I'm sorry that what I say is such cold comfort. But think of it in these terms — every voice raised, even in their supposedly confidential confines — is another voice that will bring about the day when they will have to confront these cases with the compassion the Church boasts of. If not, it will be the secular state that in the end tells them to live up to what they claim to be."

She laughed. "My God, you're beginning to sound as angry as me."

"I'd be very pleased if I could take some of your anger onto my shoulders," he said.

"You're not such a bad poor bastard," she said. "Earnest, anyhow. Notice I talk like a taxi driver now, and you'll just have to put up with it. But you must have had a decent mother at some stage."

"I did," said Docherty. "When I was a young priest, I was preaching at a parish in Sydney before they sent me to India. I gave a sermon on marriage and thought it very well constructed, first-class oratory. But when I got to my mother's place for lunch that Sunday, she took me aside and said that if I ever gave such a stupid sermon again, or pretended to know the first thing about what she and my father, or any other couple, had been through in their marriage, she would disown me. If every mother of every priest gave such good advice, the world would be a better place."

She shook her head, beyond words now.

"So, will you talk to a professional?" he asked her. "You can see already the effect of talking to me. Even if you have to see this out on your own, an ally is an ally, and you shouldn't pass up the chance of making one, no matter how professionally dispassionate. The right person might help you to direct and dissipate your fury. You *can* live a life. Believe me! Please! That's the only doctrine I'm going to press on you today. I'm no catechist, but I'm a fairly good psychologist."

"So," said the cabdriver, "you argue I should open up about it, come forward, that I should let the Church know about him. But he *is* the Church. *Monsignor!* The very word means 'My Lord'!"

He wrote out and gave her the name of the clinical psychologist he had studied with at Sydney University. She took the piece of paper. "How much longer are you here?" she asked Docherty.

"A little over three weeks. Summer break

— the academic year's ended in North America. I've got some of my family to visit." He paused. "Look, I'm not being prudish, but you use these men in a style that's part of your victimhood. That doesn't seem much good for you or them."

She weighed this.

"I'd better get back now," he told her. He began to rise.

She frowned and after a time said, "My name is Sarah. You don't need my surname."

12
DOCHERTY'S BENGAL CRISIS

1961

After his ordination in 1960, Frank Docherty was sent by the Order to teach in its school in Calcutta, Bengal.

The India he entered did not seem to be the India of Gandhi. Leaving the airport, he passed slums which, in their crowded and chaotic variegations of material, were almost too much for the eye and the conscience to take account of. These masses would not, however, be the subject of Father Docherty's educative endeavors. The school he was to join sat in ordered grounds; stuccoed classrooms suggested the Spanish Jesuit St. Francis Xavier's ambition to bring Indians to Christ in the sixteenth century. Nearby was the dusty vista of the Maidan, and in the hazy distance the wedding-cake exuberance of the Queen Victoria Memorial glimmered like a fevered dream of Empire.

The children who attended the Divine Charity campus were the well-scrubbed and handsomely fed offspring of wealthy Hindus, Muslims, and urbane Zoroastrians, descendants of Persians, as well as some Goan Catholics of Portuguese-Indian origins. The parents of these boys wanted their sons to straddle cultures and religions with composure and worldliness, and exposing them to Catholic priests helped with that. The priests argued that they were imbuing humane principles into India's future leaders, which would be itself an expansion of Western Christendom in one way or another.

Docherty was given the task of teaching English and history to the boys in the junior years of the high school. He would need to get older before he found himself teaching the senior forms. He felt a fraud, and had none of the customary confidence that his ordination had empowered him to instruct children wisely. As well, he soon began to feel that these privileged Hindu and Muslim boys were the ones in India who needed him least. He thought of the inhabitants of the shantytowns as the true Indians, the true target for an order like his, and felt these places were where Christ would have located himself.

He tried to resist the inherent pride of such suppositions, and of the idea that he had some spectacular, noninstitutional role to play as a sort of theological guerrilla. But he had read of priests who worked in squalid factories in Belgium, laboring beside people in their own grim environment, bearing witness to their industrial degradation when no one else did. And he had read of that extraordinary French legionnaire who became a Benedictine — Charles de Foucauld. As a monk, de Foucauld had traveled with the Tuaregs of Algeria on the same principle as the priests of Belgium had toiled. There was something in Docherty that was attracted to such absolutes and humilities, that was embarrassed by the comfort of his life. Was it the hidden, proud zealot in him, or was it a true impulse?

Earnest young Father Docherty studied Hindu culture, made a pilgrimage to the house of Rabindranath Tagore, and found that his own romanticism, as well as his hopes for humanity, were drawn to Gandhi.

"Where the mind is without fear and the head is held high / Where knowledge is free," wrote Tagore, ". . . Into that heaven of freedom, my Father, let my country awake."

As for Gandhi, even Indian priests in the Calcutta school would make ironic comments about his overstatements and the contradictions of his life. The line "It took a lot of money to keep Gandhi living in poverty" was often quoted. They did not understand that Gandhi was a prophet, and thus like Christ he spoke with prophetic hyperbole. But Gandhi, and a disciple of the fabled Maharishi Mahesh Yogi — whose transcendental meditation center Docherty came eventually to attend weekly — were helpful not only in suggesting to him methods of protest without violence, but also in allowing him to maintain peace with his own sexuality. For many in the West transcendental meditation was a fad. For Docherty, it had the coloration of a deeper necessity.

The Hindu government of West Bengal was kind enough to consider Christmas the basis for a school break, so in December the school emptied and the Indian priests of the Order went back to their home cities. The corridors resonated in the unpeopled school in a way that made you wonder if they would ever take on life again.

This period coincided with a rare state of mind and soul for Docherty — the dark night of which he had been warned about but barely experienced before. He felt an aridity, a sense of being blighted, and with it there set in the most severe spate of primal sexual temptation he had ever suffered. Wrestling with serpents in his own desert, he was too distracted to avail himself of an invitation to a Catholic boys' home on Christmas Day. He could barely sit through the radio news with the priests who were left in the house.

This paroxysm of want was so intense that it seemed to Docherty it could only be solved by death or sex itself — he felt he had no intermediate stratagems. On what was, by the standards of Calcutta, a windy night, he took a bus from Park Street through the center of town to the north of the city. He had chosen to wear a hooded jacket, khaki pants, and casual shoes. He left the bus near the Marble Palace and went walking.

Soon, such a ridiculously small way from his college and order's house that he could have walked there, except for his fear of perhaps being identified while prowling, he reached the streets of Sonagachi, where women displayed themselves in almost continuous ranks along the facade of dwellings, brothels, and small shops. Some of them were unbearably beautiful and could be had for a price in rupees that even he could afford many times over. But he was so deeply ashamed to be even thinking of trading for flesh in the street, it was as if he lacked the language or valor to negotiate the exchange — one for which he had never been trained or even contemplated making.

A young Indian man in a cricket sweater and smelling of cloves came up beside him, a healthy face half-glimpsed, hair sleeked but not flashy. The man spoke to him tenderly, in good English. "I can see," said the silken voice, "that sir has a natural delicacy. Perhaps the gentleman would permit me to find him what he requires."

"I don't need help," said Docherty, his face raging with heat. He felt nearly cured of his concupiscence.

"Sir, forgive me if I seem to intrude. But I own an establishment. I have no desire to grasp any supplementary stipend from the sahib. Nor would you be prevented in leaving should you not be suited."

To get away from him, Docherty turned a corner, passing a blur of young Indian womanhood, girls from the country — some, it was said, sold to brothel-keepers by their parents. In this sea of prostitutes he felt revulsion and need in equal and towering proportions. He found he had not escaped the young man, and what was shameful was that he *did* want this man to

168

present him with what his blood considered requisite, and to extract a price before or after the improbable transaction.

The man indicated a door. "If you please, sir," and he turned to face Docherty, looking in his Oxbridge sweater and scarf for all the world like an Indian provincial cricketer. I can follow him, Docherty thought. He has sufficient subtlety.

Up a staircase with orange walls a bulb shone on the first landing, and beyond that was a curtain, which the young cricketer parted, letting Docherty into a corridor. The smell was of incense, the sounds utterly normal, nothing exotic, dishes clanging from a kitchen, water running. Their banality did not calm the beast that roiled in his belly.

The young man gestured Docherty into a claustrophobic room with garish yellow walls and unframed pictures of Tantric copulation between Indian lovers. Immediately he felt chaste again. He could escape when the man was gone, bounce down the stairs, walk past those colonnades of used women, catch the bus at the Marble Palace, and locate himself in the busload of humans making boring, unwracked journeys.

But the man was back, his hand on the

169

shoulder of a slight figure he pushed forward. Docherty avoided looking at her for some time, but he now knew that sex must be done. When he did look, she was not a woman. She was a thin country girl, a flimsy child even by the standards of Bengal or Rajasthan. The circle of vermilion on her forehead was like an admission of powerlessness, a surrender to God. Her eyes were pretty, her jaw thrust forward prognathously. She was perhaps twelve.

The man had mistakenly read Docherty's hesitancy as a desire for a child rather than a woman. His stomach heaved.

"My God," he managed to say. "What's her name?"

"Tell the sahib your name!" said the young man.

"Rahini," the child said in a reedy voice.

"Excuse me," said Docherty, and turning, he was aware as never before of his impotence in the greater world in the face of sex. Here, his priesthood and his lust were hollow boasts against reality. He rushed down the orange stairwell into the street and set out south. The Marble Palace swam towards him. On the pavement outside it he vomited as people looked at him with a level of suspicion that the equivalent illness in an

Indian would probably not have evoked in them.

That night he tore release out of his body. Willing to die in the midst of the spasms, the dark paroxysm, he found it joyless and stupefying. A young girl lived in slavery in Sonagachi. She had no part in his fantasy, but now his fleeing her seemed unforgivable. Priests could bind and loose, absolve and consecrate, and pontiffs could pontificate, but throughout all such earnestness and posturing Rahini was one of thousands of children alone in Sonagachi.

He did not say Mass the next day, and sought absolution for his range of vices, lust the least of them, from a Jesuit in the church near Xavier College. In the confessional, the priest said, "I have found Hindu meditation a great source of comfort. You should not be ashamed to look at its methods. Meditation is a human thing as well as a divine."

He was lenient, as Docherty knew he would be. "I don't think one lapse will bring down divine judgment," he said in a faint Lancastrian accent. There were many good men amongst the Jesuit brethren, and many sound jurists of morality. They were no doubt themselves flawed, self-chastened men, who, because of their own temptations, were wiser than their more rigorous, callow brethren. Docherty recalled Father Holland.

"This was not one lapse," said Docherty. "This was an act of nihilism. It was full of hate and denial. It was a display of the most horrible despair. I'm terrified it will happen again."

The Jesuit priest said, "Humans are driven to such emptiness."

"Walking away from the brothel was itself a crime," said Docherty. "I was offered a girl of, at best, twelve years. What will meditation, or my absolution, do for her?"

Yet Docherty would always believe afterwards that transcendental meditation had saved him, and had allowed him to become something like a mature priest. The classes he undertook were taught by the middle-aged Guru Surabhi in an upstairs room on Diamond Harbour Road. He began them with his critical faculties in place, but found little to criticize. TM was induced by the use of mantras, phrases expressing basic belief. Docherty found them useful, but not prescriptive. He used the Hebrew "I Am Who I Am" (*"Ehyeh Asher Ehyeh"*) as frequently as he used the Indian *"Om Namah Shivaya,"* the meditation on and submission to the female principle of the universe. He

172

was skeptical of the so-called Maharishi Effect, the belief that if 1 percent of humanity practiced meditation, there would be a resultant rise in the contentment of the entire species. That would remain to him a pleasant fable.

He took to meditating twice a day while sitting in his room in the priests' house. The exercise gave him not only a sense of healing, but a space in which he felt the emotional sinews of his seminarian boyhood were stretched to mature form. Through meditation he confronted the true scale of desire; and yet, through contemplating some of Surabhi's remarks, he began also to consider the essential unity of the world. This was no abstract idea to him. It related to how he should accept the push-pull within himself, his inner tides of hungers and recognitions. To dwell on the unity of the world and of the human entity, to experience it, or to consent to feel it as a potent essence within oneself was a liberation for a priest needing to be reconciled to himself, to what he was, the usual stray package of seemingly contradictory impulses.

For the Christian orthodoxy in which he had been raised claimed that the world did not possess unity, but was driven by dualities. God and the Devil were the poles of the earthbound creature, and on top lay the poles of the flesh and the spirit. It was axiomatic that the spirit had to overcome the flesh to avoid damnation and chaos. The soul had to dominate the base meat of human existence as Europe had dominated the African darkness. That was a dangerous and destructive division to introduce into the one planet and, above all, into the one human being. It came to him gradually that he could not continue as a priest unless he jettisoned such beliefs, and became a sort of heretic. Unless the spirit somehow welcomed the flesh in as a brother, neither could happily survive. The crucial experience that had sent him to the guru on the recommendation of the solemn old Jesuit priest seemed to prove this to him.

He remembered reading one of the Desert Fathers, an Egyptian hermit of early Christianity, who had recommended a mental exercise: when attracted to a woman, or by the thought of her, one was to imagine lying with her after death, all her beauty putrefied and stinking. The body wanted her, that was the argument, but the spirit had the power to abstract her and condemn her to death. At the time, these legends had been codified — a debate still flourished about whether women possessed a soul in the same sense as men, and that argument would continue well into the Middle Ages.

But an instinct, developed through meditation, told Docherty, and reason told him even more pointedly, that he could not "conquer the flesh"; that to represent the body as a mere lump of questing flesh reduced those who were desired — women themselves — to mere lumps of yearned-for flesh and challenged the dignity of half the human species. He could not, as St. Kevin of Glendalough had, throw women whose presence tempted him off high geographic points, and it was not his duty to imagine them putrefied. He must accept both the conditions of his life, and its coexistence with a world of beautiful and engaging women, many of whom he could have loved.

Thus meditation was for Docherty the great equalizer of body and spirit, and the great appeaser of elements. As a seminarian he had not been taught how to meditate, but simply told to do it. Now, exercises the downtown guru gave him, and even the incantation of the transcendental mantras, prepared his soul for the great totality — good and bad — and the coexistence of parallel splendors and demons. Sometimes in meditation he simply sat with Christ and the "Mother Principle," Mary. Around these avatars, too, the tensions of desire flickered, for they were also human, appeased and validated and imbued — he simply accepted this — with divine force.

He did not advertise his interest in Hindu meditation, nor did he conceal it, and the people most amused were the few Indian priests of the Order, who nicknamed him Dox, short for "heterodox," and made well-meaning but skeptical jokes about him as a levitating swami. The English deputy head-master — the headmaster himself being Irish — came to refer to him as the Guru.

His confession with the Jesuit priest brought him not only to meditation but also to the office of Dr. Fatima Deriaya. The priest had astonished him that day by saying, "There is a woman named Dr. Fatima Deriaya. A Muslim. She negotiates with brothel-keepers and buys girls' freedom. Perhaps you could discuss your concerns with her."

"I would have to tell her that . . ."

"Exactly. You'd have to confess the experience of your weakness. As a Christian priest to a Muslim woman. Perhaps that is adequate penance."

Dr. Fatima Deriaya was a middle-aged, gentle woman with large, lively features and a persuasive, ironic delivery that reminded Docherty a little of his own mother. At their first meeting in her office, he managed to tell her how he had met Rahini. He gave Dr. Deriaya the street and building to which the man had taken him, and asked Dr. Deriaya whether her NGO could liberate Rahini. He realized, he told Dr. Deriaya, that one liberation barely touched that huge bowl of ignominy. He gave her all the money he had accumulated over two years.

"Can you afford that, young man?" she said, unshocked by his confession, tolerant.

She bought out Rahini for what she considered an exorbitant price, and the brothel-keeper joyously held the money and declared, "For this I can buy two new girls."

In a fallen world, it was hard to do unambiguous good.

After three years, the deputy headmaster and headmaster's reports on Docherty were so glowing that the Order decided to bring him home to Australia and into full-time university studies, though these would be interspersed with holding parish retreats and filling in for diocesan clergy in local churches.

He was uneasy to go, to exchange the scale of India for the smaller horizons of suburban Australian life, and had he been a man who had not taken vows to his order and its superiors to obey their reasonable decisions, he might have chosen to stay. But he was no more free to remain than a soldier with transfer orders. So he went home.

13
THE CASE OF SARAH FAGAN, 2

Early 1970s

One afternoon she heard him say idly that he hoped Mother Alphonsus could supply him with two other girls to help him out. She felt the jolt of this news, and a sickening bewilderment in the pit of her stomach; the extreme sentiments of the rejected. Yet at reason's futile level, she knew even then that he had never promised her their collaboration would be exclusive.

Later, in the presbytery office, he said with a naked suddenness, "You understand I might need to have these other girls here for appearances?"

She wanted to know what that meant but could not frame the question. Even though she could have raged like a virago in love, she maintained a calm and respectful demeanor. That was the condition of employment.

Next, with a deftness she would discern only afterwards, he said, "Do you feel there has been a special divine kind of friendship between us? That we are drawn close in a spiritual unity, perhaps like St. Francis of Assisi and St. Clare. The connection between us has a holiness to it. Do you sense that, too, Sarah?"

There was no air remaining in the room — he had used it all to frame his astonishing proposition. She wondered if she should run out, driven by the scale of what he had said.

"I like to please you with my work," she said simply. "If that is friendship, then I'm very happy."

He held up a hand and became more confiding, wonderfully so, and the fragrance from his hair or skin, or both, seemed very strong. "I know what it is, dear Sarah. You don't find home a place you want to be. Would you let me make friends again between you and your family?"

"How would you do that?"

"I could come and see you. A pastoral visit."

"A visit?" It could not be refused, but the idea of Father Leo Shannon encountering her parents was excruciating. Her father would slur and lurch in the living room, switching the television off with bad grace. Even her harried mother was now herself an element in Sarah's dread of home: she represented to her daughter the shame of having marriage reduce her, taking away her features; and her eyes had seen what could never be mentioned — her husband's sodden attempts to find a new version of his ruined wife.

It was apparent all at once to Sarah, under the threat of Father Shannon's visit, and of what might be shockingly said and revealed then, that her sole option was to become a nun. That was the utter escape from her family. Her mother, by the force of this choice, would come to forget everything she had seen on the night Sarah's father had visited her. God knew what her brothers thought about nuns, yet she felt that she could reduce her brothers and her father to a grudging and bewildered reverence. And be done with them.

When Father Shannon turned up at the house on Thursday night, Sarah was in torment at what he would discover and use to discount her. As her mother led the priest down the hallway, breathing was a challenge for Sarah; the world could at any point and in untold ways fracture. Father Shannon carried a box of chocolates and presented them to her mother, saying that his sister had said when she was little, to the amusement of adults, "There can never be enough chocolates."

"And besides," he went on, "your very efficient daughter has helped me so well to get the parish records in order. I'm going to get more girls from the convent to help me, but your daughter is the paragon."

The truth was that her father had been abstemious that day, at her mother's insistence, and though edgy, perhaps waiting to go out later, treated the inconvenient priest with a somber deference. Her brothers took their cue from their father. They made no smirks in Father Shannon's wake. Observing the ease of the priest, Sarah told herself he was clearly not shocked by the house or by the assortment of people within it, and she was infused with a sudden joy. He had cast absolution over her. There were no problems left in her life that could not be overcome by her friendship with him, and by prayer and study. And becoming a nun! She understood that he had mentioned the other girls purely to pretend Sarah was not as special as she actually was to him, or perhaps to allay some indefinable alarm in her parents at the intensity of his favor.

The survival of the visit, and Father Shannon's forgiveness of the Fagans for all their domestic flaws, physical and temperamental, exhilarated her.

Two afternoons later she was attending to the filing in the parish office when he entered as usual. "Sit down here beside me," he said lightly, and he put himself on the settee beneath the window. When she obeyed him he sighed a peppermint sigh. "Companion of my soul," he said. "You may indeed be unhappy at home." And with extraordinary suddenness his arm went around her shoulder, he moved his smooth face towards hers and had kissed her before she realized he was even contemplating it.

The kiss did not seem to her superficial. It opened her like a wound. It shuddered through her. She wondered if it was meant to be somehow disciplinary, the clerical equivalent of an electric prod. It seemed at the least a tough sacramental test.

He said, "I know that God permits us this in the light of our special love."

The line would sound later in her history like inept and fraudulent self-justification. At the time, however, it resonated with overwhelming authority. She thought it the truest thing she had ever heard, and though she was caught between flight and captivity, the challenge of interpreting his actions kept her static.

At last she was able to raise her eyes to him. His glittered. There seemed a huge theological certainty in them. He bent and whispered in her ear, "As much as this is permitted, I will go. Enough for today!"

He kissed her cheek, stood, bending a little, said that they must pray about this, and left the room.

The next day at school, after a fevered night, she felt agelessly wise. But she remained in a ferment; indeed had come close to pretending an illness so she could stay in the hated home. The very unexpectedness of what had happened, and the unpredictability of what would happen today, the afternoon the monsignor always visited his older sister in the Eastern Suburbs, kept her preoccupied. She saw Mother Alphonsus in her maths class, but knew that she could confide nothing to her; nor did she want to. For one thing, Mother Alphonsus was, above all, a practical woman, and this business superseded practicality.

That afternoon at the presbytery Father Shannon came in during her office duties, sat in a separate seat, and assured her it was licit for her to take her blouse off. *Licit!* She would sneer years later, as if it were a prissy word that compounded his crimes. But, again, at the time it had absurd power. She turned her back to him to remove the garment. He told her to face him since there was nothing hidden and nothing forbidden between choice souls. She thought, if he can accept my breasts, then there's nothing more for him to absolve. She turned. He said she was beautiful in the eyes of God. Then, curiously, she thought, he asked her to lie on his lap. As he tentatively caressed her breasts she felt in him a divine heat and he, the most measured of men, lost control of his body and shuddered beneath her, gasping. That happened twice. And then with a further caress he told her they were to go from each other in peace and without telling any lesser souls about what had passed between them.

She told herself she should feel flattered, and this response was interspersed by a surge of sensual feelings that she knew were forbidden. Yet, since they were centered on him, they must be lawful as well. She would ask him about that next time she saw him.

He reassured her. He visited the Fagan household again. He brought *National Geographics* for the boys.

And then, the following Thursday, when it was quiet and children's cries from the school yard were no longer to be heard, he penetrated her with his body. She lay like a martyr (and so she believed she should) ready for the transfixing, since it was the priest's will. It was her entry, she felt at once, into a true earth and the possibility of paradise. Instinctively, she served his purpose. She had no doubt that the chief pleasure to be concentrated on was his. She knew it was not her time, that her duty in this connection was to give him solace in the agony he seemed to suffer as he withdrew himself and emitted his fluid.

He became less and less secret with his body after that. He instructed her in the risk of conception, too, and generally pursued pleasures that made it unlikely. For this she was at least thankful; for with conception she could not become a nun — or so she was convinced.

14

MONSIGNOR SHANNON PREPARES FOR BATTLE

April 1996

Monsignor Shannon, Peter Callaghan, and Pat Lennon, CEO of the Catholic Church's insurance company, were waiting for their barrister, Mr. Roger Kermode, to return from court to his chambers in Phillip Street. It would not be a long wait, the secretary assured them. The three had had time to start a conversation about why barristers' chambers were so austere while the big companies of solicitors displayed expensive art in their offices, when a secretary told them that Mr. Kermode and his junior were ready to see them.

They entered Kermode's room. As well as a desk laden with files, Kermode had a settee and chairs, and a coffee table at which they all sat. He was tall and thin and the corners of his mouth were tucking themselves into a sort of smile, a smile that said,

"All right, get it out — but I've already heard it before." This was a very useful characteristic, Monsignor Shannon surmised. Kermode's junior was Ms. Marissa Zoldak — obviously a Polish daughter of the Church. She had an almost willfully sculpted look, a rehearsed severity she probably thought junior barristers needed to maintain.

Kermode announced that Dr. Devitt had offered to come to terms for a payment of $200,000 and the removal of the confidentiality clause. If the Church accepted the terms, it meant, Kermode said, the media would be onto Devitt immediately for an interview, with the result that many of those who had already agreed to the terms of In Compassion's Name would themselves set up a cry for a new settlement. It was worth meeting again with Devitt's solicitors, said Kermode, to try to come to an arrangement, even though Devitt seemed fixated on circumventing any confidentiality clauses.

"We know what the result will be," the eminent Kermode declared, "if the Church publicly yields to Devitt. It will be in danger of more and more legal confrontations, and larger and larger payouts, all at great peril to the archdiocese and the Church's repute."

The severity of the challenge was clear. Of course, Devitt must be fought. It was sharply apparent to the monsignor. It was a holy war. Even so, he was always surprised by the issue of money. Two hundred thousand dollars was a modest claim for a man who claimed to have been so badly hurt. It was clearly meant to signify Devitt's lack of avarice yet his desire to damage the Church in the public forum, or a civil court. For Monsignor Shannon knew by his own experience that any sum was dwarfed by a supposed murder of a soul. Whenever he had suffered guilt for having gravely harmed another soul, he had gone to confession. Absolved, he felt restored to himself, and to the light, and his purpose to amend was always there. But in the case of fallen humankind, and the version of it that he was, amendment was not always adequate. He knew he had a weakness. He knew that even had he paid out all he possessed in compensation, there was no adequate sum. His own sins were such that only Christ was able to take them on his back.

Even so, the victims did carry on! As if they were determined not to get over it. And ignorant journalists and pop psychologists claimed that the so-called abuser knew *no* guilt. There had been a period twenty years before when Shannon had heard Father Guest's confessions, and he knew that the man's sense of guilt, his repentance and concern for his victims were acute. Guest was aware of God's displeasure. He was aware of the potential ruin of young souls; that the assault on souls was too vast an issue to have a price tag.

The thing was that Guest could not stop. Shannon still hoped he had. His sins had been intermittent, his repentance sincere. His criminality was not established.

Ms. Zoldak distributed copies of Devitt's filed applications to the Supreme Court. They sought, despite the Limitation Act, to sue the archbishop and the trustees of the archdiocese for the abuse he had suffered a little more than a quarter of a century earlier at the hands of Father Guest.

Kermode took them through the sections of the claim. Psychiatric treatment in Devitt's early thirties, after a crisis in his scientific career and his marriage, suggested it was only then that he began to attribute his difficulties to the abuse he had suffered from Father Guest. By this time Devitt was deputy director of a research team and was using his laser expertise to work on the creation of nanowires, which apparently would make the computers of the future superfast, beyond the limits of conventional conductivity.

He was given indefinite leave when complaints emerged from his team members that he had begun to direct fits of rage at them, and at the personnel of government, and private research organizations as well. There were outbursts of rage against his wife, too, and she was frank about the fact their marriage had nearly collapsed.

Devitt claimed that in the early phase, when his nature first seemed to be undergoing a change for the worse, he had not attributed it to the abuse. This claim, said Mr. Kermode, explained why Devitt needed leave to sue now, in spite of the Limitation Act; why he had not sought legal relief earlier.

The limitations matter was not all the judge would be asked to address. The crucial question was whether the archbishop and the trustees of the archdiocese *could* in fact be sued.

Kermode said, "There is a clear reason why Cardinal Condon can't be sued — namely, he was not archbishop of this archdiocese when Guest committed these crimes. Even at the time of the later crimes, for which Father Guest served a jail sentence, he was not archbishop then either. He cannot be *personally* responsible. And that is the least of our arguments."

Callaghan, Kermode, Lennon, and the monsignor discussed for a while the cardinal archbishop's professional insurance with the subsidiary of Catholic Insurance, of which Monsignor Shannon was so proud. The cardinal's insurance, as head of the archdiocese of Sydney, had been taken out originally, Lennon said, in case of people slipping on the cathedral steps in wet weather and breaking an ankle or a skull. He suggested now that the monsignor should take a look at it and consider upgrading it, even at some expense, against the possibility that the Supreme Court might permit Devitt to sue the cardinal.

"The Church trust and the trustees are a different matter," said Kermode with a legal gravity he was not even aware of. "A trust has continuous responsibility for past liabilities even if the trustees change. So the present trustees cannot in law say, 'We weren't there!' But as my friend Mr. Callaghan has pointed out to me, there is considerable common law to show that trustees whose concern is the administration of Church assets cannot be sued as if they were employers of a miscreant priest. The culprit is Father Guest, and nearly all his savings went on his funeral, though his sister received a sum of three thousand seven hundred dollars from probate, along with the share of a beach cottage. Understandably, Devitt does not plan to sue Father Guest's estate. The other actionable party can only be God, given that the 'man,' as in 'man-of-God,' is deceased and God isn't."

A few dutiful chuckles were contributed. Satisfied, Kermode went on. "However, maybe the trustees who run Church land, who can be envisaged to run Church land in the manner of a body corporate . . . Maybe it *could* be decided *they,* the body corporate, the trust, were somehow responsible for Father Guest's behavior, especially if it can be proven that the Church had knowledge of Guest's activities."

"So," said Shannon, "the law that shelters us is also the one that may betray us?"

"We don't know. There haven't been many cases like this one."

A solemn sense of the historic settled in the room.

"Now," Kermode continued, "to the arguments his lawyers offer for his seeking relief from the Limitation Act. Dr. Devitt's university appointed an emeritus professor of clinical psychology to inquire into the problems Devitt began to suffer earlier this decade. You will find her report as Annexure Two in their papers. You will discover that it demonstrates both the research team's sense, and Devitt's, that his behavior changed during the nanowire project. Until then he had a demeanor some associate with unworldly scientists, and it was considered part of his character — he was a sort of kindly eccentric. This changed when he married. Marriage was a great challenge to him, according to the report. Devitt himself frankly told the university's psychologist as much — that his anxiety levels mounted before and after his marriage. And then suddenly, in May 1993, there were atrocious screaming matches with colleagues at the laboratory. . . ."

"Do you intend to argue that his psychological problems themselves make him an unreliable claimant?" asked Shannon, pleased to be nobody's fool.

Callaghan held up a hand in warning. "Surely it could be alternatively and equally argued that the problems Dr. Devitt has had with the research team and with his marriage are a sign of the scale of damages he has suffered?"

Kermode beamed. "Yes. Given that he is seeking an exemption from the Limitation Act, we are better placed arguing that he has made contradictory statements about the onset of his symptoms *and* about his awareness that the damage came from Father Guest's abuse. We can show, I believe, that he could have made the claim earlier. Because we also have a published case study — without names, of course, but it is a study of Devitt — as he consulted a psychiatrist in 1988, in the days of his graduate studies. Devitt admits the case study is of him, and in it he speaks of problems that had arisen as a result of Guest's abuse, the details of which the psychiatrist at the time could have heard only from Devitt's own lips. Thus he was aware of the impact of the abuse at that stage, yet took no legal action, even though he could have done so within the terms of the Limitation Act.

"What was the difference between then and now? Guest was still alive then. Now we have Father Guest's sister, who says she can remember Devitt turning up at Guest's quarters in the presbytery all the time, pushing himself on the man, offering to run errands, et cetera. I believe Devitt did not want Guest to explain that in defense. Altogether, Devitt is, in our opinion, *not* the sort of man who can be trusted to know his mind. The operation of the Limitation Act should not be suspended to accommodate such a contradictory and volatile character."

Leo Shannon admired the force of this argument but saw that even though Callaghan knew the reality of legal practice, he was uncomfortable at the idea; at the use of a man's own reticence and mental illnesses to skewer him.

Kermode nonetheless continued. "The defense has something, though, that I must bring to your attention now. If you turn to Claim 9 . . ."

There was a sigh and scrape of turned pages and some mutual consultation on where it was. "You'll see that the plaintiff has a witness — a young man a few years younger than Devitt. His name is Moore, as you see. Moore claims under statutory declaration to have been abused by Guest, his abuse commencing after Devitt reached sixteen and was suddenly of less interest to the priest."

The monsignor knew what was coming.

"I believe, Monsignor, that you met with Mr. Moore? You, too, Mr. Callaghan."

"No," said Callaghan. "Mr. Moore's case

didn't reach me."

Leo Shannon thought it best to combat the embarrassment head-on. It could only be countered by an air of confidence on his part and a combination of claimed compassion and good sense.

"Mr. Moore came to me at the cathedral for an introductory interview, the kind I often gave prior to taking a case on to the board. Moore had his own accusations against Father Guest."

"And you received him in your role as vicar advising the cardinal?"

"Yes. It was one of the earliest cases of this nature thrust on me. I listened to Moore, a highly intelligent young man like Devitt — at least we gave them all a good education — and was afterwards concerned about what to do. The organizational details of In Compassion's Name were being finalized at that stage. Father Guest was still in good health, and the abuse of which Moore spoke had ended ten to twelve years before."

"He claims," murmured Kermode, "that you took an arguably inappropriate option, Monsignor. You know what the evidence he'll give consists of. He claims that on his second visit to you . . ."

Monsignor Shannon believed, again, in intercepting bad news.

"Yes, I know what he claims. That on his second visit, I brought in Father Guest to meet him, and after I reintroduced them, I left them in my office alone. I expected Father Guest would make a statement of repentance as I'd earlier suggested to him, and between the two men there would be a reconciliation. Since those times, of course, we have had a fast learning curve in managing such confrontations, or even in considering the wisdom of them, but, as I say, In Compassion's Name had not yet been put fully in place, and I was still learning."

"According to Mr. Moore, he was petrified at being left in a room with his abuser, and he fled."

"Yes, I returned to find Father Guest on his own in the office."

"Moore is on record as saying that his unwillingness to confront the Church any further was due to your actions, Monsignor."

"I regret that. I don't quite see how . . ."

He was not sure to whom he was apologizing, because Kermode's manner was clinical and did not actually apportion direct blame. Yet he felt a strange prickling of the flesh. He could not deny he was embarrassed, all the more so since the incident might produce an uncomfortable question in court.

"If Dr. Devitt's claim succeeds," mused Kermode, "I believe Mr. Moore will not be far behind in taking a writ. Another example of a delayed desire to make the Church pay and do public penance. Things will then become very busy for all of us. Devitt has the capacity to begin a gold rush from plaintiffs alleging past abuse."

There was silence. Callaghan growled, "I'm sure that if the monsignor takes into the witness box the same candor and measured response he has shown us, the influence of this witness, this Moore fellow, will be diminished."

"And if the plaintiff Devitt *is* given leave to take a representative action against the cardinal and the trustees," said Kermode, "I think we are on fairly hopeful ground. But best we defeat that plea at the beginning, by referring to the contradictions in the plaintiff's evidence."

Callaghan gurgled. "Yes, we have the evidence that seems to show that Devitt had a strong sense of damage done him when his case study was produced by a psychiatrist nearly a decade ago. Why indeed didn't he advance his claim then? But it seems to me a plaintiff does not have to be a perfect, sensible sort of fellow to have a true claim for damages. There's the question, too, of whether the Church would demean itself by arguing his character instead of putting forward the other persuasive issue: that the Church as a trust cannot be sued. That's an issue that would rule out suspending the Limitation Act."

There were glances between the parties again. Callaghan is a decent man, Leo Shannon mentally conceded. Loyal to the Church, papal knight, careful counselor. Doesn't like going to town on Devitt.

"If you'll forgive me, Peter," Kermode said to Callaghan, "I think it is clear that it's in the Church's interest to do everything they can to discredit this claim."

"Except we have already acknowledged the justice of his case. That's the thing I'd say, at the risk of repeating myself."

"Your acknowledgment of his grievance," said Kermode, "was meant to restore him to the Church. When he rejected the deal, that changed."

"Well, I know that much," said Callaghan with an air of chastisement. Then he smiled, "You see I don't have the gift for head-kicking that I once possessed."

Kermode reassured him. "Peter, my dear fellow."

"I think we should talk over the weekend,"

said Callaghan. "I agree we can win. Without crucifying him."

A snatch of scripture arose in Shannon's mind. *It is expedient for one man to die for the multitude.*

He said, "The Church cannot contemplate losing this case."

15
DOCHERTY VISITS THE BRESLINS

July 1996

Theirs was a middle-class home in Sydney, with long views of the embayments of the Harbour and the Parramatta River, as broad here as most lakes, and complicated in geography. Beneath sandstone ledges, a beach glimmered sunstruck and saffron. This was the inheritance of the Breslins, and it was an exhilarating place.

There was peril in being here. If Docherty desired any woman on earth, it was Maureen. He cherished her in an enduring way. Damian knew it and had forgiven it. Docherty wondered which of them would open the door. It was Maureen. Though he had seen her on his previous visit, he was thrown further back, to when he had first left Australia for Canada, when feelings between the three of them were still very raw. So now at the door their history of shame and longing caused them to pause, to give themselves a chance to measure how things had been then, and to reduce these emotions to the present scale of accommodation between the three of them.

After this assessing pause, Docherty kissed Maureen's cheek. What fine northern European skin she had. Even the Australian sun had not marred it.

"Well . . ." she said. "Yes, I was nervous, and you were, but no need to be now the door's been answered. So fit all that into the enigma of longing, and let's have breakfast."

She led him through the house and onto the sundeck. There, tall Damian Breslin walked to meet Docherty with a stoop that was more a mannerism than an ailment and bespoke a tense wish to make his visitor welcome.

Maureen filled in Docherty about the three Breslin children. Rosie was living in Sydney with her husband and they had a daughter. She'd wanted to call around to see him but had had to go to Adelaide as her father-in-law was seriously ill. Niall was in London doing something financial Damian did not quite approve of; and their third, Joe, was an academic, a biologist at Emory University in Atlanta, Georgia. Maureen smiled with her relief that the business of being a parent had come good. She asked Docherty about Canada, and again he found himself describing the Arctic winters in his pleasant stretch of Ontario close to the Great Lakes. She asked him about his work, but seemed half-distracted, her attention drifting midsentence.

"You gave a lecture," she asserted with a sudden piercing look.

He uttered a few banal words about it and the reception it had had, and then eventually forced himself to ask, "How is the monsignor?" trying to sound as though he was indifferent to the answer.

Maureen looked at Damian, who had raised his eyes from the barbecue. "He's involved in a damages case against the archdiocese," she said. "It's been in the press."

"Ah," said Docherty. "Yes, I think I've seen something about that."

"He's giving evidence for the archdiocese. Damian doesn't approve of the Church's case. He's a most subversive Catholic, my husband." She adopted a brittle chirpiness.

"They're engaged in this," cried Damian, "like any big corporation trying to scare off plaintiffs. But it's worse. Because corporations don't *pretend* to love the world and

204

honor a moral code."

"Litigation is very bad therapy," observed Docherty. "For all parties."

"We are not as concerned as some are about the Church's temporal wealth," said Maureen, puzzling Docherty with her bleak eyes. She paused and looked into a middle distance. "Just for example," she asked after a long pause, "what would *you* do if you'd been told the name of a priest who might have been an abuser?"

By the barbecue, Damian paused. What if I know the name of an abusing priest myself? Docherty privately asked himself.

"You'd certainly let him know you had heard something of the kind," Docherty suggested cautiously. "I think it's too broad a question. Do you have details?"

He knew this could not — surely — concern her brother. It must be another grievous story.

Maureen and Damian exchanged a long look. She addressed Docherty with that same sideways flick of her eyes that had once enchanted him, and still did, for that matter. He thought that this was why marriages lasted. However a face aged, the contours of ageless intentions rose in it as freshly as ever.

"Frank, we're terribly sorry to put this

onto you when you're here for such a short time and there is so much to catch up on — so many more pleasant matters. But this is a pressing one that we need to deal with, no matter how distressing it is. We need to show you a note that's come Maureen's way," said lean, intense Damian. "As soon as we heard from you, we knew we'd need to consult you about it."

"But especially given your expertise, Frank," Maureen rushed to say and her face had paled. "Wait a second."

She went into the house, and while she was gone Damian turned to him and said, "If the sod had taken after his sister, he might have been halfway a man."

"You mean Leo?" asked Docherty.

Damian did not reply immediately. "I'm sorry," he confessed then. "I really don't want her to have this grief to deal with. She'll feel more guilt than he will."

Docherty felt helpless to give her aid. He had earlier heard accusations against her brother, and seemed now about to be offered a kind of corroboration.

Maureen returned holding a sheet of paper, two-handed, as if it offered resistance.

"Some days ago I visited Liz Cosgrove. Do you remember Liz? She and I met in your group of Gandhi-ist revolutionaries. I believe you helped her with that drunk of a husband of hers. Do you recall? They had two boys. And now the younger one, Stephen, has killed himself. A heroin overdose of all things — he's been addicted for years. I blame that awful father of his — he drank himself to an early grave, and now his son.

"I went to see Liz to console her, and for some reason Stephen's brother, Paul, let me walk away with this." She held up the piece of paper. "It's Stephen's suicide note. Maybe it was confusion or maybe Paul wanted me to be stuck with it for some reason. And I am stuck with it. It was like carrying home a spider on my dress. I'd like to pretend I delayed before making copies. But I did make them. I sent the letter back the next day with a note of apology, saying I had taken it by accident . . ." And now Maureen looked on the verge of breaking down. "I know I don't have to say it, Frank. But I give you this copy in strict confidence."

Acutely aware of her harrowed eyes on him, Docherty nodded, reached a hand to her lower arm as if she might not be able to walk further without support, then took what she had given him and began to read. When he was finished, he handed back the letter. He wished he could reassure her in some way. But the gravity of the thing, and what he knew from the cabdriver, Sarah, prevented him from uttering the normal comforts — "I find it hard to believe" or "The accusation might be unfounded."

He muttered, "That's terrible."

The worst of cases — those in which victims were left by the predator so empty of solace that they killed themselves.

As he read, part of him was even aggrieved that he was being given too hard a test, and that if he could not rise to it Maureen would be damaged. He had heard the accusations about Shannon and girls, and now Maureen sat fretfully waiting for his word on accusations about Shannon and boys. There were abusers who did go from boys to girls, but it was rarer, as far as he knew from research he had read, for a man to go from adolescent girls to pre- and barely pubescent boys. That did not mean it could not happen. Or that Maureen could be easily consoled.

Maureen looked directly at Docherty, her eyes irreparably young under the stylish, gray-streaked coiffure. Despite his professional competence, he did not want to be a judge in this case, one that dulled her gaze with so much anguish.

"Do you think this note is reliable?" she pleaded. "Tell me, absolutely frankly."

Docherty felt that he could not manage to answer. But then he heard himself talking. "Well, I believe it should be investigated. Nobody wants anyone unjustly accused." He was saying that a lot lately. "On the other hand, this boy took his life. All I can say is . . . The sense of unworthiness, and inability to validate himself academically . . . these are certainly symptoms of some sort of emotional or other abuse. And . . . well, he mentions your brother."

There, he thought, it's getting easier. She wants candor, this honest woman.

"You asked me to be honest with you. These are all elements that give a certain credibility to the note. He was about to suicide, he evinces guilt about his family, but he can't avoid talking of your brother. Was he delusional? Anything's possible. Was he moved by malice — well, he himself was the target of his own malice.

"This other young man mentioned in here . . . Brian Wood. Do you know anything about him?"

Maureen said, "No. We've done some research, but we don't even know if he's still in Australia."

"He's got an international consultancy firm," said Damian, "and we think he's living in Hong Kong."

"I felt I must urge Liz to take it to the archdiocese," said Maureen. "I called Paul yesterday but he said she won't be persuaded, she's still irrational with grief, as she's entitled to be. The question is, what on earth should we do? Naturally, I don't want to betray my brother in any way."

Damian and his wife again exchanged glances. Despite everything, there was a steeliness in the look Damian gave her. An uxorial "I-told-you!"

"I can't send it off to the cardinal," Maureen said in a throttled way. "I don't think I can . . ."

"You should contact this Wood," Docherty suggested.

"How can *I*?" Maureen demanded. "I'm the *sister*!"

"I should let you know," said Docherty, "the coroner would have been given a copy by the police. There's an outside chance he might send it to the public prosecutor as evidence on which to charge Leo."

Maureen began to weep very softly now. Docherty rushed to comfort her, however irrationally. "Though I'm not at all sure he would, without further evidence."

"So it's back to us," Damian said. He assessed Frank Docherty almost as if weighing him for some form of combat. "We wondered if you would do it. We understand it has to be done. In case . . . Well, we know enough of these cases to know the people involved are usually repeat offenders."

"I have no standing in this archdiocese," said Docherty. "As you know."

"But you're still a Catholic priest, aren't you?" asked Damian.

"Marginally considered so, I believe."

"Then you're entitled to take it to the cardinal."

"If I did that," said Docherty, feeling a profound sadness at the fearsomeness of suicide and damage and harsh duties, "I would have to warn your brother. But the best thing would be to persuade Liz or Paul to do it."

Damian looked directly at him. "If they haven't, it's because they feel powerless. They can see the way the plaintiff is being dealt with in this trial that's in progress."

"For which, of course, you blame my brother," said Maureen to her husband — with a repressed, teary anger suddenly let loose.

"Well, I won't pretend I ever fell for His Smarminess the monsignor."

"Well, I didn't either," Maureen declared defensively. "But it doesn't mean his guilt is proven."

"Oleaginous," murmured Damian. "Smooth as oil. Sorry, my love. It's the way he is."

Docherty intervened, suddenly resolved as to what needed to be done. "Why don't *we* go together to see Liz Cosgrove?"

"She won't let me in," said Maureen. "She tossed me out when I visited her."

"We should try it anyhow. I could do it tomorrow afternoon. Would you consider that?"

Eventually Maureen agreed, but the spirit had gone out of her. A sort of dread, a weight of conflicting duties, seemed to have overcome her.

16
MAUREEN BRESLIN REMEMBERS
HUMANAE VITAE, 1968

Despite our subservience to the Church in those years, we felt, in fact, venturesome and daring. Looking back, we were honest and hopeful children, waiting for the Christmas of the cosmos. We were anti-Vietnam, anti-apartheid, and the first Australian generation to be interested in the parlous state of Aboriginals' lives, to call for the breaking down of de facto race barriers in cities, and real ones in the swimming pools and cinemas of bush towns.

Sometime after my visit to Father Docherty's confessional, news had finally begun to spread that the Vatican was considering liberalizing their birth control doctrine. Now, some three decades later, we tell ourselves that we should not have awaited the permission of old men in Rome, or even of the smooth-faced Paul VI, an urbane northern Italian and Vatican bureaucrat. But according to the temper of the times and the nature of our upbringing, we did wait, and grasped every rumor about the Pontifical Commission on Birth Control, which was said to favor the dictates of modern science and practice. Our attitudes were no less or more absurd than those of long-serving members of the Communist Party, accepting the swerving and contradictory policies of the Comintern. It is interesting that the year of crisis of belief for both Communists and Catholics was 1968 — for Communists the Prague Spring was followed by a Soviet repression, which alienated many true believers.

In the months leading to the release of the expected papal encyclical on birth control, the press was full of comment by leading clergymen, especially Germans and Canadians, Dutch and Americans, who seemed much more progressive than our rather dour bishops, proclaiming the good sense of a new direction on a matter not only substantially altered by modern technological discoveries but also necessary for both the poor of the Catholic world, and the prosperous children of Italian, Polish, and Irish immigrants in the countries of the New World. Frank Docherty's advice to me on conscience seemed validated by this speculation.

In that happy season, Damian and I did not waste time on thermometers. We did not weary our desire. We went for it. Meanwhile, it seemed there were unlimited signs of renewal in the world. We were invited to a friend's house where, he said, a priest of his acquaintance would honor us with a family liturgy — that is, a Mass said in the household, without a boring sermon from an elderly priest with cemented views; a ceremony in which the people, along with the priest, were very nearly the co-consecrators of the bread and the wine. It seems tame now, I know. But in that other world, it said to me that the Church belonged to the people, to normal people, not only to the anointed on high at St. Mary's and St. Patrick's cathedrals, nor to the College of Cardinals, nor to the Pope alone, but to a young woman with three children.

The young priest who said the Mass in a friend's lounge room turned out to be Father Frank Docherty, my former confessor, invoker of *my* conscience. I watched him. He had a pleasant face, a little gaunt, and he was more than six feet tall. He began to recite the new English-language liturgy with earnestness. When it came to the consecration, he asked us to recite the words with him, as if we all shared in the priesthood. This was heretically exciting, the suggestion that we, too, might help to change the bread and wine into the body and blood of Christ.

When the Mass ended, we all watched Frank shed his vestments, and the excitement of seeing these ancient garments laid aside with reverence in an ordinary living room — the chasuble, the alb, the stole, the maniple — seemed to me as blatant a statement of revolution as did anything from Che or Timothy Leary. These vestments, representing power, had descended amongst the people.

Frank, as he insisted on being called, sat around with us and drank his glass of Moselle dutifully. It became apparent, not through priestly assertions but in the course of conversation, that he believed the Vietnam War immoral and unwise, a great sin of the West only equaled in recent years by the overthrow of Patrice Lumumba in the Congo. He thought — as did we — that our system of conscription was as unjust as the Americans', each being based on a lottery. And there was another important issue: a referendum was proposed to give the federal government the power to legislate for Aboriginals, based on the belief that the parliament would reform the patchwork of laws relating to the Indigenous across this enormous continent — *their* continent, after all, as many of us believed — according to a new pattern of justice, dignity, and equity.

Frank did not *pronounce* at great length on these issues — he was not the loudest authority in the room. One of the reasons, I felt then, was that unlike other men in the room he did not have in him a head of leftist anger built up during twenty years of government by a conservative Coalition. Frank's moderate voice was even shouted down by others, including Damian, in whom Vietnam had raised a fury.

That evening, of course Frank gave no sign of having encountered me in the confessional. I was only a little embarrassed that he might remember or identify me. I wondered whether he had permission from his superior, the head of his monastic house, to perform liturgies, since he was a member of a religious order rather than one of the regular parish infantry of the archdiocese. Or was he once again acting on the basis of the independent biddings of conscience?

One woman in the group brought up the matter of the contraceptive pill. It was not us comfortably off women who needed contraception most, she said. "It is the African and South American women, who give birth to more children than they can feed or educate. It is women who die because they believe they must beget or be damned. Talk about martyrs for love! Surely the Vatican doesn't think it glorifies God for that to occur?"

Damian and I began to attend a parish church in Longueville — the same church in which I had first approached Father Docherty's confessional — to listen to the sermons he gave there during his Mass. Again, my description of Frank's near-heresies and his skating along the edge of the unorthodox, a mysterious and unexplored landmass for us, might not seem surprising now, but then . . . We were as a nation so easy to impress. Ours was the last generation of the postcolonial cringe. At school we were still taught that it was the northern world that produced clever things, and the northern world that had taken the trouble to explore, possess, and define the destinies of the southern world. Thus our destiny and our boasted-of identity was to harvest wheat and shear sheep and extract minerals for the northern world. We did not need to be a venue for fresh ideas, thank you very much. Up there they had enough of them already.

My brother, as I have said, instinctively

gave sermons that did not shock faith, rouse enthusiasm, or shake the pillars of a comfortable society, and to that extent he was an unexceptional Australian priest of his day. Frank Docherty was not. He was by nature a pillar-shaker. I remember a day he took on the text about rendering unto God the things that are God's and to Caesar the things that are Caesar's, and he did so with the innocent, barefaced intention of telling us that we should listen not only to the government on the issue of Vietnam but also to the Vietnam moratorium groups, and to the mothers of Save Our Sons. We should consider whether the military conscription lottery was a Caesar-sanctioned, state-ordained form of Russian roulette, and we were entitled to ask of Caesar whether it was just. Even in liberal democracies, bad laws could be passed and Caesar could be reprehensible. Did God want us, at such a time, to concentrate on our personal piety or to be sufficiently vocal in reasonable complaint to bring Caesar back to the moral order? It was the duty of citizens to stand up against law that was at variance with the laws of universal brotherhood. But when one stood up to bad law, it ought not to be done with the self-indulgence of anger or violence, but out of love both for those who suffered the damage of that law and for those who enacted and enforced it.

It was well established, he would say on later Sundays, that against the proposition of St. Paul's that the greatest commandment was love, the fact that in South Africa there prevailed a regime which denied proper human status to the majority of its residents was an outrage. And having inherited our land from an indigenous race, whose dispossession we had not yet faced, we should neither imitate apartheid nor fail to condemn it. It was one of the counsels of Christ that no government should legislate to exalt one race over another. Yet only when the world was persuaded to condemn apartheid would it end. Indeed, Frank said, it would be interesting to ask if we in Australia would ourselves have passed an apartheid law had there been many more Aboriginals than whites.

To many in Frank's congregation, meanwhile, the African National Congress were godless Communists, and some would feel after his Mass either the moral duty or the small-minded malice to write to the cardinal archbishop about controversial Father Docherty.

The Sunday night before the foreshadowed

birth control encyclical was at last released, Leo came to tea. As I've said, my brother was more sacerdotal, priestly in the accustomed way, than someone like Frank. Leo reminded us of our uncle Flynn, who had been a real-estate agent in the Eastern Suburbs, and had the same Irish guff. Nor was Leo free of vanity — or at least he had a different kind of vanity than a man as worldly and yet ingenuous as Father Docherty.

That Sunday evening after our three children had been put to bed, the question was, would the Pope give his blessings to the new contraceptive pill?

"I tell you, Leo, women are ready for it," I ventured.

"Well, not all women," said my brother with his smooth casuistry. "Not women past their time. Not Aunty Patsy."

I see now that the question weighed lightly on him. But he said then, "I know it would be of great comfort to many women if he did accept its use. But he has faith and tradition to take account of."

"Either way, John XXIII would certainly have let contraception through."

"How can you know that?" my brother asked.

"Because he recognized that our lives now

221

are drastically different from those of medieval peasants who had to repopulate Europe after the Black Death."

"I've never heard that argument," he said with an air of exceeding, yet perhaps tender, patronage.

But then I asked the real question, the one that covered all eventualities. "What of individual conscience?" I asked it almost as an experiment. "Can individual conscience ever trump a papal encyclical?"

To give him credit, he did not mind being quizzed like this. It was something he was used to from me. He would come home from the seminary full of his clerical pomposity and I would challenge it as a younger sister should.

He asked me the question I had been all too ready to ask myself. "How can we separate genuine conscience from our expedient and selfish wishes?"

I asked, "How can the Pope himself, for that matter?"

"The Pope can because he's directed by divine wisdom. You're lucky you didn't ask the nuns that question when you were a kid."

Damian, who had been silent, said, "I hope, Leo, the poor bloody women get some genuine mercy out of this."

"Oh, Damian," warned my brother memorably. "There are questions of sexual morality. And then there is mercy. As we all know, they don't necessarily coincide."

Later, when Leo had driven off and we were getting ready for bed, I said to Damian, "He can jump either way, whatever the Pope says."

He answered, "I still can't tell which way he himself expects the axe to fall."

We slept naked, as modern people did. We wanted to be modern because that was our world. We wanted to be Catholic because, in an even more intimate sense, that was our world as well.

In the middle of the northern summer of that year, in Rome — or in Castel Gandolfo, where the Pope had his summer residence overlooking the lake — the word of the Lord, or of the Pope, came. It was the headline in the *Herald* on 26 July 1968. The edict itself was dated the day before, but we lived on the other side of the timeline and Europe was hours behind us, or as Damian liked to say, "We're twelve hours ahead and a hundred years behind."

We were clubbed by the headline. Pope Paul VI had forbidden any method of contraception but abstinence and the dreary, unwieldy rhythm business.

I surprised myself, for amongst my sadness I felt an immediate rebellion. I found out later this had been the reaction of many women. The news would cause people to leave the Church, but amongst those who did not it gave a salutary lesson in the limits of papal authority. The tendency to rebellion would be railed against by churchmen, but since that day it has proved to be irreversible at least in the West, with which we Australians, though in the far south of the world, nonetheless like to associate ourselves.

It seemed the Pope had moved in and reassumed the moral globe. There were people who praised the fact and saw the encyclical as a long-overdue curb on contemporary influence. The urbane Cardinal Suenens of Belgium had reacted like me and said, "I beg you, my brothers, let's not have another Galileo affair. One is enough for the Church." *Humanae Vitae,* he warned, was an unscientific mistake on the scale of the Vatican's dealings with Galileo, and it was a comfort to me that in the far north of the earth such a warning was sounded.

American and other bishops howled, too, foreseeing the reaction from their flock, and were affronted that they had been invited to the Vatican to have their collegial say, yet much of what they *had* said had been ignored. Some Canadian bishops pushed the idea that the encyclical was only one of many authorities to be followed in this matter. Those who did not agree with it, they said, and who used modern contraception at the sanction of their own conscience, should not be separated from the Church.

I realize now that *Humanae Vitae* was not only a prohibition laid down on women. It was a prohibition against looking at the world in a new way. All the wisdom and liberal spirit of John XXIII's Vatican Council seemed to have been quenched at a stroke. Pope John had given us citizenship of the world, and — despite the fact I had gone to the confessional and doubted my judgment — we had taken the liberties he had foreshadowed and looked on ourselves anew. And now there were no more diverse voices. The old world of a sole commanding voice was back, and I found that, to an extent I could not have predicted, I did not want it back. However, as if from ancestral conditioning, I simultaneously felt I was bound by the encyclical, with its neutral language of serene authority.

I read reprinted paragraphs in the newspaper that morning while our three children were eating. Niall, dressed in his convent-blue shirt and navy-blue pants, and Rosie in her virgin-blue uniform were ready for school. Damian offered sensible advice about staying calm until I had read the whole thing in the *Catholic Weekly,* that staid old rag that would be sure to reprint it in its entirety. But I could not imagine how the paragraphs I'd read in the *Herald* could be saved by any qualifying clauses packed away in other passages. I looked at combative Rosie, a kindergarten child, in her confident blondeness, which she got from my husband (had a Viking had some input into the genetics of Damian's Celtic fore-bears?) and I felt a pulse of weight tug at my heart. Rosie would be subject to this edict one day, too. Should I take her out of that blue uniform and send her to a vigorous secular school, deliver her from the burden of so-called faith?

When Damian sat down to breakfast, he began to read the reports and I saw him growing angrier. He knew he had to go into the Department of Health, where he was working in those years, and be teased by his peers at this latest display of papal authority. Eventually he turned on me as if I were the cause of his outrage.

"I hope your brother enjoys reading this," he said.

"What's it got to do with my brother?" I asked him.

"I bet my bottom dollar he'll be quietly pleased. Gleeful in that smarmy way. More interested in denial than giving humans permission."

"Even if it were true, is that my fault?"

He returned his eyes to the page and I thought that it was probably true. Leo was happiest to have rules clear, defined, and enforceable. He had been like that since childhood.

I put the kids in the car and Damian was with me — I was to take him to the station. We were silent, but when we had delivered Niall and Rosie to their classes, and with Joe asleep in the backseat, we were pleased we had time to talk, as if it could mitigate the facts.

"Sorry about what I said about Leo. Even though . . ."

"Yet it was Leo who sent me to that Father Docherty," I reminded him. Why had Leo done that? Had he perceived me as a potential rebel and chosen Frank because at least Frank was a priest and could permit an innocent play of ideas, now to be put aside given that the authoritative word had come down?

"He might have done it because he loves you and wants to see the rules softened for his little sister," Damian decided, with perhaps too much charity.

Then his rage was back, centered on the question itself, not on me or my brother. I put out my left hand and touched his wrist.

"What does the Pope think," he asked, "when priests masturbate? Isn't that contraception?"

It was a shocking question — it had been the unspeakable sin during our adolescence.

"Does he think that is birth control?" he persisted. "Because when you put the old fella in your hand, there's no possibility of conception!"

"How do you know priests even do that?"

"I know because they are human. Only the ones who are inhuman don't." And he smiled. "Or the liars. If the Pope himself hasn't ever done it, it goes to show why he'd write such a grotesque document."

He looked at me sharply. "I'm not kidding. There are genuinely asexual personalities, and they're always messed up with politics, the military, or the clergy, which are perfect for them. Perhaps the Pope . . ."

"For God's sake don't say that when they tease you at work."

"It's getting to a stage where my friends don't have to try too hard to make the Church look ridiculous."

"Just the same, we should wait," I said, finding myself the voice of moderation now because I was scared of Damian's rage. "As you say, we haven't read it in full. There may be something there . . ."

"There's something there all right. They want us to go back to married celibacy. It would have been more merciful if I'd been a monk, and as for you . . ."

I rang my brother during the day but he was not in. Later he called back. "I know what you want to talk to me about," he said. "I think we should read it in full first, and I haven't had a chance."

"I said that to Damian."

"It isn't the first time people have been dismayed by the Vatican. I think we were all expecting too much."

I felt a sting of anger. "What would you tell a woman with eight children, married to a laborer and suffering from hypoglycemia?"

Leo said, "Maureen, you find me a woman in that situation in your parish and then I can answer the question."

"Please," I begged him, "don't be a casuist today."

"All right. The Pope has enunciated a

principle of faith and there are few exemptions from such a principle. And that's all I can tell you. Let's read the thing."

We were horrified to see on the ABC that night my gynecologist, a bland man, courtly with women, a flatterer of the bravery of pregnant women, being an apologist for the encyclical; acknowledging that Catholic women would need to go back to the rhythm method, and accept as God's will the child who was born due to the method's significant inaccuracies.

"I wish I had an outstanding bill from that bastard," Damian told me. "I wouldn't bloody pay it."

The man's hands had delivered my three children and had suddenly declared himself — against us, for us? I felt *against,* but couldn't be sure. It depended on who the *us* was. Everything was in the air.

After I had Joe, I had to go into a rest home for ten days and be knocked out by sedation, displaying a weakness that was beyond the understanding of my mother, who had begotten six and lost two in infancy, and who had somehow absorbed her grief in making jury-rigged clothes and scraping together enough food for us.

To ensure this collapse did not happen again, I spent the better part of two years on the Pill, at the urging of our GP. I had my confidence back, I'd had no troubles, I had taken the Pill for what I thought of as a sensible length of time. I think the reason Damian was furious was that my brief illness had so frightened him, and he wanted to protect me, and the Pill had been a valid way I could protect myself. Now, given that the encyclical invoked eternal truths, our options — taken with a certain subjective wisdom — were dammed.

So it was in a lather of conscience that I approached the full text of the encyclical. To give it its due, it did not read like an arrogant document. Inevitably it began with a florid greeting, but it acknowledged medical changes in past years. It acknowledged that there were differences of opinion amongst the papal commission, some members of which were married couples.

In those opening passages a phantom hope revived in me that Pope Paul was actually going to say yes, regulate your conception according to the new technology, while praying for ancient wisdom. But then slowly he invoked the natural law and said it was immutable. For the natural law was also God's law, and God's law, as passed down by the Church under its divine mandate, was that nothing artificial was to come between man and woman.

The argument about sex between couples who could not have a child, the sterile or the aged — that was also dealt with. No unnatural means should be used, and no contraceptive methods of lovemaking, such as ejaculating outside the womb, were permitted. All sexual cunning and sexual technology were ruled out. Then the utterances grew a little crazy. Paul VI called on scientists to turn their attention to researching the natural rhythms, for they allowed a form of contraception that gave no offense to the laws of the universe. The encyclical seemed to have cut off all excuses and all choice.

17

DOCHERTY MEETS THE BEREAVED MOTHER

July 1996

Damian picked up Docherty from the monastery the next afternoon. He drove them both back to the Breslins' house to collect a solemn Maureen. She seemed grievously reconciled to this task of urging Liz to instigate some sort of investigation, even an internal Church inquiry, into her brother's guilt or innocence.

Damian dropped Maureen and Frank at the Cosgroves' and said he would wait in the car. Liz's house was on a downhill slope, and framing its door were large honest grevilleas full of winter birds discussing the wonder of near year-round nectar. Docherty knocked, and when Liz appeared in the doorway she stood there, mute, not seeming to recognize him.

"What does this mean?" she asked, staring at Maureen. Docherty was shocked at how much older she looked than the young woman who had gathered the group to take part in Vietnam and anti-apartheid demonstrations with him; her features austere as if from a lack of interest in life.

"I wanted to discuss Stephen's suicide note," said Maureen, jumping straight to the point. "I feel dreadful about it, and I think the matter must be pursued, even if it's my brother."

"And who is this man with you?"

"You know, Liz. It's our friend Frank Docherty. Father Frank. He's visiting from Canada."

"I do remember," she said listlessly. "My drunken husband accused me of foisting you on him. You couldn't help him though. The clergy haven't been any sort of blessing to us. So, I know where this is going, don't I?"

"He's an expert," said Maureen as fast as she could get it out, "on the sort of abuse your son said he suffered."

"So am I," said Liz.

She had no peace, no means of approaching and engaging her grief, and Docherty felt the familiar anger emanating from her. He did not generally encounter it three times in a week, yet he had come home to find it in familiar suburbs where he had

234

expected to have a holiday from it all.

"Liz," he said, "your loss is terrible. But Maureen and I believe you should take the note to the cardinal. In case it's true . . . Maureen couldn't feel more grief for your son."

"Yes," said Liz, her hands hugging her own upper arms and trembling, and still not inviting them in. "Yes, in case it's true. Because the dying always make up stories, don't they?"

"Not this sort of story," Docherty assured her. "Not usually."

"I'm fully prepared to admit," Maureen declared, "that it may be the truth."

Still they were not invited to enter the house.

"My advice," Docherty persisted, "for what it's worth, is that you give your son's letter to the archdiocese. To alert them. Because there might be others. It's painful for Maureen to accept there might be, but she recognizes the necessity. It is a hard document to dismiss. But through it your son can allay the suffering of other victims."

"Do you think they'd act on his letter?" she asked. "The cardinal? I don't believe it. I don't want to test it."

"I would certainly urge Cardinal Condon to act."

"For God's sake," said Liz. "Face it: they'll do nothing. They'd rather save the monsignor than listen to my son. Where have you people been living, that you believe that the cardinal . . ."

Docherty held up his hand. "I know it's a poor solution. But the letter itself is convincing. If the cardinal asks experts — and he will — they'll tell him that. And then he'll have to investigate the monsignor. This man your son mentioned in the letter? The other victim. Perhaps we could talk to him. He may even offer corroboration."

"Perhaps," said Liz bleakly. "But you see how it's all going for that poor young scientist. Catholic lawyers tell me the Church fights dirtier than any corporation. *Catholic* lawyers say it. Did you read that the dead priest's sister is saying Devitt threw himself at that mongrel Guest? Did you see that? That's what happens if you sue the Church."

"The options are not perfect . . . not what they should be," Docherty said.

"Her brother is a board member of this In Compassion's Name," said Liz, her head jerking about with confirmed animosity. "So what chance do we have . . . ?"

"There are of course the coroner and the police, and perhaps the public prosecutor," suggested Docherty. He heard Maureen's intake of breath by his side.

Liz also inhaled profoundly. Her cheeks were bluish with a sort of oxygen-sapping grief. "You know it would be hard for a prosecutor to make a case that implicated her brother in my son's suicide. The police have always been part of the problem — there are so many Catholic police here, and they weren't abused so they don't believe the worst. For God's sake, tell me to do something that does honor to my son's misery. Tilting at windmills won't do that."

She turned to Maureen. "And what are you doing, showing my son's letter around? It was only as he left the world that he could tell *me*. Paul unwisely left that copy with you because you're the ogre's sister, and suddenly there's another priest here."

"I don't think you can actually say," protested Maureen, her cheeks reddening, "that Frank is just another priest."

"Beside the point, Maureen! I do not plan to spread this news that my son was poisoned at the root. Paul may. I don't. Because Stephen wouldn't have wanted me to. Didn't you hear me earlier? He felt safe in telling me only after he'd died. He wanted us to know and to forgive him. He didn't want to be on the front page of the *Herald*.

So, please go! And respect my son, for Christ's sake, Maureen. No more passing the news around."

Maureen hung her head, defeated and bewildered.

"I'm sorry for the huge suffering that's come your way, Liz," said Docherty. "I met young Stephen . . ."

"I remember that," she said, suddenly almost indulgent. "It was when I still thought we had a chance."

Docherty lowered his voice. "If I can do anything, I'll be here a few more weeks. Maureen can contact me."

"Just go!" said Liz.

She closed the door briskly and they were alone on the doorstep. They spent some time absorbing their shock before they made their way silently out of the bird-filled garden. Damian was parked at the corner, reading a book.

"Despite what she says," Maureen said, "you have to take the letter to the cardinal."

"I don't know exactly *what* I have to do," Docherty admitted. "Her reason for not making it known is pretty authoritative."

"She won't know you've spoken to him."

"If I were to, I'd need two copies," said Docherty. "As I said, I don't believe in telling the cardinal without confronting your brother, so I need a copy for him, too. And this Wood . . . I think we have to contact him."

"Oh God, what a sister I am," said Maureen, and seized his upper arm to support herself. Docherty was tempted to encircle her.

At that moment Damian pulled up beside them. "Forgotten me?" he asked through the window.

And they had. Maureen's humiliation and confusion, and their old habit of companionship, had driven him from their minds.

The Breslins dropped Docherty back to the monastery. He went to the television room and was drinking beer with Eismann when the doorbell rang. Docherty answered it and found a frowning brown-haired young man in a business suit and loosened tie. "Good evening," said Docherty. "What can I do for you?"

"I'm Paul Cosgrove," said the young man. "My mother told me you'd visited."

"I fear I wasn't very welcome."

"I don't think she realized it did some good."

"Would you like to come into the parlor?" suggested Docherty.

"No. You want to tell the cardinal, don't you?"

"I feel I must."

"I'm with you," said Paul. "Leave it to me to persuade my mother, and I take full responsibility for now if you go ahead. Let's at least see how they react. If they don't take notice . . . that could be another matter."

"Come in and have a coffee?"

"I have to get back to her," said Paul.

"I'll appraise Monsignor Shannon and the cardinal of what's in the letter, then. I think it's the right thing."

"Good. That's what I want."

"What about this other man? Wood?"

"He's got offices all over Asia."

"That's good to hear," said Docherty. "In a sense."

"Last I heard he was living in Hong Kong."

When Paul had left, Docherty returned to his room and left a message at the cathedral for Monsignor Shannon saying he wanted to speak to him on an important matter, something that could have an impact upon In Compassion's Name.

There was a desktop computer in the front office of the monastery to allow technically adventurous monks to send and receive emails. Since most of the priests were

240

Docherty's age or older, the email traffic was low. But that evening Docherty did find a message from a friend in his monastic house in Waterloo, Father Tubby Enright, Yorkshireman and former infantryman in Northern Ireland.

I wonder how you are traveling in the wicked Antipodes. All here is summer torpor half of Canada has gone to Disneyland. How did the Australians receive your suggestions about handling abuse? I'd love to hear you say that they were wide open to your ideas. Seeing any rugby league while you're down there? You blokes are the best in the world, as you're very quick to tell everyone. In the English summer, my crowd are playing a Test series against the West Indies and doing it indifferently. Four Yorkshiremen, though, in the England team! What would they do without us despised northern English, refugees from pit, plant, unemployment and the army. . . . May I say, I regret the papal embargo on the idea of purgatory. I'd like to think Maggie Thatcher could spend a lot of time there. And are you sure in that fancy mind of yours that death itself was adequate Hell for Hitler?

241

One of Docherty's heretical ideas was that death might be what Hell was. In any case he enjoyed hearing from this sane friend. It was all anyone needed for balance. One sane friend, and a gift for meditation.

He had not intended to go online, however, to collect his emails. He tentatively typed Brian Wood's name into the search engine, adding the tag "financial services," and was rewarded by the Yahoo listing "Wood and Associates, operational and corporate restructuring," and an address in a new glass tower in Chifley Square. When he clicked on the entry, the company website came up. It was well designed, as only rich corporations and universities, with their many and varied IT specialists, seemed to be able to manage. The website declared:

WOOD AND ASSOCIATES are a leading corporate consultancy in the southwest Pacific area, with offices in all the Australian capitals, New Zealand, Singapore, Kuala Lumpur and Manila. Our task is to bring to the operational restructuring of our clients innovative solutions for all business challenges — from those offered by changing world and domestic markets to the refining of priorities arising from amalgamations. To this task, our team brings unprecedented energy and concern for the needs of those we serve. Our repute depends on supplying you with models that will suit you in uncertain times and at any level of corporate growth.

Docherty clicked on "OUR PEOPLE." No one in the management team looked more than forty-five years old. None was bald except a director who had obviously and willfully shaved his head. No one had gray hair or carried excess weight. Bright-eyed and authoritative-looking young women were notable amongst management and the board. Docherty knew that his mother, born in different times and under different stars, could have been such a woman — she had the clarity of mind and the will for it.

The managing partner was Brian Wood, who looked at the camera with authoritative whimsy. His dark hair shone. He looked like a man who rode his bike at dawn and visited the gym in the evenings. His gaze showed no signs of trauma, no acknowledgment of old molestations. His sleeping dogs seemed to lie passive, or had wandered away entirely. Docherty knew the risks of approaching him and did not like to take them. To make Wood revisit his childhood could evoke disabling sorrow and rage, and this young man, if once a victim, had made himself and his corporation into an international force, and most probably had a desire to forget.

In any case, Docherty dialed the Sydney number. Everything he said after he opted to speak to the receptionist seemed half-demented to him.

"Hello? I wondered, could I get a message to Mr. Wood? Yes, Mr. Brian Wood. My name is Father Frank Docherty: D-O-C-H . . . That's right. It's about the death of a former classmate of his. A Stephen Cosgrove. P-H, yes. Could Mr. Wood call me, I wondered?"

The woman said, "Mr. Wood is in Hong Kong at the moment. He's due back tomorrow but he may not be in the office."

"If you could get the message to him, I'd be grateful."

Conscious of the environmental immorality of printing out the website page — even the forests of Canada, let alone Tasmania, were not limitless — he did so, and then printed the letter from Tubby, purely for the self-indulgence of clinging to it as to a talisman.

In his letter to the cardinal, Docherty made the point that in light of the accusation the monsignor was facing, the cardinal himself had a duty to inform the police, even if they already had the letter. It was a duty not so much to inform on the alleged perpetrator as to notify the authorities that children might be imperiled. This was the way the law operated in Ontario, at any rate; he did not know if these things worked in the same way in New South Wales, but he intended to make inquiries.

Docherty further pointed out that the Cosgrove family, though resolved to privacy as yet, could at any time release to the press the news of the enclosed letter (on which Docherty had blacked out Brian Wood's name), and thereby the Church's defense in the Devitt case could be prejudiced. Not that he was concerned, by this stage, if it was damaged, but he did not think it wise to make that point to the cardinal. However, he did tell the cardinal that, rightly or wrongly, Stephen's mother was outraged that the monsignor was a notable witness for the defense in this unfolding case; and he believed that the cardinal, if not open to the accusation itself, would be open to the possibility that if there were a scandal, the Church might need to abandon its defense and yield to the plaintiff.

It was on these reasoned grounds that

Docherty expected an earnest reply. He was uncertain whether he should add to the letter that by pure happenstance he had met another person who claimed to have been preyed on by the monsignor. He spent some time weighing whether this would give greater credibility to what he wrote, or less, but in the end he feared it might allow the cardinal to suspect he was actively collecting evidence against Shannon as some form of clerical vendetta. He decided it would be best to mention it only when the cardinal made contact. He felt that he had already wandered far from the comfort of guidelines — given that Liz Cosgrove had not wanted her son's letter shown to others, and was skeptical of the value of doing it; and the taxi driver, Sarah, was just as uncertain about where to take her outrage. Sarah did not want her name mentioned yet. Whereas, in the case of Stephen Cosgrove, names could not be avoided, and the accusations were pressing enough, he felt, to override all etiquette.

18
MAUREEN BRESLIN AFTER
HUMANAE VITAE, 1968

After Paul VI's encyclical, I went to Father Docherty's confessional again. I had a foredoomed sense he could do something for me. My situation was that I could see no way to disobey the encyclical and remain a Catholic, and if I did not remain a Catholic, I would be spitting on my ancestors' Mass stones of Donegal.

When I told Frank I was there to talk about the encyclical, he said, "A lot are. Others have been driven away by it, too."

"Is there anything I can do but obey?" I asked him.

There was a silence. I had a fancy that he had vacated the confessional, gone off to consult further authorities. Then he said, "It throws a different light on everything, doesn't it?"

I said nothing.

"I'm still asking for enlightenment on this business," he said. "There is no doubt that an encyclical is authoritative. You're quite right — the way the Church has developed for good and ill, the Church we live in, makes us acknowledge that."

Still, I had nothing to say.

He launched into an almost annoying disquisition, in which he appeared to think history had reached an interesting point rather than an impasse for the flesh and spirit, mine and Damian's.

"The idea of basing the moral law on the natural order is something I haven't thought about a lot, and that hasn't been emphasized in my experience. It's a little like politicians who speak of 'the will of the people' — they're often the least worthy to invoke it. But let's look at the natural order of things. There have been plenty of changes in the natural order — interventions — which have been considered lawful but have changed the essential nature of things. The creation, for example, of hybrid plants by the biologist monk Mendel. Why wouldn't the Vatican see that as an interference with the natural law? I don't know the answer. I admit I can't come to a confident conclusion either way."

He sighed. "Sorry," he said. "You don't need a lecture, you need relief. Look, I think we have to wait for the dust to settle, as it will. In the meantime, my counsel is to take account of the encyclical, but also of your conscience. Nothing you have said seems indulgent or malicious to me. I will absolve you without penance."

"But no one else except you has ever told me to follow my conscience," I said. "I still feel that relying on it is a crime."

He laughed sympathetically. "In any system of rule there's a tendency to emphasize certain matters and de-emphasize others, and the Vatican *is* a system of rule, as well as a spiritual realm. But if you look at doctrine, you'll find the Vatican doesn't quite agree with you that your individual conscience is no good for anything. It's just that at the moment they're trying to regain authority — they feel things have gone too far, with home liturgies and liberation theology and the rest. Still, the fact they want to reassert their authority doesn't mean that what you decide in good faith is invalid. If our conscience is not to be believed, why are we given such a faculty? By the way, forgive my asking, but did you have any problems with the births of your children?"

"I was weak, I'm afraid. I ended up in hospital with postpartum blues after the last one."

Frank breathed out audibly. "That's an

important factor in your decision. A factor the Pope doesn't take account of in the encyclical, as far as I've read."

I began to weep. Because I did not believe in the concept he was pushing. On one level, it frightened me.

There was a silence, which he must have thought impolite to break. He said at last, "The week before the final vote on papal infallibility on 18 July 1870, the Church was still the Church. Had the doctrine been voted down, by American bishops and others, the Church would still have been the Church. A fortnight ago, the Church was still the Church, and your conscience told you it was acceptable for you to take the extraordinary medical advance represented by the Pill. And in a fortnight's time, the Church will still be the Church it ever was, and your conscience will be the same, as well. You believed only a little time ago, before the Pope spoke, in your individual conscience. And now you're telling me you don't. If your conscience was right then, it's right now. So was it right then?"

I wasn't used to having genuine conversations in that cold, salutary place, the confessional. I was certainly not used to arguing for the sinfulness of this and that — the priest in the confessional had been all too willing to do that for me in childhood and through my adolescence. Frank Docherty, the most modern priest, assumed the faithful had something to say for themselves.

"Might the Pope think you a heretic?" I asked.

I heard him laugh lowly. "Maybe. No. I hope not."

But it remained very hard for me to resist the idea that my conscience was in Rome, that it resided at the Vatican and was mediated to me by bishops.

In his brave preaching at Longueville, Docherty introduced us to the living standards and work hours of the weavers of Bengal. In one of his sermons, he praised Dr. Fatima Deriaya's work and called her a just Muslim. The normal doctrine, he said, was that people outside the Church were saved because their invincible ignorance was forgiven by God. But surely they might earn redemption not by forgivable ignorance but by merit, and because the same spirit breathed on them, too.

This was but one of the sermons that would turn out to be reported as heterodox to the cardinal archbishop. It was a mixed electorate we lived in, and some of the old conservatives clung to their fear of rampant

Asiatic Communism if we did not "stop them" in Vietnam. So we knew not everyone liked Father Docherty's eloquent sermons. Now the question was, would he preach on the encyclical?

On the Sunday eight days after my confession, Father Docherty committed the ultimate bravery of doing that. He was wary, he told the congregation, of laying down the law on marriage. He knew that he understood nothing practical about marriage. Even many married people understood little enough, he said, to laughter. Laughter was not a common reaction to sermons in Catholic churches in those days. I look back once more with astonishment at how cowed we were and how every small relaxation of the spiritual regime refreshed us, just as Father Docherty's home liturgy had.

He went on to read passages from *Humanae Vitae,* and its exhortation that the natural phases of fertility were the only lawful means of contraception.

"I know just enough, however," he said, "having taken excellent medical advice, to say that this method cannot suit all parties, and that unchosen conception can be a threat to a woman's psychiatric and physical health. The Church surely can't mean

252

that it expects women to immolate themselves. No God of mercy could want that."

Then he read a passage from, of all people least designed to impress the conservatives of the parish, Gandhi. A Hindu! Gandhi exhorted those who were going to their deaths to accept it with dignity, a dignity killers did not have. It was a noble thought and Gandhi was by definition a great soul. But did that moral position really work if, for example, you were under the heel of the SS? If you were able to reject death and bring about an escape, had you violated Gandhi's principles? Was, in fact, he exaggerating for dramatic effect? Of course he was. He was exaggerating in the tradition of the prophetic parable. And might not the Pope thus similarly exhort his people in absolute terms since that suited the nature of an encyclical letter while being aware that, appropriately, married people would have recourse to their own consciences and circumstances. Was the Pope, indeed, giving us a counsel of perfection rather than an iron rule?

Those in the congregation who were not stunned were, after Mass, gathered in the churchyard gossiping or discussing. Docherty had gone one step further than he had gone in his reasoning to me in the

253

confessional. He had brought up the idea that the Pope might exaggerate.

A strange and surprising change began to take place in me after Father Docherty's sermon. For me the encyclical had shown the absurdity of the rhythm method as it sought to consecrate it, and since personally this was such an important issue, I found that the more I pursued what was clearly a commonsense, if rebellious, option, the more my conscience supported it.

At the time I was reading some of those groundbreaking feminist authors who took our world by storm, including the furious young Melbourne woman Germaine Greer. *The Female Eunuch,* two years after *Humanae Vitae,* changed the perception we had of ourselves. Warts and all, fury and all, it changed the argument; it created a space in which we could speak. Like all revolutionaries, these women tended to speak with fury. *The Female Eunuch* was the anti-encyclical. Pope Germaine put a secular spin on our opposition to *Humanae Vitae.*

That we should see our bodies as beyond the control of the celibate Church still did not come as easily as we wanted. But once the idea had been argued by Greer, it became obvious. I wasn't rancorous immediately. The alternative proposition I embraced was not in my case accompanied by an angry loss of faith. Considering myself lucky to have got so far, I was at ease with my story, my three children.

Damian was making a similar journey, but he continued to voice a touchy if curiously faithful anger at the Vatican. One mealtime, when we were eating alone after sending the children to bed, he said, "I think we should send the kids to a public school so they don't grow up as neurotic as us."

More than I would admit to myself, if I was anything in those years, I was a Docherty-ite. Not so much a dissenter from *Humanae Vitae* as someone who felt validated in standing aside from it. Frank had no desire to be a religious leader, a seer, or a swami (in line with his Indian experience), but had he been a man of conceit he would not have found it hard to play any of those roles. For we are persuaded into our position by both reason and the force of personality, and his unassertive personality was forceful in its own way.

He initiated, without trying to, a benign sort of cult. Damian and I were influenced by him: I was profoundly so, of course — more, as it turned out, than I would have foretold; Damian at a remove. Still, despite his anger, Damian did choose to exercise our contemporary politics within a Catholic framework, joining the Docherty-marshaled groups of parishioners who attended Vietnam moratorium marches and engaged in other forays of conscience. Many of us were paid-up members of the South African Aid and Defence Fund, contributing money to the legal defense of South Africans, white and black, who had been accused of treason. In 1971 we held a vigil to protest apartheid outside the Sydney Cricket Ground on the evening before a South African Springbok rugby tour. Passing drivers honked at us. Some shouted profanities; some encouragement. Father Docherty maintained his Gandhian composure, and so did we.

We continued to be disturbed in conscience about Australia's Indigenous people, who were subject to apartheid themselves not only in terms of where they could bathe and sit in cinemas, but also with housing and travel; they even needed documents to move about: they complained of them as "dog licenses." Members of our group had enthusiastically voted yes in the Aboriginal civil rights referendum, even though, because of the realities of urban settlement, most of them had never met an Aboriginal.

Around this time my friend Liz Cosgrove, who also attended Frank's services at Longueville, took up the cause of child sex slaves in Calcutta. She volunteered to run a subcommittee that Frank had set up, which raised money to be remitted to Dr. Deriaya. Dr. Deriaya had remained an efficient activist, working on her liberations of child prostitutes, writing a newsletter, calling around the troops — by now she had recruited women from all over the world.

It was Liz and I who came up with the idea of a weekly meeting with Frank. We asked him if, amidst his studies, he could spare a night a week for a discussion group involving members of the parish.

"You don't need a priest to preside over that," Frank told us. "You don't need a priest to validate your opinions."

I understood his point exactly.

"We don't necessarily need a priest, but we need you. Consider yourself a catalyst."

The first evening meeting was held at our place. It was made up of couples for whom theology and politics were two faces of the one entity. These people were repelled by religion attempting to establish absolutes of conscience, the one strict gate to the vision of God. One middle-aged man complained that in Australia, pious observance and obedience to the law's letter were considered the measure of the soul. They, like me, were in rebellion against that, against the priestly authoritarianism that had ruled their childhoods. And yet . . . we had invited a priest! What was obvious to Frank, I think, was our love of the Church as a community. We were not theological serfs who accepted the word, any word, of Rome as truth; we were anxious for a new, sophisticated, and transforming theology.

19
DOCHERTY'S INFATUATION

1972

Docherty's infatuation, if that was the name for his profound feelings of attachment, began with an innocent sense of the enrichment Maureen brought to their collaboration, and the feeling he had of intense comradeship in dazzling causes. He had felt desire for other women, but now, for the first time, he confronted the scale of what he had blithely sworn away: his right to a life companion and to a longing that suddenly seemed to him unanswerable and as destined as laws of gravity.

Later, he remembered this desire as having a specific beginning. It was a dull day in the print room of the monastery and Maureen was helping him compose, type, and print stencils calling on parishioners to join Catholic students at Sydney University in a demonstration against Vietnam. Joe was

259

sleeping on a sofa in the room. Maureen typed earnestly and not entirely competently, he noted, and he saw like a revelation the unique way she compressed her lips when addressing herself to the next word. Within this instant he felt confused by her childlike application, charming in a grown woman. He was enchanted, too, by the fuzz of hair at the nape of her bent neck. It was an unutterably wonderful and compelling phenomenon. What it commanded of him was, he felt in a rush, adoration and a career of cherishing. He felt chosen for the task and fortunate to be called to observe and honor the movements of a person so elevated.

He wondered, could meditation contend with this new hectic conviction? As a man on the island of rationality against which tides of natural enchantment were rising, he knew he was being subjected to an unavoidable impulse, a delusion that was realer than the world and was the fuel for a long-running sexual devotion. This was not his woman, and the child in the print room not his child; he was nonetheless convinced of his ownership. Maureen's marriage to Damian seemed a side issue. Or if it were large, its scale did not at that moment need to be considered. Her marriage, and the child on the sofa, were for now remote, and she was present. Her occasional attention to Joe irrationally yet convincingly seemed to Docherty a thing of delicious significance, a proof of her exorbitant quality rather than of prior fidelity.

He worked as well as he could while she made a call to the Vietnam Moratorium organizers, and then as she briskly reported to him and they went through the list of events she had been working on at the typewriter. She will go soon, he thought, and felt frantic despite himself, as if something pressing must be said before that. She raised her head from the stencil she was incising with her typewriter keys, and he saw her gaze. She looked away and then back, and, as if understanding him, exhaled, her shoulders slumped. Like an orphan, he thought. Then she smiled weakly and began typing again.

When she was leaving, she briskly gathered her belongings and the boy and his toys. She did not look at him. She said, head down, "Frank . . . I *know.* I know what you feel. I feel it myself. What do you think will happen?" She had reddened and her lips were contorted but still she enraptured Docherty.

He could tell her things he couldn't manage to tell himself. "I know what will happen. Rationally, only one thing can happen."

Joe lay heavily asleep in her arms.

"Is there a rational level?" she asked. "I hope so. It's a bad joke — the priest and the woman of the parish."

"But it doesn't seem a bad joke to us, does it? You have three children, and a good husband. That makes this ridiculous on one level. But something in me says, 'So what?' "

For it seemed to him, suddenly, a physical law, akin to gravity, that they should be together. He had the idea, banal when perceived in others, that this was ordained: the great obsession that his priesthood existed, in part, to prohibit and counsel against.

She kissed him for a second. It was almost like an assault. It might have been a foredoomed absurdity when he muttered in her wake, "I love you." Yet it seemed to him an utterance of the law.

20
THE CASE OF SARAH FAGAN, 3

Early 1970s

When Sarah remembered the expressions of special friendship between Father Leo Shannon and her, she remembered they often did not involve her body but instead his instructing her how to pleasure him. This form of friendship ran for months, and at no stage did she persuade herself she felt anything but flattered, though the daring of it all took her breath. She remembered a sense of election more than sexual feeling, and the illimitable affection she had when he emitted the white fluid. For in the seconds beforehand he was like a pathetic creature: he had descended from the altar to become a whimperer, in the way Christ had descended to face his redemptive sufferings with tears of blood.

He assured her many times at every encounter that there was nothing wrong with their sessions of friendship and that she need not mention them to any confessor. And yet, by a kind rule applying only to the closeness of soul they felt between them, he authorized her to receive the sacrament of the Eucharist, the Communion host.

She did not seek his Masses. One week the monsignor would do the early ones and Father Shannon the later, and the following week the order was reversed, and she did not take particular notice of this rhythm of priestly duty. But her mother wanted to be at Father Shannon's Mass, and when Sarah received Communion from his hands, he seemed inadvertent, as if she were simply another communicant, another schoolgirl. She was unspecial at the altar rails, where he was at the summit of his power, but special on the Thursday afternoons in the parish office when he was bound to her. The other girls he had mentioned were sent away to deliver this or that letter and then go home. They were simply tokens.

At school, Mother Alphonsus boasted that girls made up half of the Sydney Law School. A study of the state's medical schools offered similarly pleasing statistics. She suggested to clever Sarah Fagan that she ought to apply for a scholarship for further study. Yet, for reasons mysterious to outsiders, the convent had presented itself to Sarah as a personal means of escape. There, she would be one of a number of sisters, and she was sure she would never again be called on to be as intimate a friend in spirit and body as she was to Father Shannon.

As soon as Year 11 ended she expressed her ambition to him. One more year of high school education, and then the novitiate!

"Which order?" he asked her.

She said she had not quite decided, and he promised he would look into possibilities for her.

"Our friendship has now been perfected," he told her after a December session, one of what he called "particular friendship." "You will become Christ's now, and you will need your time free in the coming year for study."

This was true enough, but she felt immediate pain at the idea of being once more simply an ordinary parishioner and student.

"It is very rare," he told her, "that God allows a friendship like ours, but He always sends us a signal when it has reached its close."

Sarah was about to leave, and was gathering herself to stand, when there came a tentative knock on the door.

"Wait, please," he said. Then, "Well," like

a family doctor as he stood up at his desk and ushered Sarah to the door as if it were the end of a medical appointment.

Coming into the corridor, she had sight of a window at the back of the building under which sat a girl she knew, a pretty, brown-haired girl named Angela. Year 9. Angela carried sheaves of letters in her hands. Father Shannon must have realized that Sarah had seen Angela: he squeezed Sarah's arm and said, "My new aide. Since you'll be busy with studies. But I'll never again have a friend like you." He squeezed once more as if to emphasize that this girl would not be afforded the special friendship he'd extended to her.

She nodded, desiring to believe him and managing it. Even so, her mother asked her when she got home teary, "Why are you letting on like that? You've got what you wished for. God knows you'll be a loss to me. You were always my dear girl."

Over the Christmas holidays her mother remarked that Father Shannon hadn't called in recently; however, he summoned Sarah and her mother in late December to the presbytery. They entered that atmosphere of calmness and floor polish, and wearing his august cassock, he ushered them like strangers into his office, a place of a different geography to Sarah now that formality had intervened. His body fortified his godly lineaments, the cologne and aftershave, against any of the old special ardor.

He told them he had met with the mother superior of the Sisters of the Holy Blood. Everything Sarah needed, should she choose that order, the order that ran her school, would be provided to her under a bequest from a generous Catholic. The novitiate was on the North Shore in a redbrick cloister amongst eucalypts, and the training, Mrs. Fagan could be assured, was very sensible, since the sisters were a teaching order with schools all over Australia.

A week later Sarah drove a friend's car on learner plates to another parish, there confessing in tears to a priest she had never met what had happened, and that it had been a priest, and therefore she was doubly guilty. She was expecting fury. She evoked what seemed an awed silence.

"Did you do anything to encourage this?" he asked, softly even by the standards of the confessional.

She didn't know, so she said she must have.

"But were you conscious of doing something?" he asked, and the anger began to show now. The irritation at being held up by an inconvenient girl.

"No," she said, because the confessional was a venue where a lie to say yes in this case would negate the effect of absolution.

"How old are you?" he asked.

"Sixteen," she said.

"You did not tell him to stop?"

"He said it was God's plan."

"Oh dear," said the priest, no longer petulant. He was silent a long time.

It was always a matter of celebration when a Catholic got a lenient confessor and so it was now, for in the end he said, "The greater sin is that man's, and he must repent of it. There isn't anything you can do in that regard. But you must be careful now, and you must always be critical of what men say to you. In these matters, they tend to lie. Even priests."

She was relieved when he continued and did not entirely exempt her from blame. "There must have been somewhere in the back of your mind the knowledge that this was not God's will. From now on, always allow *that* voice to emerge."

It was that good priest, and even now she thought of him in those terms, who had taken the burden from her. He made it possible for her to go ahead as planned. Later, however, she wondered whether her anger would have been called forth earlier if she'd encountered a more severe and unyielding confessor. In any case, at the time she considered herself cured of sexuality. The term "cured" was her own; she rolled it around her mind like a lozenge. She never heard it used by any of the retreat masters, priests who came in to officiate over special periods of silence, the periods in which mealtimes and recreation were entirely silent as well. She was grateful that this monastic environment still existed. She was able to be sociable but was best on her own. Indeed, she began to wonder if she really wanted to go out into one of the Order's schools once she had taken the vows. Should she join what they called a "contemplative order," one devoted to meditation and prayer and the singing of all, not just some, of the Liturgy of the Hours?

Sarah daydreamed, during this time, of Mother Alphonsus, and of the adoration girls had of sturdy, learned women such as she, women who could have been anything but had chosen instead to go amongst uncertain young girls to give them direction and sustain them in faith. From the marks of favor Sarah had already received, she had no doubt this role was meant for her, too.

In her last year of high school, Sarah absorbed herself in her studies, and the memory of Father Shannon sank like a stone to the bottom of her consciousness. Nuns who knew that she intended to enter the novitiate on the North Shore the following year took her aside and warned her about the severity of that three-year experience. Mother Alphonsus herself told her, "Remember to obey the spirit of the rules. Anything more, and the rules might break you." Indeed, some nuns shook their heads when they mentioned the words "novice mistress," as if these specially chosen women were the regimental sergeant majors of God.

None of that frightened Sarah; she was determined to go. When her mother became more and more wistful as Christmas passed and the day Sarah must leave home came closer, Sarah hardened her determination. She was not bound to her mother's destiny. If she waited in that household and grew mature, what might her father do then? Her family confused and angered Sarah, and made her grateful for the sure route of escape she had chosen.

The day before she left she took her eldest brother aside and told him to protect their mother against the old man. The boy solemnly promised. He had been quietening down, had grown earnest, and he shared her abhorrence for their father, the incarnate weakness.

The entire family came for her entry into the convent — her shuffling father, her brothers, and her mother, who for once had certainty of things going right. In the Order's chapel they saw their child being invested in the habit, the clothing of the congregation.

Thus Sarah Fagan became a junior novice, a postulant. After a full year she would become a novice, and at the end of that year take her first vows of poverty, chastity, and obedience. And she thought, within her new robes, that her mother could surely no longer remember the night the father placed a hand on his child's breast. The tapes of the past would be wiped. Father Leo Shannon would become barely a murmur in her memory, a dark entity subject ultimately, she was sure, to obliteration in the depths of her soul.

21
DOCHERTY AND THE COSGROVES

1971

Liz Cosgrove had the finest instincts, and considerable hope, yet Docherty could perceive her fragility. Her husband was a lawyer, she told Docherty, and worked for one of the largest city law firms. Barely beyond thirty years and a little old-fashioned in manner, she seemed already to have a shadow on her. One of the elders of the group, discussing many things with Docherty on one of their meeting nights, articulated it: "Liz Cosgrove's husband. Clever man, university medal. But a ruinous drunk."

Liz was passionately engaged with Fatima Deriaya's cause. She would collect books from deceased estates and sell them to the secondhand bookshop in Crows Nest. She baked cakes and sold them in the main street on Saturdays. She told her children's teachers that she was raising money to buy Bengali children out of slavery — she thought that some of the nuns need not be troubled by an exact definition of that slavery — and asked them if once a term they could raise funds from parents.

She wrote to Dr. Deriaya and was invigorated by the letters she got back. Yet there was premature stress in Liz's face. On one occasion there was a cut to her eye. No one questioned her about it. They didn't ask because they knew it was no accident, and if she claimed it had been, they wouldn't have believed her. They kept silent to save her the demeaning lie.

Docherty did not have a telephone in his room at the monastery, but one night he was called to the communal phone by the secretary. It was Liz Cosgrove. Distressed, she asked Docherty if he could come over to their house, saying simply, beyond artifice, "My husband and I need you."

Another priest drove Docherty. He was dropped off and Liz answered the door in her go-to-town clothes. Her face was bruised — by blows and tears miserable and hard to confront.

"Come in," she said. When they entered, Docherty could hear a child crying and a glottal male voice calling and consoling. In the living room a man of about Docherty's age sat on a lounge with a small boy. The man was pale, he wore good but much-scuffed shoes, and he rose and muttered, "Father."

"Let me put Stephen to bed," Liz said neutrally. The man kissed the child inexpertly, a long, somber kiss on his temple. Docherty saw that the bruise beside the child's eye socket threatened to spread and encircle the eye.

"I'm Matt," said the man, rising to greet Docherty. He took a long, acidic swallow. A drinker's swallow.

Liz and the child were gone but much of the man's attention was still on the door.

"Matt," said Docherty. "Is it true you both wanted me to come?"

"Yes," said Matt. "You see that damage to the boy?" He swallowed a great deal more, and coughed. "I did that. That's my work . . ."

"An accident?" asked Docherty.

"It can seem like an accident to me. But it was deliberate. That's when we said, 'Enough!' Liz screamed it. I said it in despair. And we said, both at the same time, we've got to talk to someone and . . . Well, who? Priest? Doctor? And your name came up because Liz thinks you're genuine.

Authentic. In fact, more than that. I don't know, but I can't be a chooser, can I?"

"You must feel rotten," said Docherty, wondering if bitter repentance after violence and ripe self-accusation weren't themselves part of the disease.

Matt shook his head. "I've got a ferocious headache and I'm still pissed but I don't think anyone should give a damn."

"I won't jump in with glib reassurances on that," said Docherty.

"You're trying hard to be a cool priest, aren't you?"

"Of course. The reason is I'm really a very awkward and clumsy person. But I know how you feel. I don't mean the headache. I mean the guilt."

Matt, not subjected to the priestly chastisement he had hoped for, put his head in his hands.

Liz came back. Her husband looked up. "He said, 'Daddy had an accident,' that's all," she said briskly. "Wanting to console me, you see."

Matt raised and shook his head but said nothing.

"Our other son's staying with a friend," said Liz. "So that's good."

Liz asked Docherty if he could pray with them.

"Yes," said Matt, almost brightly, as if pleased to have a plan to consume the next few minutes.

So Docherty settled in to do it, wanting the phenomenon of prayer to have at least a small efficacy rather than the shallow comfort of archaic forms and old pronouns; with a submission to what could not be fought rather than with a solitary connection with the divine. His theory of prayer had arisen from his Indian experience. In the seminary, prayer had been an egocentric and almost neurotic attempt to attract divine attention.

As he spoke, leaning forward as he gripped his chair, he surprised himself by feeling uncomfortable, in this age when priests were more likely to be asked to act as social workers (a task for which they were woefully underequipped) than as invokers of divine guidance.

"*You* know," he addressed the Ultimate, "that in the phenomenal souls of human beings there are elements that do not yield to the powers of our will; that there are lesions that can be cured only by submission . . ."

He wondered, meanwhile, whether he'd be able to teach Matt Cosgrove meditation. There was help in that. There was help in AA, too, if Matt could bring himself to submission. You could tell that he was in the phase of the disease in which he saw every disaster as unrelated to the next, disconnected from drink. Docherty could see that Matt still believed that next time he would simply say no to the striding Scotsman, the man in the kilt, the black and white terriers, to the authority of this or that blender whose name was signed on the bottle. Without knowing it, Matt wanted a prayer that spoke not to submission and loss of control, but to his willpower. That is, he wanted a prayer that would let him go on as an alcoholic. Docherty would not give him one. "These children of the Father suffer forces that are larger than their deliberate intentions. . . ."

Yet to an extent Docherty felt foolish pursuing theories of prayer while this man and woman were drowning. He might just as well use familiar mantras and well-worn incantations to get them settled, adjusted. Next, therefore, he suggested a decade of the rosary. The "Hail Mary," the "Glory Be" were recited with great hopeful clarity by Liz, with half-abashed mutters from Matt, and with the crispness Docherty felt he owed his public orisons.

"So," Liz said when that was done, reaching out for one of Matt's clenched hands.

All of the astounding but bewildered tolerance of good women was in that gesture. "What's to be done?"

She looked at both men. The silence stretched.

At last Matt said, "We're used to the priest leading the discussion, Frank. That's how it was when we were kids."

"So the person who knows least of what's happening speaks first?" asked Docherty with a smile, but looking at Matt to let him know *he* understood what Matt was doing. That, again, he was reducing this to the normal priestly intervention, comforting at the time it occurs, ultimately ineffectual. This man was racked with guilt at bruising his son and wife, but he did not even know he was hoping for future frenzies of booze that would be purer, that would fuel his true self, his eloquence and good nature, and not his squalors of soul. That would make him tolerable to himself. But Docherty did not want him to forget the intolerable outbursts that inevitably and abundantly followed. Docherty did not want him to believe that after this priestly intervention he could return to the malign rhythm of his life.

"Well, we still want it that way," said Matt, not aware that this was a confession.

"I think Matt should try AA again," Liz said.

"It does harm, too," said her husband.

"Harm?" Liz asked, in a soft exasperation, raising her eyebrows.

"Yes," Matt kept on. "When they find out it can't help them and they despair, and . . ." He cast his hands up, implying a grim end.

"For God's sake," said Liz, testy at last.

"I can't do the twelve steps," said Matt, perhaps a little too plaintively, but saved from accusations of being dramatic by his obvious shame. "I don't have a problem with repentance. I've been repenting since I was a kid." He sounded bitter about that fact. "It's the surrendering to a superior power."

"Don't you believe in one?" asked Docherty.

"I don't believe in the Catholic God," said Matt. "Why should I? When he permits such shit to reign on earth?"

"Then what do you believe in?" asked Liz. "We asked Frank to pray. Tell me what you love."

"My God is a god of vengeance," said Matt. "And given what I've done tonight, it's just as well."

Despite himself, Docherty intervened. "But there's a transcendence inside you.

This is not bullshit, Matt! You know there's something, deep beyond the *you* you're disgusted with. Beyond the next binge you already have in mind."

"What do you mean by that?"

Docherty ignored the question. "Your God of vengeance is yourself. Your son knows that. But beyond that, there's the big unknowable. Couldn't you surrender to it? God almighty, I don't know what we are! But we are beasts when we believe we can do it all ourselves, and we are saved when we know we can't."

"What if there isn't any transcendence?" Matt challenged him with sudden bitterness. "What if there's nothing and I'm just a throat? I think, in fact, I am just a throat."

"It's all right to condemn yourself that way," said Liz. "It's not all right to condemn me and the kids. I don't think you should consider yourself unique. I think you ought to find like-minded reformed drinkers, people who are obviously agnostic. Find out how they do it! Find out how they did it!"

So Matt was compelled, and it was resolved, and Docherty gave way to the temptation to talk about his passion for meditation as a means of calm submission. In Liz, hope soared. Poignantly. Because if he were honest, Docherty would have admitted he felt tragedy impending.

Matt returned to AA but, feared Docherty,
with the air of a man trying a plunge into a
forlorn hope before consigning himself to
the pit. Three weekly meetings went by.
Docherty gave Matt, Liz, and their sons
Communion at the altar rails. Then, when
he had returned from Sydney University
one Wednesday afternoon and was beginning to study, there was a knock at his door.

"There's a man asking for you. Not too
politely, either. Do you want me to ring the
police?"

" 'Here we are, here we are, here we are,' "
sang Matt when Docherty entered the
reception area of the monastic house.
"Father Frank, I present you with the
inevitable. I'm not going home and belting
my kids, though, so I thought I might turn
up and belt you, for being such a po-faced
bullshitter."

"You bastards," he went on. "You raised
us to believe that the sacraments are the
cure for human life, that we can solve
anything through them. But it's all bullshit,
isn't it?"

"I'd like to think not," said Docherty.
"But, yes, there's been a tendency to credit
them with too much effect."

There you go, he thought, despairing of himself. A prissy answer when all the man wants is a fight! "You're trying to harry me into giving you the answer neatly wrapped," he said. "Or else you want to be condemned by me. I'm sorry, Matt. I can't insult you because you haven't wronged me. All you've done is set out to prove you can't help yourself. You knew you weren't going to succeed, because you'd already decided you wouldn't."

"Damn you," shouted Matt. "I don't want a priest who knows nothing and says so. I want the old-fashioned ones who breathe fire and . . . and . . . certainty."

The enunciation of "certainty" had been quite a test for Matt and he rested for a while. Then he started up again. "I want to be condemned to Hell. I want you to tell me to confess and be chastised and get some sanctifying bloody grace into me. And with that aboard I can face every peril and beat the world and the Devil and mend my bloody ways. So for Christ's sake, just tell me I'm a sot. Invite God to strike me down."

"Too easy for you," said Docherty.

"Listen to me, you prick," said Matt with the earnestness of the drunk, "I'm not a failure at AA because I think I'm better than other drunks. I'm a failure because I know

I'm not as good a man as them. I'm *not* as good a man."

"You're too intelligent for AA, or you're too far gone for it. Which is it, Matt?"

He was bewildered. Docherty pursued him.

"I saw your ordinary shame the other night. If you were a bad man you wouldn't have felt it."

Matt fell back on his original argument. "The sacraments do the whole bloody job. That's what I was told as a kid. With the sacraments aboard I need fear nothing. And you're telling me the sacraments are powerless! I wish you'd all told me that when I was seven."

"Listen," urged Docherty, "the sacraments are like gates. We walk through them. But they can't help you, because you've decided nothing can help you. You *can* pull yourself from the pit. AA, meditation, the whole arsenal . . . Who cares as long as you save yourself, one way or another."

"Jesus!" said Matt in disgust.

"There is a you that's an observer, and he's looking down upon the you who can't stop drinking. This is the fantasy that's got you here — that you're the angel looking down on the pigsty, and as much as your wife hates it, you hate it worse. In fact, the angel in you thinks it's too superior to be involved in your drunkenness, and it just wants to be quit of you. It's a proud Satanic angel. Well, listen, Matt, you are *not* the witness to this. You're *in* it. All of you. Don't take that snide angel with you into AA. Take yourself. Then you've got a bloody chance, Matt. Until you do that, nothing happens."

Matt drew breath as if he had been the one making the speech. "Christ in heaven!" he roared.

Docherty worried about the woman in reception, whether she would be so alarmed by the exchange she would call the police.

"Tone it down, Matt!"

"What did you say?"

"You're not entitled to make a scene!"

"You're the one making the scene," cried Matt. He descended on Docherty and punched him wildly on the jaw. Docherty's teeth rattled, he bit his tongue, pain and blood filled his mouth. He grimaced, swallowed the blood, and in one furious gesture found his handkerchief to staunch the flow.

Matt's lucky punch, Docherty discovered, had dislodged a tooth. An incisor sat glistening in the red on his handkerchief. He offered the damage for Matt's inspection. At the sight of it, Matt began to vomit. The smell of liquor semirendered by human digestion afflicted Docherty like a parallel pain.

The receptionist was indeed now at the door, looking from Matt's retching to Docherty's bloodied mouth. Docherty had always had a sense that she considered him a monastic oddity, inadequately priestly, and here was the proof, in a parlor violated by vomit and blood.

Two policemen arrived very fast and seemed anxious to charge Matt. One of them insisted on inspecting the damage to Docherty's face and yelled at Matt, "Hey mate, you, do you go round beating up priests? That's a dingo act, you cunt."

Docherty explained that Matt was a member of the parish. He'd come for help and there'd been an exchange of words. "It'd be a betrayal of trust to let you charge him," he told the two policemen.

One of the two cops, who must have been a Catholic going by his outrage at the idea of punching a priest, whispered, "You don't have a thing with his wife, do you, Father?"

"No, nothing like that," said Docherty, not even embarrassed now that the revolutionary age was here and any man was entitled to talk to any other man so frankly.

In a private conference with the constables, while Matt sat bedraggled and defeated in a corner, Docherty suggested that he would accompany them to Matt's home.

"Do you know he won't whack his wife?" one of the policemen wanted to know.

"I don't believe he'll do it now," Docherty said.

The policemen drove them back to the Cosgrove house, and after issuing a stern warning to Matt, they departed. Docherty stayed on. Matt sat in a corner, unstrung. He fell asleep on the settee. Stephen and Paul came in to inspect their father ambiguously, a fallen hero or a threat, of whom, for the moment, they did not need to be afraid.

A month later, Liz Cosgrove found her husband in the bath, his wrists slashed. Ambulance men rushed him to North Shore Hospital and he recovered. Docherty visited him but Matt seemed depleted of all conversation.

He retired from life after that: spent three months in a clinic, received a pension, and most of the time lived, by agreement between himself and Liz, in a hostel near Anzac Parade run by the Sisters of Charity, with other debilitated Catholics and a certain number of alcohol-damaged priests. He died of a stroke in the late 1980s. Maureen wrote to Docherty about it.

Liz continued her work raising money to

free children from the brothels of Calcutta. If she considered herself an available woman, she was by now too severely frightened of violence to trust a male around her boys. And so her life was written. It seemed the Cosgrove family had remained blighted ever after.

22
THE PAST SINS OF
MONSIGNOR SHANNON

Early 1970s

He did not approve of his past sins, and in the penitent season after his being absolved of them he hoped they would never return to him. But sometimes they did, as he slept or in waking hours, and they induced desire.

As a young man, Leo Shannon felt he fitted the priesthood as a hand fits a glove. Even in the seminary he loved it all — the fraternity, the monastic chapel, the debates on morality, the lectures delivered in Latin, which gave him a sense of secret knowledge. The liturgy of the Mass impassioned him. The words of consecration. He believed absolutely then — though he did not quite dare ask himself later in his career — in transubstantiation: that at the words of consecration uttered by the priest, the very natures of the bread and wine were transformed into the body and the blood of Jesus

Christ. Essentially, he liked the ecclesiastical trade and its routines — the evening Masses and confessions on Saturday; the Sunday morning Masses and sermons; the dinner at his parents' place and — as he got older — at his sister's on Sunday night. The gossipy golfing Mondays spent with other priests before the sacramental and administrative business of the week.

He found it hard in a parish to occupy himself on a Tuesday. The parishes of the city of Sydney in the 1970s were not like the Irish parishes of which his great-grandparents had spoken, nor their continuation in the sparse settlements of the New South Wales bush. In his grandparents' day the priest trudged or rode from farm to farm, and there was always a peat fire (or one of eucalyptus boughs) to sit at, and always someone to speak to and to spiritually elevate. But now even the sick weren't what they'd been when he was a boy — there were not as many of them. It had been a good arrangement in the old days, with the priest too busy to inquire into what he himself really thought.

Despite his facility with theology and Thomistic philosophy, he had not wanted to pursue further research and study. So Shannon found himself an urban priest in a generation in which both parents worked. He walked amongst the children in the playground of the parish school, and the kids cried out to him, and he spoke to them. But he did not want to spend his afternoons talking to classes, offering them the primitive theology appropriate to primary school students. He wished profoundly and earnestly he could imbue them with certainty just by touching their hands, but that was not the way of things. So even a visit to the school was, more frequently than not, simply a tedious outing which, though it might have convinced the schoolkids, did not convince him.

He joined a suburban tennis club, and took a little pride from the fact that the players said to each other, "You'd never know he was a priest." But they did know he was, and that gave him mystery and potency, two qualities he had an appetite for. They had expected him to sermonize them, but he was of the school, like most priests, that the best sermon was your own normality. Though his lucky backhand smash down the line at the net in a game of doubles was no different an entity than one delivered by an agnostic, he felt it reverberate like a mystery of faith amongst the other doubles players.

Leading by example was not, of course, what it had been on the island of his forebears, a monotheistic society in which the mildest human virtue of a priest was bruited about the Irish consoling themselves for their dependence on the clergy, and the clergy deigning now and then to demonstrate their membership of the human race.

The city parish Leo Shannon worked in had been founded towards the end of the First World War, and it struck him that its records and management were chaotic, despite its priest's air of being in command of all elements. So this was the task to which he devoted himself: to get the records indexed, to make an archive of bills paid, and to restore order to bills payable, so that the monsignor would see what a splendid job he had done. He enjoyed it. Bringing order to the records was like bringing order to the soul.

He had to give an occasional talk at the nearby girls' college, a school of considerable reputation. It was an experience — girls in their second year of high school, respectful, faithful, and not yet worldly. Those with a smear of acne on their faces wore it like a deeper uncertainty about the future. They possessed unconscious beauty. That did not mean that some of them did not surmise their future power over men, but they were still uncertain of its dimensions. He had a conversation with the sensible headmistress, Mother Alphonsus, and developed the idea, at that stage without any consciously questionable intent, of recruiting some of the cleverer girls to help him organize the parish office.

The girl who succeeded Sarah Fagan was the one named Angela Galvin. He began to prepare her for the grand proposition, the special friendship involving special liberties. She was a different character from her predecessor, not as solemn, not as intellectual, but at least, perhaps more, emotionally agile. The sort of girl described as effervescent. The trouble with effervescence is that it is talkative. Sometimes it is also knowing. This girl — to use an Americanism — knew the score.

At the end of his seventh afternoon working with Angela, her father came to the presbytery. He was a trade union official — one of the new breed, not created on the shop floor but by way of law and industrial relations degrees. He asked the housekeeper if he could see Father Shannon. Shannon was out at the time, but later he called the man and arranged a meeting, suggesting a local coffee shop. Galvin told him, "I'd rather speak to you at the presbytery, Father, for fear of what might be overheard."

Leo Shannon felt a certain dread. He had a sense that the man might denounce him and the idea caused sweat to break astringently from the pores of his neck and arms.

Angela's father turned up at the presbytery the next morning. "Can we speak confidentially somewhere?" he asked Shannon.

Shannon invited him into the parlor, closed the door, and pointed him towards some easy chairs by the window. From the school yard the distant fracas of girls at the convent, boys at the Brothers school, reached them. The man sat — it was an accommodating, enveloping seat, but once in it he became aggressive. "You know, living like this, you jokers should take a good look at yourselves!"

"What exactly do you mean by that?" asked Shannon. He had his aura of justifying dudgeon in place.

"I mean, that you choose to live in this sterile environment, in these cold rooms, with every comfort except the one that counts. Playing it austere. And then you reach out to my daughter to try to give yourself some life. But not *my* daughter! Not my daughter, Father!"

Father Shannon maintained the bluff. "I don't quite see what you're implying. I'm a priest and my pastoral care extends to —"

But Galvin said, "Stop it. Stop it, now. I'm a Catholic. Not due to anything you've done. But I'm a Catholic. Let us say it finishes here. My daughter. And it stops with any other girls, too. Be assured, we are watching. I have spoken already to Mother Alphonsus."

"Whom I'm sure was appalled by your suggestion!" said Shannon, very worried by the strange, chastening worldliness in the man's eyes. Of course, Shannon thought. Industrial relations. He would have seen champion bluffers before.

He went on making his protestations, declaring that he was above all this. He acted out rather than felt hostility towards Galvin, who then made the calm point that if no more convent schoolgirls were called in to work with Father Shannon, there should be no further problem.

"But, again, you should be clear: we are aware, Father," said the man. "Let this be a wake-up to you."

So his breezy, lively, chattering daughter had chattered enough to alarm her parents. Shannon maintained his dignity and his denials. Mother Alphonsus did not alter her demeanor towards him. But he knew he must be careful now.

A month later, while he heard confessions, he encountered an eleven- or twelve-year-old boy whom he believed he knew. The boy's mother was Liz Cosgrove, a friend of his sister. Married a drunk, and he'd given her two fresh-faced, earnest boys, this one the younger.

It was simply part of the routine of the confessional to be concerned about masturbation and the young, and whenever a wholesome boy mentioned temptations of the flesh, Father Shannon asked automatically, "The lower part of your body? Do you ever find yourself tempted to touch it?" It was taken for granted that a boy this age would understand what was meant by that.

Shannon did not challenge the orthodoxy that said the young must be helped to fight off the temptation to practice what his moral theology textbook called *manustrupatio* — hand-rape. He did not utter the question with any malice. His training had instructed that this was the first of the real sins, and the young must be helped to avoid it. He himself had been helped by prayer and wise counsel to get very nearly through his teenage years before understanding what this sin was, and falling to it almost out of curiosity. These days, after his confrontation with Galvin, Shannon lived in chastened purity, fortified by prayer.

The boy seemed confused by the question. Shannon felt a pulse of sympathy. Then he felt something else: an awareness that he could help this child to get beyond that first sin, that he could comfort and accompany him through it; an awareness he had chanced on a treasure — his ability to guide this child. He paused and waited for his breath to return. His wariness, his repentance — the repentance of a man who decides he has offended God on a technicality, as a breach of theological etiquette, rather than by harming his young fellow sinners — had disappeared, and a fever was taking its place. It was a fever to which he had not known until then he was susceptible. Galvin had slammed the door on one desire. But here was another door.

"I believe that because of your intelligence," said Father Shannon, "you might encounter special problems. That's why I would like you to attend the presbytery, where I can advise you and hear your confession in privacy. Do you think you would like to do that, to come to the presbytery for confession?"

The boy said he would like to do that. The authority of the clergy is not quite dead, Father Shannon assured himself.

"I have one last question for you. Do you love your father?"

Shannon himself didn't know why he wanted an answer to this, but for some reason he did. The kid obviously thought that he was subject to a moral ambush, and hesitated.

"Please, please," Shannon soothed him, "I merely ask because I know that your father struggles."

The boy said, "I told my mother once that I hated him. She said, 'No, you hate the demons in him.' "

"So you love your father?"

"I do hate the demons in him. They make him break things. They make him hurt us."

"I'll send a note to your headmistress. See you at three o'clock tomorrow afternoon. You'll be there?"

It was disgraceful that he had an erection as he said this. But my intentions are good, dear Mother, he pleaded with the Virgin Mary. Help me, Mother. Help me help this boy.

The child seemed a near-translucent being to him, an angel with just enough flesh, whose voice had a questioning yet fresh-minted quality to it. He could have identified its especial strand amongst any playground hubbub.

He did exactly that when he visited the parish school that afternoon in his role of chaplain — behind the raucousness of the playground, he watched Stephen Cosgrove speaking sagely on a bench to other less riotous classroom mates.

Shannon hand-delivered a note to the headmistress of the school, a middle-aged nun called Sister Frances.

"It's all in the note," he said. "But, as you know, the Cosgroves are a troubled family, and I want to do what I can to prevent that marring the life of young Stephen."

The next day the boy arrived at the appointed time, three minutes after Shannon had positioned himself by the parlor door to answer the ring before the housekeeper could even leave the kitchen. Stephen stood in his school uniform, adorned with his shining prefect badge — the nattiness-next-to-Godliness with which his mother had sent him from home apparent in him, heartbreaking and demanding desire.

The boy also possessed an old-fashioned awe of church, which Leo Shannon himself would have felt at that age if summoned to the presbytery. It was intoxicating to observe. The boy had no idea that it was Shannon who trembled, who felt he hung giddily by a wire stretched across the sky and might fall from it at any instant.

"Come upstairs," Shannon said. "We can talk properly there."

He showed Stephen into the office beside his bedroom. The sofa he had used for the guidance of Sarah and Angela was still in its place. He had enough self-reflection to be amazed that he was about to take part in another act of beneficence.

He had set on a side table a glass of milk with a beaded doily covering it, and shortbread.

"I thought you might be thirsty and a bit hungry," he suggested. He removed the doily. The boy dutifully drank some of the milk and ate a biscuit. He had not come expecting to be fed, however, and he munched and sipped distractedly. Shannon did not turn his full attention, at least in an obvious sense, to him yet. He looked through papers on the desk, ticked a few, even wrote a check and put it in an envelope. He would address it later, though, for he did not have enough focus left for the task. The boy had put the glass and the shortbread, half-eaten, aside.

"Well," said Father Shannon. "You and I

are under the seal of the confessional now. You don't tell your parents about what happens in the confessional, do you?"

"No, Father."

Shannon settled in his chair, turned and looked at the boy on the settee.

"Because you are a special boy," he told him, "I need to see your private parts. To know that they are normal. It is very important to know that a boy's parts are normal. Do not be afraid. The cardinal has given me special permission to make such an inspection."

The boy looked bemused in a particular way, as a fawn-like creature unexpectedly ordered to jump through a ring of fire. Shannon knew the boy was fearful, but his pity was swept up in hunger. Once, in obedience to the Church, the boy had risen and had lowered his trousers — yes, Shannon insisted, his underpants, too — Shannon was aware that he had the casual power he wanted.

At the priest's command the boy took his own timid penis in his hand — "It is important to know if it functions properly" — and it was clear that he had not done such things very much, for when Shannon demanded that he do so, his massaging of himself was token and timid.

From then on Shannon told every lie. It was required and lawful in God's eyes that the boy become more strenuous, put in more effort. It was necessary that Shannon should show him how, and important the boy should see his own, Shannon's, full erection, and enclose it in his hand.

When it was over, a stain of shame began to invade the former exaltation as he told the boy that what they had done was not wrong; that he, Father Shannon, had a special dispensation to deal with these cases. That this was a great secret to which few were admitted.

Shannon cleaned himself and the boy up. Then he drove Stephen home, leaving him at his gate. He was certain from the boy's demeanor there would be no talking. Stephen remained awed, which did not evoke any guilt in Shannon. But the boy was also bewildered, and that did cause the priest some unease.

Having seen Stephen go inside, Shannon drove two streets and stopped in the shade of box trees as a disabling sorrow swept through him. He laid his head on his hands and wept. When he had recovered somewhat, he drove to Father Guest's parish, confessed to him, swore sincerely that this had been an aberrant afternoon and that it would not occur again, and received the beloved balm of absolution which returned the soul to its proper course. He went on a retreat at a monastery in Kangaroo Valley and after a week of silent prayer believed himself appropriately chaste.

It did not last. He returned for a while to Stephen. In fact, over a decade of fall and penitence and fall, there were three boys with whom he shared a series of these intimate pastoral exchanges. In each case a natural progression led them from the confessional to the presbytery, where Shannon would greet the boys in his own quarters when the monsignor was away. When Shannon told them there was nothing abnormal about them, that he himself was the sufferer, and that they were merely helping him with his special problems as the archbishop had sanctioned, he believed absolutely for that half hour that this was the case.

It was when a boy he did not know approached him in the confessional and mentioned Father Guest, curate of a neighboring parish, and raised the question of what Father Guest had done to him, that Father Leo Shannon saw a remarkable and further confessional possibility.

23
MAUREEN BRESLIN REMEMBERS THE EXPULSION OF DOCHERTY, 1972

One night there was a knock at our door. When I answered it I discovered the least expected of visitors, especially for that time of day. Father Frank Docherty, a little doleful and looking thin. We had not seen each other since the afternoon I'd made that berserk statement to him. To be honest, I don't know if that was virtue or cowardice, on my part and his. I had half-expected a call from him to adjust, or enlarge on, or renounce what he had said and done at our last meeting. I owed him one myself. But in the absence of us communicating, I had found the means to tell Damian what had happened, a recital no doubt all the more hurtful and annoying because of the idea the love-stricken have that the enchantment they are under is unchosen, an accident. Damian had seemed more acerbic than bitter. He said he had seen it coming but that it was a shock to hear it confirmed by me. I had a feeling he had undue faith that my attachment to him was profound, that what I was undergoing was some form of amatory influenza. He saw the affliction as temporary, a cloud on the face of the waters — in no way the waters themselves. I was not in a position to argue this point with him, to urge him to greater distress and threats and yelling.

But now he must be aware Docherty was at the door, because Frank, when he spoke, was not muted.

"Good evening, Maureen."

Frank seemed to be announcing unabashedly his arrival for anyone inside the house to hear, as well as assessing and testing me. Was this a continuation of our last exchange? I wondered. Was I still the woman who'd made that stupid, obsessive statement?

He said, "I've had a time of it, I'm afraid. I should have called before coming. But I think you'll understand."

I wondered, would I understand? I would have welcomed distracting everyone — Damian, myself, Frank — with a fury. Yet I thought of my sleeping children. And he had reached out and patted my upper arm, like a consoler, or else like a man about to wreak havoc and apologizing beforehand. It

304

seemed impossible to be angry, impossible not to invite him in.

"Damian knows," I told him.

I saw his lips compress as he entered. He was paler than I had ever seen him. I wondered who would initiate the dreaded scene. I could not have said how I wanted things resolved. As I followed him into the living room, I could see Damian's eyes glittering.

"Father Frank," said Damian. "Take a seat."

All three of our kids emerged from their rooms, one by one. With their tentative smiles they sought reassurance the world was still in place, and in return we gave them endearments and blandishments to go back to sleep. I saw them to their beds and wondered what was happening in the living room. When I returned the two men were seated with glasses of wine in their hands. Damian called, "All quiet on the Western Front?" and I said it was.

"I've come to say goodbye," Frank said now, straight off. "I've been examined and found wanting. I'm required to leave the archdiocese of Sydney. My order is sending me somewhere else."

He looked at me. I thought he might be saying, I've done this for you. This is love.

Yet immediately I thought it was also abandonment. Abandonment of me. And, I decided at that second, as some kind of antidote, also the abandonment of the group. He had provoked our rebellion, mine and Damian's. Our new conscientious daring, whatever you called it — the combination of progressive theology and politics in which we were finding a place — was connected to Frank. He had, however, become at the same time the fabric of what still connected us to our forefathers' and, let me also say, foremothers' religion.

We sat aghast, awaiting a justification.

"You've chosen to go," I accused him.

He said, "No. But I couldn't expect to be allowed to remain here forever." He smiled that smile that seemed to belong, despite his long adult features, to a thirteen-year-old at the Christian Brothers. I wondered, is that the way men become priests? By remaining boys?

"Where are you going?" asked Damian. "Is it too far for us to drive?"

"I fear so," said Docherty. "I'm going to my order's house in Ontario. They've found a spot for me there. And a job."

"*Ontario?* Ontario in Canada?"

"Well, there's one in California, too," with his annoying exactness, venerated by me.

"But I'm afraid in this case it is Ontario in Canada. There's a university there, in a town called Waterloo. You know I've been working on my master's in behavioral psychology."

We had only the dimmest sense that he had been.

"Well, they want me to embark on a doctoral degree there."

We were still bewildered as to why such a radical geographic relocation was necessary. I, as a putative lover, wondered even more so.

"Do you *want* to go to Canada?" asked Damian, as if he himself thought it too far a reach to make amends for the crimes I had already admitted, crimes of merely potential desire.

"Look, I don't have a choice," Frank said, as if he had not uttered an earlier choice, and for me.

"You don't have a *choice*!" I called out, loud enough to bring the children back, though they did not come.

He stared bleakly at me. Damian could see it, that stare.

"I don't have a choice. I have overreached myself. I am an arrogant man. I've done more harm than good."

"Bugger you!" I said. And an absurd

afterthought came straight to my lips. "If we write to your superior general," I suggested, "do you think we might sway the damned cardinal?"

I was aware that as a member of a religious order he had a superior general who might be pleaded with.

"Not in this case," he said. "Look, I might as well tell you. You may remember a thin man who sat in the choir loft. Mr. Dryden, straight black hair, and a part that could have been made by an axe."

We had seen him.

"One of the parishioners tipped me off that the man was taking notes during my sermons. I believe that he did so because someone in authority — in the Church, I mean, or maybe in a political context — told him to. So that's the story. Cardinal Scanlon has suspended my faculties to say Mass and give the sacraments within the diocese. My superior general is embarrassed by me, but he's also embarrassed *for* me. He's tolerated me as a young turk. But the cardinal has a harder time. I can understand it. He's a scrupulous man, and he's been worried by me for some time, fearful I'd harm the Church's relationship with the government by my opposition to Vietnam. And Mr. Dryden was not on his own — the cardinal had quite a dossier on me from a number of sources. I keep on forgetting about the Democratic Labor Party people and their terror of Communists, and their reports of my Vietnam sermons showed I was one.

"So that's it. Things are changing, but not that quickly. You mustn't think badly of anyone involved in this. I've had a valuable education in what is possible in the future. I will be far more careful."

"So you come and wake us up, Frank," said Damian. "Throw everything into the air, and then you're blithely off before any of it's even landed on the ground."

"I'm sorry. But it's not my choice."

"I know. 'Orders from above'! The SS excuse!"

I sensed his anger was because I was one of the items thrown into the air, and I certainly hadn't landed.

"Why don't you just leave the bastards?" he asked. "Give up that hopeless priesthood. We all know it's full of noble fools and dolts, and the dolts always win. Leave and make yourself an honest man, for God's sake."

I frowned away in the shadow of Damian's outrage. He wanted Frank to become a private man. And then what? I would be part of the debris, and I did not even know, despite an undeniable longing for imperfect Frank, where that would put me.

"But it's *my* Church," said Frank, identifying his fundamental love. "If I let myself be ejected, what does it say about me? And it may be . . . it may be a fortunate thing. Look, none of us get to a plateau of certainty where we're sure of everything. We're always in transit and always confused. I'm sorry."

"Jesus," said Damian, "show a little anger, will you? You must be so bloody angry. If you're not angry, you're not human. Listen, I know it! My wife loves you. Or if not, she is mightily distracted by you."

Damian saw my gestures of denial. "I know, I know," he continued. "And, yes, three children. But it doesn't alter the fact. Old as religion! You're the prophet, she's the vestal. Don't you bloody see that?"

I saw Damian was trying to clear the air of obsession, that he was daring Frank to love, and — as improbably as ever — to love me.

Frank inhaled and lowered his eyes. "Of course I'm angry. But what would be the sense of passing *that* virus on to you?"

"Oh, I've bloody well got the virus, I tell you," said Damian. "And Maureen has the other one. I hate having been born a Catholic. I daydream of life as an agnostic. That's the life we should all have! It's the true religion of the species. And Maureen. Do you love her in the full sense? Come on, show us the truth. You're content to move on in a cloud of cheap mystery. Come clean, like we're supposed to do in your confessional. And if you say you love her like a sister, I'll bloody well punch you."

Frank seemed unequipped for this scene, his face blushing as he strove to honor Damian's right to an answer.

"Yes," he said. "Of course I love her. As a woman, and a companion. I'm drawn to her. And I can't have her and shouldn't have her. And that's that!"

"No, it isn't," Damian insisted. "This is your chance!"

I prepared myself to intervene. My fate was being bartered between the men; I must say something weighty. But on they went.

"A chance for what?" asked Frank, finding his anger. "A three-month affair? Why not? Marriage isn't ownership. You don't own her, Damian, though you've got first claim on her love. But the three children. They own her. They'd bring her back. And so, by the way, would you."

"Thanks a million," Damian said with a hack of a laugh.

"Because you're a good man."

Damian's face had become pitiably suffused now. He had decided that after all he did not want this confrontation. I suffered one of those Graham Greene moments then: what is the boundary between love and pity? Because I pitied Damian and it felt like love. I wished I could go to him and hold him.

"Well, I'm not going to be executed," Frank told us in the meantime. "A far humbler administrative fate's come into play. I'm regretful for both your sakes." He reiterated that. "For both your dear sakes."

I put my forehead against my hand. Tears were close, but I knew they'd be to no avail.

"So, no affair with Mrs. Breslin?" asked Damian, humiliating us, as he was in part entitled to.

"Damian!" I protested.

"No," said Frank. "In a parallel universe, I can't say . . ."

"This universe will do me, Frank. Typical of you to want an alternative one."

"You could say that," Frank gently admitted.

"The Church will seem less habitable," said Damian, then, as if becoming his friend again. "I mean, if you go."

"It will be just as habitable," Frank murmured. "It has you two. Lucky to have you."

Again, I wasn't sure I wanted to be yielded up so terminally to Damian.

Damian muttered in what was obviously an uncomfortable rush, "You'll have to forgive me if I said anything offensive."

Frank went over and reached a hand to his shoulder. Man to man. Once more, I felt, with a flare of annoyance, where am I in this?

I wanted Frank. I didn't take him. There was a cost in that, and I paid it. Where was the gesture, the hand on my shoulder? It was too like that ritual by which men say, "Your girl's safe with me, mate!" Did the girl have anything to say on that matter? Maybe not a girl with three kids.

"What about me?" I cried. "What about me as you two make peace with each other?"

"Don't you see?" asked Damian. "You are the arbiter in this matter. You always were."

"All I see is you two and your gentleman's agreement."

I wanted Frank so painfully. By now I had even forgotten my children sleeping a few meters away.

Frank brought his hands to his face. Easy for you, I thought. "This is my life," he said. He dropped his hands and shook his head. "Your lives are cut out for you, too."

He turned to me. "The children are a

313

decree. They can't be denied. Damian . . . Damian is too good for the two of us. And the truth is that if I want to go on being a priest of my order, I have to go. I can't stay here. And that's it. I appreciate your eloquence, Damian. It does your bloodlines credit. You should have been at the Dublin Post Office in 1916."

"For heaven's sake," said Damian, "you don't even believe in armed resistance."

"You're right. But as Yeats said, 'A terrible beauty is born'!"

"Bullshit," said Damian. "Men were turned to carcasses."

We all went to see him off at the airport. Trans-Pacific, Sydney to Vancouver. All the weekly group and activists exuberant in grief. Except for me. I couldn't afford exuberance.

"This was meant to happen," he told me, taking me aside. "For everyone's sake."

"For mine?" I asked.

Apart from that I stood back, swallowing again and again, feeling riven and stuck for words. What do you say on the rim of a great loss? I think I can claim after this passage of time, and without too much melodrama, that he was always my shadow love.

314

24
THE CASE OF SARAH FAGAN, 4

1970s

The order permitted visits by parents and family once every three months, and Sarah considered these adequate: enough for her fond mother, more than enough for her flawed father.

Her novice mistress was not the dragon some of the older nuns had warned Sarah she would be, but more or less as promised by Father Shannon: a tall, ample woman in the tradition of mother superiors in films who exuded goodwill that was more compelling than strict discipline. She laid out the rule of the Order — meditation, the recital of the Office, study, silence except in recreation and when temporarily revoked, custody of the eyes, examination of conscience, and other appropriate exercises for a novice nun.

In the matter of the examination of conscience, she said, they should not be too particular, in case scruples, the most unimportant peccadillos, began to assume a scale equivalent in the novices' minds to real crimes such as running a concentration camp or being Jack the Ripper.

There were only five novices — it was the era in which preachers were beginning to bewail the falling-off in numbers of candidates for the priesthood and orders of nuns and brothers, blaming it on television and growing secularism, rock 'n' roll, and permissive films. One was thirty-five and had been an accountant. She must desperately want to be here, thought Sarah, to abandon a career, to nullify her training and her specialty.

Sarah cherished the test of silence and contributed to a work roster, scrubbing and vacuuming in silence. The drudgery was pleasing because it produced an atmosphere immaculate but for the faint smell of furniture polish.

When the girls took their vows after their two years in the novitiate, they were moved to a house owned by the Order near the University of Sydney, where they maintained a monastic life. They were not always successful in finding a priest to say Mass in the mornings, but they would chant the

Liturgy of the Hours and spend twenty minutes in meditation. Then they went to their university classes and studied, and in the evening were allowed to exchange ideas and assertions, political news and even gossip. It was their turn to send up the students who looked at them askance whenever they entered the lecture hall in the robes of their order.

Sarah loved university life and took a form of pride in the looks other female students gave her, as if she violated the assumptions by which they lived. Many of them, she knew, would become victims of men and the marriage tyranny, or suffer a man's power to close them out and reduce their life at home to misery. She knew that none of them was immune from the peril — as educated and forceful as they might be.

Later, she would remember her own confidence at this time, her belief that she had put herself beyond damage. Meanwhile she had her four friends, and they were pretty much amiable with each other, though occasionally when one of them, Boniface, was alone with Sarah, she was acerbic about the accountant. Sarah did suffer a crush on an ancient history lecturer, but it was a thing of sentiment, not the body. It was as if her appetites had died the

317

day Father Shannon had recruited the new girl and sent *her* away.

When the young nuns were not studying or going to classes, they worked on administrative duties, and went to schools to observe in classrooms. Sarah, who by now had taken the religious name Constance, was marked out as a high school teacher of English and history. By her third year she was occasionally teaching classes, not in the formal sense but under the supposition that she was telling the girls about her university studies and thus the studies ahead of them. She had a natural rigor that the girls respected but did not fear. She knew, therefore, that she was a born teacher and a potential Alphonsus. Her heart was mute, and she was happy.

There had been a time when nuns were taught to be chary of complimenting each other on their professional gifts. Pride was a sin exceeded in perniciousness only by lust. Pride could lead to disobeying one's superiors. But the Order was almost by instinct trying to be kindlier and warmer to its young nuns — there were so few it seemed ill-advised to drive them away with accusations of conceit. Hence Sister Constance was much praised for garnering university distinctions year by year.

Not that on visits to the Order's schools everything progressed with sisterly sympathy and concord. Some of the other teachers were reserved, some waspish in an unhappy way. At morning tea at her old school she could tell which members of the group would welcome her back when she had finished her training, and which wouldn't. One might say with an unappeased rictus of the mouth, "I hear you got a distinction in modern history. Oh my, you'll be too grand for us." If she had been honest she would have said, "I shall devote my time to taking the shine off you."

But four out of ten teachers in the schools run by the Order were in any case lay-women, with husbands and boyfriends and a social life. Though she did not desire to share their state, she was aware that in a way they humanized and diluted the old, intense atmosphere, and did not have quite the touchiness of some of the older nuns whose tempers verged on hair-trigger.

In her third year at university, her supervisor suggested she continue to an honors degree and thesis. Having graduated with a high distinction and two credits, she was the star of the group of novices, who were now about to take their vows before they were sent out into schools. But Constance felt there was no time for an honors thesis — not yet, anyhow. The Order had nurtured her and put her through her education, and she could not delay repaying them.

"You'll get the big one," Boniface told her, by which she meant the chief city school of the Order, their alma mater. "It'll be Fourth Form somewhere else for me," Boniface insisted. It turned out as she had predicted: Sister Constance was assigned to the school where she had been a student. This return brought her close to ecstasy, as if she could remake her own girlhood through the students she taught. The priests in the presbytery who sometimes appeared in the high school or said Mass for the nuns were not Father Shannon, and thus had no intrusive reality for her. Father Shannon had been promoted and moved on.

Sister Constance was energetic. Girls liked being in her classes, and in her presence. She had the support and esteem of Mother Alphonsus, still in charge at the school, which caused resentment amongst some of her colleagues. But to be admired like Alphonsus suited Constance's vanity, as did praise from the parents of her girls, who would say on parent-teacher nights how much their daughters got from her classes. She repented of this vanity and devoted all her successes to the honor of Christ and his Virgin Mother.

Occasionally there was an echo from the labyrinth of complex tunnels beneath the mountain of her career. A dream she had frequently was that she had somehow murdered a girl she could dimly remember, and the police knew it and had charged her with it, and Alphonsus knew it, too, and all Constance could do was lie and lie, existing on the knife edge between what they knew of her guilt and what she knew but denied.

At the age of thirty she was made head of the English Department, with four nuns and nine lay teachers under her administration. She suffered her periods with good grace, in the old-fashioned way — as an endured offering. She didn't miss children. She had the ones she taught. She thought it a virtue at the time, that she so closely fitted her narrow condition and that she was able to suppress her more extravagant flashes of seemingly unrooted anger, and her brief spasms of discontent.

It was a parent-teacher night. She was thirty-three years old, confident, a near-legendary figure to her girls. By now the Order was dressing its nuns less traditionally — in a calf-length skirt, stockings, black shoes, a white blouse with its insignia on it, a blue cardigan, and a blue veil. She acknowledged that the new garb made sense for a busy woman in a busy high school.

Genial Mother Alphonsus began these nights with a cocktail party, at which Constance talked to parents just a few years older than her, enjoyed their conversations, soothed their anxieties about the academic and social futures of their daughters. She got into conversation with one father about the Australian poet Les Murray and the Irish bard Seamus Heaney. She thought both were demigods and she was disturbed and delighted by the world-weary way this man spoke of them, as if he were a pilgrim in a dark valley where those two voices gave him his direction. He was raffish, untidy, with a whimsical, reticent, growling voice — an interesting fellow indeed; a doctor, she believed. He looked weary, but as if substantial matters, not trivial duties, explained it. His name also had a raffish quality. Anton Spignelli.

Later, in a classroom, she spoke to him and his wife, a smartly dressed woman, about their daughter, who was clever and exemplary. Sister Constance noticed to her amazement that her exchanges were directed at the saturnine father more than the conventionally pretty wife. Thus he was the first male since Father Shannon whom she did not perceive as part of life's crass undergrowth. This frightened her but also gave her unanticipated delight. She had lived in a neutral and untroubled condition, the one she had chosen, the condition of a bright child. Spignelli had ended that just by being in her classroom. She understood in an instant that she would see her life now from a new, anguished perspective. Yet she felt that if this was the price, it had to be met.

The couple got up to go. The wife was at the door when Spignelli took Constance's hand and muttered something about a hard-beaked rock and Sweeney being seasoned and scraggy. She recognized it: "Sweeney's Lament on Ailsa Craig." Just two apparently innocent lines he uttered with knowingness. He nodded and slouched out like a hero from a Graham Greene novel. The lines he left unsaid she remembered: "We mated like a couple / Of hard-shanked cranes."

Two days later, after carrying the image of hard-shanked cranes in her head every hour, she received a letter. It was from Spignelli. A more traditional Mother Superior than Alphonsus would have read it before passing it on, but it came to Constance apparently unintercepted. "Why would I refer you to such an off-putting image?" wrote Spignelli in apology. "I did not escape the baleful influence of Catholicism. But we are not cranes. We are not hard-shanked. We are angels."

The following evening she was told there was a telephone call for her. The convent had reached an age of liberalism when it was considered unexceptional for a nun to take a call. Anton Spignelli was on the line.

"Sister Constance?" he asked.

He had barely introduced himself before he said, "You know why I'm calling."

Sarah knew. She had spent the days since meeting the Spignellis in a frenzy of sensual feeling — there was no higher quality to it. She allowed herself now to acknowledge that a definite and profound lust had settled on her. It was as if she were inhabiting a different country with an unknown but turbulent climate. She had never felt anything approaching this, certainly not for Father Shannon — of whom she thought for a mere nauseous instant, only long enough to realize that in his case all her favors had been duties of her body accompanied with pleasure as an occasional guilty side effect. The compass of her flesh had not turned in his direction. It was, however, now turning in the direction of Anton Spignelli.

"I know what you are," he said. "A good woman. But these things are impossible. . . . I saw it all happen to you, too. The awareness. What happened to me."

"I think I know what you mean," she struggled to say, yet she felt unabashed. Without any warning, almost twenty years of her careful, invulnerable life was being consumed in a day's hunger.

"Tell me," said Spignelli, "what can you do? By way of seeing me, that is."

"I can be at the State Library tomorrow," she said. It was reasonable enough that she should be there: she had used it to introduce girls to research methods, and had prevailed on the archivists to show them special documents, convict records, the logbook of the *Bounty,* the Old Bailey papers.

"Good," he said. He seemed to feel an imperative that allowed only for the simplest discourse. There was no poetry in it, nor did she seek poetry. She was agape to meet him. "Where in the library?" he asked.

"The manuscript reading room," she said. "I have a ticket. I'll watch for you to arrive."

"I'll appear at the door at a quarter to five," he told her. "I'll make contact, then

325

turn away. Follow me to the car park on Hospital Road."

"All right," she said.

The certainty of seeing him, the certainty of animality, caused her to teach in a detached, automatic way — canny on Shakespeare, wise on Judith Wright: the curriculum had grown so enlightened that even the sublimely erotic "Woman to Man" was available for study.

> This is no child with a child's face;
> this has no name to name it by;
> yet you and I have known it well.
> This is our hunter and our chase,
> the third who lay in our embrace. . . .

She caught the bus to the State Library and was in the manuscript reading room when Spignelli, his clothes hanging with a loose, unstriven-for style from his bones, his head topped with a thick silver mat of hair, raised his chin beyond the glass, ventured in to the archivist's desk, and looked down the angle of his face at Sister Constance. She gathered up her notebook and left the microfilm machine on which she had been following the correspondence of a colonial governor named Belmore, and his relationship to anti-Irish hysteria after the assassination attempt on Queen Victoria's son, Prince Alfred, on a beach in Sydney Harbour. She followed Spignelli downstairs, out of the front door, down more steps, and along the street behind the library. Opposite lay the expanse of the domain and the great Moreton Bay fig tree under which state politicians traditionally stood in front of television cameras to deliver their pronouncements. She entered the grounds of Sydney Hospital and turned to the car park. There Spignelli held the lift door open for her. There were no other occupants. As they descended he spoke.

"What were you reading in there?"

She filled him in. "Research for a possible honors thesis," she said. "On the Irish in the 1860s."

It seemed as remote from her as was last week.

"I believe you women have short hair now, since Vatican II. Baldness is no longer de rigueur."

"No. You're right," she said, foolishly short of breath.

"Take off your veil, then. For the drive. We're going for a drive."

"It might look a bit scraggy by modern standards," she said. She realized she was speaking like an asthmatic, with gaps between words for breath.

He put his hand on hers.

"Don't be stressed," he said.

"Why do you send your daughter to a Catholic school?" she asked.

"Tradition. Her mother went there."

"And are you a believer?" Indeed, she suddenly wondered in panic, was she?

"I'm observant," he said. "You are if you come from a big enough Catholic family. Weddings, baptisms, funerals come round so often that they make you a regular churchgoer."

She did not feel she had a tormented exclusive right to him as she had had with Father Shannon. She began to work on the pins that held her veil in place. "I'll still look weird," she said. "The rest of me's not fashionable either."

Yet she was blazing and ecstatic and ready. She wanted to put her hand on his upper leg, purely as an opening bid. A Vietnamese at the gate waved through Spignelli and the woman with tousled brunette hair. She hoped he was a Buddhist rather than a Catholic.

"Are you a doctor?" she asked.

"Yes," he said. "Ear, nose, and throat."

He spoke in bulletins.

"And have you ordered other nuns of the

Order into cars?"

"Only Mother Alphonsus," he said, with a crooked half smile.

Did he utter the name of her superior, her headmistress, as a test of her humor? She was willing to tolerate it. Nothing was as large as her want.

The drive was short. At Potts Point he turned in to an underground car park. There were still many perils of being seen, but she was willing to risk them. As Spignelli parked, an elderly woman decanted grocery bags from her car, a task that claimed all her attention or perhaps all her eyesight. Constance felt the contempt of the soon-to-be-sated for this mere consumer, this customer.

In the lift he took her to him; he had Satanic luck, which she shared, their madness unobserved. The floor they reached had only three doors; Spignelli led her to the nearest and deftly unlocked it, and then they were inside and the madness could run.

The flat was art deco — glitteringly restored, a balcony beyond it looking up harbor. A thick-walled flat, she thought. She was sure about how things would go. She imagined herself yelling with satiety. He asked, would she like to use the facilities first? If she did, she could use his bathrobe, he said.

A first minute quantity of reluctance entered her.

"I'll go in myself for a second," said Spignelli.

"I'll sit here," she said, taking a chair that showed her the view and gave no hint of neighbors.

"Yes," he said. "It is very beautiful." He placed a hand on the nape of her neck. "Like you."

She liked his hand and the words. But she didn't know where to look. She thought it best to tell him. "I'll help," he said softly. "Tell me, do you want to go back?"

"No." It came from an emphatic quarter of her soul.

"All right," he said. He went into the bathroom of the flat and she waited in a sort of static, avid confusion.

After a considerable time she heard him come out again and could hear as well his breath and, as if by the displacement it caused in the air, his solid body.

Since she did not fully look at him as he presented himself to her, she saw him in fragmentary ways. He was well built, though there were some marks of negligence and coming age in his abdomen, a struggle between athleticism and a modest paunch. He leaned down and kissed her and she did not resist that, forming a devouring mouth. There was some ravenous clawing at each other, though he left her clothes alone for a time, as if, with residual Catholic suspicion, he thought they possessed an inviolable holiness. But then he unbuttoned the neck of her blouse and slid his hand down to envelop her left breast.

"Very handsome," he said. "Come to bed."

Before they went she began with a hectic alacrity to remove her cardigan, the blouse, the sexless spencer beneath that. The chaste bra, already partially dislodged, she unhooked. Where did this willingness, the urge to expose herself, come from? I am managing this, she thought, with a joy that ran beyond the bounds of all theology, and of the careful years. Where have I been? she came close to asking herself aloud.

"What is under that long, long skirt?" he asked.

"Long, long, sturdy underwear," she said. "A slip."

"Fear not," he said. "I am not a man for glamorous lingerie."

Her uncertainty returned, though, the instant she unhooked the skirt and sat down on the bed in her slip.

"Would you leave all that ugly underwear to me?" he asked. Indeed, she felt too weak to assert herself further. She could not think of what to abandon next. She had taken herself as far as her self-counsels could run. She lay back on the bed while he kissed her breasts, a wonderful yet strangely familiar sensation, as if a faint memory was stirring within her, despite the years of abstinence.

His towel had come off as he half-knelt on the bed in front of her. She was obliquely aware of it but she felt she could not look at or assess anything. He sought her right hand and he placed his penis in it. There was an instantaneous reversal of the world as it had been to that second, and she was revealed to herself in her ridiculous posture, in her fatuous half-nakedness, in her absurd Virgin-blue slip. Her mouth flooded with bile. She heaved herself from the bed and careened into the bathroom, slamming the door behind her. She began vomiting in spasms too violent for her to ensure that all of it got into the bowl.

When the chief gush had ended, she stayed on her knees panting, and found he was standing behind her in the doorway.

"Oh my God, I'm sorry. How can I help you?"

He was in his way a decent man. He was

not as conceited, as self-regarding as Father Shannon.

She said nothing.

He said, "I can see now how presumptuous ..."

But she put her hand up. She did not want to hear any eloquent confession.

"I completely misread the signs," he said. "Sometimes innocence is so profound it can look like worldliness. I'm so sorry."

"I know you have a wife," she said.

"Is that what made you ill?"

"No. But you have a wife. And a daughter."

He helped her up and took her into the small kitchen. He found a bottle of whiskey and gave them both a short measure. He was firmly wrapped in his dressing gown. She had, in the sitting room corner, gratefully reassumed the neutrality of her clothing.

"I must have been crazy," he said dolefully. "Absolutely crazy."

"Not just you," she said. She was absorbing a revelation. She knew now that she could never marry or be a lover. It was an important revelation. The fact that she was a professed nun had not meant that her capacity for marriage was lacking. That it was there as an unlikely and undesired op-

333

tion created a degree of meaningful tension in her life, as it did in the lives of the other women of her order. She had thought, therefore, that she was an orb of choices, that she occupied poles of choice. But no. Nun or not, she could never marry or be a lover.

"You have given up the normal life of women," a retreat master, any retreat master, all the retreat masters had told them. But she had given up nothing. Her range was straitened. She began to rearrange her clothing and told Spignelli she must catch a bus home. He'd only be a second, he assured her. He would drive her. She could tell Mother Alphonsus he had recognized Sister Constance at a bus stop and given her a lift.

She let him take her back to the convent — they might have been a nun and her brother. But she knew now she no more belonged there than she did in the street, or as a wraith under that tree in the domain. She felt terrifying doubt in her own existence. The core had evaporated into some other soul. She had no home and she dwelt nowhere. This was a genuine terror in knowing that if she could not find at least an ounce of solidity at the center of her being, she must kill herself. Everything was so suddenly gone, all certainty, all haven.

She did not speak to Spignelli during the journey or when she left him. She told him where she wanted to be dropped, walked into the convent, and made her excuses to the cook and Mother Alphonsus, feeling neither guilt nor rededication — not anything. Migraine, she said.

And so back in her cell, as the room she had always found quite habitable was called, she lay on her bed in the dark. She mimed sickness the next morning and escaped Mass. It was not that she believed she needed absolution before she could take Communion. It was more frightening than that. She did not know why she should make any confession in the first place, seek an absolution, meaninglessly consume the host at a meaningless Mass.

She rose somehow and taught the morning classes as automatically in her numb condition as she had in the fever of the previous day. At lunchtime she sought out one of the Jesuits in the old priests' home down the road, where retired clergy came and went. The old man sat in a chair in a corner of the sanctuary and she told him. She noticed remotely that he was not as astonished as she had expected he would be. It was as if she were doing this from ancient habit, not from conviction, accessing the rite of the release of sins so that she could take the sacraments like an innocent nun until she decided what to do — to hang herself or leave or stay.

The old priest could not have been wiser or calmer. He said wonderfully banal things.

"We have all come close to lapsing. We have all had these temptations, and you did well through the grace in your soul to resist them. What would our calling mean without such powerful tests?"

She was too exhausted to argue with him, contest his amiability, or tell him that she now saw this supposed sacrament from another angle. Yesterday she had been a believer; today she was a woman who could see a device of manipulation as quickly as the next woman.

Thanks to her numbness, she taught her way through two weeks. Nobody seemed to notice the altered nature of her soul, so strong was their belief that everything came to her easily and with grace.

Then one night after midnight Alphonsus found Constance unable to speak or move beneath the stone Gothic stairs in the entry hall of the convent.

25

MONSIGNOR SHANNON FIGHTS THE GOOD FIGHT, 2

May 1996

The proceedings of the first day of Dr. Devitt's attempt to sue the cardinal of the archdiocese of Sydney and the trustees of the Roman Catholic Church drew considerable interest, especially when Devitt began to give his evidence.

Monsignor Shannon and Mr. Callaghan sat behind the Church's lawyers and observed throughout the first afternoon the scientist's questioning, and his demeanor, alternating impressively between ferocious memory and calm reason.

Early on, Devitt was asked to identify Father Guest from a photograph that loomed large on the courtroom projector. Guest's imprisonment was discussed, and Devitt's lawyer, Conlon, a young man, leniently asked his client whether he felt consolation at Guest's punishment or whether he was roused to even greater fury to see that, though the man had been disgraced, he had not paid for the full catalogue of crime.

Devitt agreed to the latter.

His counsel was the first to ask him when he decided that the abuse had affected him seriously and he ought to approach the Church for justice.

"I became particularly aware of the harm when I got engaged and was at the same time under stress in my work with the research team. But as for approaching the Church, that idea came when I saw a report of Guest's death in 1993."

"So you became aware of the scale of the damage around April 1992 but did not think of approaching the Church until Guest died."

"Yes. I think my psychological reports bear this out."

"Why did you wait until Father Guest's death to seek any recompense?" asked Conlon.

"Because at that point I realized there was no chance he would ever confess what he had done to me. I always imagined a public confession, but after he died I couldn't delude myself."

"The Church has agreed to make an offer

to compensate you for these assaults, hasn't it?"

"Yes, but I would have been bound to confidentiality if I had taken it."

"So why do you now take this action in the public forum?"

"To get them to face up to the reality of what's been done in their name. Of what is almost certainly still being done in their name. In the name of the Father and of the Son and of the Holy Ghost, Amen."

"Why do you object to a confidential settlement?"

"I don't think it's just that I'd be muzzled about what has happened. Mind you, when it first happened, I didn't want anyone to know. But when I was ready to speak, it seemed alien and intolerable to me, the idea that if I took the terms of their settlement I could never again speak of the abuse by Father Guest."

"What would you say to people who might accuse you of latching on to Father Guest's death and, since he is not alive to deny it, falsely claiming, for monetary gain, that you were assaulted by him?"

"If that had been my motive," he said, as calm as counsel wanted him to be, "what the Church offered me would probably have satisfied me. For the Church has itself acknowledged I have a valid case."

"The Church has acknowledged that?"

"Through the chairman of In Compassion's Name, Mr. Callaghan QC. It was also stated by Monsignor Shannon. They offered me more than the normal payout of fifty thousand dollars. They wouldn't have done that if they thought I was a fake."

There was an objection, an argument about the terms under which Mr. Callaghan and the monsignor had said such things. It ran on between counsel and the judge.

Monsignor Shannon was sweating inside his lightweight clerical suit. He was distracted by the prospect of committing a convenient perjury when it was his turn to give evidence, but rejected the temptation. He did not hear the counsel's next question, to which Devitt answered in his level way.

"The sole motivation for coming forward when I did is that by then I had demonstrations of what Guest had taken from me. What he had been guilty of was measurable in my professional life and in my marriage."

He uses slightly odd terms, Shannon thought. *Demonstrations of what Guest had taken from me . . . .*

The defense counsel then attempted to forestall any claim against Devitt of mental

340

disablement by taking him through the question of his marriage and his falling out with his research team. Devitt frankly and effectively explained his relatively sudden irrational rages against his wife and in his laboratory. His regret for them seemed unfeigned. He had been treated with understanding both by his wife and his peers, and was now part of a team at Macquarie University researching the same area of laser and computer technology. The counsel read and tabled assessments of his excellent performance in his present job as an individual and scientist.

Devitt had performed well. Monsignor Shannon knew that Callaghan, such a decent man, was uneasy that the following day the Church's counsel, Mr. Kermode SC, would endeavor to undermine Devitt's reestablished reputation for stability. But, as Kermode had said when they had met in his offices, there were contradictions between Devitt's statements in various documents about when he became aware of the true extent of the damage done him.

"Of course," Kermode told Shannon and Callaghan in his debrief at the end of the first day, "you will both give truthful evidence for theological as well as civil reasons. But, Mr. Callaghan, how does your memory

square with Devitt's claim that you acknowledged his was a valid case?"

Callaghan said, "I don't think we took as
emphatic a view as he says. But under oath
I'd have to say I thought him credible. And
I probably conveyed that, informally, outside
the transcript of the meeting."

Kermode turned to his junior, Ms. Zoldak.
"Would you check the transcript of the
meeting at the cathedral, Marissa?"

She nodded and made a note, and Kermode inhaled. "But we have to look forward
to the picture of Devitt offered by Father
Guest's sister. It has to undermine credibility. So I think we should put her on first.
With any luck Devitt's counsel will decide
there's no profit in having you two in the
witness box."

Father Guest's sister was her brother's one
remaining champion on earth. Widowed in
her mid-years, she had shared the presbytery
with her brother. She was the aggrieved
priestess of his shrine.

Kermode's secretary was in the meantime
serving wine, beer, and whiskey, according
to desires. Monsignor Shannon thought he
certainly desired a whiskey, while Kermode
told them Father Guest's sister had stated
she plainly remembered how the boy pushed
himself on Guest, turning up after school,

his face aglow, insistent to see the priest. "We can make Devitt seem at least halfway a seducer."

Callaghan coughed. "I'm not absolutely convinced of her. I mean, she is his sister, and there's something about her that declares, 'My brother, right or wrong.' "

Spreading his hands, palms outward, Kermode said, "I think she deserves to express her observation of events, Peter. We can leave it to the plaintiff's counsel to make your point."

Shannon decided to intervene here. "I agree with Mr. Kermode, Peter. Surely we're entitled to make our own case, now that Devitt's rejected our overtures."

He thought that the sister's evidence, if it turned out as Kermode hoped, would show that schoolboys like Devitt have the desire in them, the same desire that came to Shannon himself. I took their sins on me, he thought. I took the sins of the girls and the sins of the boys. On me. I risked my soul so that they would not have a squalid experience in a suburban toilet. But I will never be thanked.

The second day continued with Devitt's evidence. He now faced Kermode, who rose with habitual smoothness and an air of natural, amused authority. Yet Devitt, self-possessed as ever, seemed settled in the witness box. It was obvious to Shannon that though having temporarily lost the management of his soul around the time of his engagement, Devitt was in calm command these days.

Kermode referred to the report on Devitt prepared by the Church's clinical psychologist. According to that, Shannon noted, Guest had declared to Devitt at one stage that he was saving Devitt from sinning with heedless men in public toilets; he was generously willing to take the shame and guilt on himself, said Guest further — on his own body, to bear the double sin. Devitt had told the psychologist that Guest fed him gin and lemon, and it became the sweet anesthetic, the sacramental numbing before he was instructed to remove clothing, and endure the mutual tests of their private parts to which Guest had introduced him.

"Did you feel, then, while you were with him, that he was doing you damage?"

Devitt thought for a number of seconds. "No. Though I certainly felt, even then, as if I were carrying a wound. I thought it was my fault."

"But you told the psychologist that you didn't like the extent to which your own

344

body enjoyed the encounters. So . . . your body liked them?"

"Of course there was reflex pleasure. One abominates the memory of it. One is guilty. But —"

"But for many years you did not perceive damage in what had been done to you?"

"I knew there was damage and that I was wounded, but I did not identify or assess the wounds."

"That is a convenient argument, Dr. Devitt."

"I think it is a clear distinction, Mr. Kermode. And apart from that, had I possessed the capacity to analyze the damage, I wouldn't have known at that stage it would entitle me to any legal claim."

"And the case study in 1988, when Father Guest was still alive. You felt there had been damage?"

"Yes."

"But you didn't come forward then?"

"No. I explained the distinction in my evidence to Mr. Conlon."

"At least we can say you *tried* to. So for a considerable time you didn't appreciate that you had suffered damage?"

"No. I didn't appreciate that it was Father Guest who had done the damage. In 1988 I still thought I was largely to blame."

"That means that until the early 1990s, you knew you had been sexually assaulted but did not believe it had had an adverse impact on you?"

"I didn't say I wasn't vaguely aware of an adverse impact."

"Well, you are a man for making distinctions, aren't you? Tell us in your own words about the adverse impact that you recognized before you ever thought of approaching the Church."

"A sense of unworthiness, which kept me a recluse through my high school and university years. I didn't relate to too many people then."

"And you did pretty well out of your reclusiveness, didn't you? I mean, the Shields Medal for Physics, first class honors, and the rest?"

"Study and exams were my sole validation. But you can't live like that in the big, real world."

"You say you began to feel the damage as your research life became more active?"

"I felt that I was stuck in exile behind a pane of unbreakable glass, and all my colleagues were unreachable across that barrier. They looked at ease in the world. They looked to me like its inhabitants. I suffered a terror because I didn't feel I was amongst

346

them, and I feared they would get to know it and discount me, and write off my research as well. It was an upsetting realization. And through no fault of my then fiancée, it seemed to be triggered in part by meeting and growing closer to her. I blamed her for it all at first. It was exactly as Oscar Wilde said — 'Each man kills the thing he loves.' She seemed by her generosity, by her decency, to show up the . . . the dreadfulness of those Father Guest episodes."

"This sudden upsetting realization made you depressed, then, at the time of your meeting your wife?"

"Yes, it did."

"Did it make you angry?"

"Yes. An anger even then without a target. Myself at first, maybe. I certainly thought of suicide."

"And this was four years ago? That you got engaged."

"Yes."

"What month?"

"We were engaged in July."

"And you say around then you began to identify the Church as somehow to blame?"

"I think it was even before then — earlier in the year — that I began to blame my sense of separation from human beings on Guest and not entirely on myself."

"Did you feel that your trust in Father Guest had been abused?"

"Yes, of course I did. And my father had told Bishop Modena about it, and no action was taken to prevent Guest attacking other boys."

"But you told a counselor at your university that when you first started having problems with your research team there, you made no connection between the abuse and the problems you were suffering, isn't that so?"

"That's not right. The worse my behavior became, the more I began to realize that the abuse had created the anger, the volatility. And that hellish feeling of separation. From the living."

"Yet you told In Compassion's Name that you did not feel a connection between Father Guest and your problems until last year?"

"I think you're misinterpreting what I said. Last year was when I resolved to approach the Church. But I had felt damaged by the abuse much earlier. Not, however, early enough to pursue any legal remedies."

"But the point I am making is that you keep on contradicting yourself about the date on which you became aware of the damage of Father Guest's contacts with you."

"Not at all. I've tried to say something honest about the growth of my awareness."

"So you claim."

Kermode then picked up and quoted from the report of the university's counselor. " 'It was a gradual, inchoate awakening. It became explicit perhaps at that time, but had been gradually dawning since the abuse ended when I was fifteen.' So, Dr. Devitt, you tell us the awareness arose when you were fifteen; it was there when you began to work in the laser laboratory; it was there when you met your fiancée; it was there when you became engaged to your fiancée; and it was there last year. Could you blame the court for being bewildered? And with such a bewildered memory, why should you be given leave under the Limitation Act?"

"Again, you talk about awareness as if it were switching on and off a light."

"The law seeks a definite date, not the five, six, seven seasons of awareness you're confusing it with. Perhaps with your superior intelligence . . . ?"

"I have never claimed superior intelligence to anyone."

Satisfied and citing laches as a reason to dismiss Devitt's case, Kermode concluded his questioning.

On the fourth day Mr. Conlon called a psychiatrist to explain the impact of child abuse on the lives of those violated, and particularly to explain that it could take years of disquiet and problems before a victim might feel anything outright, and then to take action against the culprit. Devitt's wife was also called — an amiable, self-possessed young scientist who declared that the Church should enable the experience victims had of bringing complaints to them to be part of the healing, not part of the ordeal.

There would be another evening and, tomorrow, a morning of scarifying headlines, Shannon knew, but he must keep his head and bide his time.

The sister of Father Guest gave evidence that was saved from sounding demented only by Kermode's skill. Even Conlon went easy on the old thing and let her condemn herself with talk of Devitt's malicious stalking of her misjudged brother.

Cardinal Condon was at breakfast in the cathedral house on the morning Monsignor Shannon was to give his evidence. His Eminence said he had included Monsignor

Shannon in his intentions while saying his Mass that morning. The cardinal realized that though the Supreme Court had not subpoenaed him, Monsignor Shannon was his proxy, and he was grateful, he said, to have such a paladin. The cardinal shone redly at the end of the table, small, bald, an old-fashioned Celtic warrior like Shannon himself, a holder of the line against secularism and flimflam, and all the rubbish about gay marriage and the ordination of women. A man who was discreet, too; who knew it was better to be charming to politicians than to hammer them from the pulpit, as some archbishops had done, to little effect, in the past.

Cardinal Condon had taken his political lessons from the intervention of certain bishops in the Labor Party in the 1950s, which came about as a result of their fear of Communism and in a hunt for fellow travelers amongst non-Catholics. As he had observed, that intervention had ultimately been destructive. Though mildly leftist in his youth, Condon was now a conservative. He was what people called "a sound man," an old-fashioned prelate. It was said that few outside his family loved him, for he was passionate about the much-pilloried Church doctrines rather than matters the world wanted him to be passionate about. But that was his job, he believed — to be pilloried by the world, intractable to fashion, and to hold the line. Monsignor Shannon sympathized utterly with these objectives.

Giving evidence in the trial that day was to Shannon like being under anesthetic yet at the same time setting himself to an automatic, nimble-footed deftness. It was time out of the normal world — indeed, it was timeless, for courts were obviously little moved by the pressure of clocks. But though the monsignor was removed from time, he was also acutely aware by the second of where he trod. He had learned these things by giving evidence in other matters, some of them commercial, involving third-party injury cases against the Church, or actions taken by the Church itself against unsatisfactory contractors who had left work unfinished.

Callaghan had always told him, "Watch out for opposing counsel with Irish names. They're often lapsed Catholics and want to get even with you and Catholic theology in one go."

Since Conlon was the opposing counsel's name in this case, and the man's demeanor was ironic, Monsignor Shannon already knew he had to be wary.

The opening questions were harmless. His years as a priest. His work as a director of the Church's insurance company — "In effect, you are the proxy for the cardinal, who is one of the defendants in this case."

"No," said Monsignor Shannon, who sensed he was on firm ground. "I give evidence on my own behalf and also on that of the Church. The cardinal has entrusted the work of In Compassion's Name to me and others."

The judge confirmed this fact with a gurgle of approbation.

"How does In Compassion's Name work, then?" asked Mr. Conlon, the (perhaps lapsed) Catholic.

Monsignor Shannon outlined it. "Those who have a justifiable grievance against a member of the Church come to In Compassion's Name for a process of healing, and if their case is considered valid, they receive a confidential compensation payment and counseling."

Conlon asked why the settlement had to be confidential.

"Many settlements are confidential," said Monsignor Shannon. And then, in a level tone as good as Devitt's: "The Church is surely as entitled to such agreements as anyone else."

"How do you decide if a case is valid?" asked the lawyer.

"By the standard of the evidence, both psychiatric and circumstantial. We use the same sort of documentation as any inquiry would use."

"And the fact that, say, the abuse occurred in an institution — a home for boys, for example, where abuse has proven to be endemic — that would serve as part of the evidence as well, in terms of probability."

"Yes, that's right, though it isn't always absolute proof. But we have our own psychologist's report on the supposed victim, and we take that into account as well. There are many factors that add up to probability of abuse."

"And you come to these agreements because in the cases you settle, you consider the Church to be culpable?"

"We consider certain priests to have violated their duty of care within the non-corporate structure of the Church, and being Catholics, we have a resultant responsibility for compassion — it is there in the name of the process, and it's not mere window dressing. As for confidentiality, let me say, backtracking, that often our clients prefer confidentiality."

"I would have thought it was more in your

interests rather than the complainants' for there to be no reporting of settlements."

"We think it's best that these issues don't become overblown in the popular press or even, for healing's sake, in the minds of the complainants."

"I see. And you face the complaints of a *single* victim, who has no legal representation, with an array of Church officials, secular and otherwise, some of them lawyers."

"Sadly," said Monsignor Shannon, confident now, daring to admire the silkenness of his answer, "these are cases that test the wisdom of more than one of us."

"But you accepted the case of Dr. Devitt as a genuine one?"

"Let me say that is a complicated question. I thought his claim was a valid one, and said so purely in terms of our giving him a confidential settlement. I thought it a valid one, I reiterate, in terms of the settlement we offered him, not in terms of his taking a court case like this."

"So you think that his having taken a legal recourse makes his argument less valid?"

Shannon grew wary. He *would* be tested. There were no grounds for premature self-congratulation.

"Well," he said, with consideration, "our

evidence could show that his objection to our confidentiality requirements is abnormal."

"What makes you say that?"

"Most victims are grateful for our terms of settlement, and they happily sign a deed of release."

"Do you think he is being greedy, seeking more than you offered him?"

Monsignor Shannon had been warned by Kermode about this question. "I can't say. I wouldn't necessarily say so."

And a dreadful, scathing inner voice asked him, did he know his own motivation? He swallowed. Kermode had by now objected, but Monsignor Shannon had time to reiterate, "I can't swear to Dr. Devitt's motivation."

"So in what way do you think his taking a court case makes the authenticity of his claim less clear?"

"We offered him everything we had — compassion, a money settlement, counseling, expressions of regret. I thought that in terms of offering him what was valid and just, we had gone as far as anyone could want. Now that the court case has become a reality . . . I don't know what to say about his situation until this trial is over."

Conlon half-smiled. "That is a fine form

of casuistry," he said. Kermode had warned him of that, too — that at some stage the counsel for the plaintiff would use the word "casuistry." It was an anticlerical insult from the secular arm of the law, and it must be borne.

Kermode objected anyhow and the slur vanished into air.

"Well, let us get down to tin tacks," said Conlon. "Do you work for the archdiocese of Sydney?"

"Yes. Apart from priestly duties, I am financial vicar."

"Are you subject to the commands of the cardinal archbishop of Sydney?"

"Yes, I am."

"Is every other priest in the archdiocese subject to the cardinal archbishop's authority?"

"Yes."

"And is every church and school run by Catholic orders subject to that authority, too?"

"They are subject to the authority of the superiors of their orders as well, but in so far as they operate in this archdiocese, they are subject to the cardinal archbishop, yes."

"If the cardinal has authority over all these clerics and members of religious orders, then he must also have responsibility for them, would you say?"

"Yes. Within the bounds of what he can reasonably know of them."

"Explain what you mean by that."

"If a priest commits murder tonight, the cardinal archbishop could not be considered to be an accessory to his crime. The cardinal archbishop doesn't approve of murder. He doesn't approve of child abuse either."

"Ah," said Mr. Conlon, "but what if he knew the hypothetical priest suffered from homicidal impulses, and ignored this, or found out it had been ignored by others? Wouldn't he have some responsibility, then?"

"No," dared Shannon.

"No?" asked Conlon.

"How could he know that homicidal impulses in the person existed before that person had killed anyone?"

"Ah!" Conlon told him with assumed admiration for his subtlety, and wagging his finger almost in warning. "May I suggest that Bishop Modena knew that Father Guest was a criminal."

"There is no note on Father Guest's file about it, as there would have been had Auxiliary Bishop Modena reported it to the chancery."

"Don't you think some other Church officials must have known about Father Guest, and been responsible for moving him around as his outrages in this or that place became obvious?"

"It would depend on whether they were definitely aware of his problem and had an exact understanding of his . . ." His what? Shannon was stumped for a while and then came up with a word which gave him no comfort. "His psychosis. It is difficult to eradicate such an individual crime," he continued. "It could be said that in founding In Compassion's Name, we provided ourselves with a tool to receive clear knowledge of when abuse happened."

It is all true, Shannon reassured himself. *All true!*

"But often the priests who were validly accused were allowed to retire or move elsewhere? Isn't that so?"

"That's all gossip and hearsay," declared Shannon.

"But Guest was moved on. What did the archdiocese do to make that possible?"

"It kept a strict eye on these men, I can tell you."

"They must have gone to confession. Were they abetted by the secrecy of the confessional?"

"I don't know," said Shannon. "Since the

confessional is secret, the matter is utter speculation."

He was relieved by his own recovered glibness.

"Priests know better than anyone," he continued, "that the sacrament of confession always requires a sincere resolution not to sin again. Absolution is not automatic — as it is sometimes depicted by the ignorant. The priest any offender confessed to would demand that the sinner repent and take a new path. The confessional box . . . the sacrament of penance itself . . . is a brake on these crimes."

"Well," muttered Conlon, as if it were Shannon's fault that they *were* speaking speculatively, "we must not be delayed by hypotheticals. So you will not say now whether you think the case of Dr. Devitt is valid or not?"

"It is not my job to say whether it's valid or not. It may very well be. But that decision has now been removed from us and placed in the hands of the judge."

Conlon smiled in a way that said, "Here's casuistry again," and then let it go. "When another victim of Father Guest, Mr. Moore, first approached the Church some years ago, you arranged for a second meeting with him. Is it correct that you invited Father

Guest to that meeting?"

"It is."

"And did you tell Mr. Moore beforehand that you were inviting his alleged abuser?"

"No, I didn't."

"Why did you present the man with that fait accompli? Why did you not tell him beforehand that you were putting him in the same room as his predator?"

"Rightly or wrongly, I thought it might inhibit him from coming to the meeting."

There were complaints from Mr. Kermode about the direction and reason for this questioning, but it proceeded.

"I suggest you knew it would inhibit him," said Conlon. "That you sprang it on him for that purpose."

"No. I welcomed Mr. Moore into a sitting room at the cathedral and then called in Father Guest and left the two of them to talk together."

"That would seem an eccentric practice?"

"I don't think it was eccentric," Monsignor Shannon said ruggedly — he had been told by Kermode to be rugged.

"Say, for example, a householder was burgled, and he accused, on good evidence, a certain other person of the crime, and the police invited both parties to a meeting and abandoned the householder in a room with the alleged burglar. Would that not be an eccentric procedure?"

"The comparison is not exact."

"I would suggest it is, since in terms of your own theology Father Guest has been proven to be a burglar of young souls."

Again Kermode objected loudly, but Shannon answered bravely. "You're speaking figuratively," he said, proud of the adjective. "Morality is exact, not figurative."

"Is it now? But if you reacted to Mr. Moore in this way, doesn't it suggest that Dr. Devitt knew from this quaint example that there was little to be gained from speaking up early, before he had achieved the maturity and composure to do so?"

There was a loud protest from Mr. Kermode.

"What were you thinking of?" Conlon shouted over the top of it.

"No," Monsignor Shannon asserted, making his own protest. "I believed that it would lead to reconciliation, to an apology by Father Guest, if he were guilty — and he was the one who best knew whether he was or not — and that they would pray together."

"Dr. Devitt and Mr. Moore started praying together with the priest when they were children, and that didn't work out so well, did it?"

Shannon found that the strain of being direct and unapologetic was considerable. When he went to the men's toilet at the end of the day, he found that though it was winter and the air in the courtroom had been temperate, the underarms of his vest were sodden with sweat he had not even known he was emitting. And there was still a test to come — the evening meal with the cardinal. As the cardinal's steward and paladin, how had he performed? He had no way of knowing. But he was more constrained than secular men in that to him perjury was not only a civil crime but the loss of one's soul.

As for the rest, he clung to Christ's utterance: "Blessed art thou when men shall revile you and persecute you, and say all manner of evil against you falsely, for my name's sake."

He washed his hands and went to have a whiskey with Kermode.

The Church's psychologist was more sympathetic to Devitt, but that was inevitable, and Kermode knew there was no sense in trying to change his professional opinion. The psychologist made the point that his assessment of Devitt was based on Devitt's hope of achieving a settlement, and his recommendations at the time had that quality. Nor, he said, would he have expressed himself in the same way had he known that what he had written would be required as evidence in a court case.

Monsignor Shannon left the court that afternoon in good spirits. "Only one thing," murmured Kermode as a warning. "Best not to complain publicly of the press building things up. Always best not to mention the press. Especially when they're not on your side. Just a hint, Monsignor."

26
DOCHERTY ATTENDS
A FUNERAL

July 1996

Each morning Docherty read in the *Herald* about the progress of the Devitt hearing, which had moved to a technical issue: could the Church be sued? He did not know that to Leo Shannon this was the more admirable and less painful phase. People always complained to the monsignor that theology and the law were concerned with the number of angels dancing on the head of a pin. To Shannon that was precisely their attraction. If a human was mentally enfeebled by such concepts, he was not worth knowing.

In court, challenges were made to various sections of the Trustee Act; to the clauses that conferred upon each body corporate, or trust established under it, the right to acquire, hold, rent, surrender leases, raise money on the security of its property, and dispose of it. Did the body corporate, however, have the capacity to sue, and be sued? That was the great question. The statute vested Church property within each diocese in the body corporate to that diocese. The diocese would have power to take on lease bequests; purchase real or personal property; and to sell or exchange it, or to rent it. It also had the power to declare trusts, which would cover any religious order or community of the Church, or any association or members of the Church, for their use or benefit; and have the power either to retain the property in relation to which these trusts were so declared, or to vest the property, or any estate or interest so created, in other trustees. Wonderfully dry, fire-extinguishing stuff.

The newspaper reports also described how Shannon had sat in court while various priests who had served with Father Guest were summoned by the plaintiff to give evidence of their "friendship or association with the man." Kermode had objected that one of the problems of the plaintiff's claims was that most of the persons whom one would expect to throw some light on them were dead or had no relevant recollection.

Even as Docherty read about the hearing and Monsignor Shannon's part in it, he had yet to receive any acknowledgment from the monsignor or the cardinal of his messages, or one from the mysterious Brian Wood. But he did get a call from Maureen. She seemed tense and in no mood for pleasantries, even with him.

"The news is," she said, "that the coroner has released young Stephen's body for burial. I know that if I turn up at the funeral it will only make things worse, but I think you might be able to comfort Liz — yes, despite indications to the contrary. Father O'Hanlon from the parish church has agreed to bury Stephen. Why don't you give him a call? Perhaps you could officiate."

Docherty explained quietly, "I'm sorry, Maureen. I don't have New South Wales certification to conduct burials anymore. I'm not even able to say public Mass."

She absorbed this. "That's appalling," she said.

"Partly my fault. I let my certification lapse."

He had a sense she was weighing it, deciding whether he had been neglectful or realistic.

"I could have been more proactive," Docherty admitted, "in getting some of those functions restored to me. But it's a fair guess the cardinal will be loath to let me preach in Sydney in any church in his archdiocese."

Maureen was silent so Docherty continued. "I've tried to contact Wood, but he hasn't returned my call. I've sent the cardinal a copy of Stephen's letter, with Wood's name blacked out. His Eminence might try to sort things out secretly with Leo, without telling us. But at least he knows now."

"Oh God," she said.

"Don't worry."

"Thank you," said Maureen. "You know, Leo has always seemed to travel smoothly until now. Whereas you've always had a sort of ecclesiastic 'Kick Me!' sign on your back."

"I don't seek to have it," he protested.

"That's why it's there." She maintained a fond silence.

"I'm sorry about your brother. As Damian says, he isn't you."

There was a pause, then Maureen said, "Father O'Hanlon's burying Stephen despite the suicide."

"He's a decent man — a real human being." Docherty knew some priests who turned their face on suicides, standing with the aged parishioners who didn't like those who killed themselves to be buried from the parish church. Indeed, the Vatican had only in the past two decades — in 1980 —

advised that suicides *could* be buried in consecrated ground if there was doubt of the stability of the self-destroyer's mind, the thinking being that there often existed psychiatric and medical reasons that diminished the victim's supposed guilt.

"If you want to go and see Liz," Maureen offered, "I'll drive you, but I shouldn't go in."

"That's all right. I can get there. You have a number for the Cosgrove house?"

She did, and gave it to him.

That evening, when Paul might be home, Docherty rang the Cosgroves and was lucky that Paul answered.

"I wondered if we could have a talk," Docherty asked.

There was a hesitation but no rancor in Paul. "Yes. It's kind of you to call."

"I informed the cardinal, Paul."

"Oh? What did he say?"

"It's too early to know but I shall tell you when I hear from him. And I believe the coroner has released your brother's body."

"The funeral is Friday, eleven o'clock."

"Would you or your mother object if I came as a mourner?"

There was a long silence, Paul Cosgrove weighing matters.

"I can't officiate from the altar," Docherty

explained. "But I could serve Father O'Hanlon as an acolyte. I'm very distressed for your mother's sake and yours — that's my only reason for coming. By the way, I blacked out Brian Wood's name. In the letter I sent the cardinal, I mean."

"Well, Brian is back in Sydney. I tracked him down and I've invited him to the funeral. He knows he's in the letter. He's not too pleased at it."

"Brave of you," said Docherty.

"He called me after I left him a message. Should I show him the letter?"

Docherty said, "I have to leave that to you. But he's a party to it all, isn't he? That's what I would have told him had he called me back."

Next, Docherty phoned Father O'Hanlon's presbytery. From within seemingly cavernous depths the priest eventually answered. Docherty introduced himself. "I remember you," said O'Hanlon. "You were having troubles with Cardinal Scanlon when I was having my own."

He asked Docherty how things had turned out for him. "I know you went to Canada," O'Hanlon said. "Your case was held out to me by the well-meaning as a warning."

"I'm glad I was a cautionary tale," said

370

Docherty. "And now I was hoping I could ask you a favor. Paul Cosgrove says I can attend Stephen's funeral Mass as a mourner. I wonder, do you need an acolyte? As far as I know I'm not permitted to say public Masses here — that was impressed on me back then. But I feel terrible — Liz Cosgrove was once a friend and parishioner of mine."

O'Hanlon said, "I was at your lecture."

"I see."

"I agree with you."

"That's a relief," said Docherty.

"Please come, then," said O'Hanlon.

When Docherty presented himself at the sacristy on the morning of the funeral, O'Hanlon did look as if he had been through something wholesome but educative. His face was that of a man who knew himself and his frailties. Docherty knew that was rare in a man who did not have a wife to subject him to self-education. But there was nothing reticent in O'Hanlon's grasping of Docherty's hand. "Kind of you to come, Doctor," he said, and then broke away to talk to a young woman who had come into the sacristy. They began to discuss the Communion anthem and recessional. "This is my niece," said O'Hanlon presently. "She's the family soprano. I don't want to muddle through the Mass and consign the poor little bastard to the earth without a wonderful voice announcing his dignity."

Paul arrived, with a list of family members who would read the lessons. Cousins, an uncle, he himself. An aged parishioner dressed the altar as O'Hanlon and Docherty watched from the sacristy, O'Hanlon ready in his vestments.

"I believe there was a suicide letter," said O'Hanlon.

"I believe there was one," agreed Docherty. The old man out in the sanctuary placed the chalice, the pyx, the water and wine. O'Hanlon breathed into Docherty's ear, "I knew your father. My God, what a character! Typical Irish-Australian — telling fables and buying the wrong horse."

"That's him," said Docherty. "He was a pilgrim." He was at home with O'Hanlon, and the beneficiary of a gracious fraternity. O'Hanlon said, "All right, Dr. Docherty, let's go."

Docherty carried the missal before O'Hanlon and placed it on the stand. He saw Liz supported in the front row by three other women. It was a scene painted down the ages. Women supporting the unsupportable. He could see a figure powerfully resembling the Brian Wood of the Wood and Associates webpage, in an immaculate black suit and black tie, standing beside an extremely well-dressed and handsome woman — a non-Catholic, Docherty surmised by the way she followed his movements so studiously, like a Reformation queen ready to convert to win her king.

The Gospel reading O'Hanlon chose was the old standby. "Come to me all ye who are heavy burdened . . ."

Docherty watched Liz and Paul as O'Hanlon began the sermon. "The life of a drug addict is in many ways a life of worship," said O'Hanlon, "and in ending his life in a manner I in my own case could not brave, I dare to say Stephen was in his way a hero."

Copious weeping. And that was good.

The dead man was to be cremated the next day, privately. In the churchyard after the Mass, a neighbor Paul clearly knew said, "You boys go and have a drink for poor Stephen. Don't worry. We'll get your mother into bed and watch her."

Paul, the good son, frowned. He had just introduced Brian Wood to Docherty.

"Go," said this gracious woman in purple.

373

"It'll do you a bit of good, Paul."

Paul turned to Docherty. "Will you come, Father?"

"Call me Frank, Paul, please."

"Let's all go," said Wood neutrally. His elegant woman had left and he was alone. "Paul says you're not a bad bloke." He flashed a thin smile to Docherty, sharp as acid. Paul went and kissed his comatose mother, and she clung frenziedly to him until her arms collapsed to her sides again, as if she despaired of retaining him, or anything. Two women led her to a car. She seemed to tread the middle air between her friends like a drunk under arrest.

"Are we ready then?" asked Wood, and the three men set off.

"I got your message, Father," Wood told Docherty. "I didn't want to answer it. Forgive me, but I didn't know who you were and I couldn't see the necessity."

"Fair enough. But you know Stephen mentioned you in his suicide note?"

Wood's jaw looked set. "Paul mentioned it. He didn't do me a favor, poor Stephen."

The old redbrick vomitorium of a pub had been rendered and painted teal and lit artfully within — as could be seen through the tall windows — and retained only its former name, the Stag and Archer.

"The old Archer," said Paul nostalgically, like a man remembering a distant, less fraught youth.

Wood led Docherty and Paul into a large bar twinkling with the cheap thrill of poker machines. Designed for a garrulous, bibulous crush, the space seemed underpopulated now, with a few clumps of mid-afternoon drinkers.

As they waited at the bar, Wood said, "I suppose the coroner's got a copy? Of the letter, I mean."

"Yes," said Paul.

"Oh fuck it, Paul!"

A fresh-faced young bar manager in his all-black like an informal undertaker met them and shook hands with Wood.

"Is the Green Room empty?" Wood tersely asked him.

The bar manager said yes.

"Bring us a bottle of Black Bush, then," said Wood. "And some ice."

Wood led Docherty and Paul upstairs, through pastel lounges and glittering bars into a small room with a conference table in its midst. They were barely seated before the man was back with a bottle of Black Bush Irish Whiskey on a tray, with glasses, ice, a jug of water.

"Brian, what *is* this hooch you're trying

to get us to drink?" asked Paul.

"Northern Irish. Bushmills, where they said no papist hand would ever stir the mash. But it goes down papist gullets smoothly. A good one, I thought, to remember your brother with." And he began to pour three glasses.

"Not for me," said Docherty. "I'm an inexperienced drinker."

"No exceptions today, Father," said Wood midpour, fixing Docherty with an apparently intractable gaze. "This is my pub and I say who drinks. Except for confessed alcoholics."

Wood was choosing his words like a man testing Docherty. It was better than empty courtesy, however. He said then, remarkably softly, "A priest did it to me and a priest knows the man did it. I'm not happy about either. But that's it! I don't consider myself in this in any way. Except . . . poor damned Stephen . . ."

The glasses were poured. Docherty was allowed to dilute his with water. When each had doctored his drink to his pleasure, they looked at each other.

"An awful business, Paul," said Wood. "Give us a toast to your brother."

Paul raised his glass towards the roof. "To you, Steve, you poor little bugger!" He paused and said with sudden ardor, "And may they all suffer public shame! The dealers! The abusers."

"Oh, Paul," Wood half-protested at the unlikeliness of that.

Paul drank a good mouthful and emitted an involuntary gasp of enjoyment. Docherty sipped. The unaccustomed whiskey went scalding down his gullet, wasted on him. Wood met Paul's stare. He drank, too, with a corresponding thoroughness and a connoisseur's savoring, ensuring the liquor had time to declare itself on the palate.

"I know what you want me to say," Wood admitted now. "I'm sorry, Paul. But it's not going to happen. I won't go after Shannon. All that's dead to me. Sorry . . . but you know what I mean."

"Then no justice for Steve? He's just a junkie who killed himself, eh?"

"No one's *just* a junkie. No one *just* kills themselves." He turned to Docherty. "I wanted to see you, Father. I was genuinely intrigued by the idea of a priest leaving a message. I sort of knew what it was about. I was convinced, though, that you were an investigator from the Church, asking me to say that . . . Well, that certain monsters were blameless."

"Well, you're out of luck, Brian," said

Paul. "He's a psychologist, too, and an old friend of Mum's."

Wood switched his gaze fully to Docherty and scanned him, frowning. Docherty stood gradually and put his glass down. "Perhaps I should go. Clearly there's some talking you want to do."

"No, no," said Paul, red-faced, taking a gulp of Black Bush in embarrassment. "I expressed myself badly. Please stay!"

"Yes," said Wood, earnest enough now, in the mode of a fellow mourner. "Please stay, Father. So, you read the note Stephen left?"

"Paul showed it to me and gave me permission to send it to the cardinal."

Wood seemed to be assessing all this now and was suddenly angry. He turned to Paul, "Don't you think you should have asked me first? Before you gave a note with my name in it to Father Docherty?"

Docherty said hastily, "The family are not expecting a prosecution. I did try to reach you through your Sydney office."

"Bugger you! *Bugger you,*" said Wood. "You've sent it to the bloody cardinal?"

"Your name was inked out. I felt he had to know."

"So he'd take severe action, I suppose? So he'd read the riot act? So he'd demote and discipline the bastard?"

"At least that."

"Oh yes," Wood said in a cool sort of fury. "I imagine he'll flay our monsignor and cast him out of the temple!"

Neither Paul nor Docherty responded.

"Yes. I thought so. Pig's arse, he will! Forgive my crudity, Father. But let me say again, pig's arse!" He laughed bitterly and shook his head. "You two don't understand the beginning of it. Look, I'm an accredited success story. I'm not speaking in arrogance. I simply am. It means that companies turn to me, or the consultancy that carries my name, to help them with their restructures, their ambitions, their mergers and acquisitions and the rest. I have managed a relationship with a woman who has agreed to be my wife. And not one of those people knows what's happened to me. They don't know I was a so-called victim. I don't want them to know, either. I barely know myself! It's vanity, sure, but also I can't afford to be seen under that category. They would forgive me for becoming a paraplegic. But they would not know what to do with me as an abused child. Would you ask an abused child to help you sort out your new corporate structure and table of organization? So, just leave me out of this. It's up to you both to make sure my name doesn't get out."

Docherty felt chastened. It was true. Even those who wanted justice done for a child could not help thinking of the child in any other category but that of victim. It was a further dimension to the enduring injustice of it all.

"Forgive me for asking you," Docherty said. "But are you suggesting that you have recovered from the damage the man did you?"

Wood assessed Docherty, deciding whether to tell him to go to hell. Docherty maintained eye contact, sure that any evasion would infuriate Wood more.

"All right," Wood said at last. He occupied himself pouring more whiskey for all parties, though Docherty had not drunk much of his. "You know as well as anyone that there is damage, but it's damage I've lived with and assimilated. In the corporate world people don't wear their heart on their sleeve. So, yes, I have recovered from the damage, if it was ever your right to ask."

Docherty said nothing.

"You doubt it? Let me tell you. I'm no more fucked up than most of us who survived a Catholic education, so-called. The education you'd wish on us, Father!"

Docherty spread his hands in a conciliatory way. "I'll be delighted for your sake if that is the case," he assured Wood.

Wood stood up. "Look, Paul," he said. "This is a hard thing to say, and I'm sorry for you and your mother. But could it be that Stephen used this business as justification for being a junkie? I know I've used it as justification for being successful, so I'm not trying to be offensive. But by taking his own life, Stephen virtually lived for the man, for that monsignor. I can't and won't live for him. I can't and won't live under the terms of what he did. That's the only possible cure to get over him. To transcend the bastard. That's what I've done. I refused to remain the hapless kid I was. Your friend the priest here seems to think that's an unreliable way forward and that something will catch up with me. Well, it'll have to move bloody fast."

Paul said, "No one will hear anything about you from me. I'm sure Frank will tell you the same thing. So, good fortune to you! And may the gods smile on you, Brian. You deserve it. No one here wishes you harm."

Docherty said, "I endorse that assurance."

"And, listen," said Wood as they prepared to leave. "Don't tell me I'm putting kids in danger by saying nothing. If parents aren't wise now to what's happening with these bastards, they never will be. They're the ones who have a duty to be vigilant."

"Okay," said Paul, sounding hollow.

"Thank you, Mr. Wood. For the hospitality," Docherty murmured.

27
THE CASE OF SARAH FAGAN, 5

1988

There was a supposed living saint and outrider of the Order — a woman named Sister Benedict — who had managed to get permission to go with another nun, Sister Patricia, to service an Aboriginal community named Nullaga in Far North Queensland. Benedict was considered the Order's eccentric and had been one of the first to go by her secular name, Joan, the name she'd had as a child. Joan ran the school at Nullaga. Sister Patricia, however, had recently been laicized, forgiven her vows and allowed to leave the community and live in the world, meaning that Sister Joan was in the somewhat improper situation of being the only one of her Order in Nullaga.

After Sister Constance's collapse, and her subsequent recovery in a clinic designed for nuns suffering from "nerves," Mother Alphonsus, seeing her young colleague in a crisis of faith or soul, was willing to indulge her in any way. So, at Constance's earnest request, Alphonsus allowed her to fly up the east coast of the continent and join Sister Joan.

Constance was pursuing the instinct that tells humans distance and newness will be the basis of a redeemed self. It was a long journey for her, involving two flights by commercial jet and a third in a small charter aircraft, which delivered her to a gravelly bush airstrip. There, a man named Sam O'Loughlin was waiting for her in his truck. He was the white official chosen by the community to serve as a buffer between the government and miners on the one hand, and on the other the Indigenous people of the concrete school and scatter of tin-roofed houses, clinic, and administration buildings at Nullaga. O'Loughlin was the same age as Sister Constance, yet seemed even more wearied than she was. She wondered, when he collected her in his four-wheel drive, whether she would find Sister Joan in the same strung-out condition.

The people at Nullaga represented a number of clans displaced from further north, where bauxite had been found in the early 1970s by police. They had been evicted in the days when *terra nullius* was the legal doctrine, the belief that native peoples lacked title in, and thus ownership over, any part of the earth.

O'Loughlin told her that he and the Aboriginal Council of Nullaga had had to deal with further mining proposals on land that was considered ancestral, and for which they had made a claim in the Supreme Court of Queensland, with the aim that the people might, this time, have a say in whether to permit the mining. Yet on the issue itself the Council was divided, skin group by skin group: those less personally invested in a particular site favored the jobs that might come, and the new element in the whole equation, mining royalties. In any case, O'Loughlin seemed to consider that the action in the Supreme Court on behalf of the group was both a necessity and doomed.

Though sturdy of soul, O'Loughlin was also dispirited from dealing with police, the Aboriginal males who smuggled alcohol into the community, and a multitude of other postcolonial struggles aimed at what seemed, on O'Loughlin's part, and on the part of the Aboriginal leaders themselves, a perpetually defeated striving for justice and dignity. He had decided to leave, he confessed to Sister Constance, and had applied for a city job with an environmental agency.

"Your colleague, Sister Joan, is a woman who believes in examples," he told Constance. "She aims to make a difference simply by being here, changing things by acceptance. I wish I was like that. I don't have the patience. But I think that every night she actually thanks God for letting her live here."

Constance liked and trusted Sister Joan at once, this woman who wore a plain blue skirt, a blouse with a cross and the emblem of the Order, and a veil over her gray hair. She and Joan shared a concrete house in the middle of the settlement, beside the school of two cement-brick classrooms.

"These are dispirited but noble people," Joan told her cheerily. "They've lost their land twice — when we whites first came, and then they lost their reservation, and now that minerals have been found here, they might be moved on again, and they know it."

Sisters Joan and Constance worked to teach the Aboriginal children as far as sixth grade. Those who went on to high school were flown to Cairns and lived there in a hostel. Some of the younger men worked in other towns and at far-off mine sites, so it was in its way an unnatural township — troublemakers stayed here, said Joan, and sometimes they or whites would smuggle in booze against the ordinance of the Council, as O'Loughlin had wearily explained. Then there were beatings of women, and worse — attacks on underaged girls.

The settlement store, run by a white man called Bert, was expensive, with heavily sugared goods and canned products brought in — diabetes food, said Sister Joan. There was a cop, young Constable Goodman, very amiable, muscular, but, thank God, not a bully. It was when cops came in force that there was bullying, said Joan. The community seemed to trust, or at least tolerate, Goodman, she explained. He was perhaps two years younger than Constance, a block of a man, with a light-brown fuzz on his arms visible beneath his uniform. He was like Sister Joan — one who seemed made for this place. There was no doubt he had wisdom and forbearance that exceeded his education. He was wise by instinct, and that was a gift.

At the school Constance began to teach classes far below her qualifications. She found that Joan did more than teach — she had beef brought in fresh from a neighboring station and served it as a stew to the students, together with a balance of frozen vegetables. She told Constance she had tried to grow her own vegetables but termites and small marsupials and bush rats always ate them.

Absenteeism was, naturally enough, high at the school, but the regime of the simple teaching of language and mathematics, and the making of the stew and the boiling of vegetables were solace to Constance's exhausted soul. It hankered for such straightforward tasks. The two nuns ate what the students ate, but their diet was varied by fish caught from the beach, often by the truants, who brought their catch as an offering of expiation.

After school, Constance would walk with Sister Joan around the settlement's wooden houses. The women loved Joan and were frank with her. They quickly uttered sentences such as, "Betsy got beat up last night by that no-hoper Tiger. Had to git Goodman to talk to him and tell him silly bugger and kick your arse!"

The women did not usually call on Constable Goodman, however; they tried to settle things in their own ways.

Joan spoke to the men, too, young and old — and often old was anything over forty-five years. Some of them bore the signs of damage from an early career as ferocious drinkers, others suffered from glaucoma, others from diabetes.

If Constance had been aware that she possessed a heart, she would have grieved for these people. But she felt she was a ghost in the school and the township. She knew that the nearest clinic was thirty miles away, and O'Loughlin drove people there, and so did Goodman if it was on his way. The administration of emergency medications — antibiotics and painkillers — was up to Sister Joan or her.

One day Constable Goodman told Constance that the next Saturday he was taking some relatives of a man named Douglas — that was his European name, anyhow — from Nullaga to visit Douglas, who chose to live with his wife and kids in his own outstation. The truck would be pretty full, Goodman said, but she was welcome to come and see the countryside.

For reasons Constance could not define, she did not want to go. Perhaps one was that she didn't feel she had taken sufficient root in Nullaga. But Joan urged her, saying it would be good for her and was part of her education. In making that argument Joan showed that she thought Constance was fully present in the settlement and would make a life there, as Joan herself had done.

Constance refused to sit beside Goodman in the four-wheel drive, letting one of the old aunties take that seat. She sat in the back, in the midst of Douglas's relatives, and they jolted through the spear grass and coastal scrub. The noise these people made was all the greater because they were showing off something to her — who they were. By now she had some sentences of the language, called Guugu Yimithirr, and they asked her what she knew and were ecstatic when she uttered her words, whether they were right or not. These were the people, Joan had told her, whom James Cook had met in 1770 at the Endeavour River after his ship was hulled. These were the people from whose language came the English word for a particular marsupial. *Kangaroo.*

Douglas was reserved but welcoming. His habitation, an elegantly constructed lean-to, lay at the foot of a ridge in which the entire range of umber and deep yellow rocks were exhibited. His wife was profoundly black and limpid-eyed, and there was just her and him there — the kids were learning whitefella stuff in Cairns, he told them. He had a kerosene refrigerator and a telephone that hung on a pole and ran off solar panels. He was a man of past, present, and future.

The relatives sat about on a rug in front of the lean-to and spoke in their language — part guttural, with some sounds like birdcalls — her ignorance about which Constance had never felt more acutely than at this moment. The host, his wife, and his relatives drank tea from enamel mugs. A stranger at the feast, she did, too.

She needed to urinate. She meant to disappear unobtrusively into the bush, but Douglas's wife rose and intercepted her and said shyly that she'd show her where to go. She led her off through the scrub to a screen of hessian beyond which lay a latrine that, Constance thought, the military might have been proud of.

"We put the hessian up for you, Sister," the wife said in her silken murmur, and left Constance alone. When Constance was done and had wiped her hands on an antiseptic cloth from a sachet, she returned to the campfire in front of Douglas's habitation. On the open fire a stew was bubbling — goanna, a delicacy for the relatives because most of the big lizards around the reserve had been killed, and they were legendary meat, lean and succulent.

She passed Goodman, who was sitting on the ground on the outskirts of the group, chewing a yellow stalk of grass. He got to his feet. "What do you think of Douglas, Sister?" he asked.

"He seems to have made a good life for himself," she said.

"Know what, he's a good fellow. But he's a feather-foot. Tribal executioner. No one will ever blab on him, of course. I reckon six murders. Well, we call them murders. He wouldn't."

Of all the astonishing things she had heard up here in the great cape, this was the most startling. She knew there was a code of law beneath the fragile mesh of the white law that Goodman was meant to cast over Nullaga and its hinterland. In this law, the law of the millennia, there were penalties, Joan had explained, and they were inflicted without malice. Sometimes it was merely punishment by exacting a quotient of blood, spearing the legs of the perpetrator. But sometimes it was death. If you committed a violation of the blood laws, your punishment could be death.

In his bush cop's khaki uniform and from within his light pelt of down, Goodman grinned at her philosophically. This situation was one he knew he must live with. This acceptance was like Joan's, and the thought came to Constance: wouldn't it be pleasant to live with an open, tolerant, plain man like this? What a relief from all the serpentine things people did. She felt a futile attraction for him. Nothing, she knew with certainty, would come of it. He was a ghost, or she was. Certainly, he was constructed for another woman, and for unimaginable children who would adore him.

It was early dark before Goodman got them back to Nullaga. All the way home in the truck, as Constance listened to yawns and conversations, she felt extraneous not only in culture but in terms of the services she could render anyone in this vehicle.

When she returned to the nuns' house, Joan was in a nightdress, ready to go to bed. She asked a few questions about the journey, which Constance tried to answer. Then Constance said, "I want to go back to my birth name. Sarah. Do you mind?"

"Why would I mind? I've done the same."

"I've left it a little late, but you can call me Sarah."

"Sarah it shall be. Pass the word around. And how's that rascal Douglas?"

Joan's eyes were vivified by all she knew of Douglas as well as by all she didn't.

"Goodman says he's a murderer."

"He's not a murderer, Sarah. He's an executioner."

Joan had said good night, turned her back, and was making for her bedroom when Sarah said, "I've something to tell you. I must talk to you."

Joan could hear the intonation and said, "I'll make tea."

When they sat down, Sarah told Joan all the news of her life straight out. Even Spignelli. Spignelli was the least of it.

"Let me say," said Joan at the end, "you came here like a ghost and you have been that way since. This is not a criticism. But it did make me wonder, what damage was done to you, you poor kid?"

28
DOCHERTY SPEAKS
WITH SARAH FAGAN

July 1996

In his room — a congenial room with foliage beyond the window — Docherty called the number the cabdriver Sarah had given him. She quickly answered, in a neutral voice. He said, "It's Frank Docherty. Are you free to talk?"

"I'm driving a passenger," she said briskly. "I'll call you back in twenty minutes."

She was good to her word.

"Well, how's the monastic life?" she asked as soon as he said hello.

"Fair enough," he told her. "I haven't seen a lot of the others — one decent old German guy, though. No killing of fatted calves, but no hostility either."

She was immediately interested. "Why would there be hostility?"

"Years back I got the Order involved in some trouble with the late cardinal. Nothing too scandalous."

She was silent.

He said. "I've got to an age when it's a relief to be a man of little distinction. To be myself in my own corner — I actually like it. Peculiar, eh?"

"Did you notice that we're exchanging pleasantries?" she asked.

"Yes," he admitted. "I don't quite know what to do with them."

"It's because you did me a great favor."

"What favor is that?"

"You believed me."

"I had no reason not to."

"I almost hoped you wouldn't, though. In its way anger's a comfort. Like you, being in a corner. I admit I'm a bit addicted to anger."

Docherty inhaled at length and told her then, "It happens, absolutely coincidentally, that I've received information about the monsignor that corroborates your story."

"I thought you said it didn't need corroboration," she said, bridling.

"No, it didn't need corroboration as far as I was concerned. But it happens that I've found out the monsignor has also been accused of assaulting a boy. At least, Shannon is named and accused in a young man's suicide note, the son of an acquaintance of mine. I'm telling you this in confidence."

"A boy?" Sarah asked incredulously. "Girls weren't enough for the monster?"

"The switch isn't entirely unknown. Someone might have found out about his passion for girls. He might have altered his preference . . . accordingly."

He listened to silence for a while.

"And this boy killed himself?"

"Yes. An overdose."

"That's too big a tribute to the mongrel," she decided. Then, "What was the boy's name? Between you and me."

"Between you and me: Stephen. That's all I can say."

"Poor little bastard!"

"Indeed," said Docherty. "But, look, my position in this whole business is weakened, I think, on balance, by the fact I was once expelled from this archdiocese. Not for moral reasons. I disagreed with the cardinal's politics. Do you believe me? If you don't, we don't have a basis for proceeding."

"No children?" she asked.

"No children."

"A lover? Male or female."

He had to assess this.

"No," he was able to say eventually, and then to fill her in on the activities that had put him in bad odor.

"The point is that people could use that past conflict to discredit me in this matter and write it all off to bile. Still, I had at least to clip Monsignor Shannon's wings by talking to Cardinal Condon about the boy. And I feel I must tell him I've met a second victim. Of course, I won't mention you by name, or the fact that you were a nun."

"I knew you'd end up involving me in something like this," she told him. Her voice was weary, not reproving.

"I didn't know I would," said Docherty. "I saw this young man's suicide note just after meeting you. So I must tell His Eminence that I've received other testimony — yours. Just to put him on guard against anything Shannon might try in future."

Sarah protested, "Even if you don't give them my name, it's still more visibility than I want. Next you'll be telling me to go to the police."

"Well," said Docherty, "you should consider it. I may find on inquiry that I am obligated as a citizen to report Stephen's suicide letter to the authorities, even though they do have a copy. Look, one of the worst things about being abused is that the perpetrator not only befouls the victim's life but gives him or her the task of trying to save

398

other victims. I need to assure the cardinal archbishop I have corroboration. No names. But confirmation."

She thought awhile about this proposition. Then she said, "Yes. But I'm scared it will come to names sooner or later. And I'll humiliate myself in front of some committee or the police, and nothing will happen. And no one will be saved."

"I think they will be in this case," Docherty assured her. "I'm asking you on slim grounds to trust me. On the day I first talked to you, you were angered because Monsignor Shannon was giving his evidence in the Devitt case and it seemed unjust to you — for all the obvious reasons. The Church will have to investigate him, limit him in some way, or else they risk a humiliation on the witness stand or before the forum of public opinion."

"Some forum!" said Sarah. She sighed. Her mood had changed — it was more rancorous. "I never thought I'd say this, but you go ahead. And after that, don't ever contact me again. I'll contact you if I want."

"You don't want to be contacted to verify the accusation? Look, I have to be able to contact you to give you that option after I've spoken to the cardinal —"

"No! And by the way, damn you, Father

Docherty." He heard her laugh deeply and privately. "I wish I'd never met you."

"You're not going to do anything self-destructive, are you?"

"Self-destructive," she said, mocking him. "That's a thought. But I think I'm too scared for that. And then Shannon *would* have won. I imagine him going on breathing blandly. Like a monster. Through gills!"

"Have you an appointment with that psychologist? The name I gave you?"

"I'm thinking about it," she conceded.

"You see, you may think differently after treatment. You may decide to take stronger action."

"You're such a patronizing sod."

"I don't mean to be," he insisted.

"You're a mealymouthed sod, too."

"Yes, you've pointed that out regularly. It's a professional tendency."

"Have you any flesh to you?" Sarah blurted out. "Or has it been sublimated? As it was with me, all that time. My chastity when I was a nun was a symptom of damage, not a choice. What's your excuse?"

"I'm more or less a normal man, I'd like to think."

"Who do you fancy, then? Who makes your balls ache?"

I was in love with Maureen Breslin, he

400

was absurdly tempted to tell her.

"Come on," she said. "I've told you everything. Now you come clean with me."

"Sundry young women of the parish when I was young, and occasional middle-aged ones now I'm older."

"Do you masturbate over them?"

"You know what they say. A healthy male who says he doesn't masturbate is a liar."

"And you do that instead of having a meaningful relationship?"

An odd question from her, but he did not point it out.

"Look, the problem with me is this," he told her instead. "I don't think I *can* have a relationship with people except through the priesthood. I was conditioned to that idea as a young man. It's my self-definition. I'm also scared that in a real love affair, the sort of thing that lasts a lifetime, the kind I'm interested in, I couldn't be sure I'd stand the tests — without failing through gaucheries and clumsiness. In any case, by the time I realized the scale of the chastity problem, I was too old to alter my course, and I'm certainly too old now, as I think you observed earlier."

"Don't let me define you, for God's sake."

"All right. But while we're at it, you're a handsome woman. And a good one. You have a future."

"Jesus, I couldn't have sex with you!" Sarah rushed to say, in a sort of panic, misinterpreting his intent. "You'd take it all too solemnly. If it happened twice you'd ask the Vatican to laicize you and want to marry me. And all that's impossible with me. I couldn't tolerate the intensity of it. I'm garbage. I don't want to be cherished. And you're a cherisher."

"I wasn't suggesting that," Docherty assured her. "Besides, you know I wasn't. Life panics you, doesn't it?"

There was a silence. Then she said, "You've always got a question. I've got to give it to you, some of them are fancy. And I don't know if I believe them. Do you always have all the questions and answers?"

"A small, select bagful," he admitted. "Beyond that . . . Nothing!"

"Anyhow," Sarah said, "I wish you'd done me the service of damning me to the Devil and telling me not to malign a good man. I happen to pick out of the blue a priest who is a psychologist *and* who believes me."

"Yes," Docherty admitted. "Sorry. Bad luck! Look, if I were an affluent parish priest of the old kind, I'd pay for the treatment. But I can't. I get a good salary at the university but that goes to my order. I'm al-

402

lowed to have spending money, that's about it. Quite generous spending money by the standards of an individual person."

"The vow of poverty. I had one of those, too. Now I've taken another poverty vow. Driving a cab. Small returns guaranteed."

"And I've got to go to the airport in ten days. If I call you, will you drive me?"

"You'll have to pay me. I can't afford any favors."

"I'll pay you," said Docherty. "I'll give you . . ." But he was distracted by a sudden inspiration. "Perhaps you should meet with the mother."

"The mother?"

"The mother of the boy who killed himself."

"Are you serious?"

"I can give you her number. And she has another son. His name is Paul. Why don't you talk with them? My sense is that it would be therapeutic for her. . . . She doesn't know how to confront her bereavement. It might be very good for you, too. Between you, you might be able to work out what to do. Everything, something, nothing. I'm not suggesting this as a psychologist. Just as a human being."

After a while, she said, "Give me the number, then. And we'll see."

29
DOCHERTY MEETS
THE MONSIGNOR

July 1996

Docherty remembered his last clinical case before leaving Canada: a youngish priest who had been sent to him for treatment. The Mounties had tracked images to this man's computer, and they were images of children. Rightly or wrongly the man had been given a suspended sentence of three months and a duty to report to the police daily for the length of that sentence, as well as for a further three months. With that done, the court record was suppressed. For now, therefore, the man's family did not know of his crime. But his bishop certainly did, and he found an administrative and chaplaincy role for the priest in aged care, far from contact with children.

Pedophiles and abusers of underage children were often stoic deniers, but the young priest had discovered his abnormal appetites with the access the Internet gave him to child pornography sites. He'd become obsessed with the material. "Part of the time I was in front of the console," he had told Docherty, "I was disgusted with myself, yet I was stuck there; by the hour becoming less human — I could tell it." His appetites were, for his disorder, utterly characteristic — girls of ten or eleven years.

He said he had never succumbed to his appetite, that it was possible for him when engaged in speaking to a living and complex child to forget these tendencies. Remembrance and fantasy came later, but he could not sufficiently turn the individual child of the school yard into an object of lust. In other words, he was in his way a human being. He knew what sin and crime were, and he hated them. And yet . . . the addiction to images.

The police had been apologetic when they'd turned up at the presbytery, astounding and aggrieving his parish priest, who'd tried to order them out. The priest was abashed, he could see utter ruination. If they had left him the means, he said, he would have ended it in the cell and gone into the screaming pit to which his kind were consigned, Hell's innermost circle.

"I envied those who were tempted by

encounters with grown men and women," he said. "I wouldn't have chosen the hell of this attraction. A cop said to me, sympathetically, that he thought I was waiting for them to catch me and shock it out of my system. I didn't contradict him — I wasn't in a position to set anyone straight."

Some of the priests Docherty treated were strangely mixed, asserting their innocence despite the evidence, telling him they did not intend to cooperate with him, or retreating into the full-blown pathologies of the North American Man/Boy Love Association, NAMBLA, or a variation on this perverse philosophy that the boy-child was honored and educated by the sexual attentions of the older man. Some priests Docherty had met had rendered themselves this deluded: the child had been chosen for them by God to sustain their ministry by making possible the sexual release God knew they needed.

In his therapy, the mental exercises he set patients such as the young priest, the ones who confessed — though some might subsequently contradict themselves by playing this excuse — Docherty realized that certain people had got the idea that impulses involving children were ungovernable. Yet not every lonely heterosexual male found it an irresistible impulse to sexually importune handsome girls. Indeed, by law, he was required not to.

So that's where Docherty always began. He told them they need not touch children, even if the impulse was there. They were capable, as were most people, of abstention.

"Doctor," said the monsignor when he finally returned Docherty's call. "Are you a physician these days, Father Docherty?"

"No, I'm a research psychologist. And an old friend of your sister and brother-in-law."

"I thought," Shannon said, as if sensing a margin of peril, "you must be that Docherty."

"Yes. As I'm sure you'll also recall, I used to belong to this archdiocese — I was also a member of the Congregation of the Divine Charity. Your sister belonged to a pacifist action group I was involved with."

"Yes, I remember. As I recall, my sister lamented your departure," said Shannon. Then: "You left a message. Something about my evidence in the court case. Some factors relating to In Compassion's Name?"

"Not a direct bearing, perhaps, but an indirect one. In a very strong way. Look, could I come to see you? I need only a quarter of an hour. Or would you like to meet somewhere else?"

"Mmm," said the monsignor, as if acutely pressed for time, which he might well have been. He might also have been gauging whether it was politic to receive the notorious expellee at the cathedral.

Docherty rushed to say, "I don't think this is something we should discuss in a coffee shop or a restaurant. It's . . . Well, I think you'd call it delicate."

"Very well, then," the monsignor said, yielding with a sigh. "You can come and see me at my office in the cathedral. I am free at eleven o'clock tomorrow morning."

"Thank you," said Docherty.

"Mmm," said the monsignor again, this time as if he had no curiosity, behind that casual noise, about the unstated information this questionable priest would give him.

Sydney's Hyde Park had always been the most pleasant park to cross, to observe the old convict barracks, and the cathedral through the prism of the plumes of water spurting from the exuberant Archibald Fountain. But today the transit there from Elizabeth Street was strangely unsettling. Docherty admitted to himself that he felt afraid. He knew he was not afraid of the monsignor or the cardinal. Yet the pervasive disquiet and tension could not be argued away. His fear was that his motives would be dismissed in a facile way — that with his scraps of evidence he would be thrown back into the street. That the archdiocese — if still stuck in the mindset of the early 1970s — would vengefully deal with him: he knew that he ran the risk of never having his appeal to return to Sydney considered.

So, in approaching the neo-Gothic, Puginesque bulk of the cathedral, built rather in the style of St. Patrick's in New York, and representing in sandstone here the same aspirations of the despised Irish immigrants, he did so without the usual nostalgia. There was a questioning going on in him as to whether he was sacrificing his mother's desires for the sake of the vanity of conscience. He had to admit that out of self-interest, as well, he wanted to be readmitted to the archdiocese, to die in Australia. He had never quite managed to feel Canadian, not that he thought it was in any way something inferior to feel.

He entered the cathedral dimness, roseate and blue with the robust light from the rose window. Chartres and Salisbury cathedrals might have better glass, but the light beyond the window here was altogether more strenuous than your average northern European day. Docherty took to a pew and prayed for wisdom and for a good reception, an addressing of the issue. The place belonged to him, too, he asserted before the court of his own mind, as much as to the people to whom he was bringing his accusations. On this high altar, after all, he had been ordained a priest by Cardinal Scanlon.

At the chancery behind the cathedral, a middle-aged woman greeted Docherty neutrally and admitted him to the monsignor's office. There was a slight redolence of cigar smoke there, as if the monsignor was an occasional indulger. Docherty was standing and the woman was not quite gone when an inner door opened and Leo Shannon entered, a gloss of certitude on his broad cheeks. His hair was smooth though he was going bald, and he had the characteristic plausible face of a fixer, and of a man who belonged at the center of a church.

"Hello, Father Docherty," said the monsignor. "My sister's favorite preacher. I'm sorry things didn't go so well for you back then."

"Well," said Docherty, "it wasn't all bad. I still have my order, you see. And my teaching."

"Oh yes. Where is that?"

"It's at the University of Waterloo in Ontario."

For all that this registered with the monsignor, as he now sat down and set himself to sort a document here, a document there, it might as well have been the University of Ulan Bator.

"Take a seat," said the monsignor. "Call me Leo."

"Thank you, Leo. I'm Frank, of course."

"I'll be just a second," the monsignor said, skimming three pages from his printer, and signing the third. It was an automatic little ceremony of power, imposed on the petitioner by men who were sure of their influence.

"You spoke of the court case," he said, looking up then. "In what regard?"

"Well, I did say indirectly, Leo. Indirectly, it could come to influence you."

"Well, it's time we got past the mystery, wouldn't you agree?"

"I think you should look at this." Docherty handed the monsignor an A4 envelope in which was a copy of Stephen's note. Brian Wood's name had been blacked out.

Monsignor Shannon opened the envelope and peered with up-tilted face at the document.

Docherty said, "I'm sorry, but a copy has

been sent to the cardinal. It is the suicide note of a young man you knew. I wanted to give you a chance to read it, and to know that I'm the one who sent it to His Eminence. Unlike those who reported on *me* to Cardinal Scanlon, I'm letting you know that I'm the messenger. Of course, I'm not assuming anything about it. But there is another alleged victim mentioned in there, though the family's blotted out his name — I'm sure you would have done the same thing in the same circumstances."

The monsignor looked piercingly at Docherty, as if he wouldn't have bothered with his reading-and-signing ritual had he known this was coming. Then he set to read the letter. His head did not move as his eyes ran over it.

He coughed once when he was finished. "This is a bloody scurrilous document, and a libel," he said then, almost blithely.

"This letter has gone from the police to the coroner, and it may be sent to the public prosecutor. Without the other name inked out, of course."

The monsignor's face reddened. "They'll laugh at it. If a man were condemned on the basis of ravings like this . . . . It would be insane!"

"The document," Docherty said, avoiding

too precise an explanation of its provenance, "came to me by way of the boy's family. The mother did not want to advertise it. But I thought it was crucial for you and the Church to be made aware of it.

"As well as that, and utterly by co-incidence, I have been approached by another party, who alleges against you a third series of assaults."

"Oh well," said Leo with more bravado than conviction, and shaking his head. "Bring them all in, every neurotic you can find. This is your fabled discretion at work, I take it. And His Eminence . . . You've sent it to him, for God's sake?"

"Yes, you'll have to talk it out with him. I beg you —"

"You beg me? To hell with you, Docherty! Beg somewhere else! And not at my expense."

"The boy killed himself with an overdose after writing that letter. That gives a terrible weight to it."

"To hell with that!" said Shannon. "Look, I remember the kid all right, amongst all the other kids of unhappy households."

He remembered the child? Out of all the children he would have innocently met, he remembered this one? "They hang round a priest they like and make themselves abso-

413

lute pests." He bit a thumbnail. "The cardinal won't for a moment believe any of this about me."

Docherty inhaled. He did not like scenes of confrontation, but this one was worse than most. If Shannon mentioned his sister . . . Docherty's earlier association with her, Docherty's willingness to hurt the family of which she was a member . . . It would get very complex and perilously testing. He said, "If I was the subject of a letter like this, I think I'd want to be investigated as soon as possible."

"What a pompous bastard you are! Didn't you get into trouble over children yourself?"

"No. As I think you know, I was thrown out for my politics. It was Vietnam. It was *Humanae Vitae.*"

"And I know where you stood on that!"

"Would you have liked the letter to have been delivered to you by someone else? The mother is so angry . . . but crippled with grief, too. I've taken what I hope is a more benign path for everyone."

"And what about the Devitt case? How is it affected? By the accusation of a youth deranged enough to accuse me and then kill himself?"

As Docherty well knew, but Shannon did not, it was usual for the perpetrator — if in this case Leo was one — to point to the damage they had wrought in the victim as if it were proof that their accuser were deranged.

"Well, as I say, it's up to you and the cardinal to look at this. But you might decide it's better for you not to be involved any further in Devitt's case."

Leo's face had grown florid, his head was thrust forward. "That would be against the cardinal's wishes. He trusts me. The lawyers get on well with me. You haven't grown so rabid that you intend to send this poisonous note to the plaintiff's lawyers, have you?"

"No." Docherty was getting angry at the man and yielded to an impulse to turn the knife. "But I think the entire matter could be a risk to your validity as a witness, and that's why I said it had an impact on the trial."

"You talk as if you *intend* to make it public."

"Of course not. Only to the authorities. I haven't inquired what my duties under civil law might be."

"Don't bother. Nothing will happen. And the cardinal didn't need to see the letter either."

"I thought differently. I'm sorry. I know

this is hard for you. But the boy died, Leo."

"That is not a moral or legal claim on me," said the monsignor.

"By the way, I also asked the cardinal if he would acknowledge receipt of the letter."

"He doesn't write letters to any old priest, you know. He doesn't answer to threats. Or the demands of obscure men."

"I believe enough in his courtesy," said Docherty.

"Have you seen my sister? Have you told her?"

God forgive the casuistry of it, thought Docherty. But casuistry was the sole way out. "If she ever knows, it won't be because I told her."

"When are you going back to your bolt-hole in Canada?"

"In just over a week," said Docherty, conceding the point. "Look, I don't think there's anything more to be achieved by my waiting here. If I could be bold enough, though: I think the tack the Church is taking in this Devitt case seems technical to ordinary people. It will do nothing to heal Devitt or erase the shame of the dead priest. From a psychological point of view, the process the Church has put in place around the world has negative impacts, on the victim and the institution itself. Isn't that

416

why Devitt pursued this case?"

The monsignor picked up and considered the death note again. "Fuck him!" murmured the monsignor. "Fuck Devitt and this little bastard and all the chancers like them. They are a cancer with their loose accusations. It's becoming fashionable to single out any reputable priest and direct the poison at him. If I ever hear anything about you, any accusation, be assured, I'll be on your doorstep."

"Well, I hope I would be in a position to prove an accusation untrue. I hope you are in such a position, too."

"Do you honestly think the director of public prosecutions will go chasing after these ravings?"

"I can't say," Docherty admitted. "In the meantime, as we say in fraternal greeting, you will be remembered in my Mass."

"And am I supposed to say, 'You in mine, Father'?"

Docherty could see no need to answer and had nothing more to say. He nodded, said goodbye, and left. He came out of the chancery into a perfect winter noon, trudged up the stairs outside the cathedral, past the statue of the Irishman Archbishop Kelly, past Cardinal Moran, who had been great on social justice and marched with the 1890 strikers. He had not got far when in the shadow of a raised carpark roof he began to shudder and give way to nausea. He reached a sandstone wall and was sick at the base of it. A woman approached him tentatively, her nostrils crimped by the vomit sourness, and asked, "Are you all right, Father?"

One of the faithful.

"It's an old fever," he gasped, feeling it no lie.

30
DOCHERTY MEETS
HIS EMINENCE

July 1996

As he waited for the cardinal to contact him, Docherty meditated three times a day, read novels meritorious and flippant from the limited monastery library, and checked up on rugby league scores from Australia and cricket results from around the world. In the third Test at Edgbaston in Birmingham, England had been humiliatingly dismissed for 147 and 89 runs, and the West Indies had had to bat only once. They led the series 2–1.

Then Docherty received a call, this time via the monastery reception, from the archdiocese. The cardinal would like to see him at two o'clock the next day.

The next morning Docherty said Mass and, in turn, served the Mass of old Gunter Eismann at a side chapel. He did not eat breakfast but shaved most carefully, and

419

donned his best black clerical gear. He was again, even more than last time, acutely anxious — not of the cardinal's potential anger, but of not being believed — and, once more, consequently pervasively concerned for his mother's hope that he might return home.

Again there was little joy in seeing the spray of the Archibald Fountain and the honeycomb Gothic of the cathedral beyond it. At the chancery, Docherty waited in the parlor, which had not changed much since the day Cardinal Scanlon had called him in to expel him. A different pope on the wall, and a picture of the late cardinal, his nemesis, had joined other previous archbishops of the city in their own frames on the wall. The same patient statue of the Virgin Mary stood on its plinth.

The sound of traffic came muted through the thick old walls. He waited. Well, he'd expected that. At last the cardinal's secretary, a young man with a gleaming face, and wearing a clerical suit whose jacket was fawn, came up to him and said his name. The man extended a hand briskly, which Docherty shook with a show of unilateral enthusiasm.

When the young priest ushered Docherty into the tall office with its varnished wooden ceiling and pilasters, he found that Cardinal Condon was standing and looking directly at him from behind his desk. A stocky man, he was dressed in a cassock with scarlet piping, and a shimmering scarlet sash encased his middle. There was not going to be any show of distraction from him, Docherty judged. He would have the cardinal's instant and full attention.

The cardinal told the secretary he was not required to take notes. The young priest nodded and left. When he was gone, Cardinal Condon raised his combative jaw and issued an invitation, through lips that exhibited a kind of pain, for Docherty to sit. Docherty obeyed. Then the cardinal took a husky little breath and began. "You still believe Cardinal Scanlon did you an injustice, don't you?"

Docherty felt sick. The opening gambit confirmed to him that he would indeed be placed in the role of a suspicious informer. To make a quick answer to what they used to call an *argumentum ad hominem,* or, in rugby football parlance, going for the man instead of the ball, was beyond Docherty's gifts.

"I think you heard the question, Father," said the cardinal, still florid with prejudgment, to Docherty's silence.

"Yes, Your Eminence," he said in a tongue-tied way. "I thought I was unjustly treated then. But I've made a life elsewhere, and it has been an honorable life. And I would be very grateful if on the basis of it the archdiocese took me in again in my mother's declining years. You have a letter from me on file that says as much."

"That has to be seen," murmured the cardinal. "You've made quite a *particular* kind of life for yourself, haven't you? You spoke at the conference of the clergy last week, I believe — controversially."

"I do my best to sound reasonable," said Docherty. "I don't set out to aggrieve the Church."

"Don't you?" The cardinal laughed in a skeptical way. "I suppose your studies dispose you to see vileness everywhere, in every cleric. People in the press talk about gay-hating gays and Jew-hating Jews. Are you a priest-hating priest?"

"No. The attitude you suggest would be grossly improper. Professionally, I mean."

The cardinal picked up documents that could only have been Stephen Cosgrove's letter and Docherty's covering note. "We have in this case a boy deranged enough to take his life."

"That's right. And, I regret to say, I have

come across another individual, not mentioned in that letter, who also claims to have been abused by Monsignor Shannon. This second informant wants privacy at the moment, though he or she may come forward in the end after having had counseling."

"My God. Legal counseling, I suppose?"

"Psychological counseling," said Docherty. "And can I make the point, Your Eminence, that insanity was not the cause of Stephen's suicide? Despair was."

"Thank you for the professional note, Father . . . *Doctor* Docherty." He paused. "The monsignor is my right-hand man. You must know that."

"I was aware you relied a lot on him, Your Eminence."

"Come on!" warned the cardinal, his suntanned face, square like James Cagney's, reddening. "I've been filled in about you. Don't pull that Gandhi trick you brought back from India. You hate Monsignor Shannon. Why don't you admit it?"

"I don't hate him, Your Eminence. I am friends with members of his family. The accusation brings me no joy at all."

The cardinal held up Stephen's suicide letter and Docherty's own letter, as if they both bespoke criminal intentions.

"This is inadequate evidence, Father

Docherty. And, believe it or not, your word is not of prime value in this archdiocese."

"I don't want Monsignor Shannon to be condemned," Docherty said. "But I think he should be asked about the matters and, insofar as any investigation can occur, be investigated. There are many people still alive who might have witnessed something between him and young Cosgrove. And, as you know, Stephen's letter would have been sent by the police to the coroner, and may ultimately be sent to the public prosecutor."

"Who will very properly find it flimsy evidence and lock it away. And as for you, I'm ordering you to destroy all copies of it you possess."

"I don't need to do that, Your Eminence. I am no longer under your authority."

"But I'm archbishop of this diocese. And you want to rejoin us?"

"Very much so, if you would allow it. But it isn't the point here. Could I plead with you, Your Eminence, just to look into the matter? Simply to question the monsignor, in confidence?"

The cardinal, whose father had been a Darling Downs farmer — tough, enduring, of possibly limited but courageously definite ideas — surveyed him in that vein. It did not seem to Docherty a promising survey.

"May I tell you straight," the cardinal said, "that I've thought over my approach to your supposed evidence, and I dismiss that evidence. The monsignor is no more guilty in these matters than I am. These claims are a symptom of old-fashioned anti-Church, anticlerical feeling. I intend to report this intrusion, this foray of yours, to your bishop in Canada."

Here was the habit of total authority that resided in the cardinal. At one time it had existed in the civil sphere. It was a professional trap for any bishop to be tempted to become the commissar.

"I ask you to consider whether that's a just decision," said Docherty, angry and with a sort of disbelief. The hostility he sensed in the room seemed reckless, unintelligent, absolute, and it surprised him insofar as he knew that no one who was appointed a cardinal lacked institutional sagacity. Yet there was already enough evidence that true wisdom abandoned so many of these Church leaders when it came to *this* matter and to *these* crimes. Worldly utilitarianism clicked into place in this matter, involving lawyers and the sort of raw prohibition the cardinal had just tried to bring down upon Docherty. And a bishop, an archbishop, a cardinal took on for a time the stewardship of a measurable, quantifiable, and physical inheritance. Institutions, real estate, holdings. These men could be panicked by anything that might erode that inheritance, suggest their incompetence, leave more powerful clergy muttering on their death that they hoped this time round they would get someone competent.

"In your jaundiced way," the cardinal now accused him, standing to signal the end of the interview, "you probably think all of us guilty of baseness. But I have worked with and trusted Leo Shannon for years, and I know his caliber. I would prefer to trust his reputation than a demented last scream of some drug addict."

"Will you let me mount a counterargument, Your Eminence?" asked Docherty.

"Only if you feel you have to. And be brief."

"I'm sure you can understand how wary I have been about drawing your attention to this material. I knew I was under a shadow, and that it might seem I was being vengeful. I do not seek to be vengeful. I want to return here, to my home city and archdiocese, but I am willing to take the risk of rejection — not because I wanted to do harm, but for the sake of any potential victims. Forgive me, I know you understand this. May I ask you to maintain at least some belief that the people who have spoken to me, and given me this terrible document I've now placed in your hands, might not be lying."

The cardinal sat down again with a skeptical squeak of the lips. "I have investigated this to my satisfaction. I know the man. I have spoken to him. When these accusers come forward — I mean, the second one you mention, because I know the other one, the dead boy, won't and can't present himself — maybe then we'll look at it again. But why should I spar with shadows? Because, Docherty, you might have noticed the palpable devils of secularism are abroad. Moral relativism and opportunism prevail — some Catholics treat doctrine like a delicatessen, where you buy only the olives and sausage you want and leave the rest. And we want more priests. Yes, that's the problem! We don't want to investigate the good ones we already have, to be punitive with them. Until vocations to the priesthood revive, until we turn the corner, why would we be a Star Chamber to those who are still laboring in the vineyard?"

Docherty said nothing and dared think little. He should have known that the Church always fought this matter with a passion, impelled by their anxiety about institutional survival, as well as by a fear of the ignorant malice of a pluralist community all too ready to believe the worst.

He declared, "I may have a duty as a citizen under the reportable offenses legislation. To take the allegations to the authorities."

"You must follow your conscience, Father," said the cardinal. He picked up the phone and told his priest-secretary that Father Docherty was going. "Happy return to Canada, Father Docherty," he said as he turned to work on a laptop.

As soon as Docherty got back to the monastery, he called his cousin, Mark Docherty, who was a solicitor in North Sydney, to check on the nature of the law in New South Wales regarding reportable offenses. His cousin was a happy, gruff sort of fellow. As a child he had come down from Brisbane in the school holidays to stay with Docherty's family, and had been more than willing to inform them of the superiorities of Queensland over New South Wales. Indeed, many of the little fellow's dictums were quoted whenever the question arose of Brisbane's attractions and supposed sophistication relative to Sydney's.

"How are you?" asked Mark when Docherty announced himself. There was the normal trace of familial reproach that Frank had not been in contact for a long time.

After polite inquiries, Docherty explained apologetically that he should like to come up to Mark's office. "I shouldn't have to use more than a few minutes of your time."

"You can stay half an hour if you like. Or come to dinner at my place, if that takes your fancy."

Docherty said that he might have difficulty, given that he was going back to Canada soon.

"Don't know how you take that place!" his cousin said, and began to sing. "O Canada, glorious and free, up to our arse in snow we stand on guard for thee!"

"When it snows, it snows, and when it shines, it shines, and often it does both at the same time. Look, I can't offer you the normal fee for advice."

Mark said, "Don't be ridiculous. Family rates. Sweet bugger all. I'll see you when you get here."

So out of the monastery and onto the bus to North Sydney. Docherty wore his clericals but with a sports coat — the sort of thing the clergy wore when they'd resigned from being too authoritative.

429

When he got to the address, his cousin emerged immediately from his office to greet him. "The missing cousin," yelled Mark, laughing at the wall in front of him on which hung photographs recording his exploits as a leading rugby referee. He took Docherty inside. "I do have a client coming at two," he said. "Sorry about that. The invitation to dinner stands."

"When I'm back. I hope to come back for good."

They exchanged more pleasantries, and his cousin whimsically told him that he was still a member of the Holy Roman Apostolic and Alcoholic Church. He'd even had a bit of practice in representing drink-driving charges brought against members of the clergy.

"When I started it, I thought I was doing God's work. I thought that a good man would not repeat a vice which could place other members of the public in jeopardy. But I was wrong. An ordained drunk driver has the same mental habits of recidivist drunk drivers everywhere. So I went and saw the cardinal, and I explained that I could no longer connive in giving the signals that garnered lighter penalties for the clergy. And he sensibly told me not to. He sent a directive out to his priests reminding them that in court, as in the confessional, a sincere purpose of amendment was necessary. This directive gave those who were charged a certain air of remorse, and it served them nearly as well as my pleadings. So they still bring these cases to me. Of course, there are some police who let them go anyhow. So we still have to depend on good Protestant cops or disgruntled Catholics to lay drink-driving charges against the Catholic clergy!"

This was a story meant to amuse, but it was too familiar to Docherty to allow him to manage much jest. Docherty thought, to him I'm still the family prude, and I've just proven it again by not laughing along.

Indeed, his cousin saw his levity had backfired and asked soberly now, "What can I do for you, Frank?"

"I want to know," asked Docherty, "what my legal duty is in this state in terms of reportable offenses. I have professional immunity in Ontario, but not here. I've been made aware of credible accusations of abuse against a particular priest, and I emphasize that word. They *are* credible accusations."

"What sort of abuse?" asked Mark.

Docherty looked at him.

"Oh," said his cousin, "That kind. Jesus Christ, Frank!"

"So what's the law now?"

"I'm not an expert on this," said Mark. "Thank God, I've never encountered a case. I got through the Jesuits without encountering anything like that, and my kids, I am certain, have been fine, too."

"Is there someone you can send me to?"

"There is a man I know who works on this stuff. He joined a firm that dumped abuse cases on him to the point that he became an expert. I can call his office to let him know you'll be over."

Mark made the call and asked for a Domenico Passerelli.

"Italian?" Docherty whispered over the table.

"One of the great Calabrian diaspora," said Mark. And then, as his call was answered, "Yes, Domenico." He explained Docherty's question to the Calabrian-Australian lawyer, then offered Docherty the phone so he, too, could speak to the man, whose young voice was vigorous. Docherty made an appointment for the next day.

"Did my cousin tell you I'm a monk?" he asked Domenico.

"He did. Don't worry. The only clergy I ever charge are the criminals."

31
DOCHERTY IS MUGGED

July 1996

The old German priest Gunter Eismann had made Docherty's stay all the easier. He was good company, this refugee from a world war and Papua New Guinea. That night he asked Docherty about his work in Ontario for Bishop Egan of Hamilton, and quizzed him about the Canadian academic year. It was late by the time Docherty returned to his room, where he took a call from Sarah. "It's the cabdriver," she said. "When do you leave?"

"Four days, ten at night. Air Canada."

"I suppose you think you've done everything you could?" she asked.

"That's what I've been telling myself," he said. "I've made complaints through avenues. Today I signed a statutory declaration in the presence of a solicitor, who has sent it to the ombudsman. I can't think what else

433

I can do that's within morality and the law. Yet I feel I've failed."

"Success would take longer than you've got," Sarah told him almost affectionately, certainly without the sort of acrid complaint with which their relationship had begun. "You took on the matter inside morality and the law. Do you think the monsignor's doing that? The cardinal? They'll squeeze morality and the law into deformed shapes. Just to make sure your statutory declaration goes nowhere."

This was a grievous comment, but, as his uncle Tim would have said, Docherty could feel the truth of it in his water.

"That's up to them," was all he could say.

"Ah, so long as your conscience is comfortable, eh?"

"I'd rather be effective," said Docherty. There was a long silence. "I'd dearly love to be effective. I don't want to be a handwringer on the sidelines."

"But you might have to beat someone up to get anywhere. And it'd be against your pacifist principles."

Docherty shook his head. "You know how to rattle a cage."

She had cast all his careful consultations with Passerelli as gestures of impotence, as he knew they were.

She said, "I have to thank you for introducing me to the Cosgroves. Paul risked letting me meet his mother."

"You've been active," said Docherty. "Good!"

"Yes. It was a hell of a sight more important than that psychologist I didn't go to. Jokes aside, it was important. For me, and for her. They told me about the other man, Brian Wood, too. We've all got a common demon."

"It was all I could think of, to introduce you to each other."

"And it was a good idea," said Sarah.

"Watch out, you're veering towards approval."

"They haven't shown me yet what her son wrote."

"You should ask Paul," suggested Docherty.

"Yes. He's a good-looking fellow, that Paul."

"I don't know if he's up to your weight."

"I don't have a weight. I'm a phantom. Look, could we meet up tomorrow — that coffee shop? By the way, unless you prove terminally annoying, I promise to take you to the airport. And despite what I said . . . my shout!"

"That's very humane of you. But I'm not

certain . ."

"*You* bring a copy of the letter," said Sarah. "You can do that. I don't want to keep it. I just want to see it. I'm ready to face it."

Docherty weighed this.

"I'll ask Mrs. Cosgrove," he told her.

"No, ask Paul, as you suggested. I didn't want to read it in her presence. She's sensitive. Tell Paul I'd like that, that it would help me. Bring it to me tomorrow in a folder and I'll give it right back."

Sarah rang off. Docherty called the Cosgrove home. Liz uttered a bleak hello in a slack voice, all tension and expectation leached from it.

He told her he was leaving in a few days, but he wanted to say a proper farewell and to let her know how much Sarah had got out of talking to her.

"Yes," said Liz. "We got a lift out of her while she was here."

He could hear in her voice the paucity of that lift. He did not know whether by now Paul had reported to his mother the disheartening answer from the cardinal, or the fact that he had put Leo Shannon's name into an official record. And, God knew, that there might be charges one day.

"Is Paul there?" he asked. He was. Dutiful

son to a mother who couldn't be consoled.

"Hello," said Paul when he took up the phone. "Look, I'm sorry about Wood."

Docherty assured him on that, and asked if he could show Sarah Stephen's note.

"She didn't ask me," Paul said.

"She felt awkward asking in front of your mother. I think it might help her," said Docherty. "I understand that sounds strange."

"I suppose you can. But I think you should get it back, and I reckon you ought to destroy your copies before you leave. I don't want any stray ones lying around. I want the chief one remaining to be the one the cardinal has, burning a hole in his desk."

Docherty promised. "And I'll keep in touch. Apart from everything else, I owe your mother a great deal for all that fund-raising years ago."

"Freeing sex slaves," said Paul. "She was proud of that."

"She picked her targets well," said Docherty. "She had a fine nose about whom she could tell the truth to — and the truth was that we were buying out children from the Calcutta brothels. But some people would have been too shocked by that idea and we had to tell them we were freeing enslaved children. Both stories were the truth."

"And then," Paul murmured, "she wasn't aware my brother would be an enslaved child, too."

For a while Docherty's throat was closed off. "It's too damn sad entirely," he said eventually. "My heart breaks for the two of you. I'd say Christ's heart breaks, too."

"Frank, no offense, but if Christ has anything to do with this Church, he can shove his heart."

Docherty felt the weight of that, of the destruction that had been done beneath the great bland claim of redemption. He felt sweat between his shoulders, the fear of his life's nullity. "Well, there's the Church as we have all suffered it," he admitted, "and then there is Christ, something different. As for priests, I don't have to tell you. We've been exalted above our merits. We have been given too angelic a burden for ordinary creatures and the thing turns rancid in us. You know that."

"Yes. But don't overdo it, Frank. You're not rancid. Father O'Hanlon . . . he's a decent man."

"Yes," said Docherty. "I'm happy to be counted in his company."

■ ■ ■

The next morning Docherty took the bus with his book, Antony Beevor's *Battle for Spain,* the letter in a folder, and his Canadian contact details. He dismounted and was close to the Powerhouse Museum when he was hit from behind in the lower back. It was for all the world like an old-fashioned round-the-thighs rugby tackle. It winded him, both his hands went out to meet the pavement, and he dropped the folder. Instinctively he curled in his head as he rolled forwards and turned onto his backside. He sat there on the cement grunting, and reached for the folder. He had a glimpse of a bearlike, blond young man, the man who had felled him, but then he was gone, sprinting towards Chinatown.

Docherty got up and shook himself. He inspected the pavement. The folder was gone.

Sarah rose to her feet when he came into the coffee shop rubbing the elbow that had collided with the pavement.

"What happened to you?"

"I was mugged. In Sydney! He's going to be disappointed. All he got was the . . . Well, all he got was the suicide letter and my

439

contact details."

"He'll know better than to contact you. And if he does, he'll get you doing some sort of a Gandhi act on him. That'll teach him."

Docherty settled himself and looked at Sarah. Her hair seemed smooth as a seal's, as Maureen's had. He felt more alive for seeing it, and even for the pungent experience of colliding with a hard surface. He thirstily drank the coffee she ordered for him.

"You're all right?" she asked, assessing him.

"Yes. But that kid . . . What could he have thought was in my folder? So I don't have the letter now. Maybe Mrs. Cosgrove or Paul can show you a copy, after all. You're going to see her again?"

"Yes. Misery loves company. But, I mean . . . Do you think this was a hit man from the Church?"

"Of course not," he assured her.

"I wouldn't put *anything* past them."

"*Hitman!*" he said, laughing.

She shrugged.

"Have you thought any more about that psychologist?" he said.

"Stop nagging," she said. "I've been thinking about other things. I'm going to try to

440

go back to teaching. The state system."

He relaxed his shoulders and spread his hands. "Well, that's an astonishing development."

"Bad news for some headmaster. Or mistress. But I must find out who I would have been had I never met the monsignor."

"That's a very good thing to find out," said Docherty. "In fact, it's wonderful," he told her softly. "Yes. I suppose you call it progress."

She said, "We have to report this to the police. We can't have you knocked about in broad daylight."

"Nonsense," he insisted. "He was gentle with me. No fuss, please."

The suicide note was out there, he thought. On the street, as they say. Hopefully in a litter bin by now. He would have to let Paul know, and the realization brought him to a further plan.

"Look, why don't you *all* sit down together. Liz, Paul, you, and this Wood fellow. Why don't you talk it out together, to the limit, putting everything on the table, looking at all possibilities? You would be such a help to each other."

Sarah closed her eyes awhile to think the proposal through.

"We would if you moderated us," she suggested.

"Nonsense."

"Aren't you a clinical psychologist? You could help us reach a little further. Without interfering every time we say we'd like to see Monsignor Shannon stretched on a bed of ants."

"Okay. I would like to do that, as a facilitator. But I have to warn you, I haven't earned the right to issue instructions on anything."

She winked, whimsically disbelieving him. "I'm up for it, if you are," she assured him.

"It would have to be tonight or tomorrow night. More likely tomorrow. I'll call on Brian Wood. Though I should warn you, he may not want to be part of any discussions."

"Believe me," Sarah Fagan murmured, "I know that won't deter you."

He rose from the table, taking a second to find his right hip, to be sure it was in place to take his weight. Yes, it still held. The last, fatal fall of his life was, with any luck, some years away.

32
DOCHERTY AND HIS MOTHER

July 1996

Docherty and his mother walked around the western shore of Sydney Cove. On their right was the glittering acre of water between them and the Opera House. On their left were the museums and old warehouses of the original maritime town, the penal settlement that had been half-bond and half-free. And, challenging the imagination, off to the right lay an Aboriginal ceremonial site, so it was said — a stream that had run through bushland down to the old foreshore.

Docherty knew there had once been hereditary owners of the rituals of this place: Aboriginal priests, enactors, maintainers. A series of such folk, men and women, who had suffered the bad fortune of having the space travelers land here in 1788 and make *this* place of all places the

443

epicenter of their European penal intentions.

Docherty had first been brought here, to the environs of Circular Quay, by his mother. She was young then. Now her bad hips caused her to force her way forward, stabbing at the pavement energetically with the rubber ferrule of her stick, heaving her other leg and her upper body to keep pace with her intent. What surprised him was, despite this struggle, how young she looked; that he could see the girl behind the effort and deterioration.

Above them was the great rivet-studded arch bridge, very close, like an ancestral god of Sydneysiders. Ahead was the international shipping terminal, and still more of the old warehouses of the mercantile port. They stopped at a plaque in the pavement that commemorated what Mark Twain had to say on Australian history: "It does not read like history, but like the most beautiful lies. And all of a fresh new sort, no moldy old stale ones. It is full of surprises, and adventures, and incongruities, and contradictions, and incredibilities; but they are all true, they all happened."

"I wish it were still true," his mother told Docherty. "Australia seems a lot plainer to me. I wasn't around when they were hand-ing out the adventures and incongruities."

Docherty wanted to hug her to make up for her lack of incongruities, yet he knew it would embarrass both of them.

"How about if we get a bench and just soak this up?" asked Docherty, sniffing the air a little more theatrically than he needed to.

"As you wish, Captain Bligh," said Mrs. Docherty. She settled herself on a vacant bench and Docherty took the space beside her. On the vivid water before them a replica of either the *Bounty* or the *Endeavour*, tourists on its deck, spread its sails to the wind.

"A lot worse places to have been born, mind you," said his mother. "I admit it. And a lot worse to grow old in, for that matter."

"I can name some of the worst places. Calcutta, unless you're financially lucky. And, I tell you what, in North America, try Regina, Saskatchewan, or Minneapolis–St. Paul on a gray icy day."

"You're still a patriot."

"A climatic patriot! And, by all that's holy, a cricket patriot, too."

"Ah," said his mother. "For a dreamy kid, you were always good in the slips field. I remember that. Your father, he was so pleased you were a cricketer. He liked all-rounders." This led her to predictable themes. "You know, he didn't buy many successful horses. That's what he wanted to be, a man known for the horses he bought, and the poor fellow never got that. And I never gave his enthusiasms the time of day. I'd seen how brittle all this dreaming was in the Depression, which, let me tell you, because of the lickspittle politicians was worse here than it ever was in North America."

Docherty made an assenting noise.

"Have you discussed with the big boy your chance of coming back?" asked his mother, with apparent indifference. Docherty knew that her superficial indifference always masked intense feeling.

"In passing," he told her. "But I fear I didn't impress him a lot."

"Well, let me tell you this — I want you here. I want to expire with you in the room, not in some Canadian province. Let the bugger know that."

"I'm working on it," said Docherty.

"I get cards from your Canadian students, you know. They think highly of you."

"Yes. Mind you, I suggested as a joke they write to you to get your maternal perspective. And they did. I'm lucky. Some of them come to Mass to take Communion just to prevent a poor turnout in the parish I help in. One of them got me to officiate at the funeral of his Methodist father!"

"You love a good funeral," she said with a generous light in her eyes.

"I don't mind weddings either," said Docherty.

"Ah, the sacrament that binds two people to do each other as much harm as they can."

"Well, I know you're the expert. But is that the full story? Really?"

"By some lights," said his mother, laughter in her eyes. "In any case, I want you to do my funeral. I don't trust the others. You won't allow a single false note or any hypocrisy."

"When it comes, and if your elderly son is still living," said Docherty.

"Why wouldn't you still be living? Stop poncing around. Just say yes."

"I'd be proud to do it. I'll tell the mourners what you said about marriage. That'll get a laugh."

"Funerals are the big one," Mrs. Docherty insisted. "Everyone involved knows it's a rite of passage. It was a sacrament of humans long before Christianity."

The *Bounty* or *Endeavour,* whichever it was, was rounding the little harbor island called Pinchgut.

"What in God's name can the cardinal have against *you*?" his mother complained. "Except the old stuff. And, for heaven's sake, you were right. Apartheid's finished, and everyone says Vietnam was a catastrophe."

"Well, you see, he seems sincerely to suspect my work. If my report on pedophilia attracts approving comment from the Canadian bishops, then I might be in with a chance to come back here."

"Sometimes I think I'd prefer to have been born a Methodist," his mother said.

But then she looked up at him and her eyes had a genuine gravity. She wanted him home. He was her boy.

"Someone should sue the bugger!" said Mrs. Docherty. "For unjust dismissal."

"Declan called me from Melbourne. *He* reckons I should sue the man. And somebody else has already. This Devitt fellow. But I don't think his case is going so well."

He was aware that he had not yet told the cardinal that there was a stolen copy of the letter out in the world. That would not enhance his popularity.

By now he was tentatively chiding himself for his naïveté. He had reached certain conclusions about the young man who had tackled him on the pavement and taken his folder. The man had not looked homeless, or harrowed by an addiction. He'd looked like a boy from somewhere in the bush, come down to Sydney looking for work; perhaps driving taxis for a while. Yes, that was precisely what he looked like! And he meets Sarah at the taxi depot, and she pays him the time of day and asks him for a favor. And he does it, perhaps in part out of awe for her, never having met anyone quite like her where he comes from. And certainly boys from the bush know how to flatten a bloke without doing him too much harm. He was wondering . . . Could it have been Sarah's means of getting a copy for herself, and taking the matter out of Docherty's hands?

The next morning he called the cathedral chancery and asked if he could speak to the private secretary of His Eminence. The woman in the office told him that the cardinal was across the harbor at Manly, in the nineteenth-century stone house on North Head, the traditional out-of-town residence of archbishops of Sydney. There, Docherty thought, Condon was a little removed from what was coming to a head in the Supreme Court: the question of whether he, and the archdiocese itself, could be sued for the crimes of Father Guest.

"Could you tell the cardinal that there have been some developments in the matter I discussed with him last week?" asked Docherty.

"The matter discussed with him last week," repeated the woman.

An hour or so later he got a message from Cardinal Condon's secretary that His Eminence would like to see him the morning after next at ten o'clock at the cathedral chancery.

33
BREAKFAST WITH THE BRESLINS

July 1996

On the morning of his last full day in Sydney, Docherty had breakfast with Maureen and Damian. Maureen answered the door again, looking up at him with that questing, undefeated expression he cherished. He felt the accustomed desire, a sense of various substantial atoms in his body involuntarily seeking a true north. The wonderful line of her naked neck was still there, though more sinewy, and she carried a small hump at the top of her spine, the first hint of old age. She took him through the house, and at their kitchen range Damian was scrambling eggs and slicing smoked salmon and tomato.

"Bless me, Father!" he called jovially. An old joke, uttered by a man secure at his hearth.

"Bless you, my son."

Docherty helped Maureen carry cups and

plates and cutlery to the sundeck. It was a bright, still winter's morning. It somehow made him melancholy by its uncomplicated dazzle. It was the coming departure that gave him the blues. So we will get old, he thought, turning our bodies towards the sun, while the orbiting earth grinds us to dust with its rotations.

The question of Leo hung over the table, but first the three of them ate their yogurt and fruit salad, their scrambled eggs, and got at least one cup of coffee aboard.

Damian said, "We need you back so the right rebellious things are said at our funerals."

"My mother wants me to do hers, too. The thing is, who will say the right rebellious things at my funeral?"

The habit of life, the chemicals that promoted a sense of immortality, made even a priest think that he would somehow be around to approve of the tone of his own postmortem obsequies.

In the eucalyptus below the sundeck magpies made their gargling morning cry and a kookaburra landed at the end of the veranda, adopting that air of skepticism Docherty remembered in the kookaburras of his childhood. They deigned to visit the habitations of man and woman, but they

452

seemed to know that at best they would be offered some sort of meat substitute, not the small, live, fatty reptiles that were their desire.

Docherty relayed a conversation he'd had the day before with the dean of social sciences at Sydney University, who had made promising notes about employing him as an adjunct.

Damian said, "When you get back, I'm not sure I want to become the husband in one of those old Catholic couples who travels round with the priest friend. A ménage à trois of the Holy Spirit. I used to think they looked pretty pallid, like three tallow candles."

"When I come back, I'll get a suntan, then," said Docherty.

Maureen put aside her scrambled eggs. "What about Leo?" she asked softly.

"Maureen, I had to send a statutory declaration to the ombudsman. It was drawn up by a lawyer. But it doesn't mean —"

"It doesn't mean he's guilty," she murmured, completing the sentence for him. "Of course he's guilty. That letter reeks of authenticity. I haven't been able to think my way past it."

"Well, I have to tell you that someone's

453

stolen my copy. I dropped it by accident in Harris Street, and then it was gone. I'm sorry. I don't know why it was taken. It could be in a garbage bin somewhere."

He gathered himself and continued. "There are other accusations against Leo. I'm sorry. . . . It's all so coincidental, the cardinal thinks it a plot."

"Other accusations?" asked Maureen, frowning. "Are you actually investigating my brother?"

"No," he said emphatically. He watched her mistrust vanish but could see she nonetheless required an explanation. So he told them the tale of the cabdriver, not vouchsafing her name, and of his meeting with her, and her specific accusations. Maureen looked ill; Damian moved to her side and put his arm around her shoulder. "You are not him," he clumsily sought to assure her. "His crimes aren't yours."

The recounting had exhausted Docherty. And there was no apologizing for it. Maureen could not now keep abhorrence for her brother out of her eyes.

"Look," Docherty murmured, "why don't *you* talk to Leo?"

She looked at the floor. "I did. Angry denials, that's all. Meanwhile, this Devitt case is everything to him. It's almost as if he thinks the Church is unsustainable unless it quashes Devitt."

Docherty drank tepid coffee. It made him feel nauseated. He said, "Leo has the cardinal's full support. I don't know whether that consoles you, Maureen, or not."

Maureen roared, "Of course it doesn't console me. Why should it?"

Damian suggested gently, "Don't savage Frank. He's not the wrongdoer in this case." He kissed the top of her head, and she swallowed and composed herself.

She said, "Leo was certainly angry enough with me, and some would think his anger proved his innocence. But I know him from childhood. He has a good act. Sadly, I now know it to be an act."

With the hollowness that is no stranger to Eros, after a few more minutes Docherty pecked a farewell on Maureen's cheek. He gave Damian a positive hug, acclaim for the man he was, the man who was no fool, the loyal complainer, the just critic, the consoler.

34
DOCHERTY VISITS BRIAN WOOD

July 1996

The offices of Wood and Associates sat on the upper floors of a city skyscraper. The water-facing building owned all the desirable views northeast to the very sandstone gates of Sydney, the great promontories of the North and South heads; and, more proximately, of the Opera House, Circular Quay with the gag of the Cahill Expressway across its mouth, and the grand steel artifice of the Sydney Harbour Bridge, beneath which Docherty and his mother had recently sat. The firm wanted people to know it possessed its own rotating bank of Australian modern art — Sidney Nolan, Lloyd Rees, John Olsen, and the rest. Nolan's painting on display was of Burke and Wills, naked in what used to be called, in Docherty's boyhood, "the dead heart of Australia."

Behind reception, a stylish young woman

was obviously not accustomed to seeing clergy here. Docherty had wanted to stand out with this woman, because he felt his oddity might impress her when he said he desired a quick word with Mr. Wood. You can't send the clergy away as readily as you dispense with couriers, the homeless and demented, particularly if they are wearing the best of alpaca.

"If you just give him my name," urged Docherty earnestly and in his most tranquil tone. "He knows me. I need see him only briefly."

The receptionist looked stressed, her eyes flitting between Docherty's sternum and the piece of paper on which he had written his name. She called someone and uttered the details of Docherty's request into the mouthpiece, looking abashed, her glossed lips bloodless. She nodded, put the phone down, and looked thoughtful. She said, "Would you mind taking a seat? Mr. Wood will be here soon."

To soothe his sense of having too many schemes running at once, too many people to juggle, Docherty set out to think himself into the state of being nothing in the face of the transcendent. In nothing, of course, there is no ground for embarrassment. In nothing, there is the flawless passage of the divine winds.

Wood appeared, accompanied by two young men with dossiers. They stopped and conversed tersely, then one broke away with a familiar salute. Wood and the other stood at the mouth of the corridor speaking earnestly for a while. Wood was giving instructions without an imperious air, nodding a great deal for emphasis. Eventually both men approached Docherty, who stood.

"Father Frank Docherty," said Wood. "This is Peter Irving, my CFO."

Irving shook his hand and, this little ritual past, excused himself. Wood said with a masculine gruffness, "How long would you say we need to meet, Father?"

"Five minutes," said Docherty.

"Would you like a coffee?"

"No, thank you."

"I'll be in the boardroom for ten minutes," Wood instructed the receptionist.

"Not that long," Docherty assured him.

In the boardroom Wood sat at once, as if by habit, at the head of the table. The harbor and the brightness seemed magnified in this place, as if every window was a lens designed to allow a drench of light and a blue water view, with the summits of humbler buildings crowding up to convince Docherty of all their vertiginous glory.

Wood said, "I wasn't expecting to meet you again, Father."

"Call me Frank. I wanted to let you know, there's going to be a meeting of the victims of the monsignor. It's tonight at the Cosgroves' at seven. The Cosgroves, another victim, and . . . I'll be there, too, by invitation. It's up to you whether you come, of course. But it would have been discourteous of me not to let you know that the various possibilities for action and inaction will be canvassed by them. Not by me.

"Also, I want to let you know that I lost a copy of Stephen's suicide letter. I dropped it in the city, by accident. Your name was blanked out in it. But I thought you should know. Finally, to fulfill my duty as a citizen, I sent a statutory declaration to the ombudsman citing Stephen's letter and the information that came from the other victim, whom you *may* meet tonight. But that's your call."

Wood seemed to have held his breath through Docherty's speech. Now he exhaled and shook his head. A chestnut lock came loose on his forehead, and for a second you could see the handsome schoolboy who'd preceded the man.

"I thought all this was settled, Father . . . Frank. I have to show you something." He

459

pressed a digit on the phone in the board-room and it was answered instantly. "Bring the *Financial Times Asia* piece, if you don't mind. Just the one copy. Yes. Boardroom."

As they waited, Docherty watched Wood. He appeared less hostile than he had been in the hotel after the funeral. A young woman in an impeccable blouse and navy-blue skirt opened the door and stood with a page in her hand. Wood thanked her as she left. He handed the printed page to Docherty. A banner from the *Financial Times Asia* with a date showed the report was only three days old. The item concerned an offer from a company named Kamichi Business Process Outsourcing, apparently well known as KBPO, to amalgamate with Wood and Associates. Through its Southeast Asian and Southwest Pacific expansion Wood and Associates had become an attractive target for amalgamation on terms that would be very advantageous to it. The merger would extend the reach of both parties throughout the region. The sum Kamichi was investing in the merged entity, and the proposed cost of a new Shanghai office, were in digits Docherty's imagination could barely get purchase on. A number of commentators stated that both partners brought great strengths and promise to the table, and that the amalgamation involved "promising synergies." There was a photograph of Wood and a corporate Japanese man, not shaking hands but jolly in each other's presence.

"Frank," said Wood, pointing to the report. "I'm either this man or I'm Monsignor Shannon's rape victim. I can't be both, and I choose this one. Because . . . Who wouldn't? So, thank you, but I won't be there."

"I understand," said Docherty, but he was not convinced. It was as if there were an unexpressed tremor in the room. It belonged to Wood, but he would not acknowledge ownership.

"I hope Mrs. Cosgrove is okay," Wood told him. "I imagine not, poor woman!"

"It's kind of you to ask. Thus far she's inconsolable, of course."

They shook hands.

"Thank you for my five minutes," said Docherty.

35
THE MEETING AT
THE COSGROVES'

July 1996

At the Cosgrove house, as a prelude to the meeting Paul administered beer and wine to the company. Sarah Fagan and Liz Cosgrove had each a glass of silvery sauvignon blanc before them, and it gave the small gathering a marginally convivial air. "There's coffee, Frank," Paul told him. "If you don't want a drink."

Docherty asked for some water, as Sarah Fagan presumed to speak brightly to Mrs. Cosgrove, telling her about the school she'd been inquiring into, a real school, Liz replied, not some old fortress of prejudice and hypocrisy. Undeniably, there seemed to be a new vigor in the cabdriver. She turned at last to Docherty, the natural convener. "All right, Frank, fill everyone in on what you have been doing."

He did it — everything he'd reported to

Wood and what he meant to report to the cardinal the next day.

"I was exceptionally disturbed by losing the copy of the letter that I was bringing to show you, Sarah. But I think you might be able to put my mind to rest on that matter."

"How can I manage that?" she asked, looking at him with absolute directness.

"I can understand why you needed the letter: it was proof in written form of an injury parallel to the one done to you. I know that sometimes what happens in these cases can seem so preposterous that even the victim needs proof. You didn't intend me any harm. Look, I'm not trying to embarrass you, but I have a certain responsibility to the Cosgroves. Do you have the letter, Sarah?"

"Yes," she said. She exhaled. "Sorry, Liz."

Liz Cosgrove looked aghast, but Sarah said, "I'll keep it safe."

Docherty nearly said, "I was the one flattened by your friend." It was nothing, however, compared to the pain of Liz Cosgrove.

"I suppose it was a pretty transparent strategy I used, eh?" Sarah said.

"If it only took me a day to work it out, it must have been transparent," Docherty said.

Sarah turned to the Cosgroves. "I wanted

to keep the letter and digest it, so I had a young man take it from Frank."

Then, from the complacency and ease of her confession, her face collapsed. It seemed to Docherty more than a collapse of shame, of being caught. She let out a howl of pain and said, "I don't even know what to do with it. But I wanted to have it."

Liz reached out to her. "Maybe," Sarah said, gurgling with tears, "maybe Paul and I could go to some underworld pub and give someone five thousand dollars to execute the mongrel! That's my contribution to tonight. That's the only damn thing that will really work."

Liz was looking at her new friend with astonishment. She kept her hand on Sarah's wrist. The inconsolable mother had become a comforter, at least for now.

"Only if he'll guarantee not to let Shannon die easily," said Liz with a hack of laughter — to Docherty it sounded salutary, a renouncing of the proposed murder. It came just as he was proposing that they should not say such things in his hearing, for if the monsignor had a freak accident, a tumble downstairs, or a brake failure . . . Well, he had heard them whistle up the man's death.

Through all this Paul kept his restrained

demeanor, a man who did not indulge in the absolutes of the women's hate for the unjust man, for the killer of children.

"There are bad things, let me tell you," Docherty assured them, "awaiting the monsignor. He's the sort of man who would love to be a bishop, and now, on the basis of the letter Stephen wrote, he never will be. Despite everything, he's at least become a figure of suspicion. That has been brought to pass, and it's no small thing."

Sarah's temper returned and she protested, "The death of Stephen wasn't a small thing either. It was a bigger thing than Monsignor Shannon not becoming a bishop, for Christ's sake!"

Unrealistically, given the small and secret conclave of the wronged that had gathered here, there was a ringing of the doorbell. Who would want to belong to such a company? It was as if someone authoritative had been brought to the door by their criminal surmises. Docherty hoped it was not Maureen. It was a purely selfish hope — to face her in this company would be an ordeal. It couldn't be Wood, he knew.

But Paul led Wood into the room. The young tycoon wore a sheeny suit but his tie was off and his shirt collar opened.

"Good evening, Mrs. Cosgrove," he said

to the bereaved mother. He sounded composed. "And my friend Frank over there, who doesn't give me any rest."

Paul wrung his hand and the two of them embraced. Then Paul said, "And this is Sarah Fagan. She has an interest in this entire thing."

"This entire thing. Are we considering legal action? I'll foot the bill," announced Wood.

"I'm afraid I don't have any malt whiskey, Brian," Paul went on. "I have red wine."

"Did you know, Paul, that the month of July is devoted liturgically to Christ's blood? Blood and red wine cheek by jowl in the Mass."

This emerged from Wood like a statement of mild hysteria.

Paul said, "I did know something along those lines." He went to the cupboard and poured a glass of red wine and brought it to Wood, who raised it and said, "Mrs. Cosgrove, here's to Stephen."

"Thank you," she said. Wood drank a sip and the others joined in, Sarah's eye on him with intense curiosity, as if he had brought to the meeting the possibility of an option she had not yet thought of. Maybe it was that he seemed to wear his victimhood lightly.

Paul pulled out a chair for Wood and he sat. "So, what is it to be? This man has to be punished."

"We've been discussing assassination," Sarah said with a puckish lilt. "Haven't we, *Father* Frank?"

Docherty said, "Sarah is well connected in the tough-guy market. I can attest to that." He was still in part breathless from the Wood apparition.

Sarah declared, "If the Church's lawyers are able to prove this nonsense that the Church as a trust can't be sued, we can't succeed legally anyhow. Isn't that the case, Paul?"

"That, I'm appalled to say, seems to be the case. If Devitt's plea is denied. But what if we agitate for criminal proceedings? Make a noise they can't ignore."

"No," said Liz. "I couldn't live through that. The lawyers being snide . . ."

Now it was Sarah's turn to stroke Liz's forearm.

"Perhaps not now, then," said Wood.

Paul said, "My mother and I have agreed to disagree on this."

"Please," said Liz plaintively. "If Stephen were depicted as a liar, or was blamed in any way — and he would be, as an addict — I don't think I could bear it. And the monsignor could walk away in the end. With the court's apology. Now that is something I really could not bear."

Wood said, "It would be harder for them to dismiss him with the court's blessing if I gave evidence." There was dead silence in the room. "I'm not boasting. It's just a matter of fact."

"All your instincts seemed to be against that," Docherty observed.

"My instincts were. But I was wrong. I fed you a line of bloody nonsense, Frank, and I haven't been able to concentrate since this morning. I said I could be the great corporate facilitator or a victim. But of course I am both. I wish you hadn't come near me, but you did. And you challenged my equilibrium."

"I feel the same way," Sarah Fagan told him. "I picked him up at the airport in my cab. If it hadn't been for him, I wouldn't be in the place we all are now. Caught between stools."

Wood spread his hands in a what-can-a-person-do? way. "The thing about you is that you set off quite a chain today. A sequence. I'd just seen you off when two very polite coppers, *extremely* polite and sensitive, arrived in the office. I think the receptionist thought they were tracking you,

Frank. I took them into the same conference room. They told me I had been named in a suicide document as a victim. They wanted to know if I would press civil charges. And you know what I told them? I told them I thought not. Of course, they said, think about it. But I said *no.*"

The others were awed and Sarah frowned.

"I said no because that way's not adequate. That way's absurd, as this Devitt man is finding. But I have to *get* the monsignor. I have to see him on *his* knees. I want to see him grieve as we've grieved."

Sarah said, "That's been our fantasy. The monsignor on his knees before the world. All of us who could have sued him in a civil court are being choked off by the trust defense the Church is running. We shouldn't be in a position where we have to hope a wise judgment will emerge from the court. We shouldn't have to wait for that. Even then, suing Shannon isn't enough. And we've rejected killing him."

"Stop saying that, Sarah," Docherty told her, but she ignored him.

"So there must be a third way."

There was silence.

"I was ashamed to declare myself a victim," murmured Wood then, a low voice but with its own authority. "I was uncertain about the woman I love and intend to marry. I was uncertain about my clients. I thought of the Filipino corporations, and the Hong Kong ones, many of them riddled with orthodox Catholics. I think the Indians would just be confused. And the Japanese . . .

"But too bad! I must discuss this with my associates. Subsequent to that, without any apology to anyone, I'll get Shannon. I will make a police investigation inevitable. Stephen's last letter will appear before the court, backed by me."

Wood looked at Liz. "Why should we hide it, Mrs. Cosgrove? It was Stephen's *word*. It is a weapon for the rest of us. Let's wield it. Please."

She frowned, yet to Docherty, and perhaps to the others, she did seem to have become reconciled, having never seen the letter as Wood saw it.

Wood said, "You, Frank, Father Frank, you are not to tell the cardinal of any of this. As far as you know it's simply talk on my part."

"What will you do, though?" asked Sarah Fagan.

"So you were used by him, too?"

"Yes." She laughed darkly. "They can't accuse the mongrel of not being bisexual."

At this outburst, Liz made a sound that was part lament and part yelp.

"I was his schoolgirl," said Sarah. "From a buggered-up family. Was your family buggered up in some way?"

"I have to say, not exceptionally," said Wood. "But the monsignor knew my father, through business, and my father had him at his dinner table as an entertaining cleric. It is a vanity of Catholics in business to be able to exhibit what passes for an urbane cleric at their dinners. Enter the monsignor."

"Yes," said Sarah, absorbing this history. "Yes."

"We should meet here tomorrow night," said Wood.

"I'll be on the way to Canada," Docherty reminded them.

"I can keep you up to date by email, Frank. As a courtesy. Beyond that, it isn't your business."

"That's fine," said Docherty. "But I have to see the cardinal tomorrow morning. My mother wants me to come back to Sydney, and the cardinal is looking for reasons to deny me reentry as a priest of this archdiocese. Am I to behave as if this meeting didn't happen? Can't I tell him, as encouragement to him to take a different tack, that

471

the victims intend to take any action they can?"

Paul said, "Our discussions tonight have been confidential, and you have an understanding of confidentiality, I know."

Docherty rose. "I don't have the legitimacy to be here. And I do think you have the right to discuss things confidentially."

They all looked somberly back at him.

"I wish you well, and I feel for you, and for Stephen," Docherty continued. "I'm glad you're here, Brian, because it will make for many more possibilities than otherwise. I hope to come back and see you all. May you have the blessings of what we used to call an omnipotent God. That's still a defensible description in some terms. But you may ask, 'Why didn't that omnipotent God intervene when we were at the mercy of the abuser?' I ask it myself. All I can say is, Christ be with you. He also is a sort of victim of the Church."

There was silence, then Liz Cosgrove said, "Thank you, Frank, for your good intentions."

"That's all I'm capable of," said Docherty. "The final and appropriate humiliation is to find out one's intentions don't add up to much. Good night. I know the way, Paul. Don't break up the meeting."

He was on the pavement outside the garden gate when there was a noise at the front door and Wood came running out. Docherty prepared himself to be damaged. Wood had been angelically wise and temperamentally calm, but of course he had to snap.

"I just wanted to say, Frank," Wood said, "leave it to me. I'll get the bastard. You'll find out how!"

36

DOCHERTY SAYS GOODBYE
TO HIS BROTHER

July 1996

Declan was up from Melbourne on legal business that he had made sure coincided with Frank's departure. He had long since invited Docherty to breakfast at the Inter-Continental Hotel on this his brother's last morning in Sydney. Docherty, dressed for his next confrontation with the cardinal, presented himself in proper canonical-form dog collar, the black alpaca that had worked perhaps a little on Wood. He wanted to look as conventional as he could, in the hope that it might earn him points in the cardinal's weighing and measuring.

At the breakfast table in the great loggia created by grafting the old colonial Treasury buildings onto a modern block, his brother looked precisely as Docherty would have wished him to — a healthy, tennis-playing paterfamilias, with the gloss that only a good

474

life in a satisfying profession and on a peaceful hearth can give a man. As Docherty arrived, his brother rose to meet him, hand out, an Order of Australia golden on his lapel.

"Frank," he said, but not with any loud, implausible fraternity. Docherty shook his hand, and once he was comfortable they arranged between themselves what they'd order. "Never face a cardinal on a skimpy stomach," Docherty told his brother. He added, "I saw Herself."

"Yes. I'm taking her to the opera tonight. Do you really think you can come back here? She's pretty keen on it."

"I'm hopeful," Docherty said. "At least I think I am. But, for several reasons, His Eminence is suspicious of me."

"Ah," said Declan, producing a folder. "This is a gift to you, of a sort. I have not been able to get the Church's records on you, although I'm sure we could if we really went for them. But this is an opinion, which I got some of our brighter young things to draw up, on the unjust dismissal of priests from their functions by church authorities. Happy Christmas."

He pushed it across the table in front of Docherty. "It's only July," said Docherty. "But thank you very much."

"The cardinal dismissed you in the early seventies, but the Church can't do that on moral grounds anymore, simple as that. Whether the cardinal wishes you to be his best mate or not, under various headings he cannot deny your claim of having been unjustly dismissed, or fail to provide reinstatement and court-ordered or agreed-upon compensation. It used to be that only workers in industries under an award system had a claim. But the latest legislation encompasses enough to include you. At state level, we have a fair work ombudsman who could take up the case. You are not without friends, in court or out. In the Devitt case the Church is using state law to its advantage. You can do the same thing. So I'm doing this for the old girl and for you."

"And that's the law?" asked Docherty.

"That's the law."

Docherty was touched that his brother would set his clever young colleagues on this issue. Coffee arrived and the brothers drank as Docherty leafed through the opinion.

"Now what I want to know," asked Declan, "is whether I could represent this situation to the cardinal as it really is, and in modern terms. Would you let me join your expedition to see him? He's hardheaded;

476

he'll try to reiterate what a loose cannon you are. And what a pleasure it will be to shake you off. I must be there to tell him he can't, and to let him know *you* know the game's changed. If they can use lawyers, so can you.

"I read a piece you wrote for the Toronto *Globe* in which you said priests are citizens as well. They are required to be and they are entitled to be. This gives them responsibilities under the law and access to the law. If you believe that . . . ," Declan leaned across the table and lightly tapped the folder, "he can't tell you to get lost when you bring your legal adviser, your brother, into the room. I'm proud to say that he knows I'm trouble." Declan winked at him. "What do you think?"

Frank shook his head. "I'm tempted to do it for the sake of Herself!"

"Why not?" asked Declan, sniffing the air combatively. "He certainly knows about our company. We've been involved in a few cases of unfair dismissal by Church schools. I think he'll give me a high-handed audience. Which will be fine."

"I have to see him about some . . . well, some other matters first," said Docherty. "But it's kind of you to offer to do this."

"I want to go to more cricket with you,"

said his brother. He grinned. "Wouldn't the old lady approve of us fronting him!"

"I believe she would. You're brave to call her the old lady. But she thinks you're a genius."

"And she thinks you're a prophet. She wouldn't want to tell you that in case it encouraged you. But for a polite fellow, you can't stop yourself getting into trouble, can you?"

"I'm a bit amazed myself at that," Docherty admitted.

His brother looked across the room. "I don't know how you manage at all, Frank, this celibacy thing. Not that I'm looking for answers."

"And not that I've got much to tell you. No sainted illegitimate children, no life partner. You see, I've got no evidence I could maintain a lifelong partnership."

"I think you might manage, Frank."

"Well, like everyone, I've had my moments. But you wouldn't wish it, that relationship, on a woman. A priest's woman. There are noble ones, let me tell you. Easier to manage if you're diocesan clergy; not so easy if you live in a house of priests. But you really wouldn't want it to happen to your daughter. Besides, I took the vow."

"It must sometimes be a relief to say that.

I took the vow."

"Maybe it's my bolt-hole," Docherty conceded.

Declan whispered, "Should we have some Irish whiskey in our coffee before coming to knuckle with His Eminence?"

"No, thank you," said Docherty. "Very kind. But I like to take cardinals straight."

As they walked, two men seemingly relaxed, towards the cathedral of sunny sandstone, Declan said, "You should spend time with Catherine." Catherine was his older daughter. "She's interested in the Church's culture, the way the structures of the Christian liturgy still prevail in civil life. She's writing a humanist honors thesis on it. On Church rituals and Masonic ones and ones that are purely societal, like our remembrance of the dead in wars. It's a pup out of Derrida, and she'd love to publish and get noticed by the major deconstructionists. If she got noticed by Susan Sontag or Harold Bloom or Jacques Derrida she'd feel she'd made it. If you were back in Sydney full-time, she could just call you up. She could come up here, go to Doyle's for lunch with you and rabbit away, uncle and niece."

"I can't imagine anything more delightful," said Docherty. And he could not. But the center of his respiration seemed to be stuck in his throat. The old awe of prelates, grander than God, was upon him.

In the outer office of the chancery, they were met by the cardinal's private secretary, and Docherty explained that in the second half of his audience with the cardinal he wanted to ask about his potential return to Sydney, and that he had a friend in making those pleadings, his brother, a Melbourne lawyer whom he believed the cardinal would know of.

Declan calmly handed over his card. The secretary nodded, and said quite pleasantly that he would give the cardinal that message. "Just wait," he murmured. "The boss is still at breakfast, but he won't be long."

Docherty and Declan sat together, shoulder to shoulder, and five minutes later the young man called Docherty into Cardinal Condon's office. Entering, Docherty found the cardinal was dressed in a black suit, red stock, and collar, no doubt ready to attend some civic event on behalf of the Catholic Church, or to give a lunchtime speech. He extended a hand, and Docherty yielded to protocol and bent his knee in a slightly slovenly, embarrassed genuflection, to kiss the cardinal's ring. The democrat in Docherty protested, "Kiss no master's hand," but he was in a complex situation this morning. The cardinal would receive more shocks, and it was best not to begin with one.

As soon as this ritual was concluded His Eminence retreated to his side of the table and sat down. He motioned for Docherty to do the same.

"So, tell me what's happening," he said.

Docherty cleared his throat. Since they had last spoken, Docherty told him, he had sought legal advice on his responsibilities as a citizen who was in possession of certain information, and thereafter he had made this information available to the ombudsman. He had no protection in law, he said, if he did not do so.

The cardinal rumbled, "If every unfounded accusation was the subject of a statutory declaration to the . . . to the *ombudsman,* the new looser and binder of sins . . . God help us!"

"I'm afraid that I had a file snatched from me in the city. It contained few pages, but amongst them was Stephen Cosgrove's suicide letter. I think it was a mugging." True enough, even in light of Sarah's confession. "On top of that, I've become aware that the other victim named in Cosgrove's confession knows about his letter and might, for all I know, consider action of his own."

"Action of his own?"

"He's an eminent citizen," Docherty said. "He won't be easily dismissed."

"More eminent than Devitt?"

"Even more so, yes."

There were some marked nasal exhalations from the cardinal. "You know what distresses me? Let him be whatever he is. What worries me is that at the center of all this is *you*, Father . . . Dr. Docherty. Letting a piece out here, a piece out there. I feel an orchestration going on. Aimed at a dear friend and trusted aide."

Docherty felt anger, a heat down his arms and in his face. "That is a misconception, Cardinal," he said firmly. No *Your Eminence* now. "I wanted none of this news to come my way. Since it did, and since one of the victims is particularly influential, I think you should take steps to prepare for the possibility that the accusations will become public."

The cardinal took these assertions of Docherty's surprisingly well. Perhaps he preferred directness. He said, "Have you asked yourself if Dr. Devitt's lawyers are behind all this? Is it an attempt to discredit the monsignor and the Church in the middle of these hearings?"

"I have to say it would be a delusion to believe that," Docherty asserted. "You might wish to warn Monsignor Shannon of what is impending, too. He won't welcome the news from me."

"Well," said the cardinal, with a pained rictus of his mouth, "I can't say you haven't been frank with me. But it is the frankness of a fool, Docherty, a man who does not know how the Church works. A man who has learned no lessons . . ."

Docherty thought that this was a good point to intervene. "I genuinely regret that you hold such a poor opinion of my actions, Your Eminence. I cannot quite see myself how I have in any way wronged you."

"Scandalmongering, sir. That's how. Undertaking the ruin of a good priest's reputation."

"Your Eminence, to my mind what I've done is to warn you of dangerous possibilities. If the monsignor's unjustly accused, then that is appalling, of course. But so is the opposite."

"These sorts of rumors always follow priests," His Eminence declared. He means it, Docherty perceived. It was as Passerelli had explained to him. The cardinal could not imagine anyone he respected doing such things. "Priests are the victims of infatuation by unstable people. It's always been the case. These claims have never had substance, or at least not as much as you think they do!"

"How wonderful if it were all lies," Docherty conceded. But now, given that the cardinal's suspicion of him was incurable, he thought it was time to attack the question of a return.

"Part of my concern about your assessment of me," Docherty pressed on, "arises from the fact that my mother is now aged, as I believe I mentioned the last time we met and in my letter earlier this year. Her health is not what it was and she has no daughters — just the two sons. She is hopeful that when I retire from my academic post I will reapply to be incardinated here, in Sydney, so that I can be with her in her advanced years."

Cardinal Condon actually whistled for a few seconds. "Well, I'm afraid there is little chance of that, Father Docherty. Perhaps my predecessor was hasty in getting rid of you — although it was a time of high political color, as I remember it. But you have done nothing to convince me that I'd want you working or preaching or giving the sacraments in this archdiocese."

"In that regard, however," Docherty pressed on, "I have an advocate. I would be grateful if Your Eminence took the time to hear him. It's my brother, Declan Docherty, who is a —"

"I know of him," said the cardinal. "He's an industrial relations lawyer in Melbourne."

"That's him, Your Eminence."

"I didn't know he was related . . . So *you* think all this is a matter of industrial relations?"

"That didn't occur to me as an aspect of the issue. But he has commissioned a legal opinion you might wish to pass on to your lawyers. If you consent to hear him . . . He happens to be in the office outside, because we met for a farewell breakfast. My plane leaves tonight, you see."

Docherty observed the cardinal hesitate. But he proceeded to phone through to his secretary to tell him that Mr. Docherty should be let in.

Declan entered in his good suit, looking uncowed. Docherty noticed that the demeanor of the cardinal changed a little. His Eminence was used to clear and unquestioned authority over priests. Industrial relations lawyers who had, however, caused problems in Catholic diocesan schools in matters of alleged unfair dismissal were a far more dangerous quantity, and it was as though the cardinal felt there was a balance of honor, of respective successes and losses, between him and Declan. That seemed to make him wary and to think he would give a weight to this encounter that he had not brought to his earlier discussions with Docherty.

The cardinal extended a hand. Declan did not kiss it in the loyal Catholic manner but shook it, and the cardinal did not seem outraged. Declan held the file with the legal opinion under his free arm.

"Your brother mentioned unfair dismissal," said the cardinal, with an air of near amusement at the concept.

"And denial of natural justice," supplied Declan. "Frank told you about our mother's health?"

"Yes. He did."

"It would be merely justice if you reversed the ruling of your predecessor and took Frank back into your diocese. What's the danger in that? He might give an unconventional sermon or two . . ."

"I believe that can be guaranteed," said the cardinal almost affectionately. *Good old Frank.* Again, though, he was not closing doors on Declan as energetically as he'd closed them on Docherty.

"Basically," Declan explained, "the unfair dismissal laws of this state lay down three principles. One is whether there is an incapacity to do the work; the second is whether there has been improper conduct on the employee's part; and the third is the case of redundancy. None of those principles existed in Frank Docherty's case."

"Ah, but we aren't a trucking company or a retail store," the cardinal said with alacrity. "The Church is a voluntary association, and judges have shown little appetite to say otherwise, whether in our case or in that of the Anglicans or of the Uniting Church, or in Judaism, or whosoever."

"Well," said Declan, "for that very reason, the issue hasn't been fully tested in our courts. An English court has found the claim of an Anglican vicar to be justiciable, but the vicar died before he could bring his case. My opinion is that the courts could find Frank's case well worth a run. In fact, if my brother were not allowed to return to this diocese to carry on normal pastoral work to the extent he chose and was capable of, my partners and I would be willing, on the basis of this opinion, which you are welcome to keep, to test the matter for him in the courts. But I ask you to look at him.

He is not a litigant by nature, and, in any case, you've had to close the major seminary, haven't you? The young are no longer becoming priests in the old numbers."

"There are just as many called," the cardinal asserted. "But the world is so loud now, and the young cannot hear."

"Well, however you like to interpret it, Your Eminence, you have a shortage of personnel. You're bringing in priests from the Third World, where the priesthood is still a going concern. And that's a fine thing. But here is a man willing to work on modest terms, a man of unstained repute and considerable intellect, willing to visit parishes and keep them alive. He would, of course, live in his community, his order's house, where he is staying now, and he might have some lecturing duties of the kind that would give great luster to the Church."

Cardinal Condon turned to Frank. "You'd be ready to stand by while your brother's law firm attacks the archdiocese?"

"I am not utterly comfortable about it," Docherty admitted. "But I do believe I was denied natural justice. Then there is the matter of my mother, and there I have a primary loyalty."

"But you've got a sweet posting in Canada . . . with tenured status at a university."

"I believe," said Declan, "we could find expert witnesses who would testify that my brother could have found a similar post here until the late cardinal, your predecessor, left him with only two choices: either to be laicized, or to go to some other area where his order had a house. Yet he stayed a priest, and that, I think, was pretty admirable. Don't you?"

The cardinal weighed this and made an ambiguous mouth. "We've all stayed priests, Mr. Docherty. But what I don't like is your giving me an ultimatum: restore him to the archdiocese, or else!"

"Yes," said Declan. "But I don't want to reach a point of coercion, and neither do you. It strikes me that the defense in the Devitt case must be costing you a great deal more than a settlement would. And the same would certainly be true in this case. Frank is not seeking any settlement other than the right to be a priest here. As well, he would be required to get certification from the superior of his order in Canada, and from his bishop, that he has performed well there. I somehow think he'll get those without difficulty. I spoke to a parish priest in Ontario, an older man Frank helps. He said he wouldn't be able to keep the place going without my brother. For one thing,

Frank offers the parishioners free counseling two nights a week. But he does the more traditional duties as well.

"As for his fellow priests in the Order of the Divine Charity, they have nothing but good to say of him even though some of them have theological arguments with him. But theological arguments are permissible in the modern Church, aren't they, Your Eminence?"

The cardinal shook his head but said nothing.

"So," Declan pressed on, "dare I say, if I were you, I'd show your lawyers this opinion I've given you. Needless to say, if you took my brother back, we would be prodigiously grateful. And my mother would call down blessings upon your head."

Now Declan put the opinion on the cardinal's desk, reached for the man's hand, took it, and kissed it earnestly. "I think that just about covers it for now, Your Eminence," he said.

"Thank you for seeing my brother," Docherty told the cardinal.

"I've known starting price bookmakers who aren't as slick as you two," His Eminence muttered, but his tone had some concession and certainly did not blot out future possibilities. He even told Docherty, on parting, to have a safe journey back to Canada.

Walking out of the grounds of the cathedral, Declan turned to his brother. "Now you know why lawyers drink too much — we are always slithering around other slitherers."

Docherty said, "I don't know how you do it. He was beating me to a pulp, and you came in and played him like a flute."

"Please," said Declan Docherty. "Not like a flute. Not anything involving lips." He gave a small shudder. "Let's make it a cello."

"Yes," Docherty agreed. "But it's a tremendous skill, and I don't have it."

"People wouldn't love you if you did."

"Your family seems to love you."

"At least they forgive me."

"You're talking like Uncle Tim used to."

"Uncle Tim was no fool."

Back outside the hotel, with the air from the harbor rushing up Macquarie Street from the direction of the Opera House, the brothers embraced. This men-embracing-other-men trick was something that had not existed when Docherty was young, when men considered affection a weakness. He had tried to learn its protocols, the unambiguous fraternal embrace — even some of his fellow priests and members of the Congregation of Divine Charity were aficionados of the hug.

"What if I pay your way up to business class tonight?" his brother asked.

"I don't think that would go well with who I am."

"Maybe not. I'll tell you who you are, Frank. You're unconventional, but you're the real bloody deal."

37
DOCHERTY LEAVES SYDNEY

July 1996

After he had said goodbye to his new friend Gunter Eismann, Docherty was taken to the airport by Sarah Fagan — it seemed now to both of them a sacrosanct arrangement.

"At the risk of giving you a big head," she told him as she drove, "it was . . . fortuitous I met you."

"*I* feel fortunate to have met you, Sarah," he said. "I wouldn't have missed all your free character assessments!"

"For God's sake, accept a compliment. How can you be fortunate to meet me? I'm only partly on the way to becoming a human being."

"I could name plenty of people who haven't even begun."

"Brian Wood. I don't quite know what will happen with him. It could be everything or nothing."

493

"That's the normal human arrangement, isn't it?"

"No, it's not," Sarah said. "Most people are nothing or a bit of everything. Very few are absolutely everything or absolutely nothing, so that you can't tell what to expect. He'll either reverberate or disappear. But it cheers me up that he's much more ruthless than me."

"And, as he said, he can afford lawyers," Docherty murmured.

As dusk came on, she dropped him outside the international terminal in the midst of the contest for car and cab spaces, the chaos of harried, distracted drivers and passengers making it no venue for earnest goodbyes. Sarah proudly found him a luggage trolley he didn't have to pay for, and their farewells were terse. She touched his arm and he found himself leaning to kiss her cheek.

He was at the long queue for Air Canada economy before he had fully said goodbye. And Sarah Fagan, prospective high school teacher, cabdriver for now, had disappeared to rejoin the banal melee of the city.

Docherty was pleased he had an aisle seat. He was beside a retired couple going to Canada because, the husband said, he'd seen a picture of Lake Louise in a *Saturday*

Evening Post when he was a child in the bush, and it had seemed the most improbable and desirable place on earth, imbued with a glamour intensified by the dourness of Australian life in the 1950s.

Docherty read a newspaper report of what had happened the day before at the Devitt trial. The senior counsel for the Church had argued that the trust and trustees could not be sued. There was an opinion piece in the *Herald* by a lawyer with whom Docherty had been to school, who was well known as a media commentator. It urged the Church to abandon the trust defense and, at any cost, to have the trial heard on its merits. Docherty agreed, and was reminded by the weight of these fretful matters that transcendental meditation was very handy both when faced with the gravity of human absurdity and with an overnight economy class flight.

Between sleep and conversation the flight was pleasant, with an esprit generated amongst the people in his area of the plane based on sharing the limits of cheap economy seats for a preposterous number of hours. Somewhere north of Fiji, they crossed that filament known as the date line and the day slipped back by one from Sydney's.

As the sun rose over the North Pacific, Docherty was oblivious to the scandal that had broken out in Sydney and was still blazing away at midmorning, taking up the nation's oxygen.

Brian Wood had bought a full page in a Murdoch tabloid, an imperfect tool, but sufficient to publish Stephen Cosgrove's suicide letter. Above the letter a heavy typescript read:

In June this year, a school friend of mine, Stephen Cosgrove, suicided by drug overdose. He wrote a farewell letter in which he mentioned me while accusing a priest of abusing both him and me. I can verify Stephen's claim, and thus I indemnify this newspaper of any action that might proceed from their publishing Stephen's pitiful document.

I take no delight in appearing before the world as a victim of this priest. But I am aware that by acknowledging the truth so publicly, by sharing it so widely with others, I can prevent further wrongs, and achieve a sense that the burden I have carried too long has been taken from my shoulders. I ask those who have loved me unconditionally to this point of my life to continue to do so. I invite those who have favoured my company, Wood and Associates, with contracts, to continue to do so. Wood and Associates is unchanged.

He had placed his address, according to the requirements of law, at the base of the advertisement. And below this was a line to say that he would not be taking up any requests for elucidation.

By afternoon, as Docherty waited for his connecting flight in Vancouver, the Church had agreed to settle with Dr. Devitt, whose terms proved modest but certainly exceeded the Church's original offer.

And the monsignor had been made available by the cardinal of the archdiocese to answer questions from the police.

38
MORNING MASS

July 1996

Docherty's flight to Toronto descended in a lavender dawn. He had that long-haul sense that his brain and major organs had somehow been sundered from his body.

He still had a bus ride to reach the Order's house in Waterloo, and on finally arriving there he found to his delight two of his fellow priests, including Tubby, waiting for him. So this is homecoming. . . . Perhaps I do belong here, he thought.

Later, he ate with them in the monastery dining room, exchanged the news of the summer, and talked about Jean Chrétien and his opposition to Quebec separatism.

"Did you cause trouble down in Sydney?" asked Tubby Enright.

"I'm still not popular with the boss down there. I'll fill you in when I've got more energy." Then they all drank a beer and eased their way off to their beds.

In the corner of Docherty's room sat his personal computer like a comrade. It was shrouded with a cover — its last night of rest before his invigorating work recommenced. Seeing it he remembered with exhilaration his graduate seminar in behavioral psychology in two days' time, the fact that it would sweep him up and energize him. Tomorrow was not too early to do further drafting of his work for Bishop Egan, a chance to redeem the stigma he bore in the eyes of Cardinal Condon of Sydney.

From a profound, exhausted sleep, he woke early the next morning. Although he did not quite know what time it was in Sydney, his body was falsely declaring itself alert to begin the day and he still felt the terrible dislocation associated with a transglobal migration.

He had not only his own PC but a fax line in his room for university communications with students and staff. And he had not been long awake when it began to stutter forth new pages to join some weeks of unanswered messages, in urgent and emphatic black, in the tray. There seemed to be a wearying number of them. And this for the quiet time of year!

The first page that emerged was handwritten and had Sarah Fagan's name on it. He read the message. It had been sent the morning after she'd seen him off.

Dear Frank,

I still feel bad I had my young friend crunch you. As you know, I have traveled a long way in a little time and I hope you didn't mind traveling the short drop to the footpath. I decided to play it as hard as them, so you'll have to forgive me. Remember the card you dropped on the cab seat the first time I met you? It had this fax number I'm trying, so I hope I've reached you with the news. Wood's gone public with Shannon's name. It's astounding. Justice in one hit! Nowhere for the man to hide! I found it easy to come out once Wood had set up a way of doing it for us. See attached. And thanks.

He watched other pages edging for Wood, pages with text and images. He was impatient for them all to download in a way he could not remember having ever felt in the old days when communications took so long, so many days and weeks.

On the first of the pages was a photograph

of Sarah Fagan herself, rather photogenic, looking at the camera unflinchingly, comfortable with her accusations, her support of the evidence of Stephen Cosgrove and Wood. There was a picture of a harried Monsignor Leo Shannon. For, according to the article Sarah had sent, the cardinal's office said it was only in recent days that accusations against the monsignor had reached them, and, it went on, that archdiocesan authorities had considered withdrawing Monsignor Shannon from the Devitt case. It seemed that Leo Shannon would, for the first time in his career, find himself reduced and written off, even before any charges arose. He, too, would have an education in archdiocesan expediency.

Independently of the investigation, the Church had announced it intended to abandon the challenge to Dr. Devitt's plea for the suspension of the Limitation Act and would enter into negotiation with his lawyers. And on the next page he saw the text of Stephen Cosgrove's letter in the tabloid.

Docherty shaved distractedly, too many developments to absorb. Maureen would be shattered, he knew. Should he call? What would he say? What time was it in Sydney? Nine in the evening. Not too late, given the circumstances.

He dialed her number. The only answer was the redolent Australian dial tone, then Damian's recorded voice inviting him to leave a message.

"I don't know what you two must be feeling," Docherty told the cold telephonic vacancy. "Maureen . . . you don't deserve . . . you deserve to be free of your brother's shame. I'm sorry. I send my love."

He was guiltily relieved that he had not needed to speak to them. Why were they out? Had kind Damian taken her away for a road trip? Was she sedated?

Docherty set off to walk the few kilometers to the parish church, St. Anthony of Padua. The pleasant streets were empty, unaware of the Sydney ferment, the birds in the white pines not yet awake. He felt strangely exposed. What if the tabloid had followed him here? His fellow priests might not be amused. He also marveled and his blood raced, however, to know that a great and necessary blow had been landed, that complacency had been routed, that secrecy and legal fictions would not serve.

He came into the yard of the parish and went to the back of the presbytery. Mrs. Cerretti would have arrived to make Father Madelena's breakfast. She did not live in the presbytery, yet it was confidently suggested by parishioners that she and Father Madelena were or had been lovers. So be it. Madelena was a good and attentive man and a fine parish priest to his people, a man of acceptance and not of exclusion. If love had taught him that, who could condemn him to Hell?

Docherty could see her, a dumpling of a woman, through the lit kitchen, chopping shallots as if for an omelet. He knocked on the door.

"It's me, Docherty."

She opened up with her slow, shy smile, the antithesis of the dragon women who'd guarded presbyteries when he was a child.

"How's Gene?" he asked as she ushered him in.

"Overworked," she said. "How are you? How did you get on Down Under?"

"I got into trouble with the cardinal archbishop of Sydney."

"Why do I believe that?"

"All jokes aside, is Gene well?"

"No. He's had the flu. He's been given another parish to run. We'd be sunk without you guys from the monastery."

"Do you want to let him sleep and I'll say morning Mass?"

"Well . . . I've got to call him soon."

503

"Why not let him rest? Let me do it. I've got jet lag and I'm wide awake. Ready to go dancing."

"All right. You'll have a congregation of about fifteen. I'll be one of them. I'll deal with the criticism from him when it arrives."

"You have an acolyte, I take it?"

"Oh, Mr. Meaney. He's here."

"Good."

"He'll already be over there at the sacristy. He has the keys to unlock the church."

"What a man!" said Docherty. Meaney was old, and of indomitable faith. Post-Famine Irish, his family had come down the interminable St. Lawrence on a fever ship — so he had told Docherty. They had died by battalions in the quarantine station of Grosse Île off Quebec. Mr. Meaney's grandparents were descendants of the survivors.

Docherty went across from the presbytery, traversing the nearby school's basketball court, and entered the standard sacristy — like one found anywhere in the English-speaking world: dim, austere, clean, with its drawers of vestments. It had always been the side-room sanctuary of the traditional second-class citizens of the New World, the Irish, Italians, Poles, Ukrainians.

Old Mr. Meaney, waiting on a chair in the

corner, stood up and growled, "H'llo, Father. You on today?"

And now here we are together, thought Docherty warmly, in the dark years of the faith of our forefathers, in an age when working mothers no longer slave to have the honor of their sons as altar boys, when Father Madelena had wisely fallen back on the option of the altar boys of yesteryear, represented today by Mr. Meaney.

"They said you were in Australia," said Mr. Meaney, as Docherty washed his hands.

"Just back, Mr. Meaney."

"And your family there well, I hope?"

"Not too bad," said Docherty. "My mother's in a retirement home. But she seems undefeated."

"Ah," said Meaney, "that's facing me, too, if my kids have their way."

"Green vestments, isn't it, for today?" asked Docherty.

"The same the whole world over," said Meaney with a sort of weary but proud certitude.

Docherty began to robe himself according to the garments of ancient Roman princehood — in an amice and the long white alb, with the cincture tied around his waist, and the stole around his neck, crossed and held by the cincture. With Mr. Meaney's help, he

505

placed the chasuble of green over his shoulders. These were considered the robes of supermen when he was a kid, though they had through the follies of the Church since earned a more ambiguous response.

As he robed, he said the old Latin prayers to himself — he was keen on Latin, though he could not as a democrat refuse the validity of an English-language Mass.

Meanwhile, Mr. Meaney had put on his own surplice and was dressing the chalice and preparing the wine and water cruets. It was said that altar wine was designed to be so bad that even alcoholic priests did not look forward to the consecration and consumption of Christ's blood.

"Thank you for that," Docherty told Meaney as he took the chalice in his hands.

Meaney now preceded him and opened the door on to the sanctuary. The congregation that stood for him was precisely as he expected: the few widowed men, the pious women of over sixty, and an obsessive-compulsive young invalid pensioner, who sometimes went to two or three Masses at various churches in a day as a belt and braces form of achieving salvation. Docherty had counseled him and assured him that observance once a day was more than enough. The young man had cheerily agreed with him and continued to seek Masses around the place.

At the bottom of the symbolic mountain made by the stairs of the altar and the little mound on which the altar stood, Docherty turned to the congregation and greeted them, these hallowed few; no less hallowed than the thousands entering the morning commute, some of them making the long daily trip into Toronto, but these had come to share the rite, and thus were the most immediately precious to him, these members of a minority club. He felt love for them stir in him habitual, unrequited, and irreducible, and for Christ his brother, the redeemer, Jesu, Joshua, Jesse, Jesus, the man who had laid down a ruthless rule: "If you do this to one of the least of my brethren, you do it to me."

Such was the Gospel according to the Bedouin-brown Jesus, better honored by many unbelievers than by those who loudly claimed to be his men, his women. Docherty had always had fellow feeling for unbelievers, because in a parallel universe, without having begun life as he had, he would have been one. But through accidents of history and birth and even immigration, this was *his* mystery. And he would never abandon his misrepresented and abused brother

Jesus, brought into disrepute by the apparatchiks of the Church, and, of course, a day past in Australia, by Monsignor Shannon. What of Maureen? he wondered again. How is she handling the reflected shame? For she was, of course, a victim, too.

"As you and I were there in the beginning, let us be there at the end of things, my brother," prayed Docherty. He didn't care if it was literal sense. It made sense to him. It was the correlative of all his sensibilities.

It was home.

ACKNOWLEDGMENTS

This book of demons had its beneficent friends. My wife, whom I was not primarily attracted to for her editorial skills, nonetheless continued her work as a gifted editor of first and last review of this text. As always, it is not her fault if the results do not shine.

The equally genial editors Meredith Curnow and Catherine Hill also helped me push the virtues of the text as far as they would go.

My enduring and valiant agent is Fiona Inglis. It is just as well I can write well enough for her to keep me on the books, because life without our friendship would be bleak.

My friend Kara Shead, a criminal law practitioner who has prosecuted a number of the cases involving child abuse by clergy and others, helped me with legal advice, and to the extent the material as I have deployed it is accurate and credible, I owe it to her. Any solecisms are, of course, my own.

There have been many books on the crisis in the Church. Some that I read during the period of writing and that contributed insights to this narrative include Richard Sipe's *Sex, Priests and Power: Anatomy of a Crisis* (1995) and the same author's *A Secret World: Sexuality and the Search for Celibacy* (1990); David France, *Our Fathers: The Secret Life of the Catholic Church in an Age of Scandal* (2004); and the much-criticized but valid John Cornwell, *Dark Box: A Secret History of Confession* (2014).

I would like to mark the death of a dear friend, Father Pat Conner, Society of the Divine Word, expelled from the archdiocese of Sydney for no crime but the most pacifically stated political opinions. An exile in the United States until his death in 2015, an authentic thinker, meditator, and believer, his book *Whom Not to Marry* was described by the *New York Times* as the ultimate word on the subject, and his activism and spirit intrigued and compelled all his Australian and American friends. You were not Docherty, Pat, since Docherty is utter fiction. But I like to think you and Docherty would have been friends, had he existed. It was above all your example that caused me to retain a belief in the authenticity of Catholic spirituality, even if I am no archbishop's model Catholic.

Lastly, as all we writers must, I salute the reader.

ABOUT THE AUTHOR

Thomas Keneally began his writing career in 1964 and has published thirty-three novels since, most recently *Napoleon's Last Island, Shame and the Captives,* and the *New York Times* bestselling *The Daughters of Mars.* His novels include *Schindler's List,* which won the Booker Prize in 1982, *The Chant of Jimmie Blacksmith, Gossip from the Forest,* and *Confederates,* all of which were shortlisted for the Booker Prize. He is married with two daughters and lives in Sydney, Australia.

The employees of Thorndike Press hope you have enjoyed this Large Print book. All our Thorndike, Wheeler, and Kennebec Large Print titles are designed for easy reading, and all our books are made to last. Other Thorndike Press Large Print books are available at your library, through selected bookstores, or directly from us.

For information about titles, please call:
  (800) 223-1244

or visit our website at:
  gale.com/thorndike

To share your comments, please write:
  Publisher
  Thorndike Press
  10 Water St., Suite 310
  Waterville, ME 04901